DEEP FOCUS

THE DEEP SERIES - BOOK FIVE

NICK SULLIVAN

Cover design by Shayne Rutherford of Wicked Good Book Covers
Cover photo by Zenobillis/Shutterstock.com
Copy editing by Marsha Zinberg of The Write Touch
Proofreading by Gretchen Tannert Douglas and Forest Olivier
Interior Design and Typesetting by Colleen Sheehan of Ampersand Bookery
Original maps of Little and Grand Cayman by Rainer Lesniewski/Shutterstock.com

ISBN: 978-0-9978132-7-2

Published by Wild Yonder Press
www.WildYonderPress.com

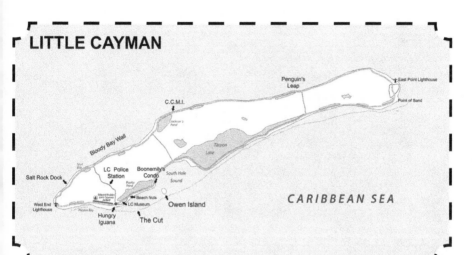

LITTLE CAYMAN

Penguin's Leap

East Point Lighthouse

Point of Sand

C.C.M.I.

Jackson's Pond

Tarpon Lake

CARIBBEAN SEA

Bloody Bay Wall

LC Police Station

Boonemily's Condo

South Hole Sound

Salt Rock Dock

Booby Pond

West End Lighthouse

Beach Nuts

LC Museum

Owen Island

Pirates Bay

Hungry Iguana

The Cut

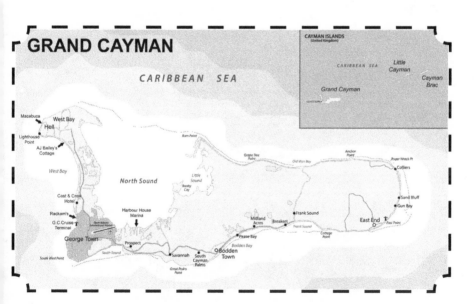

GRAND CAYMAN

CARIBBEAN SEA

CAYMAN ISLANDS
(United Kingdom)

CARIBBEAN SEA

Little Cayman

Cayman Brac

Grand Cayman

Macabuca

West Bay

Hell

Lighthouse Point

AJ Bailey's Cottage

West Bay

North Sound

Rum Point

Grape Tree Point

Old Man Bay

Anchor Point

Roger Wreck Pt

Colliers

Little Sound

Booby Cay

Sand Bluff

Gun Bay

Cast & Crew Hotel

Rackam's

Harbour House Marina

Midland Acres

Breakers

Frank Sound

East End

East Point

G.C Cruise Terminal

George Town

Prospect

South Sound

Savannah

South Cayman Palms

Bodden Town

Pease Bay

Bodden Bay

Trent Sound

Cottage Point

South West Point

Great Pedro Point

To Dawn Lee McKenna. Your life story inspired me to spin stories of my own. Your fellow authors will miss your humor, kindness, and wisdom, and your fans will miss your wonderful writing, compelling characters, and well-sculpted plots.

Deep focus / noun: *(cinematography)*

a photographic technique in film that keeps all elements of an image in sharp focus, simultaneously capturing key activities in the foreground and background.

Nobody will ever notice that. Filmmaking is not about the tiny details. It's about the big picture.
Ed Wood, filmmaker.

1

"And... action!"

Leather boots filled the closeup shot, as the camera's view followed the worn footwear across the wooden deck until they came to a halt. Camera One panned up, taking in a man dressed in garish pirate's attire, black greatcoat flaring out from his flanks. A red sash was cinched below a bulging belly, a stubby cutlass tucked into one side. Rising higher, the camera focused on the man's face. The black eyeliner and a single gold earring were certainly eye-catching, but the pièce de résistance was his beard, dyed a shockingly bright cobalt blue. With a flourish, the man swept a tricorn hat from his balding head and sketched a lazy bow.

"Arrrr, mateys... welcome aboard the *Jolly Robert*! The greatest rum cruise in the Caribbean! I be yer cap'n, Robert Bluebeard! Yaaaaarrrr!"

Suddenly, a furry figure jumped into frame, dropping onto Bluebeard's shoulder. The new arrival gave a shriek, then busied itself picking at the edge of the pirate's beard, grooming the bushy expanse of blue hair. The capuchin monkey was outfitted with three items of apparel: first, a tiny pirate hat atop its head, mirroring Bluebeard's own; second, a bandolier, strapped diagonally across its scrawny chest, the belt adorned with numerous tropical drink umbrellas, closed and awaiting use; and third... a diaper.

"This here be Ulysses, first mate and bartender-in-training." He pointed off camera. "You there!"

Camera Two provided a wide shot of those in attendance: college co-eds surrounded Bluebeard, the majority of their tanned, supple bodies clad in bikinis or board shorts. Many held plastic cups of rum punch. A muscled frat boy was the target of Bluebeard's index finger, and he stepped forward.

"Extend yer drink to the first mate, my good man."

The youth looked over at his friends, a goofy grin on his face. He turned back to the monkey and held out his rum punch, a skewer of pineapple slices and dayglow cherries sloshing against the rim.

"Ulysses! Bartend!"

The capuchin shrieked, then deftly slid a paper umbrella from his bandolier, opened it in his tiny fingers, and popped it into the man's drink, the toothpick of the decoration piercing the topmost cherry. The drink-holder laughed and returned to his friends. Mission accomplished, Ulysses returned to grooming his master, who planted his fists on his hips.

"Thar be a few rules on me ship, so listen up, ye scurvy dogs!" he bellowed. "One! No smokin', fightin', or throwin' yer trash overboard. If I see any cups floatin' in our wake, ye'll be joinin' 'em! Two! Only three drinks per person! Each of ye has three wristbands and once ye've handed them over, it's sodas or water for the rest of the voyage, so make yer rum ration count. And three! See to it that ye be havin' fun, or ye'll be walkin' the plank!"

"Ohmigod, so lame," muttered a girl off-screen, the youthful voice flat and nasal.

Camera Two pulled back and up, showing that the partygoers stood on the deck of a pirate ship—or a cheap, modern-day knockoff of one. Overhead, a black-and-white Jolly Roger fluttered in the breeze. Under the grinning skull, not crossed bones… but crossed beer bottles.

Camera Three focused on one of the college girls, a petite blonde sporting glasses and a ponytail; in her hands, not a drink… but a book. Heaving a sigh, she gazed off toward the horizon, looking like she'd prefer to be anywhere else. Beside her, a buxom brunette nudged her bare shoulder.

"Lighten up, Sarah, it's a party boat!" the brunette cajoled in a nasal voice. "And ditch the book, nerd. You're not in school today."

Sarah sighed again, and Camera Three zoomed in on her flawless face as she opened her full lips to speak her first line.

"This drunken barf-fest is not my idea of fun, Cindy. I wish—"

"Aaaahh!" a voice shrieked off-screen. "Bloody hell, he did it again!"

With its lens still pointing at Bluebeard, Camera One could see what Camera Three could not: Ulysses, bored with fruitless beard-grooming, had extracted another umbrella, opened it… and jammed it into the pirate's ear.

"Cut!" a voice shouted.

The actors on set relaxed—a few of the background extras had been sucking in their guts to look good in their swimwear, and the exhalations were audible. "Bluebeard," whose real name was Daniel Wolfit, clawed at his ear.

"If I hadn't twitched, that malodorous little shit would've punctured my eardrum!" Gone was the ludicrous pirate's brogue, replaced with a theatrical British accent. The actor extracted the umbrella and hurled it aside, a droplet of blood adorning the point of the toothpick.

Ulysses, his artistic talents spurned, shrieked into the recently cleared ear, eliciting a wince from Wolfit.

"Someone get this devil monkey off me! And change his damn diaper! I was inhaling the unholy reek of his feces all through my speech."

The animal wrangler extended an arm and the capuchin dutifully leapt across to receive a treat.

"You're *rewarding* him? The wee bastard jabs me in the ear and—"

"Enough, Daniel." A gaunt man rose from a director's chair. Appropriately, the word "Director" was emblazoned on the chair's canvas backing. Heinz Werner dug a cigarette out of a pack and fired it up. "Dario, if you please, let us take fifteen and reset. Daniel's beard is starting to run, anyway." The director's voice had a droning quality, a strong German accent tugging at the consonants.

The first assistant director—1st AD—clapped his hands. "Fifteen minutes, people!" Members of the film crew relaxed, boom microphones carefully set aside and camera lenses covered. "Hair! See what you can do about the streak of blue dye."

A stout woman with a shoulder bag of brushes, spray, and a hair dryer waddled over. "Took too long setting up the shot," she muttered. "It's ninety degrees and humid—what did you expect? Should've shot this in the States."

"I left the Royal Shakespeare Company for *this*?" Daniel Wolfit appealed to the sky as the lady from the hair department took a look at the streak of blue dye that ran down his neck.

"It's on his skin now. This is makeup's job." She wandered off.

"*Gott im Himmel!*" the director swore. "We will lose the light!"

"The light's the least of our worries, Heinz," Alan Novak, the gray-haired cinematographer said, pointing out to sea.

On the horizon, a cruise ship was making its way into the bay that lay alongside George Town, the capital of the Cayman Islands and the largest town on Grand Cayman. The *Jolly Robert*—a converted party-barge on loan from Jamaica—was currently anchored in the bay. The film crew had wanted to shoot this particular scene at a pier, but they'd had difficulty finding one that could accommodate them without securing additional permits. They'd settled on a mooring in the bay with a clear shot out to sea, but this newcomer would likely fill the background, since the moorings to either side of the *Robert* were already occupied.

"*Scheisse,*" Heinz Werner hissed, before looking at his watch. "Time is a harsh mistress and she makes cruel demands of us. But we needs must obey."

Novak merely nodded. He had worked with Werner on three previous movies and was accustomed to his odd way of speaking. Atop the stilted, almost pompous, verbiage lay a thick accent. The director hailed from the Czech Republic, specifically the region of Bohemia, where a substantial portion of the populace was German.

Werner looked up from his watch and squinted out at the arriving cruise ship. "Did we get all of Bluebeard's opening speech before the untimely simian assault?"

"We'll check the gate," the cinematographer offered. "The humidity and salt air can be tricky on the lens, but I think we got it."

"Let us hope so. For now, we will focus on the closeup coverage and avoid that looming monstrosity." He waved a dismissive hand toward the oncoming ship. As Novak headed back to a bank of monitors, Werner looked around. "Dario, where is my 'Sarah'? Where is Brooke?"

"I think she went to crafty to grab a water," the 1st AD said, referring to the craft services table, where a steady supply of drinks and snacks was maintained. Dario tilted his head down and spoke into a mic. "Jerry, could you bring Brooke Bablin back to set? Heinz wants a word."

"Can I get out of this blasted pirate coat?" Wolfit asked, a member of the makeup department dabbing at his neck with a foam sponge. "I'm going to get heat stroke!"

"*Ja, ja*... I will focus on my lead actress's scenes," the director said. "I may need you to deliver some lines to her from off-camera, so don't sojourn too far."

The rotund actor snorted, nodding his head to the ocean around them. "Not bloody likely." He started to clomp off the set but a crewmember—rounder around the middle than Wolfit—stopped him.

"Where are you going with that?" the prop master asked, pointing at the cutlass. "Weapons don't leave the set."

"It's duller than a butter knife!"

"Weapons don't leave the—"

"Here! Take the blasted thing." Wolfit disarmed himself and left the set in a huff. "At least they let me cut the eyepatch," he grumbled. "Felt like that eye was going blind for real."

Jerry—the second assistant director—came up to Werner, with the blond actress who played the bookish college student following close behind. Gone were the spectacles, and she now wore a lightweight dressing gown over her bikini. She stopped in front of the director, raising a sculpted eyebrow expectantly.

"Ah, Miss Bablin. Good. I wanted to—"

"What did I tell you about smoking around me, Mr. Werner?"

The director was momentarily thrown. He held up the cigarette. "*Mein Liebchen*, it has been a long day, and the relentless march of tedium is trying to the soul. Perhaps—"

"No smoking within twenty feet of me, unless it's part of the movie. It's in my contract." The defiant actress lifted her chin, locking eyes with the director. At only five feet in height, she usually had to look up to stare someone down. "Shall I call my agent?"

Werner summoned up a brittle smile. Brooke Bablin was the nearest thing this mid-budget sci-fi movie had to a movie star, and he needed to keep her happy. "My apologies, Miss Bablin." He turned and flicked the cigarette overboard.

The 2nd AD winced, stopping himself from making a mid-air grab at the smoking butt. Instead, he furtively glanced over toward the representative from the Cayman Islands Film Commission, hoping the man hadn't seen the blatant act of littering. No such luck. The Caymanian shook his head and made a note on his clipboard. Another $500 penalty added to the budget.

Heinz Werner clapped his hands together. "Now, Miss Bablin… your first scene—"

"You mean, the scene that psychotic monkey just screwed up? I still don't know why you didn't go with a parrot."

Werner sighed. "As was explained in the table read, the monkey is vital to the greater arc of the story. In addition to accomplishing a number of plot points, the monkey itself hearkens back to our own evolution… and this symbolism ties in to the evolution that occurs in the creature at the heart of our movie."

"Whatever. You're the *visionary*." The way Brooke said it, it didn't sound like a compliment. "So, are we going to shoot again?"

"Yes… and no. We have an unwelcome maritime guest encroaching upon the framing for the wide shot, so for now we will focus our efforts on your coverage."

"Fine by me," Brooke said, shrugging out of the dressing gown and revealing a toned body that only a near-starvation diet and a full-time personal trainer could achieve. The eyes of several nearby crew were helplessly drawn to her as she plucked her prop spectacles from where they dangled from her bikini top and slid them onto her face. Brooke held the gown out to the side.

Dario, the 1st AD, took the gown from her fingers and shoved it into the hands of a passing intern. He triggered his mic. "Call everyone back to places, please."

While cast and crew scrambled, Werner took out the pack of cigarettes. They were scarcely out of his pocket when he caught Brooke looking at him with a raised, perfectly sculpted eyebrow. He returned the cigarettes to his pocket, turning aside to stare at the sparkling waters of the Caribbean.

American movie stars… they will be the death of me.

———◆·◆———

"All right everyone, this is now officially dinner. Most of you are wrapped for the day, but those of you in the two interior scenes, be back at the dock in one hour."

The 2ⁿᵈ AD glanced at his clipboard as members of the cast and crew disembarked from the two tenders, freshly docked at the northernmost pier of Grand Cayman's George Town Cruise Port. A group of extras gathered to one side, and Jerry turned his attention to them. "Background, you're all wrapped. See you at Base Camp tomorrow at six a.m. sharp."

Brooke Bablin held out a hand and the assistant director took it, helping the petite actress step across to the pier. "Great work today, Miss Bablin."

"It's why they hired me, Jerry."

"Are you eating with us, or do you need a car?"

"No and no. I need a drink. See you tomorrow."

Snugging a ballcap onto her head and donning a pair of sunglasses, Brooke strode away from the pier, leaving behind the cast and crew as they bum-rushed the nearby restaurant the producers had rented, jockeying for position at the craft services buffet. She'd eaten there last night and the spread had been decent, but right now she wanted to find a nice tropical beverage—heavy on the rum—and then get a solid night's sleep.

The cruise ship terminal was in George Town proper, south of the popular stretch of sand and hotels known as Seven Mile Beach. Unlike many Caribbean islands, Grand Cayman did not allow the cruise ships to actually dock at a pier, requiring them instead to shuttle passengers ashore via tenders. Groups of vacationers milled about, waiting for outbound transportation.

Walking north along North Church Street, Brooke passed small groups of tourists strolling along the road. With the hat and shades, she felt fairly anonymous, but she turned her head aside all the same when the father of a family of four swiveled his head in her direction.

Ahead, she spied an outdoor bar and restaurant named Rackam's. Situated on the water, it would provide a nice view of the rapidly approaching sunset. Settling into a corner table, she ordered a piña colada and a tropical salad with blackened chicken. Once she'd put aside her hat and sunglasses, Brooke breathed in a lungful of the salty air. The frothy frozen drink arrived just as the sun kissed the horizon and she took a lengthy pull on the straw, stopping just shy of brain freeze. The drink was delicious, and they hadn't skimped on the rum.

Looking down at the drink's fruit garnish, she snorted a laugh. A paper umbrella adorned the side of the glass. Watching a monkey jab that pompous ass in the ear had been the highlight of her day. That fat has-been couldn't go an hour without mentioning his Hamlet or Richard the Third. Brooke took another sip. True, her own body of work tended toward the salacious, but she was far more successful—and famous—than he would ever be.

As if to prove the point, a man in a garish Hawaiian shirt approached her table. He looked to be in his late thirties, but with a boyish face. "Please to excuse, but you look familiar," he began, an atrocious accent from some Slavic country mangling his English.

"I get that a lot," Brooke said, wishing she'd kept her sunglasses on.

The man snapped his fingers. "Oh! I know! You are American actress! You are very popular in my country. I love you in that movie... *Seven*... uh... *Seven* something *Sins*..."

"*Seven Sexy Sins.*"

"*Da!* You are very good in this. Please, if I may be so brave... would you give autograph?" He dug in his pocket and came up with a pen. "Please, my wife, she love this movie too. It would make her very happy. Oh, but I have no paper."

Brooke granted the man a smile. The quicker she gave him an autograph, the quicker he'd leave. "I can help with that." She set her small credit-card wallet on the table and extracted a business card with her headshot on it. She took his pen and quickly scrawled her autograph on the back. "There you go."

He came around the side of the table to take it. "Oh, thank you, Miss... Brooke Bablin! Yes! It is you!" Suddenly, he raised his smartphone. "Smile for selfie!" He snapped a photo but stumbled and bumped the table.

"Hey!"

"Oh, please to forgive! I knock your little wallet to floor. Here, hold phone!" He ducked under the table and came up with her card holder. "I am so ashamed. I go!" He took his phone and hurried off.

Brooke sighed. *At least he didn't spill my drink.*

The sunset was good, the salad even better, the piña colada the best. Brooke paid her bill and had the restaurant call her a cab, enjoying a pleasant rum buzz as she waited alongside the road with an evening sea breeze caressing her skin. A taxi arrived and in minutes she was at her villa complex. Most of the cast had been put up at a hotel on Seven Mile Beach, but Brooke had insisted on her own accommodations. She walked through the courtyard, its tropical trees lit by tastefully placed spotlights. Reaching her corner villa, she slid the room keycard from her card wallet and swiped it through the lock, eliciting a green light and a click.

Stepping inside, she tossed her sunglasses and ballcap on an entry table and approached the gloom of the living area. She flicked on a light and gasped. Across the room, near the door to the patio, stood a solid-looking woman, her arms well-muscled, her hair cut short.

"Who... who are you?"

The woman smiled. "Why, I'm just your biggest fan," she replied in some form of Upper Midwest accent. She held up a familiar-looking business card. "Thanks a bunch for the autograph. Betcha this could fetch a lotta money."

"But not as much as actress herself," came a voice from behind.

Brooke whirled to find the foreign man from the restaurant. She opened her mouth to scream, but he pressed a wet rag over her mouth and nose; a sweet, chemical odor permeated her nostrils.

"You really were good in that movie," the man said, as his face lost focus and Brooke's vision faded to black.

2

Boone Fischer gently kicked his right fin, adjusting his orientation to the gap in the coral that he hovered beside. He shifted his grip on the pole spear to a spot just behind the three-pronged tip, stretching taut the elastic band attached to the butt end. Exhaling slightly, Boone generated a touch of negative buoyancy in his body. Descending slowly along the wall, the business end of the spear came into line with the quarry he'd spotted. Inside a niche in the coral, the diaphanous fins of a lionfish fluttered in the shadows. This fella was a large one, its reddish stripes almost black at this depth. With no natural predators in the Caribbean, the invasive fish seemed unconcerned with the triple-pointed death that edged closer. A nearby slipper lobster was more sensible, scuttling away from the approaching spear points.

Boone glanced over at his dive buddy to make sure she was clear. Occasionally, a skewered lionfish would thrash—between spearing it and tucking it into the storage container, a careless diver could get stuck with one of the numerous spines that adorned its dorsal, anal, and pelvic fins. While a lionfish was venomous, and there were a handful of cases of necrosis on record, its sting was rarely lethal; allergic reactions or infections were the primary concern. Regardless, a sting still hurt like a son of a bitch, Boone knew only too well.

Amelia Ebanks floated alongside the wall about fifteen feet away, a pole spear of her own held in a loose grip. She watched Boone intently, flashing an "OK" sign at him when she saw him checking on her. Amelia was a Caymanian, born and bred. Her coffee-colored skin spoke of a mix of origins—her father being descended from the original Ebanks family on Little Cayman, and her mother hailing from Jamaica.

Satisfied, Boone tossed a single nod in her direction before returning his focus to the lionfish. Lining up on the target, he moved the paralyzer head closer to his prey. The Department of Environment in the Cayman Islands had strict requirements for lionfish culls, requiring licenses, training, and only allowing DoE-issued spears. Boone found the barbless three-prong design a bit tricky for gripping a lionfish—a particularly energetic specimen could pull itself free from the tips—but at least the lack of barbs made it easy to transfer it from spear to catch-tube.

Once the spearpoints were a couple of inches away from the target, he simply let go of the shaft. Propelled by the elastic band, the spear shot forward through his fingers, skewering the lionfish. Withdrawing the pole, Boone expertly brought the thrashing creature to the Zookeeper containment tube at his side, pushed it through the one-way funnel at the top, then stripped it from the spear by pulling the points back through the small center hole in the plastic funnel. He looked into the clear side of the tube— the Zookeeper was nearly full. *Room for one more.* He checked his Shearwater dive computer. *Plenty of air.*

Pivoting, he caught Amelia's eye and tapped the side of the tube with his pole spear, then raised a single finger on his free hand. She flashed an "OK" sign and started looking.

In less than a minute, they spotted another. Not surprising, really. The lionfish was a voracious, Indo-Pacific species, and had no business being here... but they were here all the same, and there were a *lot* of them. In the mid-1980s, there were no lionfish in the Atlantic and surrounding seas. Then, in 1985, one was seen in South Florida—possibly the result of release from an aquarium or collector. Then, more and more were discovered up and down the coast. The Caribbean was next. Now they were everywhere: from the Flower Gardens of the Gulf of Mexico to Trinidad and Tobago, from Belize to Bermuda, and as far up the US coast as Massachusetts. Even the Mediterranean was facing an invasion.

Venomous spines might be the primary concern to humans, but that was far down the list of reasons they were such a problem. First, their appetites: lionfish ate anything and everything they could fit into their mouths and their stomachs expanded to allow it. One scientist found a specimen with parts of sixty prey inside it. In addition to having no natural predators in the Caribbean, prey fish in this part of the world hadn't adapted to recognize the lionfish's predatory tactics, making them easy pickings. Second, they reproduced at an alarming rate: a lionfish became sexually mature in less than half the time of most fish species, capable of reproducing every four days, and a female could churn out over two million eggs in a year.

With all of this in mind, Boone didn't hesitate to kill them every chance he got, despite their beauty. And every delicious fish taco made from lionfish was a fish taco that *wasn't* made from grouper or snapper—fishes that belonged here. A motto had gained traction: "Eat 'em to Beat 'em." Many islands across the Caribbean organized lionfish culls, and the Cayman Islands were no exception. Here, on the Sister Island of Little Cayman, the dive shops held a cull every Wednesday afternoon.

This Wednesday it was their turn, and Bubble Chasers Diving would do their part. Boone lined up another shot and bagged his last fish of the dive. Drawing the speared lionfish out of the coral, he sensed a rush of movement behind him. Turning, he spotted Amelia, eyes wide, a flattened hand atop her head, fingers up—a well-known underwater dive signal: *Shark.*

Without even bothering to look for the shark, Boone quickly secured what had likely attracted it, thrusting the lionfish into the tube. Only then did he spin around, putting his back to the coral. *There.* A "reefy," the sleek predator circling the pair of divers. Caribbean reef sharks had once been uncommon off Little Cayman, but after years of lionfish culls, the bold, gray-brown sharks were seen more often. This one wasn't big, but it wasn't small either. Boone took a deep breath, then let it out slowly. Several years ago, on the island of Saba, a diver had been bitten by a reefy while spearing lionfish. Boone nearly died freediving down to save the man, losing consciousness from a shallow water blackout. He had suffered a few panic attacks since then, when elements of that day had presented themselves, and this set of circumstances seemed right on the nose.

Selfishly, he wished Emily were down here with him instead of Amelia. One look in Em's eyes would calm him. But Emily Durand had already done plenty for Boone, having suffered her own issues after a far more harrowing ordeal. Em had found an excellent therapist and had shared some of her advice and coping techniques. Boone was relieved when the panic didn't surface, and he observed the shark with a calm, analytical mind.

The reefy's back was arched and its pectoral fins jutted downward. *Aggression... or frustration.* Boone reversed the pole spear in his hand, extending the butt end outward. The shark was only doing what predators did, and it had every right to be here... no sense wounding the animal. He gestured to Amelia, beckoning her to join him against the wall. She reversed her spear as well, finning up beside him. The shark circled to their left, then abruptly cut in along the wall, heading their way. Boone calmly nudged its nose with the spear-butt and it turned away, heading for the blue.

Amelia let out a muffled sound of relief from behind her mouthpiece. Boone turned and raised a thumb, pumping it toward the surface. Amelia nodded eagerly.

◆ ◆ ◆

Emily Durand reclined on the starboard flybridge bench of the *Lunasea,* enjoying the glorious day, her favorite pair of lime-green sunglasses sitting unused on the dashboard beside the wheel. Anyone who knew her would find that unusual—it was a rare sight to see her outdoors in daylight without some form of shades shielding her brilliant green eyes. Working in the tropical outdoors for a living, she also tended to cover up, but today Em was allowing herself to soak up a little extra vitamin D. A yellow bikini speckled with green polka dots stood out in marked contrast to her lightly tanned skin, and her braided blond hair shone in the sunshine.

Just a little longer, she thought. *As soon as they pop up, I'll cover up.* Many sunscreens had been found to be detrimental to coral reefs, so she went without, limiting her exposure to the tropical sun to short bursts.

Emily glanced across the flybridge to the opposite bench—a shining pair of brown eyes looked up at her from the shade beneath. Brixton, a potlicker mutt they'd rescued on the Belizean island of Caye Caulker, raised his head expectantly.

"Not yet, Brixy," Em said. "A little more snooze time, yeah?"

Brixton lowered his head back to his paws. Boone and Emily didn't often bring their dog on the dive boat, but lionfish culls were one of the few times when their Delta Canaveral didn't have paying divers aboard, and Brix loved his time on the *Lunasea*—although Boone had to carry the dog up the flybridge ladder if the pooch wanted to be topside.

Tilting her head south toward shore, Emily let out a lazy yawn and squinted toward the flat little island. She had experience with quiet, out-of-the-way places… but if she had thought Saba and Caye Caulker were sleepy little isles, Little Cayman had revised her definition of "quiet." Smallest of the three Cayman Islands, "Little" was by far the least populous; its population fluctuated, but usually hovered around two hundred residents.

A splash and the sound of a diver clearing their nose signaled the return of Boone and Amelia. Brixton scrambled out from under the bench, nearly upending the water dish Emily had set out. Brix barked and wagged his tail excitedly.

"Permission to come aboard?" Boone called up as he made his way toward the stern, dragging the lionfish catch-tube along the water beside him. He looked up at her. "Don't you look comfortable!"

"If you get to kill, I get to chill," Em sang back, rising from the bench and standing at the starboard rail. "How many'd you get?"

"Twelve. A couple are whoppers." He looked up and abruptly halted his swim, treading water. "Haven't seen *that* one before…"

Em smiled, adjusting a thin strap of the polka-dotted bikini and leaning over the rail. "Oh, this old thing? You've seen me in it before."

"No, I haven't."

She bit her lip, a grin dimpling one cheek. "You sure? Gee, maybe I bought it in Grand last week. You like it?"

Boone blew out a breath before resuming his sternward swim. "I do indeed."

"Good. Then you can come aboard." Emily stepped back from the bench and threw on a lightweight cover-up she'd picked up in Cozumel, threading a couple of buttons into their loops as she headed for the ladder. "Brix, stay."

"Little help?" Boone called out playfully, lifting the tube onto the swim platform.

"Ooooh, that's a good haul," Em remarked, lifting the tube and setting it into a mesh gear bag to keep it from rolling around before sliding it under the starboard bench. She turned to find Boone still in the water, taking Amelia's pole spear and helping her climb aboard.

"Boone let you spear any?" Em asked, as she guided their new co-worker to a slot for her tank. "Or did he hog them all himself?"

"I got a few, and Boone and I had to double-team one, but I prefer to just watch," Amelia replied, settling into the spot on the bench and removing her gear. "I know they're invasive, but…"

"That's okay. You just don't have Boone's bloodlust."

"Wait'll you dive a cull with Em," Boone said, as he settled across from them. "She's like a lionfish serial killer down there." He set the two pole spears at his feet.

"I am not!" Em handed Boone a pair of orange foam cylinders.

Boone pinched the paralyzer tips together and carefully slid each cylinder onto a spearhead. He'd learned the hard way not to try this if the boat was in rough water, but today the seas were quiet.

"Either of you ever get stung?" Amelia asked.

"Couple times," Boone said. "Once, while tucking one into the tube. And over in Belize, when I thought I'd make some ceviche and was careless clipping the spines. Hurts like holy hell."

"Had to take him to the clinic," Em said. "Cried like a baby, 'e did."

Boone grinned, shaking his head. "Needed some antibiotics, but it isn't too bad. Hot water sorta deactivates the venom, so they had me hang out by the sink for a bit."

Em rose and went to the padded camera table set into the center of the deck behind the *Lunasea*'s flybridge ladder. She picked up a clipboard and flipped the pages to the back, where they kept their cull log. "You got twelve, yeah?" She looked toward shore. "What dive site is this again?"

"Something to do with a penguin," Boone said. This spot was outside the Marine Park and they didn't get this far over very often.

"Penguin's Leap," Amelia said.

"Bit of a funny name, that," Emily said, jotting it down. "Seen plenty of red-footed boobies, but I think Little Cayman's a bit warm for penguins."

Amelia laughed. "It's named because some famous American actor had a house on the shore, just to the west of Ken Hall Road. My grandfather says he met him a couple times."

"Not sure how we went from penguin to actor..." Boone said.

"Oh! You mean he played *the* Penguin?" Emily's face lit up. "On that old *Batman* show on the telly in the 1960s?"

"Yes, that sounds right," Amelia said. "But I can't remember his name."

"Burgess Meredith," Emily supplied without hesitation. "Also was the boxing trainer in *Rocky*."

Boone laughed, unfolding his lanky frame from the bench and standing to stretch. "I can't believe what a nerd you are," he said with a grin.

"I never hear you complaining when we crush it at Beach Nuts' Trivia Night."

"Got me there."

A whine came from above and Boone raised his head. "Oh, sorry Brix! Stay right there! I'm coming up."

"Amelia, you wanna drive?" Em asked. Emily usually skippered, but they were still training the young Caymanian.

"Of course!"

"Take the wheel!" Emily ordered.

"We're so close to CCMI, let's just swing by and give them the cull," Boone suggested. "I can pick the tube up later."

"I'll give them a call on the radio," Em said, and the three of them ascended the ladder to the flybridge. Brixton was overjoyed.

———◆◆———

Later in the afternoon, the Central Caribbean Marine Institute's RIB—rigid inflatable boat—sped away from the *Lunasea*, returning to shore. CCMI didn't have a dock, so they'd come out to the Bubble Chasers dive boat to grab their catch. The researchers there would examine the lionfish—weighing and measuring them, examining stomach contents, etc. Often, a fair amount of the cull would be delivered to various restaurants, particularly the Pirates Point Resort, for their lionfish sushi night on Fridays.

Boone gathered Brixton on his lap and sat side-saddle on the starboard bench, letting the dog enjoy the sea breeze as the custom Delta Canaveral built up speed. "Take us home, skipper!"

"Well... just to the entrance to the lagoon..." Amelia clarified.

"I dunno... you're gonna need to learn to run the cut sometime," Boone said. "And the seas are pretty chill today." Most of the dive ops on the island were located in South Hole Sound, a protected lagoon on the southwest side of the island. The channel in the fringing reef could be challenging... though not as challenging as the one in Cayman Brac, which had even less room to maneuver. Still, leaving the lagoon in Little Cayman was occasionally tricky—*entering* it, even more so.

"We'll take a gander at the channel when we get there, 'Melia," Em said, rearranging Brix's water bowl under the port bench. Boone had affixed a patch of Velcro to the deck beneath the bench, and a corresponding patch under the bowl, but sometimes the stainless-steel bowl came free, the Velcro being an adhesive-backed type they'd found in a crafts store over on Grand.

Amelia took them back across the reef, turning the wheel to port and heading west toward Bloody Bay Wall. As they reached Jackson's Point, Amelia turned the wheel further to port, taking the boat along the coast, which ran west-southwest. Off the port bow, a dive boat was moored in the shallows.

"Looks like Reef Divers is out late," Boone remarked, noting the Newton 42, the name *Island Sister* on the front of its flybridge.

"They're at Cascades," Em noted. "Betcha they came back from the drop to La La Land and spied some spotted eagle rays in the sand near the boat."

"Good reason to burn the last of your bubbles," Boone agreed.

"I thought the eagle rays were at Eagle Ray Roundup," Amelia said.

"You and every diver who asks to go to that dive site," Boone said. "They used to be there in large numbers, one of the older divemasters told me. You can still see eagle rays at Roundup, but nowadays your odds are better here at Cascades."

Boone and Emily had only been in Little Cayman for six months, but in that time, they'd learned a lot from the other dive ops about the many sites around the island. Cascades had numerous mini-walls and sandy slopes that "cascaded" down to the drop-off. The sandy areas drew stingrays and eagle rays, and the site was also known to draw a shark or two.

Emily rose from her bench and waved across at a figure on the opposite flybridge, but the person appeared to be dozing.

"Who's up top?" Boone asked.

She shrugged. "Can't make 'em out. Might be taking a kip."

Boone chuckled. The individual did appear to be napping, and odds were good they also would've understood Emily's British slang. More than half of the current Reef Divers staff hailed from the United Kingdom. Emily had grown up in South London, and her blue-collar accent and impish antics made her quite popular at the Beach Nuts Bar, situated near the Reef Divers dive shop. While self-governing, the Cayman Islands was a British Overseas Territory—there were quite a few Brits in the diving industry in Grand, Little, and the Brac.

"I see something, I think," Amelia said. She pointed toward the open ocean to the northwest.

Boone squinted behind his polarized shades, then lowered Brix to the deck and rose from the bench. "Pretty far out. Looks like a small boat." There wasn't anything unusual about seeing a boat out on the ocean, but something about it nudged Boone to give it a closer look. *Is it movement? Something blurring across the top?*

He turned to grab his binoculars from a compartment alongside the wheel, but Emily had anticipated him and already had them in hand.

"'Ere you go, Boonie. You've got some extra altitude on me, so let's have you give it the looksee, yeah?"

"Thanks." Boone smiled, taking the binoculars. At nearly six-four, he certainly had the height advantage on his partner, a pint-size powerhouse an inch under five feet. "Amelia, bring her down to idle for me, please?"

"Aye aye."

As the *Lunasea* slowed, Boone braced himself against the bench and raised the binoculars, aiming them at the distant boat. He immediately lowered them. "Emily, take the wheel and steer for that boat! And floor it... they're in distress!"

3

"There's a man waving a beach towel back and forth," Boone said, as Emily took control of the *Lunasea* and pushed the throttle to the stop. Below, the Caterpillar C 12.9 transitioned from rumble to roar, and the converted Delta Canaveral poured on the speed. Obtained from a police auction in Belize, the *Lunasea*—originally named the *Alhambra*—had come from a dive op in Honduras that had been a front for drug running. The 985-horsepower engine could push the customized Canaveral with its subtly modified hull up to thirty-five knots—in theory, at least. There was only so much the cartel could do with the base hull-form, and if the seas were rough, she had trouble attaining those speeds.

"Wonder if their radio is down," Emily mused.

Boone verified that their own VHF was set to Channel 16. It was, and there had been no distress call. He grabbed the mic and thumbed the talk button. "Small craft off the northwest coast of Little Cayman, this is the dive boat *Lunasea*. Do you read?"

After a silent pause, Boone triggered it again. "Small craft, in the event you can hear but not transmit, we see you waving a towel and assume you are in distress. We are inbound."

The radio came alive with a Welsh-accented voice: "Lunasea, *this is* Island Sister. *That you, Boone?*"

"It is indeed. Heya, Rhys. You copy all that?"

"Yes, ah do. I still have divers down, but can assist once they're up."

Emily reached over and pressed Boone's thumb onto the button. "Eagle rays, yeah?"

The voice on the radio laughed. *"There she is!* Prynhawn da, *Emily."*

"Good afternoon yourself, Rhys!"

"Yes, several spotted eagles down there. Back to your radio call... let us know if you need assistance."

"I don't see any smoke or anything," Boone said. "I think we can handle it. Let you know if otherwise. *Lunasea* out."

In three minutes, they pulled up alongside the vessel, a small fishing boat with the name *Bob's Bobo* along the bow.

"Funny name, that," Emily commented as she brought the *Lunasea* down to an idle.

"*Bobo* is a Caymanian word for a dear friend or loved one," Amelia offered. A smile crept onto her face. "You're Boone's bobo."

"Hear that, Bobo Boone? I learned a new word!"

"Wonderful," Boone deadpanned, a small smile escaping the corner of his mouth as he descended the ladder to the main deck.

Across the way, *Bob's Bobo* bobbed on the waves, its bow facing east toward Cayman Brac, the neighboring Sister Island not visible at that distance. The figure who had been waving the towel stood at the gunwale, looking quite relieved. The man was blond, a rosy glow of sunburn making substantial inroads on his pale skin. "Hello! Thank goodness you saw us! We couldn't get the radio to work."

"You've got someone else with you?" Boone called across.

"Yes! Willis is down below, trying to fix the engine."

"I'd be happy to take a look, if you'd like."

"Yes, please! I'm Leonard, by the way."

"Pleased to meet you. I'm Boone. Amelia and Emily are up top. I'd like to tie up to you. Normally, I'd just step across, but you're drifting and we're already pretty far offshore. Emily can use our engine to keep you more-or-less stationary."

"Whatever you think is best," Leonard said, nodding uncertainly.

"Em, bring us alongside," Boone called up to the flybridge, deploying the dive boat's fenders on the port side as Emily came about. Amelia descended to join him, and he directed her to the stern line. Kicking off his sandals, Boone stepped up on the gunwale, skirting the wheelhouse coaming on his way to the bow.

Little Cayman was far too small to host a Cayman Islands Coast Guard vessel, and with Grand Cayman ninety miles away, it made sense for Boone to take a look before they called it in. The boat appeared seaworthy, and Boone had considerable skill with marine engines. Back in Bonaire, he'd been Rock Beauty Divers' go-to guy when an engine needed repair.

Boone looked astern and watched as Amelia tossed her line across. Leonard muffed the catch, but managed to get it on the second try. Watching the man look around for a place to tie off, Boone quickly realized he had a landlubber on his hands. "Em, nudge us in... I'm gonna step across."

"Right-o!"

As Emily brought the *Lunasea* close with a gentle hand on the wheel, Boone's long legs bridged the gap with ease. Stepping onto the fishing boat's bow, he quickly tied off to the cleat there and made his way astern, tossing several orange ball fenders over the

Bobo's starboard side on the way. Leonard had found a cleat and was trying to tie a knot that would arouse either pity or rage in any sailor witnessing the attempt.

"Here, I got it," Boone said, leaning down and unravelling the mess, then cleating the line properly.

"Thanks," Leonard said. "The only boat I've been on before today is the Staten Island Ferry in New York."

Boone looked off to the west. "You came across from Grand?"

"Grand?" Leonard wrinkled a sunburned brow. "Oh! Grand Cayman. Yes. I hired this boat in Grand Cayman."

Leonard pronounced the island's name the way most Americans did, hitting the first syllable and tossing away the second, the same way Boone had when they'd first moved here. It hadn't taken long before a local had corrected him. With Grand Cayman and Little Cayman, you were supposed to stress the second syllable, and it sounded more like "mahn" than how he used to say it. But when referring to the Cayman Islands, or to Cayman Brac, locals stressed the *first* syllable. It had taken Boone a while to wrap his brain and tongue around that, and he still got it wrong from time to time.

Boone looked around at the interior of the vessel, clearly a local fisherman's boat. Grand Cayman's protected North Sound, where many of the island's boats were docked, was nearly eighty-five miles from where they were now. "Bit further than I would've gone with this boat," Boone remarked.

"Willis said we'd be fine. I wanted to check out the Sister Islands for possible locations."

Boone raised an eyebrow. "Locations for what?"

"Mistuh Leonard," a voice called from below, "I can't fix it!" A Caymanian teen popped his head up. "Oh. Hello, mistuh. Who you?"

"Hi, I'm Boone. Willis, is it?"

"Yessuh."

"Not Robert? Or Bob?"

The youth looked confused. "Robert's me fadduh's name."

"So, I'm guessing *Bob's Bobo* belongs to your dad."

Willis sagged, resting his arms on the deck outside the engine compartment. "It were pure stoopidness to t'ink I could take it across myself," he muttered.

"Wait, what?" Leonard reddened—an impressive feat, considering how much the sunburn was contributing to his present complexion. "You said this was your boat!"

"It is de family boat," the youth explained.

Boone quickly crossed to the hold and sat on the edge. "No worries, Willis. I'm good with engines. Mind if I take a look?"

"Yes, please, t'ank you," the young man sputtered.

"What happened when you broke down?" Boone asked, lowering himself into the cramped engine space. Standing there, his upper body was still above the deck.

"De overheat light came on and de engine jus' died."

"Okay, thanks… that gives me a starting place." Boone glanced up at Leonard, noting the anger on the man's face. *I think Willis could use a little distraction.* "Hey, Em?" he called across to the *Lunasea*. "Come on over! Meet the crew."

———— ◆ ◆ ————

Leonard Berezinski ground his teeth. Things were not going well. Even before he'd left the pier in Grand Cayman, rumors were flying that the film's starring actress had bailed, and the shoot was in doubt. And now this: marooned at sea in a broken-down fisherman's boat. He watched Boone as the tall young man ducked out of sight into the engine compartment. Willis sidled up beside Leonard.

"I have fixed her before many a time," he said.

"So what's different this time?" Leonard asked heatedly.

"I don't know, suh. Trouble don't blow shell. Sometime she catch you unaware."

"What the hell does that mean?"

"Ahoy the *Bobo*!" a British-accented voice called. "Permission to pop aboard?"

Leonard turned and felt his jaw involuntarily slacken. Poised on the dive boat's gunwale, one hand holding the cowling alongside the wheelhouse, a stunning blonde cast a shining smile across the tiny gap between the boats. Leonard guessed she was in her late twenties, but her French braids and a playful set of dimples on either side of her lips made her seem even younger. She was wearing a lightweight, cream-colored cover-up but it hung loosely open, revealing a petite build, curvy in all the right places, as the green polka-dotted yellow bikini made clear.

"Or I could stay over here," she said with a little shrug. "But I figured you could use some company while Boone bangs about in the bilge."

Leonard snapped back to reality. "Oh, sorry, yes! Please, come over."

"Right-o." Despite her diminutive height, the young woman effortlessly stepped across, her bare feet slapping onto the deck as she hopped down from the gunwale. "I'm Emily Durand," she offered, looking up at him. "Leonard, right?"

"Yes. Leonard Berezinski. And this is Willis... umm..."

"Ebanks," the youth said.

"Hey, whaddaya know?" Emily exclaimed. "We've got an Ebanks, too! Amelia up there at the wheel."

Willis smiled. "One outta fourteen Caymanians is an Ebanks, my teacher say."

"You a fisherman, Willis?" Emily asked.

"Sometimes I help my dad. He hurt his foot last week. But de movie people offered good money to rent de boat."

"Okay..." Boone's voice rose from below. "I see the problem." The divemaster's head popped up, forehead drenched in sweat. "You've got a broken drive belt. It happens with some inboards. Think your dad kept a spare?"

"I dunno. Wait! I t'ink I seen one somewhere." He turned and went into the little wheelhouse, pulling open a cupboard built into the side.

"So... what brings you two to Little?" Emily asked.

"I came to look at the Sister Islands," Leonard said. "I'm a location scout for a movie that's being shot down here."

Although the blonde's eyes were obscured by a huge pair of light green sunglasses, Leonard was pretty sure they widened as Emily's face lit up. "A movie? Ace! What's it called?"

"*Man O' War*," Leonard said.

"What, like sailing ships with cannons? Horatio Hornblower, that kind of thing?"

Leonard laughed. "No, nothing like that. The name refers to..." He trailed off. "Actually, I'm probably not allowed to reveal that. But it's a sci-fi horror movie. We have an amazing director. Heinz Werner."

"That sounds familiar," Boone said. "Wait, is he that German director who did the documentary about that guy getting eaten by grizzlies?"

"No. Completely different person."

"So, who's in the movie?"

"Mostly unknowns, but we've got Brooke Bablin in a starring role," Leonard said, before realizing that the film might *not* have her anymore. The actress hadn't shown up for her six-a.m. hair and makeup call and her villa was completely empty, with the exception of a single note written on the condo complex stationery: *I QUIT.* Frantic calls to her agent hadn't yielded any explanation, their office claiming they were equally baffled by the sudden departure.

"Brooke Bablin? Blimey!" Em struck a pose, reaching back to flip aside a braid, then tipping her sunglasses down on her button nose and peering over them with brilliant green eyes. "I'm a girl with a very particular set of skills," Em rasped in a seductive voice. "*Sexy* skills."

Boone burst into laughter. "Wow. Good thing you have a day job."

"Sod off, Bobo Boone, that was good!" She smiled at Leonard. "Couple of my mates always said I looked like her."

As Leonard smiled back at this stunning young woman, a light bulb went off. "Emily... how tall are you?"

4

Fifteen minutes later, Boone climbed out of the engine compartment and helped Willis slide the deck panel back into place. "That spare belt seemed a bit brittle, so let's take it real slow. Em, can you skipper her? I'd prefer if you were the one bringing her through the gap."

"Gap?" Willis asked. "You mean between here and Grand?"

Boone shook his head. "You're not going back tonight. The sun would be down before you got halfway home, your radio is on the fritz, and I don't trust that belt to hold. The gap I meant is usually referred to as 'the cut.' It's a channel into Little Cayman's lagoon on the south side. Most of the dive shops are inside there. You can stay over and we'll find a better belt for you. Between Bubble Chasers and the other dive shops, we'll get you fixed up. And I'll call a guy who repairs electronics on the island to look at the radio."

Leonard nodded, distracted, looking at his smartphone. "Okay, sure. Thank you. Hey, how often are the flights from Grand Cayman? I can't get a signal..."

"Yeah, service is spotty up here on the north side," Boone said. "As for flights, depends on the day, but there are about twenty-four inter-island flights a week. Cayman Airways operates puddle jumpers that go from Grand to Little to Brac, and back again."

Leonard put his phone away. "How long to get to this lagoon?"

"Not long," Em said. "It's 'round the bend, on the southwest side. We don't want to bust the belt, so I'll keep the speed around eight to ten knots. Probably take thirty or forty minutes." She turned to Boone. "You gonna let Amelia try her hand at entering the cut today?"

Boone thought for a moment. "Nah, I'll do it. I'd rather she try it on a day when you're aboard with her."

Em grinned, holding up a finger to get Leonard's attention. "You'd rather she run the cut with *me* aboard because...?"

Boone chuckled. "Because you're the better skipper."

"And don't you forget it! Not to worry Leonard, I'll get *Bob's Bobo* safely to our dock, easy peasy."

"Amelia and I will keep pace," Boone said, stepping across to the *Lunasea*. "When we reach the channel, I'll take over the wheel and follow you in."

"So, Mr. Location Scout," Emily began after she and Willis had cast off the lines and brought in the fenders, "what exactly are you scouting for?"

"Mr. Werner thought the shoreline in Grand Cayman was far too developed a background for some of the scenes. He asked me to check out the Sister Islands and see if things looked a bit more... uninhabited."

Emily laughed as she took her place behind the wheel of the fishing boat. "Well, you picked the right one! Cayman Brac has ten times the population of Little. Here, we've got large stretches of the coast with no houses at all. And as for the buildings we have, I'm not sure I've ever seen a structure with more than two stories."

"I have to admit, there's not much to look at over there," Leonard said, holding up his phone and shooting a short video of the shoreline. "Which is probably what Werner wants. It's all so flat."

"Yeah, Little Cayman is mostly sea level," Emily admitted. "If you'd made it over to the Brac, you would've seen some cool cliffs. They have caves over there, too. But here? Here, we've got Bloody Bay Wall!"

"Yes, I heard about that! Great name!" Leonard looked toward shore. "Whereabouts is it?"

Em laughed. "Right under you."

Leonard smacked a palm against his forehead, wincing when it impacted the sunburned surface. "Oh, of course. Duh. A wall dive."

"*The* wall dive! We're situated on the Cayman Trench and the wall here is nearly vertical in places. Just a sheer drop into the abyss. You're swimming along the sand at eighteen feet and then *boom*! The bottom drops out!"

"How deep does it go?"

"Y'know, we had quite a row at Trivia Night over that question. Depends on who you talk to. I've heard a thousand feet… two thousand feet… two and a half miles. It's *deep*."

"That might make for a fantastic backdrop…" Leonard mused. "How's the visibility?"

"Fantastic! A hundred feet, most days."

"The movie has a number of underwater scenes in it. We're working with the Cayman Islands Film Commission and we've got a permit to shoot in a few places. That wall sounds perfect."

"Well... right here we're inside the Marine Park. It might be easier to get permission to shoot further back to the east. We were actually diving there before we found you. A spot called Penguin's Leap."

"Odd name."

"That's what *I* said! Apparently, it's named that because Burgess Meredith had a house on the shore there."

"Really? That campy *Batman* villain? Oh, wow, our property master will *love* that! He's obsessed with those old shows." Leonard squinted an eye and gritted his teeth, laughing through the grin. "Hwaa-hwaa-hwaa!"

Emily had only seen the show a few times, during a late-night YouTube video binge-fest, but she recognized the distinctive laugh immediately and burst into laughter of her own. "Brill impression, Lenny! Are you an actor, too?"

"No... I'm terrible at memorizing lines." A contemplative look crossed his face. "How about you, Emily? You ever do any acting?"

"Me? Well... Boone always says that when I give my dive briefings I put on an entire play. Although I'm not sure he was being entirely complimentary." She laughed. "Oh... I *am* an Emmy Award winner."

Leonard perked up. "What?"

"There was one time where I was doing an impression of a grouper getting groomed by a cleaner shrimp, and the whole boat lost it laughing... so at the end, they gave me an "Emmy." Y'know, cuz I'm Em. The trophy was just an orange from the snack cooler that they drew a goofy face on. I kept it 'til it rotted."

"Oh. So... no actual acting, then?"

"Well... I did a couple Christmas pantos back in the UK."

"Pantos?"

"Pantomime. Kind of like a family-friendly variety show. My amateur dramatics group did some when I was at university. Oh! And I was in *A Christmas Carol* right before secondary school. Played Tiny Tim."

Leonard raised his eyebrows. "Umm..."

"Well, I didn't have *these* yet," Emily laughed, flashing open her beach cover. "And my height was right."

"Four-foot-eleven," Leonard recited.

"Gold star to Lenny!" Em said. She nodded to shore as they trundled slowly southwest along the coast. "There's McCoy's Beach Bar. Most of the bars and restaurants are on the south side; that one's cornered the market for the north coast. Used to be a resort. Might be a cool location for you. Locals like that place."

"If we had to bring in any equipment to Little Cayman, where's your port?"

"Port?" Emily laughed. "You'll see it in a minute or two." Soon, she pointed across the water to a square chunk of concrete against the shore. "Salt Rock Dock! We usually get a barge from Grand on Wednesdays. Anyone who's expecting something drives out there to pick it up from the containers. Sometimes, when the seas are rough, it might be weeks to get a shipment."

"Oh my..."

"Yeah, if you need to bring in anything for your film, might be safer to charter a flight in. Or bring it over on a rented boat. Preferably one with longer legs than this one."

The minutes ticked past as *Bob's Bobo* made her way to the western tip of the island and Emily swung the wheel to port. "And around the bend we go!" Emily looked back and gave a wave to Boone and Amelia, who were a hundred yards off their stern, pacing them. Boone waved back.

"Here comes a plane!" Willis called out.

"That's the last one of the day," Em explained. "It'll drop off a few passengers and continue on to Cayman Brac, where it'll sit overnight before coming back the other way tomorrow morning. Little Cayman's airstrip is over there to your left. And the lagoon is just ahead! See those breakers? There's a ring of coral that forms a little atoll. Great shelter for boats when the seas are rough... but getting in and out can be a bit of a wild ride. There's a channel on the southwest corner of it. Once I start my run, be sure you're holding on to something."

"Will my father's boat make it through?" Willis asked nervously.

"Oh, yeah, no worries," Em said, biting her lip. "Provided the belt holds."

Boone watched as Emily positioned herself south of the channel and pivoted the fishing boat into line with the cut in the fringing reef. He'd made the transit often, and most of the time the trip through was uneventful. The trick was to time the swells, gunning it at just the right spot, cresting each wave in turn and slaloming down to tackle the next one. When you hit everything just right, it was exhilarating; but if you were off, it made for one hell of a bumpy ride. And if you were *way* off, a wave could spin or roll you and send your boat into either side of the cut. One year, a sailboat had decorated the reef for nearly ten days before conditions calmed enough to remove it. And another time, a plucky new police constable had crunched into the coral to the east of the channel; it was one of the reasons Little Cayman didn't have a police boat on island, relying on one next door at Cayman Brac.

"Ready to take over?" Amelia asked, offering Boone the wheel.

"You mind?"

Amelia laughed. "Not at all! I'm nervous enough for Emily!"

"She'll be fine." Boone took the wheel and swung the boat out to sea a bit before turning to port and lining up behind *Bob's Bobo*. Truth to tell, he was a tiny bit nervous for Em himself. She'd been running the engine low and slow, but when she came to the swells she'd have to throttle up. He hoped that crusty old spare belt would hold.

"There she goes!" Amelia shouted, gripping a handhold on the side of the wheelhouse. Ahead, the water churned behind the fishing boat's stern as Emily pushed the little boat toward the first swell.

Boone held his breath, only letting it out when the fishing boat rose over the first swell before dashing down into the trough. "One down... and..."

"Ooh!" Amelia winced as Emily took the next swell just below the crest, sending up twin walls of spray on either side of the bow. The thumping smack was audible across the water.

"All's well," Boone said. "I've done worse a hundred times. And the last one is usually easier..."

"Whew! She's in!"

Boone relaxed as he watched the fishing boat level out and turn to starboard, heading for their dock past the Southern Cross Club. "Okay... our turn. Do you mind sitting on the deck and grabbing hold of Brix?"

Amelia knew the drill. She sat down, grabbing hold of a bench brace with one hand and gathering Brixton against her with the other. "Ready."

"Here we go…"

————◆•◆————

Ten minutes later, Boone brought the *Lunasea* alongside their pier. Emily and Willis had already tied up *Bob's Bobo* on the opposite side and Leonard stood just outside the cockpit, gathering his things.

"How'd it go?" Emily called up as she caught the bow line. "Did he botch it?"

Amelia was giggling as she stepped across with the stern line. "He smacked into the first swell so hard!"

"Yeah, yeah…" Boone said sheepishly, as he cut the engine.

"So exciting!" Leonard said, stepping onto the pier and setting a bag at his feet. He fished his phone out of his pocket. "Emily, you made for quite a heroic figure during the crossing!" He opened his photos and showed her the smartphone screen. "I hope you don't mind that I took a few shots."

"Not at all, long as you send me these!" Em said, admiring the photos. "Smashing pics, Lenny!"

"Willis… would you take a photo with me and our captain?" Leonard handed over the phone and sidled up to Emily, holding her against him with an arm around her shoulder. "And could I trouble you to remove those sunglasses?"

Emily shrugged, taking them off. "It's nearing sundown, so I s'pose I can oblige."

"Em tends to make faces when you try to capture her on film," Boone called down. "So be sure to take a bunch."

Emily stuck out her tongue at Boone, then proceeded to mug for the camera for two or three shots before finally subsiding into a respectable smile.

Leonard looked up at Boone. "Did we get one?"

"Eventually."

Em broke free of Leonard, cinching closed her cover-up. "Oh, you love it, Bobo Boone."

Boone grinned as he brought Brixton down the ladder before stepping over to the pier and releasing the dog. Brix bolted for shore, looking for a place to do his business. Boone gestured to the small complex of buildings. "We run our dive shop out of the first floor of the condo we're renting here. We've got a guest bedroom and the living room has a fold-out. Em, why don't you get Leonard and Willis settled while I call around for a spare belt. Amelia, can you track down Fitzroy? See if we can't get the radio fixed."

"Your condo," Leonard asked, engrossed in the photos, "does it have Wi-Fi?"

"It does indeed," Emily said. "This way, gentlemen!"

5

Heinz Werner stubbed out the smoldering remains of his cigarette, adding its corpse to the rest of the butts in the ashtray. "Play it back one more time," he sighed.

"You got it." The editor returned the timeline to the beginning of the scene and restarted it. Hovering over their shoulders, Alan Novak, Director of Photography, stood with his arms crossed.

Werner leaned forward, trying to keep his mind on the action playing out in front of him. Occasionally he scrawled a timecode and a note on a pad that lay beside the ashtray. When the playback reached the end, he nodded to the editor. "Acceptable. Let us take a ten-minute break, then we'll look at the next scene. I need a moment to collect my thoughts."

Chairs scooted and rolled as the technical crew cleared the small, dark room. One man paused expectantly.

"Not you, Dario. Sit over there, please."

The 1st AD nodded and plopped down in the corner, out of the director's line of sight.

Werner leaned forward, propping his elbows on the workstation as he massaged his temples. This production was shaping up to be a disaster. The decision to shoot in the Cayman Islands had seemed like a grand idea at the time, as one of the principal producers was an influential resident in Grand Cayman. Indeed, George Town had a reasonable amount of infrastructure, and the local producer's contacts had helped keep costs in line. And with this movie being a seaborne creature feature, you just couldn't beat the vibrant blues of the Caribbean Sea, and the underwater scenes would benefit from a visibility far superior to anything they would have gotten in the States or across the pond in the Mediterranean.

Furthermore, with the prospect of shooting a movie in paradise, most of the actors had been happy to accept minimum scale—although many of the cast members were relative unknowns, and negotiating the lower salaries hadn't been a heavy lift. Werner enjoyed the challenges of molding inexperienced young actors. Natural talent, unmarred by old habits or ingrained mannerisms, was far more to Werner's liking. That being said, the producers insisted he needed a name on the marquis other than his own. After some searching, Brooke Bablin had been brought aboard. Werner found her difficult to work with, but the pint-size bombshell had a huge following, and that would translate to big bucks at the box office. They'd also managed to score a B-list action star for their male lead. Cliff Van Dorn was thirty-five playing twenty-five, but he was in good shape and Werner found his acting better than average.

The production had started well enough. But then things began to go wrong.

First, there had been a mix-up with a cargo container of filmmaking equipment shipped from Miami. When the container was unloaded and opened, it was found to contain two tons of coffee and multiple pallets of stuffed animals and action figures. They were still trying to track down the missing container, but replacement equipment had to be rushed down in a privately chartered—and very expensive—flight. Next, Cliff Van Dorn had been mugged in New York City the night before his flight. Despite demonstrating exceptional martial arts abilities on the big screen, he'd showed no prowess at all on the security camera footage outside the bodega, where two unarmed, masked thugs had beaten the holy hell out of him. It would be a long time before he appeared in front of a camera again. Police still had no leads.

And the casting issues weren't over yet, for no sooner had they recast their male lead and brought a promising young actor down to replace him, than Brooke Bablin decided to "pull a diva" and walk. Werner had been forced to shift today's shoot schedule to one of the other storylines—one that didn't involve the character of "Sarah." Nevertheless, the troubles continued. Today's shoot had suffered numerous technical difficulties—a series of equipment failures that baffled the technicians. Finally, Werner had called it a day at four in the afternoon, retiring to the editing room to go over what they'd managed to shoot.

"I won the Jury Prize..." Werner said into the smoke-filled air of the editing room.

"Sir?" Dario asked from the darkened corner he currently occupied.

"The Cannes Film Festival."

"Yes... I know. For that docudrama about the pool hustler."

"*Stripes and Solids.*"

"Yes. Wonderful film."

"And now I direct monster movies."

Dario remained silent.

Werner sighed. "Fate leads and I follow."

"Umm… this is a *very* good script, Heinz."

"I know. I rewrote much of it. Now, if the universe will allow me to *film* it!" Werner's phone buzzed from the workstation, vibrating the ashtray and making the cigarette butts dance like Mexican jumping beans. "Get that, please."

Dario rose and answered the call, then held it out to the director. "It's Leonard Berezinski."

Werner took the phone. "What is it, Leonard? We're going over the dailies," he said, referring to the raw, unedited footage of the day's shoots. "Wait a minute, why are you calling? You should be back now, *ja*? Just come to the editing room."

"Actually, Mr. Werner… the boat broke down."

"*Gott im Himmel*… of course it did." Werner pinched the bridge of his nose, sucking in a long, calming breath. "Misfortune continues her spiteful dance. This movie appears to be laboring under the weight of some form of curse."

"Well, actually… this breakdown might be a blessing in disguise," Leonard said.

"Explain."

"Any word from Miss Bablin?"

Werner ground his teeth, grabbing the pack of cigarettes that lay on a tray beside the monitors. "*Nein*. She has 'flown the coop,' as they say. No one has heard from her since she left the downtown pier after yesterday afternoon's shoot. The producers contacted her agent; apparently her impulsive decision was not something she had discussed with them. They are trying to track her down. Recasting at this late stage would be… difficult."

"Maybe not. Check your email."

"One moment." Werner set the phone aside and tucked a cigarette between his lips, lighting it as he looked around the darkened room. "Dario, bring me my laptop."

The 1st AD brought Werner's computer, setting it beside the editing board and opening it for him. Heinz Werner went into his email and found a message from Leonard with three photo attachments. Taking a drag from the cigarette, he tapped the first one and it filled the screen.

A stunning blonde smiled out at him from the laptop, dimples at the corners of her mouth and mirth in her eyes. Werner's immediate impression was: *She looks like Brooke Bablin!* Even the height was similar. Leonard was standing alongside her, and her head only came up to his shoulder. A loose cover-up hung open over a polka-dotted bikini revealing a very attractive figure. Not as gym-toned as Brooke's body, but close. Her facial features were softer, less sculpted, but Werner actually found her far more appealing. He tapped the second photo.

In this shot, the young woman was in profile, gripping the wheel of the fishing boat the production company had rented. The picture had been taken from slightly below, as if Leonard had been seated on the deck when he took it. In the background, a wall of spray filled the air, the horizon tilted as the boat pitched up, likely on the crest of a wave. Her French-braided hair was speckled with shining droplets of seawater.

Werner opened the third photo, a full shot taken from further back. In this dynamic shot, the blonde's bare feet were planted firmly on the deck, her tanned legs bent at the knees as she skippered the boat through the rough waters. Werner returned to the previous picture and zoomed in on the young woman's face. A pair of enormous lime-green sunglasses obscured her eyes, her smiling lips pressed together in a look of determination. The girl's overall expression was a mixture of concentration... and glee.

An inchworm of ash fell from his forgotten cigarette and Werner blinked. He grabbed his phone. "Leonard... who is this girl?"

"She's a divemaster on Little Cayman. Our rented boat broke down off the coast; she and her boyfriend were on their dive boat and spotted us. They're trying to repair our boat as we speak and I'm staying over. As soon as I saw her, I knew I had to contact you."

Werner flipped back to the first photo. "It is uncanny."

"I know, right? Even the height."

"Does she have any acting experience?"

"Not unless you count Christmas shows when she was a preteen."

"Well, that is something, I suppose. What about her personality? Did she seem like the sort of person who can think on her feet?"

"Absolutely. She's extremely funny. I had a hard time keeping up with her. And yes, she's definitely someone who makes quick decisions. Seemed smart as a whip. And you should have seen her navigate this crazy gap in the reef! Oh! And the island itself... it has long stretches of coastline without a building in sight, and I'm fairly sure you'll want to shoot the underwater scenes over here. There is a sheer wall dive that—"

"Leonard," Werner interrupted. "I'm going to mute you for a moment." He tapped the icon to silence the call and set the phone beside his ashtray. Steepling his fingers over his nose, he closed his eyes for a long moment.

"Sir...?" Dario asked from his corner.

Werner opened his eyes and reached out to touch the image on the laptop screen. "When fortune deigns to bestow a gift, only a fool refuses it." He turned toward the darkened corner. "Dario. Cancel tomorrow's shoots. Tell the crew to spend their time ironing the bugs out of the equipment and have the actors run their lines. The stunt coordinator can rehearse the big fight scene again. And for the love of God, see if there are any other trained monkeys on the island." He shifted his gaze to the door. "Jerry!" he bellowed. "Get in here!"

The door banged open and the 2nd AD burst in. "Yes, Mr. Werner?"

"Find out when the first flight to Little Cayman is and get me on it."

"Yessir." He started to go.

"Wait! That young actor we hired to replace Van Dorn... uh..."

"Billy Faust."

"Yes. Get him a ticket as well. I want to see what sort of chemistry these two have."

Jerry looked confused. "Which two?"

"Why are you still darkening the door? Go book the flight! *Schnell!*"

As Jerry scampered back out, Werner returned the phone to his ear.

"This young woman... what is her name?"

"Emily Durand."

6

"Brixton... leave that hermit crab alone."

The dog looked up from the crustacean he'd been nudging, cocking his head at Emily. *Who, me? I wasn't doing anything.*

"C'mon back, Brixy," Em called. "There's a teensy piece of bacon in it for you!"

Boone didn't know if Brixton understood the word "bacon," but it sure seemed like he did. The brown mutt dashed across the sand to the patio table under a Cayman broadleaf, where Boone and Emily had set themselves up with a simple sunrise breakfast. Nearby, the bright red blooms of a flamboyant tree rustled in the sea breeze. Brix danced on his hind legs, eyes locked on Em.

She laughed. "I haven't even broken off a piece yet, Brix."

"Doesn't matter," Boone said, sipping his coffee. "You've awakened the Bacon Madness."

Emily held out a piece and Brix practically inhaled it, then sat in the sand, staring intently at her. "That's it for now, Brix."

Em poked a spoon into some yogurt and fruit. "I'm surprised the smell of coffee and bacon didn't rouse our guests."

"I'm not. Did you see the sunburn on Leonard? Bet they're both pretty sun-sapped from yesterday." He shrugged. "They can sleep in. Fitzroy is coming to take a look at the radio around ten."

"What about the drive belt?"

"Found one on the Brac. Since we're not booked for any dives today, I'll pop over after Fitz looks at the radio. I need to pick up a couple things, anyway."

Emily nodded. Cayman Brac had a wider variety of stores and shops than Little, and sometimes they took the *Lunasea* next door to restock. Their fellow Sister Island was less than five miles away—ten miles, dock to dock. Grand Cayman had far more in the way of stores, but Grand's West Bay was nearly ninety miles distant, so they rarely boated across. But when they did, they filled the boat with goodies.

Boone took a sip of the strong coffee Emily had brought back from Grand the last time she'd been over there. "Damn, this is good."

"It's Hacienda La Minita from Costa Rica. AJ recommended it! She helped me find some at that new Foster's in Camana Bay."

Boone cocked an eyebrow. AJ Bailey was a British divemaster on Grand Cayman who had been tremendously helpful when Boone and Em had made the move from Cozumel. "Do any of you Brits actually drink tea?"

"Me mum always teases me about being a traitor to my people. But tea just doesn't give me the eye-popping, sun-greeting jolt I need. AJ feels the same."

"You're still obsessed with her, aren't you?"

"I am not!" Emily hid a smile behind her coffee mug. "Well, not as much."

"Mm-hmm." Boone took a leisurely bite of bacon. "You gotten the tattoo yet?"

Emily laughed. "Given our near-nightly activities, you know very well I haven't!"

Boone leaned back in his chair. "You're getting a mermaid, aren't you?"

"None of your business! I haven't decided! Yes, probably!"

Emily had taken quite a shine to AJ when they'd first met. The Grand Cayman divemaster had a striking look, with vivid tattoo sleeves on her arms and blond hair streaked with purple. Adding to Emily's obsession was the name of AJ's company: Mermaid Divers. Em had a thing for those mythical fish-femmes and had even debated incorporating one into their own dive op on Cozumel. Ultimately, they'd gone with Bubble Chasers Diving—a reference to the technique of following a group of divers' bubbles during a drift dive. Cozumel had whipping currents, and drift dives were the norm. Here, on Little Cayman, dives were made from fixed moorings, so the name didn't make as much sense. But neither one of them felt like repainting the company name on the boat or changing the website, so they'd stuck with it.

They'd been here in Little for quite a while, operating as they had before: chartering small groups of divers and subbing when other dive shops needed an additional boat. They didn't need to work all that often, thanks to unexpected windfalls from their last two island homes. On the Belizean island of Caye Caulker, they'd discovered a priceless Mayan sculpture, which they'd handed over to Belize's National Institute of Culture and History. The government and several international archaeological groups had rewarded them—in part because Emily had nearly died as they fled the jungle near Lamanai with the artifact. That monetary gift had been generous, but it didn't hold a candle to what they'd received from the shipping magnate Karras Othonos, after Boone and Emily saved the lives of his eldest son and daughter off the coast of Cozumel.

After a month in Grand Cayman with multiple trips to the Sister Islands, Boone and Emily had settled on Little, seeking the quiet solitude of that tiny island—although Emily claimed her vote to live there was because she didn't want to "step on AJ's toes" by setting up shop on Grand. That being said, she flew across to visit her friend fairly often. Em had been threatening to return with a tattoo for some months now.

"I'm thinking... ankle." Emily sipped her coffee, gazing out at the waters of the lagoon. Their patch of beachfront was on a bend in the southern coast, and they faced directly east, where the sunrise was bathing the shallow waters in a pink-orange glow.

"An-n-n-n-n-nd... cue the sunglasses."

Emily smiled as she plucked the oversized shades from her T-shirt and slid them on. "You know me so well."

Footsteps in the crushed coral gravel around the condo drew Boone's attention. Leonard and Willis approached, each with a steaming mug in hand. "Oh, good, you found the coffee. Pull up a chair. Emily's taking suggestions for tattoo locations."

Leonard was caught mid-sip and coughed a burst of coffee into the sand. The pair sat down at the table just as Boone rose.

"Can I get you some breakfast? Just bacon and eggs, yogurt and fruit."

Willis waved a hand. "Oh, no, don't trouble—"

"Yes, thank you," Leonard said quickly. "Scrambled, please."

Boone tossed Emily a quick look, a smile on his face. "Scrambled it is. Be right back."

Emily stabbed a hunk of papaya with her fork. "So, gents. We've got someone coming at about ten to fix the radio, and Boone says he can get the right-sized belt for your engine from next door on the Brac. He'll have to go fetch it, but he may be able to get it sorted by early afternoon."

Leonard nodded, looking at his phone. "Yes. Good. Say, Emily... can you drive me to the airport?"

"Uh...sure. 'Airport' is rather generous. Airfield or airstrip, maybe. Why, whassup?"

"I told my director about... about the island. And he's coming over to get a look at you. At it. The island, I mean."

Emily tilted her head. "Okaaaaay... what time?"

"Seven o'clock."

"Oh! Like... in half an hour."

"Yes, if it's not too much trouble."

"No, no trouble. But you'll have to inhale those scrambled eggs you just ordered."

Heinz Werner leaned forward in his seat at the front of the little cabin, looking between the pilots, eyes locked on the approaching island. The ocean was a deep indigo in most places, but surrounding Little Cayman were brilliant bands of turquoise. The rising sun was just to the left as the small turboprop plane began its descent.

Beside him, in the seat to his right, Billy Faust gasped. "Whoa… it's beautiful," he breathed, his cheek pressed against the window, trying his best to see their destination.

Werner grunted, raising his phone to his face and tapping the Memo function. "The island is flat, infused with green and rimmed with blue. Robinson Crusoe could have found himself on these shores. Ideal for the Act Three portion of the script, although the infrastructure will not be suitable for many of the more complex scenes."

The plane landed with a gentle bump and taxied to its right, pulling up alongside a small building, where a man in an orange vest rose from a chair and grabbed a wheeled cart, making his way toward the aircraft as its propellers slowed to a stop. The airstrip attendant chocked the wheels, then opened the side door and lowered the stairs. Opening the luggage compartment, he removed a few bags before the plane's second leg to Cayman Brac.

Three passengers toward the back of the cabin deplaned first, before Werner stepped down into the morning sunlight. Breathing in the heady mixture of salt air and aviation fuel fumes, he waited for Billy Faust to join him. The young actor exited the aircraft and looked around, a pair of small backpacks in his hands.

"Thanks for inviting me along, Mr. Werner. Not sure why you *did*, but I'm happy to be here!" Billy, being a recent addition, made the mistake of anglicizing the director's name, saying it the way it was spelled.

"It is pronounced '*Vair*-nur,' William," Werner corrected.

"Oh, jeez, I'm sorry, sir."

Werner waved the error away. "The reason for your accompanying me will become readily apparent. Just beyond this building, I suspect." He started forward.

"This has got to be the smallest airport I've ever seen," Billy commented.

Rounding the corner, Werner spotted Leonard standing beside a white soft-top Jeep Wrangler. Leaning against the back was the purpose for his visit: Emily Durand was dressed simply in a faded T-shirt and shorts, with bright green tennis shoes on her sockless feet, and matching green sunglasses atop a button nose. Gone were the French braids, and Werner was pleased to see her hair hung down just beyond shoulder length. Leonard said something to her, and her face lit up in a smile as she waved.

"Whoa. She looks a lot like Brooke," Billy observed.

Werner smiled, a rare expression for his face. "I know."

"Welcome to LC!" Emily announced as the pair approached the Jeep. "I'm Emily Durand, Mr. Werner. I'll be your taxi for this morning."

"Pleased to make your acquaintance, young lady." The director gestured to the young man beside him. "This is Billy Faust, our new leading man."

"What happened to the *old* leading man?" Em asked. When the pair gave each other an uncomfortable look, Emily quickly pivoted. "C'mon, hop in! Do you need anything from the store? It's right over there." She pointed down the sandy road as she went around to the driver's door, positioned on the left-hand side.

"We are fine, thank you," Werner said.

Leonard opened the front passenger side door for him, and the director climbed in beside Emily. Billy and Leonard got in the back. A loud squeak sounded from the back and Leonard yelped.

Emily laughed. "Sounds like someone met Marlin. That clown-fish is our dog's favorite chew toy. I was wondering where that'd gotten to." She put the key in the ignition.

"I would have thought your steering wheel would be on the right," Werner commented.

"Yeah, this being a British territory, you drive on the left side of the road, but plenty of vehicles over here come from the States. Boone and I are used to having the wheel on the left, so we went for that. Not a lot of traffic on Little, anyway!" She started up the car. "I miss our crazy Volkswagens we had in Cozumel, but it would've cost more to ship them than to just buy something here. Wish I could've found a Jeep in a color other than white, but our choices were limited."

"White is pure," Werner intoned. "The absence of color provides a blank canvas for the mind's eye."

"Well, my mind's eye would prefer a bright green," Emily replied without skipping a beat. "Leonard said you'd booked a suite at the Southern Cross. Beautiful place. You want me to take you there, then?"

"Actually, Miss Durand... I wonder if I might be so bold as to request an island tour."

"Oh! Sure! Won't be a long tour, I warn you!" Emily pulled away from the airstrip. "Right now, you're in Blossom Village, the only real town on the island. We'll start our tour there on the right... The Hungry Iguana. Tasty grub. Good breakfast. And Paradise Villas, lovely cottages there. Little Cayman Divers... good op! One of their boat captains is a novelist—how cool is that? Now, I could turn left here and cut across to the Bloody Bay Wall side, but let's keep on keepin' on, shall we? This is Guy Banks Road we're on. It runs along the south coast from end to end."

Emily slowed as they came to a long, one-story building on the right. "That store I mentioned? Right there in the middle. It's the only one on island. Actually, that building has our grocer, hardware store, pharmacy, liquor store, post office, and bank all rolled into one."

"I would imagine things are expensive over here," Billy said, leaning forward between the seats.

"Well, things are pretty pricy in Grand Cayman, too! You'll pay an arm and a leg for a packet of crisps. One of the pitfalls of island life." Em pointed to a building on a low, grassy rise on the right. "Next up is our very own Little Cayman Museum! A lot of cool exhibits, including the Bloody Bay Wall Mural project. It's a huge, life-size multi-photograph exhibit of a massive section of the coral reef wall."

"My cinematographer would no doubt enjoy that," Werner remarked.

"The museum's a great place to learn about the history of Little. I recommend it." Em sped up, continuing east.

"What a charming chapel," Werner said, as they passed a simple, powder-blue church with a steeple in front. "What denomination?"

"It's Baptist, I think. I'm an Easter-and-Christmas semi-heathen, but they're very welcoming. Lovely people there."

"What is this body of water through the trees on the left?" Werner asked. "The ocean is to our right, no?"

"Oh, that's Booby Pond. And before any of you three blokes start snickering, the name refers to the red-footed booby. Over a third of their entire Caribbean population lives right here on Little Cayman. That shallow pond is brackish water and fringed in mangroves. Perfect habitat for them."

Werner lifted his phone to his face and spoke. "Booby Pond. Shallow inland water feature. Birds. Mangroves. Possibly a good location for a shoot."

"Uh... two things," Em said when he lowered the phone. "First, the pond is a protected nature preserve. And second... the mosquitos would suck you dry."

"Noted."

From there, Emily continued along the coast, pointing out the resorts and condominiums as they passed. "Most of the accommodations for tourism are along this stretch. The lagoon provides protection from rough seas, so the majority of the island's docks are in there. Little Cayman Beach Resort is probably the biggest operation. The Southern Cross where you're staying is right there past the Conch Club... and next door is where Boone and I live."

"Boone. Unusual name."

"I'm quite partial to it, but I'm biased," Em said. "His mother is from Tennessee and she's apparently descended from a famous backwoodsman, 'Daniel Boone,' so... she named him Boone."

"Is he your boyfriend?" Billy asked from over her shoulder.

"Long as he keeps giving me foot rubs," Emily replied.

They continued along the coast, Emily pointing out the few sights along the way. They paused briefly at Point of Sand Beach on the eastern tip, then swung north to the East End Lighthouse, which was essentially a pole with a light on it. Cayman Brac was just visible across the waves. From the lighthouse, Emily took them back to the west along the northern coast. There was almost no development along this stretch, the rough road thickly lined with sea grape and cockspur.

Emily braked and slowed to a stop at a familiar sight up ahead. "Iguanas have the right of way. And he's a big boy."

Crossing the road was a sizeable iguana, bulky head held high, a dewlap dangling down from its chin. Its overall color was a gray-brown but its snout had a bluish tint.

"What a majestic creature," Werner breathed appreciatively. He fished a pack of cigarettes out of his pocket. "May I?"

"Uh... sure." Em loathed the smell, but the top was down so what the hell.

"*Danke.*" Werner ignited one and blew a cloud of smoke out to sea. "I appreciate your indulging my weakness. It has been a long, trying week. Now, this lizard... tell me more."

"That's a Sister Islands Rock Iguana; found only here and on the Brac. That one's a male; you can tell from the big dewlap. They're endangered and a lot of them get hit by cars every year. Feral cats go after them, too. There's a gal at the museum who knows everything about them. She's also an expert on the invasive green iguana that's messing with our local lizzies, trying to interbreed with them. You'd like her! She's German, too."

"I am not actually German. I am Czech."

"Oh. Sorry! I heard the accent, and your name..."

"No, no, your instincts are good. I am from the Bohemia region in Czechia, so my ancestry is German." Werner turned to look at her. "What about you? Where are you from?"

"I'm from England," Em said, watching as the iguana finally made its way into the sand at the base of a thicket of sea grape.

"I suspected as much, but your accent is deceptive too, yes? Is it... Cockney?"

Emily smiled. "No, but probably got a bit of that in me, yeah? I'm from South London."

"I see. Out of curiosity... can you... change your accent?"

Em glanced over at him before returning her eyes to the road. "How d'ya mean?"

"Well... if you were an upper-class girl attending Oxford... how would you speak?"

"What, y'mean talk posh?" Emily shrugged and took a stab at it. "I suppose I could, my good man." Emily giggled, enjoying the game. "I say, shall we meet for high tea at Harrod's at half three?"

"Acceptable..." Werner said to himself.

"Okay, guess it needs some work," Em said with a laugh. "It's a good thing I'm not an actor, innit?"

"I thought it was good," Billy commented from the back.

"Much obliged! Oh, speaking of actors..." Em slowed, pointing to the right at the brilliant blue of the sea through a gap in the tropical scrub. "Over there is a dive site called Penguin's Leap... and it's named that, because somewhere around here the actor Burgess Meredith had a house."

"Ah... very amusing," Werner said. "Because of that superhero television show. Although I remember him better for his Oscar-nominated performance in *The Day of the Locust*."

"I thought you were gonna say *Rocky*," Em said. "*Day of the Locust* sounds scary. What, is that like a monster movie with giant locusts attacking people?"

Werner wrinkled his brow. "No. The film is a harsh and unrelenting denunciation of the shallow and ultimately unfulfilling world of the film industry. It depicts Hollywood as a cesspool of excess, delusion, and broken dreams."

"Wow. So... not a popcorn flick."

Billy Faust snickered, and Werner cast a baleful gaze his way. They continued on along the northern coast, Emily pointing out the few remaining sights, many of which she'd shown Leonard the day before. Finally, they reached West End Point, where Emily started back along the southern coast toward town, pausing only to point out the Iguana Reserve just before the airstrip.

"And that's it!" Emily said, when they returned to Blossom Village. "But to *really* get a feel for Little Cayman, you need to take a tour *under* the water. The Cayman Islands have so many dive sites, you can hit a different site every single day of the year! If you're certified, Boone and I can take you out to Bloody Bay Wall."

"A tempting offer, and your tour has been delightful," Werner said, "but I must be candid with you. I was less interested in the tour itself, than in how you conducted it. I did not come to Little Cayman to see the sights. I came here to see you."

"Me? Why?"

"Miss Durand... Emily... how would you like to star in a movie?"

7

"Huh... that's odd," Fitzroy said, peering at the etching on the end of a tiny cylinder.

"What is?" Boone asked.

Fitzroy glanced at his smartphone, where he had pulled up a PDF of the instruction manual for the VHF marine radio aboard the *Bob's Bobo*. "This model takes a six-amp fuse."

"Okay..."

Fitzroy held up the tiny cylinder. "This is a three."

"So, that's why the radio didn't work?"

"Well... having the wrong fuse alone wouldn't necessarily do it... but there were also some loose wires. The thimble connector for them was lying in the bottom of the housing. I guess a rough ride might have knocked it loose, but..." He held up the fuse. "This is harder to explain."

Boone turned to Willis. "You know anything about this?"

"I never change no fuse. Probably been dere since we bought it. And de radio work fine when we left Grand Cayman. I call one of my breddren on his boat as I pass dem by."

Boone shrugged. "Can you fix it, Fitz?"

Fitzroy Jenkins was the go-to guy for electronics repairs on the island, and Boone wasn't surprised at all when he replied, "No problem. I already recapped the wires and I have the right kind of fuse in my truck."

"Great! Thanks, Fitz. What do we owe you?"

"Buy me a beer, and we're good."

"You realize this boat is being rented by a movie production company," Boone prodded.

"Good point. A hundred dollars US."

"I'll let Leonard know," Boone said with a grin. "Thanks again, Fitz. I'll leave you to it. Gonna fire up the *Lunasea* and head over to the Brac to get the replacement belt. Willis, you want to come? I'll let you skipper us across."

"Yes, please!"

"All right. Why don't you hang here for a bit? I need to walk our dog, then I'll grab some water and snacks for the trip and come get you."

Leaving Willis at the condo, Boone gathered up Brixton and took the dog around the grounds. Many of the individual condominiums were empty at the moment, their owners back in the States or in the UK. Several iguanas sat impassively in the sand, sunning themselves. They were used to Brixton's daily snuffling, and the dog gave them their space—with a little help from Boone's firm grip on the leash.

Coming back around to the beach side of the complex, an orange flash of movement caught Boone's eye as an object landed on the walkway with a squeak. Marlin, Brixton's clownfish chew toy, bounced into the sand. Brix pounced on it and chomped repeatedly in an ecstatic flurry of squeaks.

"Look what we found in the Jeep, Brixy!" Emily came out of the sandy parking lot and crouched nearby.

Boone let go of the leash and the pup was off like a shot, dashing across the sand, tail wagging and mouth still full of clownfish. Emily gathered up the dog and gave him a vigorous ear scratch and a smooch on the top of his head.

"Sorry for the delay," she said. "I was giving the movie director a quick tour of the island. Dropped them off to settle in at Southern Cross." She rose from petting Brixton and dug the toe of a green sneaker into the sand, her lips pursed in a soundless whistle.

Boone looked at her. "What?"

"Hmm?"

Boone smiled. "There's something else."

"Is there?" Em asked, all innocence.

Boone crossed his arms and raised an eyebrow, waiting.

"Um… I might be in the movie."

That was not what Boone was expecting her to say, but then he remembered Leonard asking Emily to take off her sunglasses for a photo. It had struck Boone as a bit presumptuous at the time, but now it made sense. *Guess the guy was scouting more than locations.* "Wow! That's great, Em!"

"And remember when I mentioned to Leonard that some people say I look like Brooke Bablin?"

"You're better-looking than her, but yeah, I remember."

"Well… apparently she quit. And that's the part they want me for. It's a big role."

"Congratulations, Em!"

"Hold on a tick, it's not a done dealio... I have to audition first. And I'm not even sure I want to do this."

"Why not?"

"I dunno... seems kind of... stressful. And my girlhood dreams didn't include becoming a famous actress, walking red carpets wearing puffy dresses. I've got an amazing life already."

Boone shrugged. "I think you'll have an amazing life whether you do it or not. You leaning one way or the other?" Boone had seen the excitement in her eyes when she'd told him the news, so he suspected he knew the answer.

"I'm... intrigued," Em said, a smile tugging at the corner of her mouth. "Could be fun."

"One of the things I love about you is you're always up for trying something new. I'd say this qualifies."

Emily snorted a laugh. "No doubt about that!" She stood in silence, gazing out at the waters of the lagoon. After a moment, she came fully alive, her face lighting up. "Oh, who am I kidding? This is too crazy to pass up, innit?"

"Whatever you want to do, I'll back you up."

"Damn well better! Okay. I'll do it. Provided my audition isn't a total shambles."

"When is it?"

"Uh... sort of now-ish? They're coming over here in a few minutes. Mr. Werner, the director, brought over an actor to read with me."

"Okay, great. I can make myself scarce. Willis and I are going over to the Brac—"

"No, please! I want you here!" Emily's voice had a tiny quaver to it, but she took a deep breath and continued in a level tone. "Would be nice for you to stick around for moral support, yeah?"

"You nervous?"

"God, yes."

Boone closed the distance to Emily, tipping her sunglasses up onto her forehead before laying his hands atop her shoulders and locking eyes with her. "*You... you will be fantastic. I know it. You put on mini-performances every day of the year.*"

"But this is different..."

"Well, sure. But let me just say this: anyone who can grab the karaoke mic and swing for the fences like you do has nothing to fear from reading off a piece of paper."

Em smiled, rising up on her toes to kiss Boone on the chin. "See? Moral support. I'll keep you around." She tipped her sunglasses back onto her nose. "Let's go make sure our place is presentable. C'mon, Brixy! I think we'll tuck you in the bedroom for a bit, yeah?"

As the dog scampered after Emily, Boone headed for the pier to let Willis know the trip to Cayman Brac would be delayed.

❖ ❖ ❖

"Come in!" As Emily opened the sliding door, cool air rushed out; Boone had cranked the air conditioner higher than usual in preparation for their guests.

"Thank you, Miss Durand." Heinz Werner entered, a sheaf of papers in one hand and a small bag in the other.

Billy Faust was a few steps behind, smoking some kind of electronic cigarette, his eyes on several pages of script. Engrossed in what he was reading, he tripped and stumbled at the doorway. Emily reached out and caught his elbow.

"Whoa, there! Save the stunts for on-camera, yeah?"

Billy chuckled, pocketing the vape pen. "Thanks for the save."

"All in a day's work." *Good-looking bloke, that one,* she thought. She figured he was a few years younger than her. Emily ushered him in and slid the door closed. Boone approached Werner, hand outstretched. "Welcome, Mr. Werner. I'm Boone Fischer."

Werner blinked. "My goodness, you are tall."

"Uh… yeah, you got me pegged."

"Long of limb and lean of frame," Werner continued. "Very striking."

"Thanks?"

Werner set his bag down and shook Boone's hand. "And this is Billy Faust, our leading man."

"Beautiful island you've got here," Billy said, offering Boone a firm handshake.

"Where's Leonard?" Boone asked.

"I sent him to rent a car and take a closer look at several of the locations Miss Durand was kind enough to show us. And thank you for rescuing him and repairing the rental boat."

"Well, just so you know, I really only patched it. I'm gonna go grab a part later today and it should be good to go. Oh, and I got a guy to fix the radio."

"What was wrong with it?" Emily asked.

"Couple things. Tell you later."

Emily shrugged. "So, gents… where do you want me?"

Werner was already scanning the living and dining space of the open-plan condo. "This kitchen area is well lit. May we move the table out of the way and set a chair in front of that wall?"

"You got it," Boone said, lifting the small, circular table and setting it aside while Emily plunked the chair down against the far wall.

"Miss Durand, if you would like to look over the sides?" Werner said.

"Sides?"

Billy waggled his pages. "Sides are the parts of a scene being used for an audition."

"Or the portion of the script that is being shot on a given day," Werner elaborated, handing her most of the pages he held before setting his bag atop the table and extracting a retractable tripod.

Emily looked at the sides and a smile crept onto her face. "Am I 'Sarah'?" she asked.

"Yes."

She gave a brief laugh and even Boone grinned.

"Something is humorous?"

Emily shook her head. "No. I mean, yes. It's silly."

Werner paused in his assembly of the tripod. "Yes?"

"Well… it's just that one of the most famous dives on Little Cayman is named 'Sarah's Set.' It's these two underwater mounds, you see… and apparently there was this divemaster named Sarah, and…" Emily trailed off.

"Ah… very amusing," Werner said, dryly. "Will you be able to set this bawdy tidbit aside when you audition?"

Emily sobered. "Yes, of course. I'll take a look at the… um… 'sides.'"

While Werner set up his camera, Emily studied the pages. Apparently, she was a brainy, stunningly beautiful university student on a party cruise. She glanced at the second set of pages, a scene with a marine biologist character named Ethan. She read the stage directions near the end of the scene: *The tension is palpable. Their eyes lock together. The music swells and they kiss. Passions escalate and…* Emily coughed. "Um… who's playing 'Ethan'?"

"That'd be me," Billy said.

Emily reddened and looked over at Boone. *Well, I did ask him to stay. This should be interesting.* She cleared her throat. "Mr. Werner…

would it be okay to ask what the movie's about? Leonard said it's called *Man O' War*, but he wouldn't elaborate, other than to say it was a science fiction horror movie."

"Yes, of course I can explain." Heinz Werner retrieved the last of the pages he'd brought, handing one each to Boone and Emily. "Provided you sign a Non-Disclosure Agreement."

Em looked at it while Boone scrounged for a pen in a kitchen drawer.

"A standard, boilerplate NDA," Werner assured her. "It is primarily to keep cast members from spoiling aspects of the story on social media."

"Here ya go," Boone said, having signed his with only a cursory glance. Emily shrugged and followed suit. Boone had uncanny instincts, and if he'd thought there were shenanigans afoot, he would still be reading it, word by word.

"*Danke.*" Werner set the NDAs aside. "*Man O' War* is a creature feature, in the vein of *Jaws*... or *Orca*, or *Tentacles*. Except our creature is a mutated Portuguese man o' war."

"Uh... you mean..." Boone held his hands less than a foot apart, to indicate the size of the creature's float "...like those blue-topped jellyfish?"

"It's not a jellyfish, Boone," Emily said, slipping into Trivia Night mode. "It's a siphonophore."

Werner's face lit up. "*Ja*, very good! It is a colonial creature, made up of many specialized animals that work together as one organism. The translucent part at the top that you indicated with your hands, Mr. Fischer? That is a gas-filled float. The ocean winds blow against it like a sail. Indeed, that is how it got its name, in that it moves much like a warship from the age of sail. It is often spelled 'man-of-war,' but it was decided that title would look terrible on a movie poster."

"And… that's your monster?" Boone asked, looking dubious.

Heinz Werner nodded. "In the real world, the Portuguese man o' war, or man-of-war, or bluebottle, is rarely more than a foot across, although its tentacles have been known to extend one hundred feet. But our fictional creature… is much, *much* larger. By the end of the movie, the flotation sail will be the size of a battleship, and the tentacles will extend over a mile!"

"Whoa, cool!" Emily exclaimed. "What made it that way?"

"Toxic spill… or alien influence. The writers are still arguing about it. But needless to say, it mutates. In the real world, the colonial organisms that make up the bluebottle carry out different functions: floating, eating, excreting, injecting venom. As our monster evolves, it keeps adding new specialized parts and new abilities. And it gains intelligence."

"Okay, I'm sold," Boone said. "I'd watch the hell out of that."

"If all goes well, you won't be alone," Werner said, returning to his camera. "Miss Durand, you play—"

"A young university student," Emily interrupted. "Gorgeous, smart, and capable. I'm on a booze cruise, from the looks of it."

"Yes. In fact, let us start with that scene." Werner powered on the camera. "Billy, you're not in this scene, of course… but would you be so kind as to read the other parts?"

"Sure."

Em started to sit in the chair Werner had requested, but then looked at the script. "Is Sarah sitting in this scene?"

"No, she is not," Werner said, adjusting the settings on his camera. "She is standing on the deck of a pirate ship party boat, the *Jolly Robert*."

"Then… shouldn't I stand?"

Werner smiled. "Yes. Very good."

Boone stepped in beside Emily and grabbed the chair, whispering "Break a leg," in her ear before retreating.

"You ready?" Billy asked.

"No pressure, yeah?" Emily blew out a breath. "Okay. Ready."

Werner held up a hand. "And... action."

"Lighten up, Sarah, it's a party boat!" Billy read. "And ditch the book, nerd. You're not in school today."

The instant Emily opened her mouth to speak, her mind flashed back to the island tour, when Werner had asked her about her accent. Taking a chance, she did her best to soften her South London dialect, channeling the sound of one of her favorite BBC news anchors. "This drunken barf-fest is not my idea of fun, Cindy. I wish we'd gone to somewhere educational."

"Educational? This is spring break, Sarah!" Then, Billy suddenly pitched his voice down. "Yeah, Sarah. C'mon, let's party!" Billy switched back with "Leave her alone, Biff. She's not interested."

Em choked off a giggle at the one-man back-and-forth and forged ahead with the scene. The script said: *Sarah sighs*, so Emily gave a sigh before continuing. "I was hoping we'd get a chance to go diving. I've been thinking of majoring in marine biology..."

Emily and Billy continued with the scene until they reached a scrawled "End Scene" in the middle of a page. Em looked up. Werner was smiling. He tapped a button on the camera.

"How... how'd I do?" Emily asked.

"Considering I just handed you those pages... you were every bit as good as I'd hoped. And I noticed you adjusted your accent..."

"Oh, yeah, I figured there was a reason you asked me about that earlier. Hope that was okay. I probably should've asked first, yeah?"

"I am pleased that you did not," Werner said. "It showed initiative and instinct."

"But... Brooke Bablin is American," Emily noted. "This is an American college class on spring break, innit?"

Werner shrugged. "Scripts change, sometimes daily. Sarah can be an exchange student." He reached down to the camera. "Now, you were a little nervous, I think..."

"Guilty as charged."

"But there is no need to be. You have a natural quality that I find refreshing. Let's try it again."

Emily repeated the scene, and the words came more easily to her this time around. Werner nodded when they finished. "Good. Let's move on to the seduction scene."

Emily's eyes shot toward Boone, who was sitting in a chair off to the side. He raised his eyebrows, the ghost of a smile on his lips.

Werner adjusted the tripod. "Billy, if you would join Emily against the wall?"

Emily opened her mouth and snapped it shut. "Uh... Boone?"

The lanky divemaster was already rising from the chair. "Hey, before you hit record, I should go walk the dog. C'mon, Brix!" He opened the door to their master bedroom and Brixton came trotting out. Boone grabbed a tennis ball and headed for the sliding glass doors. "See y'all when you're done."

Emily gave Boone a grateful look and mouthed, "Thank you." He smiled and headed out into the tropical sun.

8

Brixton sat in the shade of a casuarina tree, panting after a vigorous game of fetch in the surf. A few feet away, his shirtless, shoeless master spun, cartwheeled, and kicked.

Boone Fischer was an extremely adept practitioner of capoeira, a flashy Brazilian martial arts style that looked to a casual observer like a form of dance, incorporating acrobatic moves and flourishes to keep an opponent off-balance and second-guessing the *capoeirista*'s next move. Boone enjoyed practicing the martial art in the sand, since the shifting surface required additional concentration when executing certain moves. Emily had remarked that Boone practiced his capoeira the way some people did with tai chi; and indeed, Boone did find it meditative.

He relaxed into a *ginga* step, the shuffling footwork looking a bit like a dance move, although its purpose was to rapidly shift the center of gravity, changing the weight on the feet so that a wide variety of moves could be brought to bear in an instant. He snapped off a round of *queixadas*, alternating feet between the looping back kicks.

Emily is going to be in a movie, he thought, as he transitioned into a *macaco* backward handspring, kicking at an imaginary opponent as he bent backward and spun head-over-heels, landing in a crouch for an instant before transitioning right back into the *ginga*. Em was still auditioning, but Boone could tell that Werner had every intention of hiring her. Although he guessed other people would probably have some say in it—producers, in particular. Going from a famous actress to an unknown non-actress divemaster was likely to ruffle some feathers.

Boone cartwheeled to the side and snapped an *aú batido* L-kick into the air before tumbling back the other way and reversing the move with an inverted kick from the alternate foot. *I wonder if I'll be seeing much of her if she ends up in this movie,* he thought. Boone was the farthest thing from the jealous type, but he didn't look forward to the prospect of being away from Em for a lengthy period of time. True, there did seem to be interest in shooting some of the movie over here in Little, but Grand Cayman had far more infrastructure. Emily would likely be over there much of the time. Maybe he could take the *Lunasea* across and berth her in West Bay for a while; hang out with AJ and her crew while Emily filmed her scenes. *Like that seduction scene...*

Boone let his mind go blank as he executed a long series of movements, tumbling, spinning, and kicking as he lost himself in the dance. Sweat and sand flew from his long limbs as he ended the sequence in a handstand, eyes facing out toward the breakers along the lagoon reef. The sound of clapping from behind him broke his concentration and he flopped into the sand, looking back toward the condo. Emily stood beside Brixton, smiling proudly as Werner and Billy applauded vigorously. Leonard had returned from his scouting and stood nearby, his cell phone raised. Apparently, he'd filmed Boone's exercise.

"Astonishing," Werner said. "I have filmed many fight scenes in my time, but I've never seen anything quite like that. Almost like a dance. It's not karate or judo. What do you call it?"

Before Boone could reply, Emily jumped in. "It's a Brazilian martial art. Boone's a black belt! It's called... capicola! Right Boone?" Emily grinned, pleased with herself.

Werner cocked his head quizzically. "Capicola... is some form of Italian cured meat, is it not?"

"Oh, bugger me, I always get those confused," Emily said, not through yet. "I remember now. Capezio."

"Capoeira," Boone said, rising and brushing sand off his body.

Werner nodded, sliding a cigarette from a pack and lighting it. "Perhaps you could teach some of those moves to our stunt coordinator and fight choreographer. We have a pair of fight scenes in the film."

"Boone also knows Brazilian jiu-jitsu," Emily added. "But it's not as flashy as carbonara."

Billy laughed heartily at Emily's teasing. "Is she always like this?" he asked, addressing Boone.

"Keep your cameras rolling," he replied. "You'll have a blooper reel longer than the movie."

Werner's attention wandered out into the lagoon. "*Was ist das?*" he said to himself, walking to a spot beside the pier. Boone thought he might be referring to either the *Lunasea* or the *Bob's Bobo* that were tied up on either side, but instead the director pointed off to the right. "What is that verdant patch of land across the water?"

"That's Owen Island," Boone said. "Sometimes it's jokingly called the fourth Cayman Island."

"Is it inhabited?"

"No. Privately owned. It's about eleven acres of sand, not a single structure. Tropical plants throughout, and sandy beach all around. No dock or anything, so people just kayak over and have a picnic."

Leonard joined the director. "Thought you'd like that. The shipwreck scene, right?"

"*Ja*, it is perfect. Much better than the other location." Clamping the cigarette between his lips, Werner held up his hands, framing the flat, green islet. He shifted his hands a little to the right and left. "We can shoot from this direction… or this direction, and see none of the resorts. A deserted island."

"I already checked with the film board," Leonard said. "As long as we keep to a small footprint and leave it better than we found it, we can shoot there. The landowner would require a small fee, in addition to the payment to the film commission."

"Good. Very good. Well done, Leonard." Werner turned from the island and gestured toward the *Bobo*. "What is the condition of the chase boat?"

"Mr. Fischer here might be able to tell you better than I," Leonard said.

"If you mean the fishing boat," Boone said, "I've got some good news on that front. Fitzroy and Willis are getting a replacement part over at the airport."

"I thought you had to go to the Brac to get it," Emily said.

"Well, that was the plan… but I called Matt over at the Brac Port Authority to tell him I'd be late because you had to audition for a movie. He got all excited and said he'd run over to Kirkconnell Airport before the plane for Grand Cayman left. A buddy of his was coming across so he gave the belt to her to bring over. Fitz and Willis are having lunch at the Hungry Iguana, and they'll go over and grab it when the plane lands."

"When will that be?" Werner asked, looking at his watch.

"In about forty-five minutes."

"Then I must hurry. Billy and I have seats on that plane for the second leg to Grand Cayman."

Emily blinked. "Oh. So… you're leaving?"

Werner approached her. "Yes, young lady… I have a movie to shoot." He held up his bag and tapped it. "But more to the point, I have some audition footage to show to a few people over there. And if all goes well… you should be hearing from me tonight. In fact, go ahead and book yourself the first flight over tomorrow morning. I will pay for it, regardless of the outcome."

"You mean…?"

"I mean nothing other than what I said. I want you to have a seat on the first plane to Grand Cayman, and you will know tonight whether you will need it or not."

Boone cleared his throat. "So… the boat your company rented? The radio repair and the replacement belt will run a hundred and fifty US. And refueling… that'll run four hundred."

Werner shrugged. "Of course. Leonard, pay the man."

"Sure thing," Leonard said. "So, Willis and I can take it back to Grand Cayman tomorrow morning?"

"Yeah, about that…" Boone ran a hand through his unruly hair. "This is really a coastal fishing boat. I never would've taken a boat like this across, were it mine. Tell you what… we could use a run to Grand for some supplies anyway." He gestured over his shoulder at the dive boat. "I'll take the *Lunasea* and escort you back. At sun-up, we'll head across together."

Werner was looking at the dive boat as Boone spoke. "Your boat can manage the open ocean?"

"Yeah, she's got a powerful engine and a custom deep-vee hull, so she can handle rough seas well."

"Good. How would you like to be a chase boat?"

"What is that?" Boone asked. "You used that term with the fishing boat."

"We have several ships involved in the plot of *Man O' War*, the chase boats provide film footage from alongside."

"Oh. Well, if you cast Emily in the movie, then I suppose we'd put our diving charters on hold for a bit, anyway. In which case, yes… the *Lunasea* would be available for hire. I'd need to skipper her… and you'd need to hire our co-worker, Amelia Ebanks. She's a local, so that may come in handy."

"Agreed. Someone will be in touch. Leonard, bring the rental car over to my room; I have a plane to catch." With that, Werner turned and headed across the sand toward the Southern Cross, trailing cigarette smoke. Leonard hustled to the sandy lot by the road. Billy started to leave, but hesitated.

"Emily, it was a pleasure… working with you. Hope I'll be seeing more of you soon."

"Me too, Billy!" Em said.

Billy smiled, then turned and jogged to catch up with Werner.

"He was blushing," Boone remarked, watching the young man go.

"Probably the hot tropical sun," Emily suggested.

"There was a kiss in that scene, wasn't there?"

"Hey, we were making art." Emily smirked impishly. "I think we got it right by the third take."

———◆•◆———

A half hour later, Fitzroy and Willis returned from the airport with the replacement belt and Leonard arrived with some cash he'd withdrawn from the only ATM on the island. While Boone installed the belt and topped off the *Bob's Bobo*'s tank from several dockside drums, Emily packed a bag "just in case."

Meanwhile, in Grand Cayman, Werner and Billy touched down at Owen Roberts International Airport and were met by the second assistant director, Jerry, in the half-domed entryway.

"Welcome back, sir," Jerry said. "I have a car waiting in the short-term parking lot." He led the way toward the glass-fronted exit.

"Has the meeting been scheduled?" Werner asked without preamble, walking alongside his 2nd AD and leaving Billy Faust to follow along behind.

"Yes, I've got the writers meeting us at five in the hotel business suite. We'll have most of the producers joining us via videoconference call."

"What about Beck?"

"I texted him, but no reply as of yet."

"Call his assistant back in Los Angeles. Have her track him down. We need him there." Maxwell Beck was the field producer on the project and was in Grand Cayman overseeing much of the production, reporting back to the executive producer, a woman named Barbara Barclay. Beck and Werner went way back, the producer having worked with the Czech director on several films.

Jerry reached the hired town car and opened the back door for Werner. Billy knew the drill, and went to open the front passenger door, but halted as he realized the Caymanian driver was on the right side of the vehicle. Sheepishly, he went around to the other side. Jerry joined Werner in the back, rolling down his window when he saw the director digging out a pack of cigarettes.

"How did today's rehearsals go?" Werner asked, lighting one up.

Jerry opened his mouth, then closed it. Tried again. "Well, we got through half the list..."

"Only *half*?" Werner shouted the question and Jerry winced. "We had another technical issue, this time with the *Mako*."

"*Gottverdammt*, what now?"

"Not sure, but the engine wouldn't start."

"I expect the mercenary ship to be fully operational by tomorrow morning!"

"We've got a marine mechanic working on it now," Jerry said. "So... Mr. Werner... do we have a Sarah?"

"I wouldn't have asked you to arrange the meeting if I didn't think we did. I had no time to upload the audition, with the plane from Little Cayman departing so soon after we finished, but the moment we get back to the hotel, we will send it out to the overseas producers."

"Was she good?"

Werner hesitated. Emily Durand was by no means an actress by profession, but she had a quick mind and bold personality. He was confident that he could mold her into what the film needed. What's more, he relished that challenge. Back when award nominations came his way with some regularity—before the sci-fi and horror films filled his résumé—Heinz Werner had been known for several independent films where he had taken virtual unknowns and pulled forth spectacular performances from those rookie actors. Several of them were now stars, and in Werner's opinion, they owed it all to his talent for *creating* talent.

Instead of answering Jerry's question directly, he leaned forward in his seat. "Billy... what did you think?"

Billy looked back over his shoulder, caught off guard. "Uh..."

"Don't ruminate! Answer. What did you think of her?"

"She was great. I mean... she's never done this before, so it might take a little work, but... I liked her better than Brooke." His eyes went wide. "Sorry! I shouldn't have said that."

"No, no, it's quite all right." Werner sat back and smiled. From the first day of table-read rehearsal, it was clear to him that young Billy Faust had been intimidated by Brooke Bablin. But the up-and-coming actor was positively *captivated* by Emily Durand. *And attracted to her as well,* Werner thought. *Which will be wonderful for the film.*

9

With sunset on the way, Boone announced he was taking Emily out for an anticipatory celebratory dinner at the restaurant on the grounds of the Pirate's Point Resort. It had taken a little bit of begging, as the resort's gourmet chefs carefully planned and prepared each evening's menu in advance, and making a reservation by noon was normally mandatory. But when Boone offered extra lionfish for the resort's Friday Sushi Night, an exception was made.

"A congratulations dinner before we've heard anything... you better not jinx it for me!" Emily warned, as she took the seat Boone offered her at a table on the patio overlooking the grounds.

"Tell ya what... we won't order any champagne. Keep our expectations in check."

"Fair enough," Emily said, looking at the printed menu for the day. "But I will be getting the lobster, since you're buying."

"I'll join you on that."

"Ooh, and it's Cayman-style lobster! That dish is delish."

Em was a convert to this local recipe, even though they'd only had it a few times. The Caribbean spiny lobster was boiled, but instead of being plopped on a plate with butter and lemon, the crustacean still had a culinary journey ahead of it: the lobster was de-shelled, chopped, and added to a pan of sautéed red, green, and Scotch bonnet peppers, thyme, and garlic, with chicken stock added. Served over rice, it was heavenly.

A waitress arrived, setting down a basket of fresh bread before she took their drink orders. Emily went for some white wine, but Boone opted for an Ironshore Bock from The Cayman Islands Brewery over on Grand Cayman.

"It just occurred to me," Em said, ripping into a roll, "that with all the excitement, I neglected to eat lunch."

"Look at you, Little Miss Movie Star—skipping meals already."

"Sod off, beanpole," Emily said through a mouthful of bread and butter. "We can't all have your freakish metabolism."

"Hey, I'm just trying to help," Boone said, getting a mischievous look on his face. It wasn't often that the stoic divemaster did the teasing—that was usually her department. "Y'know... they say the camera adds ten pounds."

"Then I won't eat any cameras."

Em scanned the rest of the menu and was ready to pounce when the waitress returned with their drinks. "We'll have the lionfish ceviche and conch fritters to start. The mango and papaya salad. And two Cayman-style lobsters!"

"Excellent choices," the waitress replied, jotting everything down.

Boone raised his dark lager. "To Emily Durand and what I hope will be a fascinating experience."

Emily clinked her wine against his pint glass. "And to Boone Fischer, finding enough things to keep himself occupied while I'm hobnobbing with Hollywood. God, I love that word. Hobnob."

Boone grinned and took a sip. "You won't forget me while you're off being a star?"

Emily sighed as she tasted the wine. "I'll try not to let fame go to my head. Besides… if you're chasing me around with the chase boat, we'll see plenty of each other. Plus, maybe you'll teach a few actors some of that fancy fighting style. You know. Capillary."

Boone laughed. "That's a new one."

"Hey, we actresses have to be good with words." Emily's smile slipped as she looked out at the glorious sunset that was painting the sky and water a brilliant orange. She set her sunglasses down on the table. "Boone, I gotta be honest. I kind of expected to have heard already."

"Heinz Werner wants you in the movie," Boone said with absolute conviction. "But he probably has to run it by a whole herd of movie types. And Hollywood is a few hours earlier."

Emily blew out a breath. "Okay, yeah. Good points."

Boone set down his beer and sat back in his chair, looking out to sea. "They're gonna give it to you," he said distantly.

◆ ◆ ◆

"This… is our new Sarah," Werner said, bringing up a still of Emily from her audition. Alongside it on the screen was the photo Leonard had taken with her, her bikini-body on display under her open cover-up.

All but one of the principal producers were assembled, some in person, some remotely. Ironically, the only one missing, Jeffrey

Scott, had a house here in Grand Cayman. He was currently in the air, flying back from his château on the French Riviera. The meeting had only just begun, the gathered production team and videoconferenced producers having just finished watching the audition tapes. Two takes of each scene. Werner had deleted one of the scenes between Billy Faust and Emily, because the blond Brit was clearly giggling during the kiss.

Executive producer Barbara Barclay spoke first. She sat on her cliffside balcony overlooking the Pacific Ocean, her video-conferencing camera carefully situated to show the spectacular view behind her. Werner had been to her mansion on the bluff in the Pacific Palisades section of Los Angeles. If words for Barclay's home were to spring to mind, "ostentatious" would spring the highest.

"Mr. Werner, I want to make sure we are all on the same page, here. You want to go from a well-known, proven actress... to a complete newcomer."

"We no longer have the well-known actress," Werner said politely. "And as for whether Miss Bablin could be considered 'proven,' I reserve my judgment on that assertion."

"Her box office grosses for *Seven Sexy Sins* and *Midnight Cowgirl* are sufficient proof for me, Mr. Werner."

"Nevertheless, Brooke Bablin has departed the movie. As I am sure you are aware, no one has heard from her since. Her agents claim they are as in the dark as we are, although they may just be covering for her. In any event, from the manner of her departure, I doubt very much if she has any plans to return. A change of heart... requires a heart."

Barclay raised an eyebrow. "That's rather harsh, isn't it?"

"I believe it was an apt phrase. Deserting an entire ecosystem of professionals and putting the entire production into jeopardy strikes me as... heartless."

"What did you do to drive her away, Werner?" Associate producer Trey Sadler asked, sunlight from the setting sun blazing against the polished windows in the New York City skyscrapers behind his head. "We've all heard the stories about how difficult you can be. And the studio is painfully aware of the box office failure of your last film, as well as the cancellation of—"

"Mr. Sadler, Mrs. Barclay," Werner interrupted, "I have no doubt you have numerous eyes on me at all times. Those eyes would have seen that I gave no offense." *Other than the cigarettes, perhaps,* Werner thought. He'd made sure to fuel up on nicotine before they'd begun the teleconference, so that he could keep from smoking during the meeting.

"Perhaps if we had offered her more money," a third producer speculated, his fleshy jowls dewed with sweat. Unlike the others, he had no impressive vista behind his head, just a blank wall and the edge of what appeared to be a cat's scratching post. Werner couldn't remember the man's name, thinking of him only as Frog Face.

"*More* money?" Barclay scoffed. "If anything, we will be *taking* money from her. We will sue her for breach of contract!"

"Let's use that as leverage, then," Frog Face suggested. "I say we approach her agents again and—"

"No!" Werner pounded the conference table. "The milk is spilt and curdled, and it cannot be put back into the glass. And even if it could, one would be unwise to drink it. We have an opportunity before us, to continue the production schedule as planned."

"I agree with Werner here, at least with regard to Brooke Bablin," Barclay said. "But *not* about hiring a non-actor. I recommend we start up the casting process again, and—"

"Unacceptable!" Werner glanced around, eyes locking onto his target. "Max! What would such a delay cost us?"

The field producer had shown up at the last second and now leaned against the wall, dressed business-casual in a light blue shirt and slacks. He looked at Werner, considering a moment. The scrutiny continued, and Werner began to get uncomfortable. They had a somewhat rocky history together, but the director had always found the man highly competent. Finally, Maxwell Beck removed himself from the wall and approached the camera nearest him. "A casting delay would certainly cost us a pretty penny. Housing, food, transportation... not to mention we'd have to renegotiate every actor's contract, as some of them may not have availability after a certain date."

While the producers pondered this, Werner grabbed the initiative. "The universe is indifferent to our needs, and we must seize opportunity when it presents itself. We are here, *now*. We are ready, *now*. And we have a Sarah... *now*." He pointed at the camera. "Mrs. Barclay. Forget what you know about Emily Durand. What did you think of what you saw? Immediate impression!"

Barclay rocked her head side to side. "She was charming. A little rough around the edges, but a pleasing, natural quality. And she and Billy had some real chemistry. Plus, there's no denying she is breathtakingly beautiful. And she certainly shares a lot of physical similarities with Brooke Bablin. Although, with more of a 'girl-next-door' quality."

"Yeah, if the girl next door is super-hot," Sadler interjected. "And I must admit, I thought she was pretty good. Accent was a little weird."

"We can work on that," Werner said eagerly. "Writers! Any problem with Sarah being an exchange student?" He knew there wouldn't be, having rewritten half the script already. The writers were merely his thralls at this point, and their enthusiastic agreement to his suggestion came right on cue.

"I can't believe we're even considering this!" Frog Face croaked. "Bringing in an *amateur* to replace a star?"

"It was amateurs who made my *Amazonia Infernalis* a hit at the Cannes Film Festival!" Werner pointed out. "And amateurs who outshone the celebrity cast members in my award-winning *Under Moon and Stars*. And look at them all now; all of them... stars. You know very well my reputation for pulling a performance out of new blood. Let this Emily bleed for you now!"

Barbara Barclay grimaced. "I'm... not sure about your choice of words there, Mr. Werner. But your point is well taken."

"Actually..." Trey Sadler said, tapping a Mont Blanc pen against his lip, "the fact that she *is* an amateur... and looks a lot like Brooke... and is being brought in to replace a diva who jumped ship... all of that is public relations gold! We could plant some rumbles in social media, let the public chow down on some rumor and innuendo."

"*All About Eve!*" one of the veteran writers piped up, referring to the classic film where a young understudy eclipses a Broadway mega-star.

"All about... Emily," a younger writer supplied, leading to laughter and a high five.

"Oh, that's good," Sadler said, the pen-on-lip drumbeat accelerating.

"And...!" Werner shouted, preparing to hammer the last nail into place. "And..." he continued in a softer voice, "...we can go ahead and restart the casting process anyway. If Emily is everything I hope for—everything I expect—then we can call the casting search off. But just in case, we'll have options."

"I'm convinced," Barclay said. "All in favor?"

The vote was unanimous. Everyone voted to hire Emily Durand. Even Frog Face.

The sun had long set, and Boone watched Emily poke at her piece of cassava cake.

"So... tomorrow, Amelia and I will head over in the *Lunasea*," he said, "to make sure the *Bobo* gets back across. It'll probably take six or seven hours." He waited. The bill had already arrived and been paid. The tip lay on the table. The other diners had left.

Emily forked a piece of the cake, then let it roll off the utensil.

"Figure I'll get a slip at the Yacht Club," Boone continued. "Then I'll probably hit Foster's for supplies and see about storing my haul at AJ's place. You want to do dinner after your shoot?"

"I didn't get it," Em said quietly.

Boone was silent for a moment. "It's only eight o'clock. Hey, this is a stupid question, but... is your phone on?"

Emily raised a slow-burn glare from her dessert plate.

"Yeah... stupid question," Boone muttered. Then he froze. "Less stupid question, maybe: do they have your phone number?"

Emily set the fork down. "I... I don't know. I don't think I ever gave it to them."

Boone rose from the table. "Leonard. They probably called Leonard, figuring we'd all be at the condo."

Emily dropped her fork on the plate with a clatter, and the two of them scrambled for the Jeep. Minutes later, their tires crunched to a stop in the sandy condo lot. Leonard was amidst the palm trees, loud-talking on his phone as they arrived.

"I don't know! They were here a few hours ago, but then I got back from... oh! Oh, wait! They're here!" Leonard waved frantically. "Where have you been?"

Boone started to reply but Leonard waved him off.

"It doesn't matter! Here!" He held the phone out to Emily. "It's Heinz Werner."

Emily took the phone, her pupils wide. "H...hello?"

"Congratulations, Miss Durand. You've got the part."

Emily's attempt to reply came out as an excited squeak.

"I assume then, that you accept. I will expect you to be on the first plane over tomorrow morning. You will be taken from the airport straight to our offices to fill out paperwork, and then you will be taken to a meet-and-greet with the cast and writers."

"Okay! I'll be there! I got the plane ticket and I'm already packed."

"Good. Leonard has a script for you. There will be some changes, but I ask that you read the script once, all the way through, then go to bed. You will need your rest."

"Read script, then sleep. Right-o. You're the boss!"

"Yes. As of right now, I *am* the boss. See you tomorrow."

Emily stood in a daze as Leonard retrieved his phone. She turned to Boone, eyes full of wonder. "I got it."

"Of course you did," Boone said, giving her a firm hug. "Congratulations, Em."

Emily returned the squeeze, then stepped back and did a wild dance in the sand, finishing with an airborne fist pump.

"Save it for the shoot," Boone said with a grin. "Hey, how much are you getting paid?"

Em's eyes widened. "Bugger, I completely forgot to ask. But honestly, Boone... who cares? I wouldn't be doing it for the money."

Boone laughed. "Spoken like someone who's got a chunk of change in the bank. But you're right, it doesn't matter. We're good, as far as finances go."

"I've got a script for you," Leonard said.

"Right. Thanks. I'll read it, then get some sleep! Early morning for me."

"Even earlier for me," Boone said. "Leonard, we should head out at sunrise around six a.m. The crossing will take six or seven hours."

"Okay, I'll let Willis know. Thank you again for helping us with the boat and letting us stay here. And Boone, about the chase boat job, we'll get you a berth near some of the boats we're using in the film."

"Great!" Em exclaimed. "Then I can pack a bigger suitcase, and you can bring it across! The baggage allowance on those little planes is naff."

The trio entered the condo, Leonard splitting off to the guest room to grab the script and speak with Willis. Boone and Emily retired to the master bedroom and Brixton practically bowled them over, tail wagging.

"Hey there, Brix. We'll go walkabout in a bit," Boone said, opening a high cupboard above their closet to bring down Em's suitcase. He plopped it on the bed, and Emily began to stuff it full.

"What about Brixy?" she asked, holding up two blouses, then throwing them both in. "Can't really bring him in the boat. It's too long a voyage, and the seas can get rough."

"I already arranged for him to stay with Rhys," Boone said.

"Really?" Em asked, pausing in her packing. "When?"

"Before I took you to dinner. And I already called Amelia, to see if she's game for the crossing and the chase boat gig. And I called AJ, to let her know we're coming."

Emily cocked her head at him.

"I knew you were gonna get it," Boone said with a smile.

Em returned the smile. "One of your freaky flashes of intuition?"

"Nah, just common sense. You're a brilliant, beautiful gal who can't go five minutes without putting on a performance. It was inevitable."

Leonard knocked at the door jamb. "Here's your script, Emily. Werner asked me to hang onto it until the producers gave the green light." He offered a stack of pages held together with brass fasteners in the punch-holes.

"Thank you!" Em grabbed the script and looked down at the cover sheet as Leonard went back to his room. *"Man O' War..."* she read aloud. She flipped the page. "Oh, cool... a cast list."

"Recognize anyone?" Boone asked, reaching up into the cubby for his own suitcase.

Em scanned through the list. "No... well, except for Brooke Bablin, who's listed as Sarah."

"Which is you."

"Which is me."

"And they said she quit."

"Yeah."

Boone set the suitcase down. "Hmm..."

"What?"

Boone shrugged. "Wonder what happened."

———— ◆·◆ ————

"She's waking up."

The familiar female voice came from far away, or at least it seemed to. Brooke Bablin opened her eyes and was greeted with... nothing. Darkness. Confused, she tried to move, but found she couldn't. She tried to speak, but only a muffled sound issued forth. Fear gripped her, and she began to struggle.

"Take a pill to chill," a Slavic accent purred right beside her ear.

Brooke froze, breathing hard into what she now realized was a gag. A hand gripped the back of her neck, and the shroud of darkness was lifted as the man removed a hood that had been over her head. As consciousness returned to her fully, she realized she was tied to a chair.

"Mornin', sunshine," the woman said.

The man looked back at her. "Is not morning."

"It's an expression, Borscht-for-brains."

"Ah! Because she is wake up!"

Brooke mumbled into the gag and the man removed it. "Thirsty..." she managed.

"This I can help with." He opened a small fridge and took out a bottle of water. Uncapping it, he gave her a long drink, though more of it went down her shirt than into her mouth.

Brooke fought a wave of dizziness and nausea. "Wh... what did you do to me?"

"Well, we doped you up pretty good 'til we could get things settled," the woman said. "Sorry about that. If ya need to hurl, there's a wastebasket by your feet, there."

Brooke recognized her voice now, with its midwestern twang. Memories struggled to rise through the haze. "Who... who are you people?"

"You can call me Potluck," the woman said. "And Boris Badenov here, you can call him Tolstoy."

"You... you were in my room," Brooke slurred. "You... kidnapped me!"

"Maybe a little bit," Tolstoy said.

"Call my parents! They'll pay! Or my agent! Or—"

"All in good time, sweetie," Potluck said. "We're just gonna cool our jets here for a while."

Brooke looked around the room. The ceilings were very low, and it seemed like they were in a windowless basement. "Where am I?"

"You ask where you are?" Tolstoy moved closer, glee in his face.

"Don't say it, Tolstoy..." Potluck warned, annoyance in her voice.

Tolstoy leaned down and hissed, "You... are in Hell!"

"Oh, for the love of Pete," Potluck muttered.

"How did you get into my villa?" Brooke asked, still clearing the cobwebs from her mind.

Tolstoy laughed. "I must thank you...you make easy for me!"

Brooke tried to focus on the man. "What are you talking about?"

"Tolstoy here is a whiz with electronics and locks," Potluck said, pride evident in her voice. "We were going to try to get our hands on a keycard from housekeeping and spoof it, but that was risky."

"*Da*. And could leave record of entry that might not match time maid is working. So, I follow you from port, and you choose my favorite bar! And you were so very nice to give me autograph and selfie."

Brooke frowned, dredging up the hazy memory. "My card wallet... you knocked it on the floor..."

"Yes. Clumsy of me," Tolstoy said with a wink, then held up a small black device in the palm of his hand, its nondescript surface featureless and devoid of buttons. "I only need moment. Your room card... much safer to use."

Potluck—whose real name was Olivia—rose from her chair and headed for the short flight of stairs. They were fortunate to have found a place with something that passed for a basement; hardly any structures on the island had them.

"I'm going for groceries; you want anything?"

"Yes!"

"I'm not looking for those stupid black cigarettes, Tolstoy."

"Then just some American cigarettes. And some pizza. And rum."

Potluck paused on the stairs. "Rum? Not vodka?"

"I am, how you say... going native."

"You're going nuts, is what you're going," Potluck said, but a smile lurked at the edges of her mouth. Last year, when the Cozumel job had gone fubar, the two ex-mercenaries had hunkered down in Grand Cayman to wait for things to cool off. Their team leader, code name Angler, had gone his own way, tired of running... tired of killing. They hadn't heard from him since. After a few months in paradise, the Russian and the Wisconsinite had grown closer and decided to make a home there. That was all well and good, but Grand Cayman was an expensive place to live, especially for a pair of ex-mercs trying to keep their heads down.

So, when this job came along—the offer arriving through one of their old channels—the pair had jumped at the chance to make enough money to extend their stay. She hoped it had been the right choice. She wished Angler were still around... he'd had a nose for what jobs to take—and which ones to avoid like the plague. It was funny that she still thought of the old soldier by his call sign. Indeed, Olivia Peterson and Alexei Shirokov tended to use their code names with each other, as well; a kind of shorthand that reminded them of where they'd come from.

"Okay, Tolstoy... cigs, pizza, and rum. Seeya later."

"And I'll see you... in Hell!"

"Oh, jeez, that got old the first twenty times you said it." Potluck shook her head as she left the stairs and closed the door behind her.

Outside, island insects chirped and rasped in a strident chorus. The bugs were particularly loud and the night exceedingly dark at the end of this dead-end street, their nearest neighbor being a business that rented out heavy equipment, like backhoes and cement mixers. Potluck jumped into a battered SUV and started down Miss Daisy Lane, turning left when she reached a T-intersection. Heading east toward Esterly Tibbetts Highway, she passed a red building on the right. Potluck rolled her eyes. Illuminated in the nearby streetlight, a painted yellow sign on one wall declared: "Welcome to Hell."

10

"Amelia, how you doing over there?" Boone asked into the radio handset.

"Running smooth," she replied back.

"Okay, then let's nudge it up a couple knots. Maybe we can keep this crossing closer to six hours."

The two boats had departed just after sunrise, and they were nearly halfway across. Boone had left Emily sitting outside their condo with Brix, rereading the script with her morning coffee. The earliest flight out didn't leave until 8:50 a.m.

Amelia's voice came back over the radio. "The engine's still behaving, Boone."

"Good. How's your cousin doing?"

Amelia laughed. "Still going strong."

After they'd rendered assistance to the *Bob's Bobo* the day before yesterday, Amelia Ebanks had called her parents and mentioned she'd met a Willis Ebanks—the son of a fisherman named Robert Ebanks. The Cayman Islands equivalent of the coconut telegraph had gone into action, and by the next day, Amelia learned that Willis was a second cousin. It was decided that she would accompany her newfound kin on the *Bobo* during the crossing and compare family gossip. Rather than fly back, Leonard joined Boone on the *Lunasea* to ask additional questions about Little Cayman and to tell him what he could about running a chase boat.

At present, Leonard's pale complexion was swinging between spokes on the color wheel: from red due to the earlier sunburn, to green from the rolling of the boat. The seas weren't bad, but this was a long, open-ocean trip. Leonard applied some more sunscreen. "Should've taken that motion sickness pill the moment I woke up," he muttered. "But I think it's kicking in."

"Eyes on the horizon," Boone advised.

"There's a nice breeze up on this… what do you call it?"

"Flybridge. Short for 'flying bridge.' It's just a term for a bridge above the main bridge, usually with some duplicate controls up top. A lot of dive boats have them. Better visibility and a more enjoyable ride, but you can always retreat to the wheelhouse if the weather turns."

"This boat of yours… good speed, good range?"

"Yes to both. As I said before, we don't really make this crossing very often. Most dive boats don't even try. But the folks who made a few 'upgrades' on this boat had some open-ocean travel in mind."

Leonard didn't ask Boone to elaborate, instead simply nodding. "And she seems like she'd be a stable platform for a camera," he observed.

"Well… as stable as a thirty-eight-foot dive boat can be. But yeah, her hull is built for a decent ride."

"I'm just the location scout, but on this shoot, we've cut some corners here and there. I'll be assisting on a chase boat once all the locations have been chosen and arranged for," Leonard explained. "Some people in the photography and transportation departments will tell you everything in greater detail, but basically, you'll be driving this boat with a camera crew on board, an assistant director, and some additional support staff.

"No problem. We can carry up to twenty divers, but that's a bit cramped. Em and I like to keep it at twelve or less if we can help it."

"It'll probably be about that," Leonard said. "There will be two other chase boats, most days. One of the chase boats will also operate a drone for aerial footage. We want to get multiple angles with each take; otherwise, we'd be at sea all day."

"And what are we shooting?"

"There are three main boats in the plot, but I'll let the transpo guy tell you the specifics about each of them, if you're interested. You're actually going to pull in beside two of them and dock your boat there. We've rented an entire section of Harbour House Marina."

"Oh, great! Saves me having to pay for the Yacht Club slip," Boone said. "Wish I'd known sooner; I've already prepaid for three days."

"We'll cover that, don't worry," Leonard said.

Boone looked at his Aquinus dive watch. *Emily should be in the air*, he thought. "Hey, Leonard... got a question for you. And you may not be able to answer this, but... as you may have guessed, I'm in love with a certain kooky, blond Brit, and I'd hate to see her get hurt."

Leonard looked at Boone. "You saved our butts out there, so I figure I owe you. Ask away."

"Why did Brooke Bablin quit?"

Leonard sighed. "I don't know. They offered her a boatload of money and box office points, and the studio is sinking a fair amount into production. Heinz Werner can be… difficult. But the shoot only began recently, so I don't see how a personality clash could've happened so quickly. Plus, Brooke doesn't take shit from anyone. I doubt even Werner could drive her away so quickly."

"So… what happened? She storm off the set?"

"No! She shot for the whole day, but then she just didn't show up for work the next morning. The 1ˢᵗ AD told me her condo was cleaned out, just a note left saying 'I quit.' Even her agents didn't know about it. Or so they say. Who knows? They're supposed to be on *her* side, not ours… so they could be hiding something."

"Maybe she got a better offer," Boone suggested.

"Are you kidding? The studio would sue her into the stone age if she bailed for another gig. She's under contract. Hell, just quitting is a breach."

Boone opened a cooler at his feet and removed a pair of aluminum water bottles, offering one to Leonard. Bubble Chasers was trying to cut down on using plastic, so they'd bought a bunch of these on one of their last shopping trips. "Here, brought an extra for you. Hydrate."

"Thanks," Leonard said, unscrewing the top.

"*De nada.* Hey, you said Mr. Werner was 'difficult.' What did you mean by that?"

"Well… he's eccentric. Prone to mood swings. Sometimes goes off on tangents with the day's shoot, rewriting stuff on the fly. And he can be demanding of the talent. There's an actress who was a lead in one of his earlier films who had a complete breakdown and had to be involuntarily committed halfway through the production."

Boone raised an eyebrow. "Anyone I know?"

"Maybe, but I'm not telling. She was nice to me."

"And Werner caused the breakdown?"

"Well... drugs were involved, so... hard to say."

"Did they recast the role?"

"Nope. The studio shelved the project. Too bad—the movie was going to be fantastic."

"What was it called?"

"*Zombie Bigfoot.*"

Boone laughed. "No, seriously."

"I *am* serious. Whoever ends up making that movie will rake in the dough, mark my words. Sci-fi action-adventure horror comedy. It's like *Shaun of the Dead* had an unholy love child with *Jurassic Park.*"

Boone checked his watch again and squinted through his polarized shades toward the east. "Hey, Leonard. Take the wheel, would you?"

"Sure."

Boone stepped aside, eyes on the sky. *There.* A familiar sight came into view: a Cayman Airways Twin Otter approached from the east, the small turboprop plane being the same model as the ones that flew between Saint Martin, Saba, and Statia. Boone stripped off his dive shirt, waving it back and forth as the commuter plane flew by on its way to Grand Cayman.

"Uh, there's a guy down there waving a shirt," the pilot said. "What's a dive boat doing way out here?"

Emily, sitting on the left just behind the cockpit, quickly looked down at the sea below. A broad smile overtook her face. *Boone.* She waggled her fingers in the window, knowing there was absolutely zero chance he'd see. *But it's the thought that counts.*

"Is he in distress?" the copilot asked. "Should I call it in?"

"No, no!" Emily blurted, leaning toward the aisle. "It's okay! I know him. He's just saying hi."

The copilot looked back at her. "Really?"

"Yeah! I'd ask you to give 'im a little wing-waggle, but I imagine that's against regulations."

The copilot grinned and shook his head, returning his attention to the controls as Em returned her attention to the script that sat on her lap. This was her third read and she thought it was pretty good. Any movie that had a pirate and a monkey in the first scene was already something she'd watch for at least fifteen minutes. *Not sure how I feel about parading around in a bikini for half the movie,* she thought, absently wishing she'd held off on ordering the cassava cake last night. *Although, I didn't really eat much of it, did I?*

It was only a half-hour flight between islands, so this time through Emily skipped any scene she wasn't in. When the puddle jumper touched down in Grand Cayman, she finished the last page and stuffed the script into her backpack before sliding an enormous pair of sunglasses onto her face. Exiting the plane, she crossed the apron and stepped into the baggage claim. It was only five minutes before the few bags from the little aircraft appeared on the conveyor belt and she grabbed her small green suitcase. On a larger aircraft, she'd have been able to store it above her seat, but the Twin Otters had no overheads, and barely any room under their seats. Pausing to straighten the lightweight, yellow sundress she'd selected for first impressions, Emily made her way to the exit and was greeted with her name on a sign, held by a Caymanian man wearing a white polo shirt and black slacks. Beside him stood a young white guy, talking rapidly into a phone.

"I'm Emily Durand!" she said when she reached the man with the sign.

"Oh! She's here. Gotta go," the man with the phone said, hanging up. "Welcome, Miss Durand!"

"Hey, no need to be formal with me. Call me Emily, please. Or Em. Or Emmy, if you're feeling cheeky."

The Caymanian laughed and took her suitcase, while the other man looked confused for a second, then smiled. "Emily it is. I'm Jerry, the second assistant director. That's Gus, one of our drivers. We'll be taking you to our offices so we can get some paperwork out of the way, then straight to a quick meet-and-greet," he said, as they followed the driver to a town car in short-term parking. "Then, off to costumes."

"It's all happening so fast!" Emily said as she climbed into the car.

Jerry snorted a laugh. "You don't know the half of it." He started to say something else, then clammed up.

"Can you tell me half of the half of it? Then I'd know a quarter of it."

Jerry sighed, surrendering. "Werner wants to shoot with you this afternoon."

"What?! Is he mental?"

Jerry leaned toward her. "I think the jury's out on that. But he can be... unusual. The term 'mad genius' has certainly been thrown around. But he wants to stay on schedule, and they're still having trouble with one of the vessels from another storyline, so you may be on the pirate ship today. Assuming the costume fits."

Emily rolled her eyes. "You mean the bikini."

"Oh, great! You read the script!"

"Three times. It's good! Hold on a tick… are they putting me in Brooke Bablin's costumes?"

"Well… you are about the same size…"

Emily shook her head.

"Everything's been laundered, I'm sure."

"But what looked good on her might not look good on me! Fortunately, I brought a few options."

The car drove through a series of roundabouts, making its way across to West Bay Road behind Seven Mile Beach. Driving south for a short distance, they pulled into the lot of a five-story hotel, its roof blue and its walls painted in various shades of yellow. The surrounding area was filled with resorts and hotels, with new construction going up in the near distance.

"Here we are," Jerry announced. "This used to be a Comfort Suites, but it was sold for redevelopment. Fortunately, reconstruction is some months away, and we managed to rent the entire building for offices and housing for cast and crew. We even hired back some of the original hotel staff, which made everybody happy. Oh, that reminds me… here's a welcome packet to tuck in your backpack. The keycard to your room is inside."

"Was Brooke staying here?" Em asked.

"No, she was staying at a villa complex nearby. But they're giving you a suite!"

A few minutes later, Emily was seated at a table in a small conference room with a sea of papers in front of her, pen in hand. A by-the-books production assistant went over the essentials: apparently, Em would be joining a Screen Actors Guild union called SAG-AFTRA, and would be paid nearly $4,000 a week. After a flurry of signatures, Jerry collected Emily and whisked her across a palm-lined hall to a larger conference room, this one full of people.

"Wait, wait, wait..." Emily did an about-face, returning to the outer hall and practically hiding behind the nearest ornamental palm.

"Are you okay?" Jerry asked, sounding concerned.

"I will be. Everything just... it just hit me." She blew out a slow breath. "Went from fantasy to reality in an instant, yeah? Seeing all those people. Just give me a sec." She leaned back against the wall, closed her eyes, and focused on her breathing, recalling the exercise her therapist had given her to cope with her panic attacks. What she'd just felt was nowhere near as severe, but she figured the same technique would work just as well with a simple case of the jitters. And it did. Two minutes later, she blew out a final breath. "Right. Better now."

Emily opened her eyes and smiled at Jerry. Only it wasn't Jerry. A man in a light blue dress shirt and slacks was standing beside the palm tree, watching her. His dark hair was carefully styled with a light touch of gel, and his dark brown eyes—almost black— regarded her curiously. Em looked past him and saw Jerry on the phone. She returned her gaze to the newcomer. "Uh... hi?"

"Forgive me, I didn't mean to distract you. Meditation?"

"Oh, no, not really. Well, maybe kinda sorta. Just calming my nerves."

"Ah. A case of butterflies in the stomach?"

"Oh, yeah, big time. Although these are more the size of hummingbirds. Or maybe pterodactyls. I'm Emily."

"Yes, I know. Emily Durand," the man said, taking her offered hand and holding it. "I saw your audition." He smiled, then continued. "They're all waiting for you inside, you know. I'm Maxwell Beck, the field producer for the production. I'm one of

119

the people with an eye on the budget... and you, my dear, are a godsend in that regard."

"Um... thanks?"

Max leaned in conspiratorially, still grasping her hand in a light grip. "But there's no need to be nervous. Most of the people inside are thrilled to have you stepping in for Brooke."

"Most?"

"And I, for one, am glad to have you aboard," Max concluded, releasing her hand and entering the conference room.

"You good to go?" Jerry asked, tucking his phone into his pocket.

I was, Emily thought, watching Beck vanish inside. "Yeah. Let's do this."

11

Reentering the conference room, Emily glanced around, noting that most of the assembled cast and crew were clustered in little cliques, many of them noshing on small plates of finger foods from a craft services table against one wall. Jerry led her straight to Heinz Werner, who was speaking with a pair of men who looked so over-the-top nerdy, Emily first assumed they must be playing nerds in the movie. The heated conversation quickly revealed them to be writers. Em lurked behind Jerry, tugging at his sleeve, mouthing for him to "Wait."

"I don't want a toxic spill!" Werner declared. "If we make it a toxic spill, then we have to include those doing the spilling, and that would either require an additional ship and an additional at-sea shoot, or an additional land location... a chemical plant, or some such thing. And those aren't easy to arrange, according to Leonard."

The younger writer held up a finger, a eureka look on his face. "What if... what if it's the radiation from a ruptured nuclear reactor in a Russian submarine that mutates the creature? No additional casting needed, and we could do the wrecked sub with CGI!"

The older writer, sporting a graying ponytail, snorted a derisive laugh. "Excuuuuse me, but were you still watching Elmo in diapers when *The Abyss* came out? Greatest underwater movie ever."

Emily swallowed a laugh as she heard shades of Comic Book Guy from *The Simpsons* in the ponytailed man's voice.

"I saw *Abyss,* dickhead. That was an American sub."

"Oh, yes, the nationality makes all the difference," Ponytail replied, surfing a wave of sarcasm.

"*Nein, nein,* no submarines!" Werner barked. "Alien influence is simpler."

"But didn't *The Abyss* have..." the young writer began, but trailed off.

Ponytail took up the baton. "Actually, Mr. Werner, in *Zombie Bigfoot,* didn't you have a..."

"Stop! Do not speak the name of that travesty again in my presence. That movie does not exist, so we need not worry about borrowing elements from a nonentity. Make it a meteor shower." Werner nodded, convincing himself. "*Ja, ja... das ist gut.* We start at the edge of space, our beautiful blue planet below. The audience watches as a meteor strikes the atmosphere and burns with the flames of a hell-bound fallen angel. It fragments, pieces break off and vaporize, until finally a tiny, glowing nugget survives, and splashes into the sea with a hiss."

"Whoa, I like it," said the younger writer.

Werner continued, his voice intense. "The irradiated crumb of meteor sinks into the inky depths before brushing against the questing tentacles of a Portuguese man o' war. The primitive creature mistakes it for prey. It draws the meteor in..."

"Actually," Ponytail said, interrupting, "any part of a meteor that reaches the earth is called a 'meteorite.'"

Werner looked at him, his creative excitement extinguished and replaced with a dead-eyed glare. "Tell me, Derek... when you are on a dinner date and you begin to speak, do the women often go off to powder their nose, never to return, leaving you alone to discuss trivial facts with the waiter?"

Ponytail/Derek blinked, taken aback.

Werner turned from him and addressed the younger writer. "Write what I have described. I will allow one use of the word 'meteorite,' in the stage directions only. Get it done and bring it to the special effects department."

When the writers scattered, Emily pounced. "Hello, Mr. Werner!"

"Ah! My new Sarah is here at last! Come... I will introduce you to the cast."

Werner mounted a pair of steps to a small dais and addressed the crowd. "Ladies and gentlemen, may I have your attention, please."

The groups of people around the room turned as one, and Emily felt her heart rate increase as Werner beckoned for her to join him on the raised platform.

"As many of you know, Brooke Bablin has departed the production. But, as with many things in life, adversity can bring opportunity! As fate would have it, the perfect replacement awaited us on the Sister Island of Little Cayman! Since it is our intention to shoot some of the marine shots there, I see this fortuitous discovery as serendipitous providence! Please, give a warm welcome to the newest addition to our family... Emily Durand!"

Emily smiled and gave a little wave. While the applause didn't exactly erupt from the gathering, it seemed warm and heartfelt from most—although some glanced at each other with lifted eyebrows or mouthed phrases.

"Emily, why don't you tell these good people a few things about yourself," Werner suggested.

Em swallowed, took a deep breath, and stepped forward. "Afternoon, all! Or… morning, maybe. Is it, still? Honestly, I'm not a hundred percent sure I'm not still in bed, back in Little Cayman, dreaming all of this."

Smiles. A few laughs.

"Uhhhh… 'a few things about myself,' eh? Okay, you're the boss! Favorite food: whatever's on my plate. Favorite drink: coffee or rum, depending on the time of day. I have a dog named Brixton, a boyfriend named Boone, and a boat named the *Lunasea*. I'm a big fan of karaoke night, I dominate at trivia, and if any of you blokes play poker, I'd be more than happy to separate you from your money."

More laughs now, and she had everyone's eyes locked on her. Emily relaxed and turned up the charm, the words flowing forth.

"I'm a big fan of nature and wildlife, particularly sea life. Embarrassing fact: I'm obsessed with mermaids. Mind you, I do possess enough of a grasp of the real world to know that mermaids don't exist—that being said, I may get a tattoo of one."

She quickly turned to Werner, anticipating his reaction. "*After* the shoot, boss! I know they've got me in a bikini for half the movie, so I'll keep everything 'au naturel.' Oh, wait… that means 'naked' too, don't it? Obviously, I didn't mean I'd run around starkers—this isn't that kind of movie, is it? Blimey, I should've read what I was signing more carefully."

That got a bigger laugh, particularly from the blue-collarish crew corner—no surprise there, many of them having tattoos of their own. Even Werner chuckled.

124

"Now, some of you might be detecting the slightest indication that I am not a Yank. And before one of you asks, no I'm not Australian, either. I come from London! Although that seems like a lifetime ago. I left there after university and I've been island-hopping the Caribbean ever since. Beats the climate in dear old Blighty, that's for sure."

A plump older gentleman smiled and nodded his head. He looked like he probably played Falstaff in Shakespeare in the Park in the summer and Santa in the winter.

"So, what else, what else...? I am a divemaster by trade, a damn good one. Lost count of how many dives I've logged— though I've got it written down somewhere, I assure you. Oh! I can skipper a boat with the best of them, so... writers?" She caught the eyes of Ponytail Derek and his younger counterpart. "If you want to change something and put me behind the wheel of one of the boats, I'll do you proud, I promise."

Werner stepped forward slightly and addressed the room. "Speaking of rewrites, 'Sarah' will now be an exchange student from England."

"Well, that's a spot of luck!" Emily gushed, wide-eyed. *"I'm* from England!"

The room erupted into laughter, and Emily was led into the middle of the room to meet and greet her cast and crew. She'd only managed to talk to a few of them before Jerry once again absconded with her and took her down to costumes—but not before Em insisted on a detour to the smaller conference room where she'd left her suitcase and backpack. "In case costumes need some options," she explained.

Just after twelve noon, *Bob's Bobo* and the *Lunasea* rounded Rum Point and entered the protected waters of the North Sound. This bay was a sizeable body of water, and it was nearly six and a half miles to the film's rented marina slips, down at the southern end of the Sound. Boone almost suggested he go ahead and zip over to the Yacht Club, which was much closer to where he was planning to spend his afternoon, but he figured he ought to take a look at the boats the *Lunasea* would be "chasing."

After some jockeying to find a place for the two boats, Boone tied up alongside the concrete pier, just behind a large vessel that looked a lot like an oceanographic research ship. Boone guessed it was just over a hundred feet long. A crane was attached near the stern, and Boone could make out what appeared to be a small submersible on its aft deck. Above the three-level superstructure was a white sphere, which looked a lot like some of the radars Boone remembered seeing on Dutch warships around Bonaire and Saba. The name on the stern was *Puddingwife*.

Boone chuckled. He'd always liked that fish's name. The puddingwife was a species of blue-green wrasse, common in the Caribbean. Amelia waved to him from down the pier, then pointed at her phone. Boone took his out and found a text from her: *Staying with Willis's family. Is that okay?* Boone replied it was fine, suggesting they meet for dinner later. Amelia looked at her phone, then flashed an "OK" sign and went with Willis toward the main road.

"Boone, I want to thank you for getting us safely back," Leonard said. "I've got to get over to the offices, but we'll talk again, soon." He grabbed his bag and Boone helped him across to the pier. "Oh, tell Willis to call me! We're going to keep him on payroll and use the *Bobo* for some shoots here in Grand."

"Bet he'll be happy to hear that. You got a number, or...?"

"Oh! Right! You'd think after last night, we would've exchanged cards or something. Here." He handed over a business card, and Boone gave him numbers for himself, Amelia, and Emily. Leonard looked around and pointed at a man walking toward them from the western side of the pier. "That's Deacon. He's with transportation, in charge of wrangling the chase boats and the set vessels. He'll fill you in!" And with that, Leonard turned and jogged toward the street access to the marina to hail a cab.

Deacon approached. He had an easygoing manner to his walk, and from his clothing and heavily tanned face, Boone pegged him as someone who'd spent a lot of time on boats before this movie.

"Hey there," Deacon said. "I'm guessing you're Boone Fischer."

"Yessir," Boone said, offering his hand.

The man shook it. "I'm Deacon Brody, with the transportation department. I keep these things afloat." He jabbed a thumb over his shoulder at the *Puddingwife*, his eyes already locked onto the *Lunasea*. "Sweet boat. Delta Canaveral?"

"Good eye."

"I've been on a few. Good boat. Stable… which we like!" He pointed at the name on the side. "Ha! Clever name."

"Your film's new leading lady came up with that," Boone said. He nodded to the research vessel. "Is this one of the ships in the story?"

"Yeah. The *Puddingwife*—we just call her *Pudding* most of the time. She's on loan from a salvage company in Texas."

"Pretty high-tech looking radar dome for a salvage ship."

"Oh, that's just for show. The prop guys built it. The crane is real, though. So's the submersible. We rented that from a guy in Honduras. We'll have an underwater camera drone too, but that's the camera department's area, not mine."

"So, there are submarine shots, too?"

"A few," Deacon said. "Hey, you're a divemaster, right?"

"Yeah."

"Good to know. Might be you could make a few extra bucks on top of the chase boat rental and salary. Anyways, let me show you what you'll be chasing. We've got three main ships that play a part in the movie. The *Pudding* here is the oceanographic research ship that's being used by a group of treasure hunters, searching for a Spanish galleon. They are disguising that search by combining it with an actual oceanographic survey; so, on board we've got some marine scientist types. They end up studying the creature and find ways to fight it. Our leading man is in this storyline—that was supposed to be Cliff Van Dorn, but something happened to him in New York, so now some new up-and-comer is playing the part."

"Billy Faust," Boone offered.

"Yeah, that sounds right."

"Cliff Van Dorn… he's in all those action movies, right? What happened to him?"

"Uh… let's just say he fights better on-screen than in real life. Got busted up pretty bad. It made the news." Deacon gestured to the western edge of the pier. "Now, over here is the *Mako*."

The boat Deacon was indicating was a high-speed motor yacht of some sort; its partially enclosed flybridge was set back from the wheelhouse below, and the boat's sloping lines gave it a sleek look.

"This beauty is an Azimut 60. Absolutely gorgeous yacht. It helps when you have producers with toys like these, and the one who lives here in Grand Cayman loaned her to the movie. I'll give you a tour, if you like. Her actual name is *Prince of Tides*, but in our story, the *Mako* is run by a group of mercenaries-turned-pirates. They're secretly working with someone on board the *Pudding*, and are tracking her, waiting for her to find the treasure. Of course, the mercs are just there for cannon fodder."

"Cannon fodder?"

"Yeah. You know, the poor schmucks you throw in front to soak up all the machine gun fire." Deacon laughed. "Like those Red Shirts on *Star Trek* that were the first to die in every show. Every good monster movie needs a lot of cannon fodder. Can't go killing off the stars. Well… not usually."

"How fast does this baby go?" Boone asked.

"Right now? Zero knots. But we've figured out the problem."

"Fixable?"

"Oh, yeah, easy. Just have to replace the fuel lines," Deacon said. "Although I don't like *why* we need to replace them."

"What happened?"

"Somebody cut them."

"What?"

A flash of regret came across Deacon's face. "Hey, forget I said anything. It's getting fixed. We got enough stuff that's gone wrong on this shoot—best to keep this on the down-low. Maybe a disgruntled crew member…who knows? I've set up some security cameras on all three boats and the police are making a discreet inquiry."

Boone nodded, looking around at the other vessels at the pier. "And which of these is the third one?"

"Now *that* vessel is a lot of fun, but she's over in George Town right now. Here…" He pulled up an image on his phone and shielded it from the sun so Boone could see it.

"A pirate ship?"

"A 'party barge,' actually. They brought her over from Jamaica. We've named her the *Jolly Robert*. There's a party cruise operation in Barbados that has a pirate ship named *Jolly Roger*, so the writers tweaked the name."

"What part of the story line is that for?"

"More cannon fodder! Think the beach scene in *Jaws*, but with drunken college kids on a rum cruise. Some of them survive and are rescued by the *Pudding*. Among them, your gal, our new leading lady. In fact…" Deacon glanced at his phone's clock. "I think they're planning on shooting her first scene right about now."

12

"Where are the new pages?" Werner asked.

"Here, sir." An intern working for the script supervisor handed him a brightly colored sheaf of papers. Each subsequent version of the shooting script was printed on a different color, and the rewrites to date had been copious.

Werner waggled the pages. "What is this, chartreuse?"

Dario, the first assistant director, chuckled. "I think the business center is running out of color options."

"The script morgue will look like a *gottverdammter* rainbow when we are through," Werner muttered around the cigarette he'd just tucked into his mouth.

All around them, the deck of the *Jolly Robert* bustled with crew as they set up for a shot. The pirate ship was moored further out this time, to ensure no one could moor behind them and ruin the scene. It had been discovered that Brooke was visible in several of the wide shots, and the decision had been made to reshoot everything. The principal cast and background actors were still ashore, but the "second team" was aboard. A group of actors with approximately the same looks and height of their counterparts, the second team was there to stand in for the principals while the camera and lighting crews set up the shot.

Dario thumbed a button on the radio clipped to his belt, pressing his earpiece with his other hand. "Say again, Jerry?"

Werner ignited his cigarette and flipped through the script. He would receive a smaller shot script for the day, but he wanted to go over the revisions the writers had made. He was pleased to see that the meteor—or meteorite—splashdown was worded just as he'd laid out.

"Copy," Dario said, finishing his radio call. "The costume department has sent Miss Durand to the tender for the principals. Background has already left the dock," he said, referring to the two tenders they were using, one with the main actors, the other with the extras.

"Good. And tell the special effects department they can start working on this meteor sequence," Werner said, tapping the yellow-green script. Most of the animators were working in Ukraine, but a small team was on location as well.

"You got it," Dario said, already beginning to type the text.

Werner went to the gunwale and looked toward the approaching tender boat with the extras. "And please tell me the animal wrangler found another monkey?"

"Afraid not, sir."

Emily arrived at the cruise ship tender dock and was waved into a waiting boat ahead of the animal trainer. She stepped across, tightening the belt of the dressing gown over her bikini. She was pleased that the costumers had liked her own selections enough to let her wear one of her favorites, a solid lime-green one she'd picked up in Cozumel.

"Keep that thing far away from me," Daniel Wolfit said, as the animal wrangler stepped aboard with a small cage.

"You know, he can sense you don't like him."

Wolfit snorted. "Then he possesses more insight than training. I loathe the beast."

The handler squeezed past and sat in a corner, the cage on his lap.

"What kind of monkey is that?" Emily asked.

"He's a capuchin," the animal wrangler said. "They're common in Central and South America."

"He looks familiar. Has he been in other movies?"

"Only two, and both were filmed in Brazil. Capuchins are the most common type of monkey in movies, so that's probably why he seems familiar to you."

"Hey there, cutie!" Em said, leaning down and addressing the tiny occupant.

The little monkey gripped the bars and chittered at her.

"Oh, really?" Emily responded. "And then what happened?"

The monkey reached through the bars and Emily watched the trainer go on alert.

"I hear your name is Ulysses," Emily said, offering the tip of her index finger to the questing little hand. "I'm Emily."

The monkey gripped her fingertip and Em giggled, gently pumping her hand in a handshake.

"Pleased to meet you, Ulysses."

"His name used to be Pepe," the wrangler said, "but we changed it early on, once we had the script."

"You're lucky they haven't changed its name two or three times since then," Wolfit said, waggling the latest version of the script.

"I'm Paulo Silva," the handler said, holding out a grape to Emily. "Here, offer this to Ulysses."

"Thanks, Paulo!" Emily took the grape in her other hand and held it up. "Care for a little treat?"

Ulysses released her finger, both of his hands reaching for the piece of fruit. Emily held it closer, and the capuchin snatched it, settling down in the cage to eat the grape with little bites.

"Good boy!" Em cooed.

"He was most decidedly *not* a good boy the other day," Wolfit muttered.

The tender's engine rumbled, and the crew cast off from the pier. Emily sat beside Wolfit.

"Good to have a fellow Brit join the cast," he said. "At the meet-and-greet, you mentioned you were from London, I believe. South London I'd venture, if my ears do not deceive."

"Bravo! Deptford."

Wolfit smiled. "I thought so. I had a stage manager at The Old Vic who was from there. Loved how he spoke—very salt-of-the-earth."

"Yeah, well… I think Mr. Werner wants me to dial it down. Hope I can. You speak beautifully, Mr. Wolfit. Any pointers?"

"I'd be happy to assist, my dear. A lifetime of Shakespearean training has stood me in good stead with regard to the Queen's English. I believe you'll want to employ what is referred to as Received Pronunciation, or Standard British. I'll keep an ear out and endeavor to steer you down the correct path."

"Thanks much!"

"I couldn't help but notice, during your exceedingly charming speech at the meet-and-greet, there was no mention of acting in your curriculum vitae...?"

"Uh... not much, no."

"Not to worry, dear girl. I suspect you're a natural!"

Emily heard the engine on the tender drop toward idle and she looked across the bow. "Ohmigod, it *is* a pirate ship!"

Constructed to look vaguely like a child's vision of a pirate ship, the *Jolly Robert* sported two masts with red sails, and flew a skull-and-beer bottles Jolly Roger, the black-and-white flag fluttering over a little crow's nest that appeared to have a dummy in it, dressed in a pirate outfit. Em guessed the dummy was supposed to look like a dummy, given how ridiculous it was, one floppy arm dangling with a plastic hook on the end. The tender swung broadside to the *Jolly Robert*, coming alongside a hinged metal stairway that was lowered from above.

The actors began to transfer over. Emily rose, but Jerry, the 2nd AD, asked her to hold up. "Let the initial crush go over, then I'll bring you straight to hair and makeup."

"I was wondering about that," Em said. "Mind you, I'm not one who wears much makeup, but I figured, this being a movie and all..."

"For interior scenes, you'll do that first thing, but today we're exterior on the ship. You've got a lot of closeups and it's hot and humid. You'd sweat it all off, so we wait until you're aboard."

After everyone boarded, Emily went up the stairs and was taken to a chair in the shade, where members of the hair and makeup departments went to work. Em kept the sides on her lap, the small pages showing the order of scenes and all of the dialogue in them. Initially terrified by all the words she'd have to remember, she calmed when she realized this wasn't like a play where you needed to know them all at once—she'd only need to learn a few lines a day.

Apparently, her character wore her hair in a ponytail, which Emily was certainly used to. As makeup put on the finishing touches, a young man sidled up to the chair. "Miss Durand? I'm here to take you to set. Are you ready?"

"I dunno, am I?" Em asked, checking with the woman who'd applied her makeup.

"All done," she said. "There's a portable electric fan in a pocket of your cast chair. Use it when you're not shooting, or you'll find yourself back in this chair."

"Right-o!" She turned to the young man who'd come to fetch her. "Okay, let's go, um… what's your name?"

"I'm Phil. I'm the 2nd 2nd AD."

"I thought Jerry was the second assistant director."

"He is. I'm the 2nd 2nd AD."

Emily wrinkled her brow. "This sounds like a 'Who's-on-first' bit. Why can't you just be the 3rd AD?"

"I don't know, ma'am. This is my first film."

"Well, whaddaya know, me too! Lead the way, Second Second!"

The kid laughed and took her to the set. As she approached, Dario called out "Second Team out. First Team, rehearsal."

"What's that mean?" she asked Phil.

"Uh, the stand-ins for you and the others are the Second Team; they're there for the cameras and lights to set up the shots. And now, the main actors like you—First Team—will rehearse."

"Okay," Em said, heart rate increasing as she approached the ring of cameras and crew. She hugged her dressing gown closed, feeling self-conscious.

"Ah, good!" Werner called out, the dregs of a cigarette in his fingers. He approached her, then looked at the cigarette and went to toss it. Jerry was there to take it, popping it into a soda can. "Miss Durand, I expect great things from you! Nervous?"

"Bit nervy, yeah."

"Good! Use it!" Werner said as he turned away and went to whisper something to the 1st AD.

"All right, listen up!" Dario said. "We've got a tight schedule, so after rehearsal, return to your marks. If everyone is happy, we'll go straight into the shoot."

Emily nodded, slipping on the fake glasses the costume department had given her. A busty brunette came up alongside her and yawned.

"Hi," Emily said. "You're playing Cindy, yeah?"

The girl gave a half-smile and nodded. "And you're our new Brooke Bablin."

"Oh, well... I wouldn't go that far."

"No? Well, I guess not. She's a big celebrity after all, and you..." She shrugged. "But you do look a lot like her, I'll say that."

"Thanks."

"And you were very funny at the meet-and-greet."

Emily leaned in. "I was terrified, truth to tell. What's your name again?"

"Cindy."

"No, I mean your name-name, not the character."

"That *is* my name. And my character's name."

"Well, that's a spot of luck!" Emily said with a smile.

Cindy pointed down at the deck. "Those pieces of pink tape? That's your mark. You might want to stand there so we only have to do this once."

"Oh... okay, thanks. Toe the line, yeah?"

Boot heels sounded as Wolfit strode across the deck, a garish pirate's costume hugging his ample frame, although the front was partially unbuttoned. Appropriate to his character's name, his beard was colored a deep blue.

"Once more unto the breach, dear friends!" he declaimed in a sonorous voice. As he passed Emily, he sketched a courtly bow. "M'lady. How dost thou, this fine day?"

"Peachy keen, Mr. Wolfit!" Emily then cleared her throat and did her best to posh up her speech. "I mean... I am doing ever so well, dear sir."

Wolfit laughed, then held two fingertips close together. "Split the difference," he said with a wink, then made his way up to the forecastle.

Cindy rolled her eyes. "God, he's so full of himself. Brooke hated him."

"What?" Emily was shocked. "But he's charming! I like him."

"Hmm," Cindy said, as if reassessing Emily.

Okay, enough of this Mean Girls shite, Em thought, turning away from Cindy Squared and going over her lines again.

"Stand by for rehearsal!"

Oh, bugger, I better get rid of my script. No, wait, Wolfit still has his.

"Quiet on set!"

Emily blew out a breath, mouthing her lines.

"Background!"

What does that mean? Oh, the extras are moving now.

"Action!"

Up on the forecastle, Daniel Wolfit dropped his erudite speech and launched into a full pirate's brogue. "Arrrr, mateys... welcome aboard the *Jolly Robert*! The greatest rum cruise in the Caribbean! I be yer cap'n, Robert Bluebeard! Yaaaaarrrr!"

The scene played out, and Emily managed to hold her own. When the scene ended, Werner whisked in.

"Excellent, *mein Liebchen*! You were marvelous!"

"I bollocksed up a line near the end. Sorry."

"Your ad lib was superior to what was on the page," Werner said, taking the script from her fingers. "Now, we are going straight into the scene!"

"The accent okay?"

Werner smiled politely. "Better," he said, heading back to his chair beside the monitors.

"Last looks!" the 1st AD shouted, and hair and makeup descended on Emily, primping and powdering.

Em glanced up at Wolfit and saw the man buttoning up his greatcoat. *Guess we're doing this.* She slipped out of her dressing gown and it was taken from her instantly. Background actors shuffled into their positions. Paulo Silva brought Ulysses to set, and the little monkey reached for Emily as they passed on their way up to the forecastle. Wolfit gave the monkey a wary, side-eyed glance.

A flurry of phrases issued from members of the crew and the first assistant director.

"Picture's up!"

"Roll sound."

"Sound speed."

A crewwoman lifted a clapperboard with writing on the slate, holding it in front of one of the cameras before speaking in a monotone. "Scene two, Take one, Alpha. Mark!" She clapped the hinged stick at the top of the slate and retreated from frame.

"Background!" Around Emily, the actors playing the college partiers went into motion.

Werner leaned forward. "And... action!"

As Wolfit launched into his opening speech, Emily's mind went blank. *What the hell am I doing?*

Boone was standing in the parking lot of the Foster's supermarket in West Bay, eight canvas bags of non-perishable groceries and various non-food items at his feet, waiting for AJ Bailey to pick him up and take him to her place. This area of Grand Cayman was at the northern end of the famous Seven Mile Beach; the buildings were mostly one or two-story, and the overall vibe much sleepier than the resort-packed area to the south. AJ had an afternoon dive slated, but she'd suggested she would try to depart early and take her divers to Trinity Caves, which wasn't far from her dock. If all went well, she could grab him by two-thirty in the afternoon. Boone glanced down at his phone, checking the time. A quarter to three.

Boone raised his eyes as a Royal Cayman Islands Police Service patrol car pulled up beside him and the driver's window rolled down.

"Boone Fischer?" A Caymanian police officer leaned an arm on the door. The man looked to be in his thirties, with a no-nonsense expression on his face.

"Uh… yeah."

"I'm Constable Tibbetts. Come with us, please." The man jerked a thumb toward the backseat.

"Is everything okay?" Boone asked.

"We'll explain on the way."

"On the way to where?" Boone asked, opening the back door and doing his best to gather up the bags of groceries and set them on the seat. The officer didn't reply, so Boone finished loading the bags before joining them in the back. As soon as he sat down, he knew he'd been punked.

In the front passenger's seat sat a young woman, her blond hair tucked into a British-style policewoman's hat with a red band.

"Hi Nora," Boone said.

Nora Sommer turned, the slightest of smiles on her face. "This was AJ's idea, of course."

"Of course. So, you're not busting me for buying too much coffee and toilet paper?"

"AJ requested we roll up on you with the lights flashing, but I refused," Nora said, her voice tinged with a slight Norwegian accent. The tall Scandinavian woman was a close friend of AJ's, and occasionally accompanied her on dives. Boone had heard she'd recently joined the police force on Grand Cayman.

As Constable Tibbetts put the police car into motion, Boone asked, "So, where is AJ?"

"AJ got a late start, and the nearest moorings were taken," Nora replied, "so she asked me to come get you."

"No problem. Thanks for the lift. I could've gotten a cab."

"That's what *I* said. But AJ thought it would be more fun to misuse police resources."

Boone couldn't tell if she was joking. He himself had been accused of being stoic from time to time, but this young woman from Norway put him to shame.

"I hear Emily is in the movie," Nora said.

"Yeah, she's actually shooting right now. On a pirate ship, I think."

"The pirate ship with the big red sails?" Constable Tibbetts asked, a grin on his face. "We saw it heading out to sea on the way here!"

"They should have shot this movie in November," Nora mused. "During the Pirates Week Festival."

They went north along West Bay Road for only a moment before turning left at an Esso Station, then left again, taking Boggy Sand Road along the ocean. The sparkling water shone a vibrant blue out Boone's window. At the end of the road, they came to a stop.

"AJ left her cottage unlocked for you," Nora said, exiting the vehicle. "I will help with the bags."

Boone grabbed as many as he could, following Nora to the little cottage on the edge of the property. Although nowhere near Boone's height, she was a tall and slender woman. "How's the police work going?" he asked.

Nora shrugged. "Quiet most days. Emily's movie friends have been a handful, but they seem to have settled in. Although we got a call about someone vandalizing one of their boats."

"Cut fuel lines?"

Nora paused at the sliding glass door. "What do you know about that?"

"Nothing really. The Azimut 60 they're using had the fuel lines cut. Deacon, the production company's transportation guy, said one of the producers owns it."

"Yes. Jeffrey Scott. He has a house here. Detective Whittaker suspects it might be a disgruntled employee of the producer, perhaps one of the regular yacht crew. We are going over CCTV feeds at the dock, but so far we've seen no one but film crew coming and going from the vessel during the twelve hours prior to the malfunction."

Behind them, a squawk sounded from the patrol car's radio, and Nora cocked an ear. Boone couldn't make out what was being said, but Nora set down his bags. "I have to go. AJ should be along shortly." With that, she hustled back to the patrol car, which executed a quick three-point turn and raced back toward the main road.

Boone slid open the door and entered. The room was moderately cool, but not an icebox by any means. Like many island-dwellers, AJ kept the air conditioning set to an economical level, electricity being expensive on Grand Cayman. The sofa bed that he and Emily had used a couple times before was right beside the entrance, so he went to one side of it and tucked all the bags neatly against the wall. AJ had offered to let him keep everything here until he headed back. Although nothing was perishable, it wouldn't do to leave it in the hold of the dive boat for a lengthy period of time, and Boone wasn't sure how long he'd be in Grand.

A rumble sounded from outside and Boone stepped back out into the tropical air. AJ had arrived, currently astride an idling motorcycle. He'd admired it before on an earlier trip; it was an expensive Italian model of some sort, sleek and powerful. AJ was dressed in full gear, and Boone was put in mind of the "Black Widow" character in those Marvel movies. She turned off the engine and removed her helmet, shaking out her shoulder-length hair, purple highlights shining in the afternoon sun. She gave him a sly smile. "How was your ride?"

"Nicely done. Emily would've loved it."

"Yeah, couldn't resist."

"Speaking of rides…" Boone indicated the motorcycle. "Ever since you gave Emily a ride on that thing, she's become obsessed with getting one. So… thanks for that. If she wraps herself around a palm tree, I'll be coming for you."

AJ laughed, remaining astride the motorcycle. "Sorry my dive went later than planned."

"No worries."

"And now I've got to flake on you again. Got something I need to take care of."

"Oh. Okay. Can you do dinner? I'm trying to get Emily to join me, if that movie shoot lets her go."

"Absolutely! I want to hear all about your new cinema starlet. I've been dodging that pirate ship the past few days; curious to hear some juicy Hollywood gossip."

"How about we meet at Rackam's at seven?" The seaside bar-and-restaurant was where Boone and Emily had first met AJ, and was popular among local divers. "I'll text Em, see if she can escape from the cameras."

"Sounds like a plan." AJ hefted the helmet in both hands. "Good to see you again, Boone. Make yourself at home!" She re-helmeted herself and started the motorcycle up, heading back down the road.

Boone took out his phone and texted Emily. *AJ and her motorcycle say hi. Can you get away for dinner?*

13

"All right, listen up everyone!" Dario called out. "We're going to have one... maybe two chances at this before we lose the light. We will shoot out of sequence, skipping over the 'walk the plank' bit. We'll leave that for last."

The beginning of the scene involved a bit of fun and games on this pirate-themed rum cruise. Several guests were asked a series of questions by Captain Bluebeard. If they got them right, they got a T-shirt. If they got them wrong, they had to "walk the plank" and be forced to jump into the water. The sequence went: wrong answer, guest jumps... right answer, guest gets T-shirt... wrong answer, guest gets ready to jump... but *surprise!* The creature's tentacles grab the guest off the plank. Chaos ensues.

Because this involved some stunt people going overboard and a safety boat below, it was decided to get the action on the main deck first, right at the moment the creature reaches over the sides and attacks the people aboard.

The sun was midway down the sky and the *Jolly Robert* had been under power for the last twenty minutes, her engines chugging and her red sails billowing. They'd moved northwest, rounding the point of West Bay and turning north-northeast along the coast before slowing to a stop as they neared the popular waterfront bar, Macabuco. Rules for anchoring were extremely strict, and the Film Commission representative directed the ship's captain to a spot they'd been cleared to use. Now anchored in the sand flats inside the outer reef, they were about to shoot the "attack"—the first appearance of the creature in *Man O' War.* The mutated Portuguese man o' war itself would be computer-generated imagery, so they'd be reacting to an attack from nothing. Well... *almost* nothing.

The 2nd AD came over to Emily. "So... Miss Durand... do you think you can get through this without laughing?"

"Ohmigod, I am *so* sorry, Jerry! It's just... I mean, come on!" She gestured over to an area under an awning where three men and a woman were sitting in the shade.

The four motion capture performers wore skintight, gray onesies, their bodies festooned in an assortment of ping pong balls and patches with different symbols on them. At the moment they were unmasked, but all had hoods to pull over their faces. Emily and the cast had rehearsed on the transit up here, and when the time came for the creature's tentacles to reach over the side of the boat and grab several partygoers, those four spandex-clad figures had come cavorting into frame, silently reaching at the screaming actors. In all honesty, it was one of the funniest things Emily had ever seen and she'd lost it, laughing until she cried— which infuriated the makeup department. It also enraged Heinz Werner. It was the angriest she'd seen the man.

"I swear, I'll keep it together," Em promised. "I think I've got it out of my system." Indeed, she had managed to get through the rehearsal the second time, only giggling at the end.

Jerry nodded, not entirely convinced. "Mr. Werner needs this shot in the can today, Emily."

"He's still mad, isn't he?"

Jerry waved her concerns away. "He's always mad by the end of the day. Just relax, stay focused. You'll be amazing." He scurried back to the surrounding sea of crew.

"Quiet on set!" Dario called out. "Places, please!"

Daniel Wolfit strolled past Emily on his way to his mark. "A little corpsing happens to the best of us."

"Sorry? Corpsing?"

Wolfit paused. "To 'corpse' is an English stage term for breaking character and laughing. Aren't you British?"

"British yes, actor no. Any advice, Mr. W?"

Wolfit leaned close. "When the moment comes that we are under attack by our invisible foe, don't 'see' those people in those suits. Look through them. Then, think of something in your life that frightened you—truly *terrified* you—and see *that* instead."

"Places, *please!*" Dario repeated, more firmly this time. Wolfit left for his mark.

Emily didn't need to think long. Her nightmare ordeal on the highest peak in Saba flooded back into her mind.

The crew called out their commands and Werner barked "Action!"

This time, when the imaginary attack came, Emily didn't see spandex and ping pong balls… she saw the face of Aidan, his features dripping with rain from the oncoming hurricane, impassively announcing that he was going to sacrifice her. Emily screamed.

"Cut!"

Werner rushed forward. *"Mein Gott,* you were chilling, my dear!"

Emily blinked. "Did you get what you needed?" she asked, her heart still hammering.

"From you, yes. Everything." Werner crouched ever so slightly, looking in her face. "You are crying."

"I am?"

"Get my star a tissue!" Werner barked.

A woman from makeup appeared as if by magic, dabbing at the corner of Emily's eyes.

"You were marvelous, *mein kleiner Schatz,*" Werner gushed. "My little treasure."

Novak, the cinematographer, came up behind Werner. "I think we got it, but if you want to check it with me, we need to hurry."

Werner looked toward the western horizon. "If that take was good, we can shoot the 'walk the plank' sequence before we lose the light, *ja?*"

But Novak was already hustling back to the monitors. Werner grabbed Dario and shot off a quick, whispered command.

"Everyone stay right where you are," Dario called out. "Hold positions while we check that take." He lifted a handheld radio. "Bring the chase boat out here!"

Wolfit waved at Emily from over by the plank and gave her a hearty thumbs-up. Emily replied by clutching her fists to her heart, mouthing "Thank you!"

A second woman from makeup came up to Emily and aimed a portable fan in her face with one hand, dabbing sweat with a microfiber sponge with the other. Several tense minutes passed.

Then, "Okay! We're good!" the 1st AD called out. "Moving on! Or... moving backward to what we skipped." Some of the crew laughed at that, as Dario once more took command. "Cameras, return to the starting positions we set during rehearsal. First team, on your marks. Everyone not in the shot, please move to the stern and stay quiet."

Bodies launched into motion as everyone scrambled to reset the scene. One camera prepared to shoot the plank from the deck, while a second camera was angled over the side to catch the first "plank walker" when she got the question wrong and had to jump. The burble of an engine sounded from alongside the *Jolly Robert* as the chase boat with another camera crew and a pair of safety divers arrived from where it had been waiting near the shore.

"Okay, quiet on set! Everybody focus! We get this right, we're back on schedule. Otherwise, we'll be right back here tomorrow, understand? Places!"

Emily joined the two other "plank buddies" at the port gunwale, a nubile waif in a blue, one-piece swimsuit, and a studly young man in red board shorts. Both were stunt performers. First up would be the stuntwoman, who would fail the quiz and walk the plank. Next, Emily/Sarah would get everything right and win a T-shirt—showing off how smart she was—then the final stunt-man would get on the plank and be "attacked," hurling himself straight backward, the CGI tentacle to be added later.

The stuntwoman got onto the plank, positioning herself in the middle. Wolfit stood with one boot on the deck, the other on the step up to the plank. Silva brought Ulysses, clad in his pirate hat, drink umbrella bandolier, and diaper. He gingerly set the monkey on the pirate's shoulder, giving him a grape to occupy himself. To his credit, Wolfit remained focused on the coming scene.

Werner called for action and Bluebeard brandished his blunt cutlass.

"Arrrr, missy... ye must answer me these questions three! Question one! What... is the color of the bathing suit ye be wearing?

The girl laughed. "Blue!"

"Good! Question two! What two countries share a border with the continental United States?"

She scoffed. "That's easy. Canada and Mexico."

"Arrrr, I can see ye be one smart cookie. Very well... question three! Who is credited with the first circumnavigation of the world?"

The confidence drained from her face. "Columbus...?" she said slowly and uncertainly.

"Oh no, my dear! I regret to inform ye, the answer is... Ferdinand Magellan!" Wolfit stepped up onto the plank and advanced on her, blunt cutlass pointed at his victim. "And now, my dear, ye must walk the pl—"

A loud crack sounded and Bluebeard and stuntwoman dropped like stones as the plank abruptly snapped in two, plunging the pair into the ocean. Ulysses shrieked in surprise, plummeting after the two humans.

Emily was standing next to the splintered plank and looked over the edge. With his heavy pirate's coat and boots, Wolfit was in serious trouble. Although the Emily of a few minutes ago knew there were safety divers nearby, the Emily of the here-and-now acted. Stepping up on the gunwale, she dived overboard, knifing into the water beside the portly actor.

Wolfit spluttered, flailing in the salt water. Emily came from behind and grabbed hold of the man, keeping his head above the water. The chase boat was racing in, and the stuntwoman was already moving to assist, looking shaken but unhurt.

"Are you all right, Wolfy?" Emily asked, kicking hard to keep them at the surface.

He coughed, then managed to catch a breath. "I confess... on the list of special skills on my résumé, you will find fencing and tap dancing... but you won't find swimming."

"We've got you, no worries," Emily said, as the stuntwoman joined them. Suddenly, Em felt something pulling at her hair. She heard annoyed chittering beside her ear as Ulysses climbed her ponytail and clung to the top of her head, where he proceeded to shriek repeatedly.

"Just my luck," Wolfit muttered. "The monkey lives."

<hr />

Five minutes later, Emily stood on the deck in a puddle of salt water, an oversized towel wrapped around her body. Wolfit had been stripped of his sodden pirate's gear and sat nearby, alongside the stuntwoman, likewise swaddled in towels.

"I don't understand it," one of the crew was saying, examining the broken stub of the plank as Dario peered over his shoulder. "This was rated to eight hundred pounds."

"I may be a shade on the portly side," Wolfit bellowed, "but together with this young lady and a little monkey, we are nowhere near that weight."

"Where's the part that broke off?" Emily asked.

The crewman shrugged. "Probably floated away."

"Well... might want to get that, yeah?" Em suggested. "See if you can tell what happened?"

Dario nodded, grabbing the radio and asking the chase boat to look for it.

"Not until the divers find Bluebeard's cutlass," the prop master admonished. The man was staring over the side at the waters, a blue T-shirt with a Captain America shield stretched across his ample frame.

"The current will take that piece of plank out to sea," Em warned.

"So what? If we lose that cutlass, I'll have to get another one, and if it doesn't match what we've already got on film…"

Dario sighed and triggered the radio again. "Find the sword first."

"Miss Durand?" A costumer was looking at her askance. "Where are your glasses?"

Emily reached to her face, then let her hand drop. "Oh, shite."

Dario triggered the radio again. "Hey, once they find the sword, send them back down to look for Sarah's glasses. The wire-frame librarian glasses."

Emily sighed. "Those'll be hard to find. And the sun is going down."

"It's okay, we have a spare set," the costumer said, catching the prop master's eye. "Always smart to have a spare."

The prop master glared at her and stalked away.

"How's Ulysses?" Emily asked Dario.

He laughed. "Wet and pissed. But he'll be fine, thanks to you."

"Well, he pretty much used my head as a lifeboat and saved himself," Emily said with a grin.

"Yes, thank you so very much for rescuing that infernal beast," Wolfit deadpanned, leading to more laughter from the group.

Heinz Werner, who had been strangely absent once Emily had come back on board, suddenly stormed into view. He tossed a half-finished cigarette overboard as he reached the group beside the broken plank.

"Why are you all laughing? The shoot is ruined! We will have to do this again tomorrow!"

The crewman who'd been assessing the break in the plank spoke up. "We're sorry, Mr. Werner. We have no idea how that happened."

"Do you think this is an acceptable answer? That you do not know what caused this catastrophe? I find no reassurance in incompetence!"

Emily started to speak, but Werner whirled on her.

"And *you*! I hired you to be an actress! Not a lifeguard! We have professionals for that! If you had been injured, this entire production would shut down again."

Em was still coming down from the adrenaline of the rescue, and came right back at him, gesturing to Wolfit. "Hey, in case you didn't notice, this fantastic actor was wearing thirty pounds of costume and the divers weren't in the water yet. Maybe 'cause you were rushing everything, yeah? I acted on instinct, and *that* is a kind of acting I damn well know how to do!"

Werner blinked, caught off guard. Then he glowered and turned on his heel. "Take us back to George Town!" he shouted over his shoulder. "We're done for today."

14

oone sat at the three-sided bar at Rackam's, nursing a Caybrew, his phone lying beside him next to the Cayman Islands Brewery coaster. There had not yet been a reply from Emily, but he figured she probably had her phone off while they were shooting. He'd texted Amelia to invite her as well, but she had made plans with some of Willis's side of the Ebanks clan, and they were going to throw a backyard cookout over in Bodden Town. AJ had let him know she'd be there in a bit and would be bringing Nora, but for the moment Boone was by himself. He glanced out to sea as the sun set. Just as the blaze of orange and pink lit up the western sky, his phone buzzed. A text from Emily.

"You at Rackam's?"

He texted back that he was.

"Arrrr! Look to sea, matey! Can you see me waving?"

Boone stood up and went to the edge of the seating area. There, on the edge of the bay, the party barge pirate ship lum-

155

bered along, the red sails dark in the fading light. It was too far away for either of them to see the other.

He texted, *"You take over the ship yet?"*

Boone watched three little dots at the bottom of the message app as Emily texted something. Finally, it came through.

"Stay there! Good news, I'm off and can join you. Bad news, today was a right mess and I need a drink."

"I'll be here. AJ and Nora too."

"Ace! Three against one, Bobo Boone. We'll go easy on you. Be there soon as I can."

Boone smiled and returned to the bar. The bartender looked up from the glass she was drying. Boone didn't think he'd seen her before; a Caymanian woman in her forties with nut-brown skin and freckles on her plump cheeks.

"Another?" she asked.

"No, I'm good. Got some folks coming in a bit." Boone's phone dinged again. A selfie photo of Emily appeared. Grinning ear to ear, she was being photobombed by a visitor on her shoulder. Boone laughed aloud.

Curious, the bartender sidled over. Boone rotated the phone for her.

"Is that a monkey?"

"At least one," Boone said. "The one without fur is Emily. She's in that movie they're shooting."

"You don't say! How exciting! You know, one of the stars was in here earlier this week. Had dinner right over there."

"Really?" Boone said, glancing at the table she was indicating. It was in a nice spot, off to the side and right up against the edge, with an excellent view of the water.

"Yes! That celebrity actress who is in all those sexy movies? Let's see, what is her name...?"

"Brooke Bablin?"

"That's the one!"

"I, uh... I don't think she's in the movie anymore," Boone said.

"What happened?" the bartender asked.

"Heard she quit."

"Well, that's a shame! One of our servers got her autograph. She's famous!"

"Yeah, so I've heard."

The bartender looked up as a pair of newcomers rounded the corner from the street. "Evening, AJ! Strongbow cider?"

"Hi, Maeve. Yes, please."

Boone signaled the bartender with a subtle finger tap to his own chest, letting her know he was buying.

AJ Bailey took a stool alongside Boone, and Nora Sommer sat beside her; the tall blonde wore civilian clothes now, a simple blouse and shorts. AJ had traded her black biker's get-up and boots for a sleeveless tank, shorts, and sandals.

"I'm guessing you didn't come over on the bike," Boone said.

"Nah, brought the Mermaid Diver's van," AJ said. "Where's Emily?"

"She just sailed by. Said she'd be here shortly." Boone observed Nora scanning the other occupants of the bar and nearby tables, head on a swivel. "Nora, what are you drinking?"

"Nothing for the moment, thank you."

"You find everything you needed at Foster's?" AJ asked.

"Mostly. Couldn't find that Costa Rican coffee you got Em addicted to."

"Hey, don't blame me. It was that bloke from the Keys who got her hooked on it. Jesse McDermitt."

Boone laughed and shook his head. Boone, Emily, and AJ had recently met the man at a bar in Marathon... but Boone and Em had actually had an encounter with him several years back. "It's a small world, AJ."

"That's right, you two met him before!"

"Yeah, he plucked us out of the water near Saba. But he gave us a fake name at the time."

AJ nodded, having heard the story from Boone and Emily during an earlier visit. "Right, I remember. After you blew up that submarine."

"Submarine?" That had gotten Nora's attention. "What is she talking about?"

"Oh, you're in for a treat," AJ said.

"Nah, it's better when Emily tells it."

"You can't mention blowing up a submarine and not explain what you mean," Nora insisted. "Tell me now."

Boone shrugged. "Heck, we've probably got a while before Em gets here, so why not?" He signaled for another Caybrew. "It all started in Bonaire..."

———◆·◆———

By the end of the tale, Nora was looking at Boone with new-found appreciation. "It was very brave what you did. A bit stupid, perhaps."

"'Foolhardy' is probably the word you're looking for," AJ suggested with a smile.

"Can't argue with that assessment," Boone said with a chuckle. He noticed Maeve the bartender looking toward the entrance, a look of excitement on her face that slipped toward puzzlement.

"Oh my, I thought Brooke Bablin was back! But it's your friend from the monkey picture. Do you know, they look a lot alike? Your friend and Brooke, I mean. Not your friend and the monkey."

Boone stood from his stool and smiled as Emily entered the bar area wearing a yellow sundress that Boone was quite fond of.

"Evenin', all!" Em said as she rounded the bar. "Shall we get a table? I'm famished!"

"Here're some menus, and you can grab any table you like," the bartender said, then leaned toward Boone. "You want the meal all on the same tab?"

"I do indeed, thanks," Boone said, handing over a credit card as AJ and Nora rose from the bar to join Emily.

"Oh, this one's got a good view," Emily said, leading the other two women to a table.

Boone opened his mouth to say something when he realized Em had picked the table Brooke had apparently sat at, but decided it didn't matter. He brought his beer over and immediately found himself laughing at Emily's latest antics.

"I'm sorry, I just have to touch them again!" Em said, tracing one of AJ's elaborate sleeve tattoos with her fingertips. "I swear, I'm *this* close to getting one—I just need to commune with yours a moment longer."

AJ looked both amused and uncomfortable. "Stop it! That tickles!"

"You probably should've kept that motorcycle jacket on," Boone said. "Protect your arms from her."

"Motorcycle," Emily breathed, trance-like, still touching the tattoos. "Want motorcycle toooooo..."

AJ had had enough and scooted her chair back. Boone decided to provide a distraction.

"So... Emily..." He brought out his smartphone and opened her latest text, then showed the monkey picture to AJ and Nora. "Is this one of your co-stars?"

AJ laughed at the photo and Nora raised an eyebrow.

"Oh, yes, that's Ulysses. He's my love interest in the movie," Em said with a straight face. "Well, one of them." She smiled sweetly at Boone.

"You have any scenes with Billy Faust today?" he asked.

"No, more's the pity. But I met this smashing old English bloke named Daniel Wolfit. Shakespearean actor. He plays a pirate. Well, not really—he plays a guy who's playing a pirate. Had a lot of great acting advice."

"Like what?" AJ asked.

"There was this one scene where I kept cracking up—'corpsing,' as we actors in the biz say—and he gave me a trick that really worked a treat!"

"Which was?" Nora asked.

"Um..." Emily hesitated a moment. "It was sort of a sense-memory visualization thing. Hard to explain. Anyway, cured me of the giggles, that's for sure."

"What was making you laugh?" Boone asked, a look of expectant mirth on his face.

"Well... it's a monster movie, innit? And they do all that with computers, yeah? So, there were these motion capture blokes in head-to-toe spandex with ping pong balls stuck to them, and they got in your face with 'Grrr hands' and—"

"Wait, what?" Boone said, grinning. "Grrr hands?"

"Oh, you know... Grrrr!" Emily curved her fingers into claws and pawed at the others like a five-year-old dressed as a werewolf for Halloween. The table erupted into laughter; even the stone-faced Nora cracked a smile. "Yeah, see? Try acting with *that* in your face."

"Any other acting pointers from this fellow?" AJ asked.

"Yeah! He had some advice on film and TV acting from none other than Dame Judi Dench. And I love me some Dench!"

"Who doesn't?" AJ said with a smile.

"So… her key advice for acting on film is… 'don't do anything.'"

"This does not seem like good advice," Nora commented.

"Well, it's an exaggeration, innit? But the point is, 'less is more.' Big reactions on film look like overacting."

Boone chuckled. "Emily Durand… toning it down? You're not exactly the poster girl for restraint."

Em threw a wide-eyed, mock-shocked look at Boone, then turned away from him and addressed AJ. "I should be offended. Shouldn't I be offended?"

"I'd be offended," AJ said.

Nora simply crossed her arms and looked at Boone.

"You promised you wouldn't gang up on me," he said.

"Did I? Doesn't sound like me," Em replied. "Go get me a Caybrew."

"At once, your highness." Boone rose.

"I'll take a Strongbow," Nora said, and AJ waggled her nearly empty bottle, indicating the same.

Boone went to the bar and waited for Maeve to finish up with a mixed drink that involved a cacophonous blender. Glancing across the bar, he noted a pair of men at a table in another seating section. One was dressed corporate-casual, his back to Boone. The other wore a garish Hawaiian shirt and a ballcap. Boone wondered if he was a regular, as he looked vaguely familiar. He was speaking loudly in a foreign accent and, between blender pulses,

Boone was just able to make out "Not nearly enough!" before the whir and rattle of ice and fruit juices blotted out the rest.

"What can I get you?" Maeve shouted above the din of the machine.

"Two Strongbows and a Caybrew! Please!"

"Coming up!" Maeve snagged the bottles, popping the tops and lining them up before returning to her work on the frozen drink.

Boone gathered the bottles and glanced toward the table with the two men, only to see the one in the tropical shirt departing through the front entrance. His compatriot set down the check and a pair of US twenty-dollar bills on the edge of the bar before exiting through another part of the restaurant. Boone frowned. *Something about that...* but his thoughts were interrupted by the sight of two men standing over the table with Em, AJ, and Nora. One was a tall Asian man and the other had a muscle-head surfer-dude vibe, his frosted hair spiky from hair gel. Boone brought the drinks to the table as the latter one spoke.

"Seriously, babe, you were fantastic! And you looked amazing. Like... *really* amazing."

"Oh, thank you, that's sweet." Em said politely.

"Drink delivery," Boone announced, offering the bottles all around.

"Hey Boone! These two are with the movie," Em said. "Ray here plays one of the mercenaries, and this is..." She gestured toward the surfer-looking fellow. "Sorry, I don't know if we met at the meet-and-greet?"

"Chip. I'm the assistant stunt coordinator and assistant fight choreographer."

Boone offered his hand. "Boone Fischer. I'm gonna be piloting our dive boat as a chase boat at some point." He shook with Ray and then Chip.

Chip maintained his grip for a moment. "Wait a sec, I know that name... you're the boyfriend. The guy that Werner wants to teach us some moves."

Boone retracted his hand. "The director saw me practicing and mentioned something about that, yeah. Didn't know if he was serious, though."

"I think he was, cuz my boss told me 'Herr Werner' was all excited about putting some of your moves into the shoot. What are your styles?"

"Capoeira and Brazilian jiu-jitsu."

Chip nodded, "Yeah, the thing is... BJJ isn't flashy enough for film. Way too much rolling around on the floor and joint locks and shit. Not really compelling for a movie, know what I mean? And capoeira... well... no offense, but we're not shooting a music video."

Boone shrugged. If the guy was trying to get a rise out of him, he'd picked the wrong target.

"Boone's a black belt in both of those, y'know," Emily said.

"Cool, cool," Chip said. "I'm a third-degree black belt in tae kwon do, a fourth-degree in karate, and a practitioner of the Keysi fighting method."

"I'm a fifth-degree sequined-belt in karaoke," Em observed, pronouncing karaoke the way a Japanese tourist had taught her, *kah-rah-oh-kay.*

Chip blinked, looking at her. "I don't know that one."

"It's deadly," AJ said somberly.

"Hers, especially," Boone quipped.

"You've had some training in Ducati, haven't you, AJ?" Emily asked, referring to her Italian make of motorcycle.

Chip was just catching on, as evidenced by a slight reddening of his tanned face. Fortunately, Nora brought things to an end.

"Excuse me, but we're very hungry, and the two of you are blocking our waitress."

Chip and Ray turned around and moved aside as a young redhead approached the table, pad in hand.

"Sorry for the delay in taking your order, ladies and gent." She looked at Chip and Ray, then back to the others. "Do you need us to pull up a table?"

"No," Nora instantly replied. "But we are ready to order."

"And I'm gonna need something stronger than this beer," Em said. "It's been a *long* day."

While they waited for the food to arrive, Emily recounted the day's events, culminating in her knee-jerk dive into the water when the plank broke.

"Hopefully I'll still have a job tomorrow morning," she said, sipping her Rackam's Rum Runner. "I thought Werner was going to bite my head off."

Boone recalled what Leonard had told him of that earlier failed movie, where an actress working under Heinz Werner had had a nervous breakdown. He resolved to do a little Googling before he mentioned it to Emily. Instead, he said, "Hey, you're trained to save someone in distress. And you did it. You can't stop being you, just because someone's got a camera in your face."

"Good on ya, Em," AJ said. "I would've done the same."

"I would have punched the director in the nose," Nora said matter-of-factly.

"Weird..." Boone said, poking a plantain. He trailed off, thinking.

"What is weird?" Nora asked. When Boone didn't reply, she started to speak again.

Emily held a hand up, signaling Nora to hold up a second.

"Is this that thing he does?" AJ asked.

Em nodded, sliding her Rum Runner over. "Here, try this in the interim. Very scrummy."

Boone thought back to several separate incidents, but then his mind segued over to that pair of men he'd just observed in the other seating section when he was up at the bar. Try as he might, whatever puzzle piece he was trying to find didn't manifest itself. Finally, he looked up from his plate. "Sorry... went away there." He popped the punctured morsel of plantain into his mouth.

"Spill it," Em said.

"It's strange, isn't it? The location scout's boat breaks down— and the *way* it broke down was kind of suspicious. Another boat gets its fuel lines cut, and—"

"What?" Em blurted.

"There is a high-performance yacht in your film," Nora said. "It appears it was sabotaged."

"The mercenary boat in the script? The *Mako*?"

Boone nodded. "Yep. And then you tell me a plank on another movie-set ship snaps in two in the middle of a scene... and the crew swears it shouldn't have broken."

"Yeah, this crew guy swore up and down it could hold four grown men, easy peasy."

Boone plunged ahead. "The lead actor is beaten up the night before he boards a plane to come here, the lead actress quits after the very first day of—" Boone stopped in midsentence.

"What...?" Em asked.

"One sec." Boone rose and went to the bar.

"Another Caybrew?" Maeve asked.

"No, thank you. Question for you... what night was Brooke Bablin here?"

"Uh... I think it was Tuesday. Your waitress, Lily, would know. She served her." Maeve caught the girl's eye and waved her over. "You remember what evening you got Brooke Bablin's autograph?"

"Yes! It was Tuesday, at sunset. I was nervous to ask for it, because I'd already seen someone bother her for one. I think she was annoyed at him when he bumped her table trying to take a selfie."

"How did she seem?" Boone asked.

"I don't know... tired? But she was very polite to me when I asked her for an autograph."

"And the man who bumped her table... anything unusual about him?"

"Oh, no... that was just Lev. He was probably drunk."

"He a regular?"

Maeve laughed. "More of an *irregular* regular. He comes in every once in a while and sits at the bar, drinking and smoking. Very funny foreign guy. Always wears loud shirts."

"He here tonight?"

"He was," Lily said, pointing at the table the two men had vacated just before Boone came over to get the ladies their drinks.

"Any idea who he was with?"

"No, sorry. Never seen the other fellow before."

A gale of laughter sounded from the table and Boone looked over to see Emily doing what appeared to be a monkey imitation. AJ was belly-laughing and Nora looked on with bemusement, a half-smile on her lips.

"I better get back," Boone said. "Thanks for the info."

"Hey!" Lily said, catching him by the arm. "The blond girl at your table who looks like Brooke Bablin... she's the one who took over her part in the movie, isn't she?"

"Yeah. How did you know that?"

"It's all over the internet! Maeve said you told her Brooke was out of the film, so I looked it up." She took out her phone and pulled up an entertainment news story.

Boone took one look at it and then retrieved his own phone and found the piece. He started for the table.

"Bobo Boone is back!" Emily crowed, then sobered when she saw the look on his face. "What's up, Boonie?"

Boone sat and set the phone down in front of her. Nora and AJ leaned in to look.

On the screen was a news story from one of the UK tabloids. A photo of Brooke Bablin was juxtaposed with a photo of Emily— one that Leonard had taken of her on the dock in Little Cayman. In bold font, the title read:

ALL ABOUT EMILY
Battle of the Blonde Bombshells!

Did this Pint-sized Amateur Actress Topple
the Queen of Seductive Cinema?

Find Out on Page Three!

"Sodding hell..." Emily muttered.

15

AJ pulled into the parking lot of the hotel and let Boone and Emily off by the entrance. "Thanks for a great evening," she said. "Sorry about that gossip-page prattle."

"Stupid words for stupid people," Nora said.

"Yeah, thanks," Em replied. "Sorry if I spoiled the mood. Let's hang again soon, yeah?"

"Thanks for swinging back for the groceries," Boone said, as he wrestled the bags out of the van. "And thanks for the offer of the sofa bed, but I suppose I should take Em up on her offer of a palatial hotel suite."

Emily snorted. "The room came with a hair dryer, and the coffeemaker has packets of regular *and* decaf, so yeah. Lap of luxury." The room was better than most, but wasn't anything special.

AJ drove the van onto West Bay Road and headed north to drop off Nora. Emily smiled and waved, then sunk back into her funk.

"I can't believe they ran that story!" Em said. She was furious. The gossip piece had been full of salacious hypothesizing, implying that she could have had something to do with the famous actress's departure, even going so far as to suggest she might have seduced a producer.

"How did they even get all that information about you?" Boone asked.

"I'll tell you how. You remember that photo of me in the green bikini on Page Three?"

"Burned into my retinas."

"Yeah, well… it was an on-set still! I've got the little glasses on and the ponytail. They took that photo from the shoot. Someone in the production crew is in on it!"

"Pretty smoking hot photo, though," Boone said.

Em gave him a look. Boone wasn't often demonstrative in his compliments. "Oh, you liked that one, did you?"

"I have a pulse, so… yeah."

"Well, I'm not surprised. It appears I had a little help. Even though that photo came from the shoot, they Photoshopped it. Airbrushed extra shadows on my cleavage."

Boone laughed, then cleared his throat. "I'm sorry."

Emily led the way to a bank of elevators, and they rode one to the top floor. Emily found her keycard but fumbled it, dropping it to the floor.

"Butterfingers." Boone retrieved it for her and slid it through the electronic lock. They entered the room, stepping over a set of sides for the next day's shoot that had been slipped under the door.

Em picked them up and scanned the pages. "Hey, will you help me go over my lines?"

"Sure. What scenes are you shooting tomorrow?"

"They're going to try to finish the attack on the pirate ship," Em said. "Everyone dies except me, my best friend Cindy, the party-boat pirate captain, and the monkey."

Boone picked up the full script that was lying on the king-size bed, flipping through it. He stopped at one part and read through a few passages, his eyes widening. "Whoa. Nasty way to die." He held the script up for her.

Em looked at it. "Oh, yeah… gonna be a lot of special effects make-up tomorrow, they said. You know how a Portuguese man o' war sting leaves those strings of red welts?"

"Not firsthand, but yeah, I've seen pictures."

"Well, our fictional beastie is huge and mutated, so when it stings you, it opens up bubbling lacerations. A couple victims who get wrapped in stingers just swell up and *pop* from all the venom that gets injected."

"Delightful."

"Anyway, I'm just screaming, running around—"

"In a bikini."

"Shut up. I'm trying to get away, and one of those stingers barely grazes me, and I pass out and fall in the water. When I wake up, I'm aboard the research salvage ship."

"The *Puddingwife*."

"Yeah!"

"Lemme guess… you get CPR from Billy Faust."

Em paused. "No… but that's not a bad idea, Boonie! I'll suggest it!"

"Glad to help."

"Hey… what was up with the radio on the *Bob's Bobo*? You never told me."

Boone explained the odd situation with the fuses, in addition to the loose wiring. "Might have just been shoddy maintenance. That boat's seen better days."

"And what about the *Mako*? Her fuel lines were cut? No one mentioned that during the shoot today."

171

"I think they want to keep it quiet; not spook anyone. Might have been an employee of the yacht's owner, but..." Boone thought for a moment.

"But... what?"

Boone sighed. "Just... be careful. Keep an eye out for anything... hinky."

"Well, in order to do that, I'll have to keep my job. Let's run my lines, yeah?"

They spent the next half hour going over her scenes, and Emily was a little surprised just how *bad* Boone was, reading the other characters' lines. Although, in some respects it made sense; Boone was one of the most authentic, down-to-earth people she'd ever known, and "pretending" to be someone else just wasn't in his wheelhouse. The only time he put on a stellar performance was at poker. He was a master at bluffing—but that was only because he didn't seem to have a tell. Boone would face down his opponents with a serene, expressionless face; straight flush or garbage, he'd look the same. That being said, Emily always knew when he was bluffing, but to this day, she didn't know *how* she knew.

They had just finished going through her scenes for a third time when Boone's phone rang. He looked at the number, then answered.

"Boone Fischer. Oh, hi Deacon." He listened, saying "uh-huh" a half dozen times, while grabbing a hotel notepad and pen to scribble a few notes. "Okay, I'll see you bright and early. Oh! And get the word out... I highly recommend everybody pop a Dramamine first thing in the morning." He hung up and turned to face Emily. "Looks like they're putting me to work."

"How much are they paying you?"

"Leonard laid it out for me during the crossing. Three thousand a week, for rental and skippering the chase boat."

"Really? Gee," Em said, a mischievous gleam in her eye. "I'm getting four."

"Oh, really? So, I guess next time we're out with AJ and Nora, you can get the drinks."

"Who's that guy you were talking to?"

"Deacon? He's in charge of the chase boats and the three boats that are sets for the movie. They've been looking at the weather forecast, and things are looking very good for the next few days, so they want to get set up for the shoots in Little Cayman. I'm supposed to take the *Lunasea* and escort the *Mako*, the *Puddingwife*, and one other chase boat over to Little. Looks like your pirate ship won't be going across."

"Yeah, one of the crew said it was more of a coastal party barge and they didn't want to risk the crossing."

Boone opened his messaging app. "I better text Amelia, have her meet me at the pier first thing tomorrow morning."

"So... we might not see each other for a few days—is that what you're saying?" Emily asked, gathering the scripts from the bed and tossing them aside.

"Yeah." Boone tapped "send" on the text. "Might be a while."

Emily slipped a strap of her sundress off her shoulder. "Tell me again how much you liked that tabloid photo."

———◆·◆———

"Look at this!" Tolstoy said, gawking at an image on his phone. He held it up in front of Brooke Bablin's face. "She look much like you, yes?"

"Quit teasing her, Tolstoy," Potluck said.

"Can I... can I read that?" Brooke asked.

"Of course. Is very interesting article." Tolstoy said. He handed her the phone.

Brooke was no longer bound to a chair, her captors having shifted her to a mattress on the floor, with one of her wrists handcuffed to a chain they had attached to a thick pipe, possibly for the house's sewage. She was able to slide the chain up and down the pipe, which allowed her to lie down and sleep, or sit up and eat. Bathroom trips were permitted when needed; a little half-bath occupied one corner near a washing machine and dryer.

Potluck came over, keeping a watchful eye on Brooke as she scrolled through the story. "It's just gossip rag trash," she said.

"She looks nothing like me," Brooke muttered.

Potluck took the phone from her. "I dunno. I'd say there's a resemblance..." She squinted. "Huh."

"What?" Tolstoy asked.

"She looks kinda familiar."

Tolstoy took the phone and looked more closely at the person identified as Emily Durand. "She look familiar to me as well." He scrolled through the opening paragraphs. "It say she is divemaster on Little Cayman. So maybe we see her on this island over last year, *da*? After all..." He scrolled down to the full-length bikini shot. "...she certainly makes an impression. *Bozhe moi!*"

"Put that away," Potluck muttered. "How did the meeting go?"

"He still not say how long we..." He glanced over at Brooke and didn't finish the thought. "But I convince him to double our pay!"

"Well done. Where was the meet?"

"That bar I like. Rackam's."

Potluck shook her head. "You go there way too much. We're supposed to be keeping a low profile."

"Is nice outdoors place and has good specials of day."

"Yeah, and you call to ask about those specials way too often, Borscht-for-brains. You're gonna get us caught."

"Take a pill to chill, they think I local drunk. And they let me smoke!"

"Oh, that reminds me." Potluck grabbed one of the bags of groceries from an earlier outing. She tossed a flat black box to him. "Got your precious cigarettes."

"You found them!"

"Yeah, down in Seven Mile. A cigar bar in the middle of a shopping center parking lot had them. Don't ever say I never did nothin' for ya."

"I would never say this," Tolstoy said, extracting one of the black-and-gold cigarettes from the box.

"Hey!"

Tolstoy and Potluck both jumped, turning to look at Brooke.

"Can you *please* not smoke in my dungeon?" She jiggled her handcuffs. "Since I can't go out for fresh air, do you think you could go outside to suck on that?"

"You have fire, little one," Tolstoy said, sounding more impressed than offended.

"Yeah, she's right," Potluck agreed. "Go outside with that."

Tolstoy shrugged and went up the steps and out the door.

Potluck went through the grocery bags. "All right, Princess, what would you like to eat along with your smoke-free air? I've got ramen and PB&J."

Outside, Tolstoy fired up a smoke. He'd become addicted to the flashy Black Russians on his last mission. *The mission that went to hell in handbasket*, he thought, then laughed out a cloud of cigarette smoke. *Hell in handbasket. English idioms are very strange. What even is a handbasket?* He chuckled again, then looked down the quiet road, lit sparsely by widely spaced streetlights. "I have no handbasket, but here I am... in Hell!" he said aloud. Absently, he drew his phone from his pocket and looked again at the tabloid article. *Very pretty girl. And very familiar.*

16

The sun hadn't yet risen as Boone's taxi arrived at the Harbour House Marina. Amelia was already there, waiting for him at the *Lunasea*. Numerous members of the film's production staff bustled about the other boats.

"Get anything good?" Amelia asked, helping him bring aboard the shopping bags.

"A little of this, a little of that," Boone said. "You have fun with the Ebanks clan?"

"They throw a mean cookout!" Amelia said. "And Willis has some wild brothers and sisters, that's for sure. We had a good time. He's actually here, aboard his father's boat." She pointed across the pier at the *Bobo*, where Willis was speaking to several members of the film crew. "They're using him as a safety boat for today's shoot with the pirate ship."

"Great!" Boone managed to catch the youth's eye and gave him a wave.

After they finished loading his haul from Foster's, Boone left Amelia aboard the *Lunasea* and went to find Deacon. Walking along the edge of the concrete pier, he looked up at the *Puddingwife*, the largest of the vessels he'd be escorting across. He paused, eyes on the stern near the crane. A dumpy crewmember in a shirt with a Batman logo was standing close beside another man. Heads down, the two were conferring. Boone immediately recognized the other individual as the well-dressed man from Rackam's who had been at the table with the foreign barfly, Lev. He looked like he was wearing the same dress shirt and slacks he'd had on the night before.

"Good morning!"

Boone turned to see Deacon coming up to him. "Morning, Deacon."

"We ready to do this?"

"Gonna be exciting, that's for sure."

Deacon looked at a clipboard. "Just so you know, you'll be bringing a camera crew over with you. They need to see how your boat handles, and they may want to set up a camera rig with a gyroscopic stabilizer. Test things out on the way."

"Sure thing. Hey, real quick, can I ask who those two guys are?" Boone pointed toward the stern, but now only the pudgy crewmember remained.

"I only see one. You mean the guy in the Batman shirt? That's Adam Dozier, the property master. He's in charge of props for the shoot—anything the actors use, from pens and coffee cups to the firearms the mercenaries will have—although there's an armorer that is more hands-on with those. Production just decided to send Adam over now, since there are a lot of moving parts involved in the upcoming scenes. You said two guys?"

"Yeah, the other fella looked like he wore suits for a living, but was dressed down a little. Dress shirt and slacks... black hair."

Deacon shrugged. "Might've been the field producer or one of his assistants. The decision to shift things over to Little Cayman was a bit sudden, so he came down here early to make sure everything went smoothly."

"What boat will you be on?" Boone asked.

"I figured I'd enjoy the Azimut," Deacon said with a grin. "See how the other half lives. Oh, and Leonard is coming along. He'll probably want to go with you and ask a few more location questions."

"Fair enough. Oh, hey, just remind everyone, if they didn't already take motion sickness medication, they better do it now. Takes a while to kick in."

"Yeah, I messaged everyone about that last night. But the weather's supposed to be good," Deacon noted.

"Doesn't always matter in the open ocean, and everyone's tolerance is different. Better safe than sorry."

Nearly an hour later, the small convoy headed across the North Sound, bound for Little Cayman. The *Lunasea* was in the vanguard, leading the group of boats north-northwest toward the gap in Barker's Point. Even though their destination was to the east, the lagoon was extremely shallow, and Boone didn't trust the larger boats to navigate the eastern cuts near Rum Point. Once they reached open ocean, they would swing to starboard and head east-northeast across to Little.

Boone monitored Channel 16 until they were in open water, then had all the boats switch over to Channel 72 to keep in touch during the transit. Deacon kept an extra pair of ears on Channel 16 on a secondary radio on the bridge of the *Mako*. Amelia took the wheel and Boone climbed down the ladder to see how their passengers were faring. On board was a camera crew of four, as well as a representative from the art department, a carpenter, and Leonard.

"Everybody doing okay?" Boone asked him.

"So far, so good," Leonard said. "Thanks for the reminder about the motion sickness pills. I may make it across without tasting my breakfast this time."

"How's it coming with the camera, guys 'n' gals?" Boone asked. The two men and two women were busy affixing a large quadpod to the deck, bracing it between the dive benches.

"They're testing out a rigging that won't require doing anything permanent to the boat," Leonard explained.

"Well... that's good. Since I didn't know doing something permanent to my boat was even under discussion."

"Don't worry, it never was," an older woman said, her graying hair under a Grateful Dead do-rag. "I'm Marsha. Best boy." Seeing the flash of confusion on Boone's face, she laughed. "I realize my gender and my age make that a confusing title, but best boy is a traditional film term. I'm the assistant to the key grip."

Boone grinned and shrugged. "And a key grip is?"

"Well... a *grip* works either in the lighting department, or in the camera department, as in the case of Murray, here."

A black man in his forties raised a hand, but quickly returned the hand to what he was doing.

"Murray's job is to help with the rigging of a camera. Like, if you wanted a camera on a moving dolly, or if you had it on a crane."

"Or on the deck of a bobbing boat," Boone said.

"You catch on fast. Now, a *key* grip is just the person in charge of the other grips. And I'm the key grip's assistant. He's back on the *Jolly Robert*. And the rest of these losers are the camera operator and first assistant camera: Mike and Madge."

"Two packs of M&M's."

Now it was Marsha's turn to look confused. "How d'you mean?"

Boone laughed, embarrassed. "Sorry, that was something Emily would say, but she's not here, so you get a poor imitation." He gestured to the group. "Marsha and Murray, Mike and Madge."

"Oh! M&M's! Ha! Never thought about that."

"Hey, Boone, can you take a look at this map?" Leonard spread it out on the camera table. "I want to be sure about where we're going to put the boats."

"Where'd you get a physical sounding chart?" Boone asked. "I don't even have one of these."

"The Film Commission gave it to me. After the shoot, it's yours!" Leonard touched a point on the northwest side of the island. "When she was driving the *Bobo* for us, Emily showed me this Salt Rock Dock on the north side. Can we keep one of the boats there?"

Boone chewed his lip. "Um... I wouldn't. You could, if the weather's gonna be as placid as they think... but there's a reason why Little goes without shipments some weeks. If the seas get rough, any boat you keep there could take a battering. Most cruisers that visit anchor in the sandy lagoon."

"But... that cut in the reef... you want to take the *Mako* and *Pudding* through there?"

"Probably not, although that's only one issue. Come up top." Boone scrambled up the flybridge ladder to the radio and keyed the mic. "*Mako*, this is *Lunasea*. Is Deacon there?"

Apparently, he was down on the aft deck sunning himself, but after a delay, he came on the line. "Deacon here."

"Hey Deacon, it's Boone and I've got Leonard with me. Listen, what's the draft on that Azimut 60?"

"Just under five feet. Why?"

"I'm trying to figure out where we're gonna put her. The protected lagoon is only three to six feet in most places. And I think I know the answer to this, but... the *Puddingwife*... her draft is way over six, right?"

"Yes. Closer to ten."

"Ouch. Okay... so she's definitely not going to work inside the sound."

"The Film Commission said we could use some of the moorings if we checked with them."

"Good, that's what I was hoping. The Azimut can make it through the cut, and I know where she could maneuver, so if you want to do that for a shoot, I'll come aboard and pilot her in. But it would be best to keep her at a mooring, and that salvage ship is definitely going to need to stay outside. Grab a pen and paper and give me a moment."

Boone took out his phone and pulled up a PDF he kept of public moorings in the Cayman Islands. He keyed the mic. "Okay, given their size, the *Puddingwife* and *Mako* will need to use the thirty-inch mooring balls. Those moorings are secured to the seabed with two eyebolts instead of one. Now, all public buoys have a blue stripe on them, and the lines are yellow."

"So, we can moor at any like that?"

"Well... no. First off, we're going to want to moor on the south side, 'cause I'm guessing the cast and crew will be staying in various places in the lagoon, right?"

Leonard nodded. "Yes. We've booked a bunch of rooms, all within a mile of your condo. Mostly at the resorts, but a few rented homes."

"I count five south-side moorings that can handle the *Mako* and *Puddingwife*. There's normally a three-hour limit on the public moorings and the dive boats are the life blood of the island, so we don't want to hog any of the good ones. I'm gonna veto the Soto Trader wreck dive site; that one's too popular. Deacon, write these four down and ask the Film Commission for permission for an extended mooring on those, and ask them to contact the dive ops and let them know. Actually, while they're at it, have them see if any of the operators would be willing to hire out to ferry cast and crew to the boats, because the *Lunasea* and the other chase boat alone ain't gonna cut it."

"Good idea, thanks."

"Okay, so the moorings I'm looking at are... got your pen?"

"Ready."

"These are in order of preference: Black Hole, Patty's Place, Grundy's Gardens, Pirate's Point."

"Got it."

"When we get there, I'll guide you to two of them," Boone said. "We'll transfer whoever needs to go ashore onto my boat and the other chase boat, and then we'll go into the lagoon."

"Understood. Thanks."

Boone hung the mic back beside the radio. Leonard slapped him on the shoulder.

"Pretty damn glad we got you when we found Emily! Two for the price of one! Although, in all honesty, you can hit them up for extra pay. Doing all this with the moorings, that's going above and beyond what we're paying for."

Boone shrugged. "To be honest, anything I can do to make the shoot go more easily... I figure that makes Emily's life easier, too. And that's good enough for me."

"Quiet on set!"

The morning sun was low in the sky as Emily sat in a folding canvas chair off to the side, watching some of the other actors preparing to shoot one of the smaller scenes. There had been a last-minute change to the schedule, and Emily wasn't quite sure what was going on. Werner hadn't spoken to her since the previous day, and she feared he might still be furious with her. Phil, the 2nd 2nd AD, came over and gestured for her to follow him, holding up a finger to his lips, suggesting they go quietly.

"Where to, Second Second?" Em whispered.

"One of the CGI artists is on board. He's part of the team that does the computer animations. Werner wanted you to look at something."

Emily went into the interior of the party barge, back where a captain's cabin would likely have been if this had been a real pirate ship. A young man was sitting at a folding table, fingers flying over a laptop keyboard. He looked like he was right out of high school.

"Oh, you're here! Hi, I'm Andre, with the Visual Effects Department. Werner asked me to show you something. You remember the accident yesterday?"

"Happened two feet from me, so... yeah."

The kid laughed. "Right. Sorry. Anyway... have a seat and check this out."

Andre rose and stood to one side of the chair. Emily sat and he tapped a key. On the screen, a video began of the lead-up to the accident. There was no sound, but Emily watched Wolfit/

Bluebeard ask his three questions, then direct the stuntwoman onto the plank.

"Blimey!" Emily's eyes went wide. As the pirate mounted the ship-side edge of the plank, slender, translucent tendrils rose into view alongside, feeling their way toward the plank. As Wolfit stepped forward to poke his sword at the girl, the tentacles made contact with the plank and in the blink of an eye, seven or eight of them rushed into motion, wrapping themselves around the plank, which then snapped, plunging Wolfit, the stuntwoman, and Ulysses into the water. Hissing smoke rose from the broken edge.

"That is ace!" Emily shouted! "You made it look like the monster broke the plank!"

"Burned through it with acid, actually. It was Daniel Wolfit's idea to make use of the accident. Werner was really pissed about the shot being ruined, so Wolfit found him at the hotel bar and suggested this idea. Werner loved it. Came and found me and I got my crew of animators in Ukraine on it. We just showed it to him. He's reordering the scenes with this in mind."

"It's brilliant!"

"Well, if you like that, you'll *love* this." He found another file and clicked on it.

This time, the scene was shot from the side camera that was positioned to film the stuntwoman jumping into the water when she got the question wrong. Instead, the camera followed Emily as she stepped up onto the gunwale and dived over the side. As her bare feet left the edge, another CGI tentacle shot from the water, just missing her and striking the ship where she'd been standing. A special effect went off at the spot where the tendril stuck to the side, smoke rising as if the tendril were burning into the wood.

"Whoa!" Em cried out.

The camera followed her as she pierced the water before surfacing, her face bare, looking for Wolfit.

"Guess I lost the glasses on the dive," Em noted, continuing to watch the video.

In the background, an iridescent shape rose to the surface, its characteristic "sail" and float looking like a gigantic Portuguese man o' war. In the water around her, more tendrils rocketed out of the water, heading up and out of frame, as if they were going after the ship. Sarah/Emily swam up to Bluebeard/Wolfit, and... the video stopped.

"That's as much as we had time to do," Andre said apologetically.

"Wow. I am... flabbergasted," Emily said, stunned. "I am absolutely gasted with flabber."

Andre grinned. "That means you liked it?"

"I *loved* it!"

"Great. The writers are making some changes, and Werner said to send you to him once you'd seen this."

"Right-o. Thanks, Andre! It's positively blinding!" When Andre looked puzzled, she added, "That means it's great."

◆ ◆ ◆

Emily returned to set and saw that they were still shooting, so she made her way toward "holding," where actors often waited during downtime. There she found who she was looking for.

"I owe you a pint," Em said. "Or three."

"You've spoken to Herr Director?" Wolfit asked.

"Not yet, but I'm betting he'll be a smidge less angry today, thanks to you. I saw what the graphics gang did. Great idea you had!"

Wolfit chortled. "No, it was a great idea *you* had... to dive in and save my sorry arse before that costume dragged me down! And I simply pointed out to Heinz that the bravery and quick-thinking you displayed were far better character development than 'Sarah' answering some simple quiz questions and winning a souvenir T-shirt. I also suggested that the shock and surprise on our faces was real, and he couldn't ask for better acting."

"Well, I owe you one!"

"Miss Durand?" an intern called. "They're ready for you."

Emily went forward and Werner waved her over to the bow, where he proceeded to fire up a cigarette.

"Miss Durand, I must apologize for my unseemly behavior yesterday."

"S'all right," Emily said.

"But when misadventure strikes, opportunity is often found. Mr. Wolfit was right to suggest we include more of your own dynamic nature in the role. After a long night of revisions, Sarah's character arc has been greatly improved."

"Well, as long as we're improving the character... once I've been rescued by the other ship, can I wear some clothes?" Emily flashed her dressing robe open, revealing the bikini. "After four or five scenes, this is a little much, innit?"

"Agreed."

"So, how do the changes you've made affect the day's shoot?"

Werner took a vigorous drag on his cigarette. "The attack on the ship will happen as before, but we can do much of that without you. Right now, we will shoot several smaller scenes with

Sarah, Cindy, and Bluebeard. Then, when the afternoon sun is closer to the light we had at the time of the accident, we will be shooting some additional material in the water. The actual rescue was too real toward the end. You lost your glasses and you both broke character. Understandably, of course. But we will need additional footage."

"How will we get away?" Em asked. "If that imaginary thing is in the water with us, wouldn't it just nom nom nom, and eat us?"

Werner laughed. "First, the stuntwoman who fell in will die horribly, giving you a chance to swim a little distance away with Bluebeard. And then..." Werner smiled and beckoned her to follow him astern. "*This* will be your salvation." He gestured up at a tiny dinghy that hung from a davit near the stern. "When the creature's tentacles envelop the *Robert*, some will strike the lines that hold the dinghy, burning them like acid. It will drop into the water and you will swim for it."

"And I help Bluebeard aboard! And Ulysses, too. And then I get stung while I'm still in the water!"

"Well done! Exactly. A tendril will graze your leg. You will lose consciousness and start to sink but Mr. Wolfit will turn the tables and rescue *you*, pulling you into the boat. The boat will then make its escape from the carnage."

"What about Cindy? She gets saved too, right? In the original script?"

Werner shrugged, puffing out a cloud of smoke. "During rewrites, it was decided that we really don't need her for the rest of the plot. Cindy will die in the attack."

"But... she's in half the movie..." Em felt a little sick to her stomach. "Mr. Werner... are you saying that because I jumped in to save Mr. Wolfit, you're going to bump Cindy down to a bit part and kill her off?"

Werner's face twitched and his eyes flashed. "We have spent much of last night and half the morning rewriting and rearranging—" Suddenly, he flung his cigarette overboard. "Fine!" he shouted, a tinge of the previous day's anger resurfacing. "We'll rewrite again! Go back to holding. Someone will fetch you when we need you."

Emily watched as the director stormed off. Turning to go, she found a Caymanian with a clipboard beside her.

"Did the director just throw another cigarette overboard?"

"Uh... yeah."

"Thank you," the man said, marking something with a vigorous slash of his pen.

17

"Hey, Boone! Can you take me across to that island?"

Boone looked up from an energetic game of tug-of-war with Brixton. The divemaster's absence of a day and a half might as well have been a decade, as far as the devoted dog was concerned. "Sure, Leonard. If you don't mind getting a workout. If we took the *Lunasea*, I'd have to anchor in the sand and we'd have a wet walk, but we can grab a couple kayaks from the condo's stash and get right to the beach."

"Fine by me!" Leonard shaded his eyes, looking out at Owen Island. "Werner and Novak want me to scout where to shoot our shipwrecked survivors coming ashore."

"Who's Novak?"

"Alan Novak. He's the director of photography, or DP. The cinematographer. Worked with Werner on several movies."

"Gimme a sec, and we'll grab some transport." Boone rose and led Brixton back to the condo.

The sun was high overhead, and several of the film crew he'd shuttled over had settled into the outdoor area near the *Lunasea*'s dock. In the distance, on the other side of the surf line, the *Puddingwife* and *Mako* bobbed in the gentle seas. Permission had been granted to moor them at Black Hole and Grundy's Gardens. Boone and the other chase boat had offloaded some of their crew to other resort piers further down the shore.

From what he'd heard, some changes had been made in the shoot schedule; actors and additional crew would begin landing first thing tomorrow morning on several chartered planes. Boone's phone dinged and he retrieved it. Emily had gifted him with another photo. Boone's face broke into an uncontrollable grin when he opened the text.

Emily peered out at him from the screen, one eye squinted shut, her perfect teeth gritted in a snarl. Perched on her head was an enormous pirate hat, and she wielded a curved cutlass. Behind her, an older gentleman with a dyed-blue beard looked on with delight. Gray dots appeared under the photo, indicating she was typing.

"Yaaarrrr! Guess who's finishing up shooting in Grand today? This scallywag! See you tomorrow, you scurvy dog!"

More gray dots, and…

"Speaking of scurvy dogs, give Brix a kiss for me! Got to go!"

Boone replied, typing: *"Love you, Captain Goober."* He stared at the phone, but no additional dots were forthcoming. Looking around, he spotted Leonard and waved him toward the kayak rack.

Owen Island was only a thousand feet from the dock. Boone and Leonard skimmed across the teal waters in their kayaks as the noonday sun shone down. The undersea world was easily visible at this shallow depth; sand and turtle grass extended in all directions, and a stingray made an appearance, its dark shape moving alongside them as it rooted in the sand for prey.

"This side closest to the shore is probably your best bet," Boone said as they neared the sandy edge of the little green islet.

"Yes. We definitely want a side where there is no developed shore behind it. Supposed to be a deserted isle in the script."

As the two kayaks nuzzled into the sand, Boone and Leonard stepped into the ankle-deep water and slid their boats up onto the shore. Leonard took out his phone and started photographing and filming stretches of the beach.

"This is probably the side we'll use," Leonard said, after he'd filmed the stretch from every angle. "But can I take a look on the other sides as well?"

"Fine by me," Boone said. "I'll hang here." He popped the compartment on the front of his kayak and retrieved a garbage bag. He'd spotted a few plastic bottles and wrappers on the sand, and some more trash just inside the tree line. Kayakers and picnickers generally kept Owen Island quite clean, but the ocean tended to deposit bits and pieces of garbage no matter where you were.

Leonard spent a few minutes recording the beaches to either side of where they'd come ashore before returning to the kayaks. "Can we move further inland?"

"Sure." Boone led the way toward the center of the little island. "There's a sandy area with ankle-high groundcover right in here, and then it thickens up in a few places."

Leonard methodically documented their short journey into the interior, while Boone scanned for any more trash to pick up.

It was spotless away from the beaches, he was glad to see. Up ahead, the tropical foliage grew thicker, and as they passed a particularly dense clump, Boone suddenly stopped.

Did I see something? Uncertain, Boone backtracked a few steps. *Yes. There.* Leonard continued ahead, engrossed in his filming and photographing, but Boone carefully pushed into the dense greenery, brushing aside the fronds of a robust bull thatch palm, whose squat base looked like a pineapple capped with fans of leaves. Boone circled the tree and came to a halt, staring in puzzlement.

"Boone?" Leonard called out. "Where did you go?"

"Back here!" Boone could hear Leonard getting closer. As the location scout neared, Boone retrieved his phone and took several photos before beginning a video recording of the object and the immediate area.

"Oh, there you are," Leonard said. "What are you doing in there?"

"Found something."

Leonard started to push into the foliage. "What is that? Looks like a sign."

"Yep. A 'No Trespassing' sign."

"In the middle of the island? That's weird."

"Actually, that's not the weird part." He pointed at it as Leonard made it past the palm.

Planted in the ground was a rectangular sign, the slanted words *NO TRESPASSING* printed along the top. Below it was a name, carved into the wood in cursive, the words weathered by time.

Leonard took off his sunglasses and squinted. "I can't make the name out."

"It says 'Burgess Meredith.'"

"Cut! Adequate!" Werner entered the set. "Even Ulysses cooperated this time, thank the heavens."

They had just completed a scene where Emily—or "Sarah"—spoke to Wolfit/Bluebeard in a tight two-shot. In the previous three takes, the monkey had leaped across from the pirate's shoulder to Emily's, an action that was most certainly *not* in the script. Apparently, the little capuchin felt indebted to her for rescuing him from the ocean. Several of the crew actually liked the moment, and at least one of those earlier shots might survive the cutting room floor. Although one take certainly wouldn't; Ulysses had discovered the knot of Emily's bikini at the back of her neck, and only Em's lightning-fast reflexes had prevented an embarrassing clip for the blooper real.

The animal wrangler approached and held out an arm. Ulysses jumped over and received a treat.

"Mr. Silva," Werner said, stopping the man from leaving the set, "I am concerned about your monkey's newfound infatuation with Miss Durand. When we begin shooting aboard the *Puddingwife*, she will be in numerous scenes with Mr. Wolfit and the monkey."

"I'm sorry, Mr. Werner. I will see what I can do."

"Actually, um… just a thought," Emily ventured. "Mr. Werner, you seem like you know how to 'go with the flow,' yeah? Kinda like what you did with the broken plank."

"I have been known to allow the currents of fate to take me where they so choose," Werner said, retrieving his cigarettes from a pocket. "Go on."

195

"If Ulysses keeps coming to me—maybe because he thinks I saved him—why not go with it? Did you get film of him climbing onto my head down in the water?"

"Yes..." Werner said, eyes already beginning to gleam.

"Great! If 'Emily' can save Ulysses, then 'Sarah' can save Ulysses. And if he jumps onto me during a shot, we just go with it, yeah?"

"Brilliant!" Daniel Wolfit said. "Honestly, Heinz, I loathe the creature, and I suspect he knows it. If the monkey weren't crucial to the plot, I would have begged you to cut him from the start." He looked to Emily. "And the next time he jumps over to you, I'll just extemporize a line or two about you having saved his life... animals can show gratitude and devotion... etcetera, etcetera."

Werner turned to the handler. "Mr. Silva? What do you think?"

"It would certainly make my job easier."

"Excellent. Then that's what we'll do. Dario!"

The 1st AD joined the group. "Yes, sir?"

"What's next?"

Back at the dock, Boone and Leonard brought the kayaks ashore and stored them before retreating into the cool interior of the condominium. While Leonard connected to the Wi-Fi to send his footage and photos over to the cinematography department in Grand Cayman, Boone looked up the number for the Little Cayman Museum. They were often open for a few hours every weekday afternoon, but he thought they might have some Saturday hours. Unfortunately, he got the answering machine. *Damn.* Boone hung up.

"Hey, Leonard? I'm gonna walk Brix. Back in a few."

Boone took the energetic pup on a stroll between the various condos and resorts, sticking to the shade of silver thatch palms and casuarina trees when possible. As Brixton sniffed the trunks of several palms, Boone thought about the sign. Amelia had said that Meredith's house was all the way up on the north side, west of Ken Hall Road and ashore of the Penguin's Leap dive site. Why on earth was a No Trespassing sign with Burgess Meredith's signature on it stuck in the middle of Owen Island? His best chance to answer that would have been the Museum and unfortunately, they weren't open tomorrow either, it being Sunday; he'd have to wait until Monday afternoon.

Luckily, inspiration struck when he neared the Little Cayman Beach Resort. Cutting along the beach and through the row of thatch-roof-shaded hammocks, Boone made his way to the Beach Nuts Bar. The open-air watering hole had a sizeable roof to allow drinking during the strongest tropical downpours, and the ceiling was adorned with countless pieces of colorfully painted driftwood; visitors were encouraged to create one to add to the collection.

"Boone! Heard you were making a movie!" Lilith, a Korean-American woman from Arizona, was doing a sudoku at the bar. The afternoon dive was still out on the reefs, so things would be slow for the next hour.

"Actually, Emily's the one doing the movie. I'm just driving a boat around."

"Can I get you a beer? We just tapped a keg of Shell Shock IPA."

"Tempting, but I better not."

"How about some water for your pooch?"

"That I'll take, thank you." Boone took the offered bowl and set it beside a barstool. The sound of vigorous lapping began immediately. "Hey, question for you. The German gal at the museum? Katja? She used to work here, right?"

"Oh, Iguana Girl? You just missed her. Came over here to grab some lunch after she closed up over there. She was on her way to a possible sighting of one of those invasive green iguanas."

"She coming back?"

"Pretty good chance she'll be here late afternoon tomorrow. It's Sangria Sunday, after all!"

"Okay, thanks. Hey, can you give her my number? Let her know I need a little island history help."

"Sure." Lilith grabbed a napkin and a Bic pen and scribbled down Boone's digits.

"C'mon Brix!" Boone returned the water bowl and headed for the beach. "Back to home base!"

"Hey, Emily?"

Emily looked up from studying her sides to discover Cindy standing over her. One of the brunette's arms was crossed in front of her, gripping the opposite elbow.

"Hi Cindy. Ready to get wet?"

"Um… about that. I heard what you did."

"What do you mean?" Emily had never seen any new pages that showed Cindy getting eliminated early, so she hoped the young actress remained unaware.

"One of the writers told me. Werner was going to kill me off and you got him to change his mind."

"Oh, that. No biggie. You woulda done the same."

"No. I wouldn't have." Cindy's eyes welled up.

"Hey, don't mess up your makeup, Cindy-rella!" Em handed her a tissue from the little pack in the side pocket of her camp chair. "You don't want that makeup gal mad at you; she looks like she eats nails for dinner and nuts and bolts for afters."

Cindy laughed, the first genuine laugh Em had seen from her. She bunched the tissue and dabbed at her eyes. "It's just... this business. It's so competitive."

"Well, I'm not really in this business so we don't need to compete. Unless there's only one everything bagel left at the craft services table; then you better watch your back."

Phil poked his head around the corner. "Miss Durand? Five minutes."

"Aye-aye, Second Second!" Emily rose to go, and Cindy surprised her with an impromptu hug.

"Thank you," she whispered in Emily's ear, before breaking the clinch and dashing off to get ready.

Exiting the actors' holding area, Emily looked aft. Near the stern of the *Jolly Robert*, a woman leaned over a monitor, testing the joysticks on a handheld controller. At her feet, a small drone on a tether whirred, its directional propeller housings rotating in response to her movements. *It's kind of like our UPC*, she thought. In Cozumel, Boone and Em had encountered a revolutionary drone—its creator had called it an Underwater Personal Conveyor, but it was really a glorified scooter with autonomous capabilities. After they had saved the lives of several members of the wealthy Othonos family, the drone had been given to them as a gift: Boone called it "the spoils of war."

Emily headed forward to where the plank had been, watching the crew as they prepared to film the water shots. She went to the side and saw they already had the chase boat on station. A pair of rescue divers were suited up, as well as a two-man underwater film crew.

"Hey. 'Sup?"

Emily turned to find Chip, the surfer-dude-ish assistant stunt coordinator. He came alongside her and leaned against the gunwale, unabashedly checking her out.

"Hey," Em replied, cinching her robe closed over the bikini. "We're about to splash around and make movie magic."

"I know. That's why I'm here. Got to make sure everyone falls into the water safely."

Em cocked her head. "We already did that part. I saw some amazing special effects they put in when the plank broke."

"I know. I saw you dive in. It was hot." Chip put his back to the gunwale and leaned his arms up on the side, stretching his T-shirt across his chest.

Is he flexing his pecs? Ew.

"Yeah, so… they want some different angles of you diving in. I'll be overseeing that. Hands on, ya know?" Chip actually winked.

"I've made my living diving into the water. I'm good, thanks."

"It's a safety issue. Don't worry, I'll keep you safe."

"Seriously, I don't need—"

But Chip's eyes had already locked onto new prey; he straightened and strutted away from Emily. "Hey. 'Sup?"

Emily followed his gaze and found Cindy approaching in her costume swimsuit, the busty brunette currently without the protection of a dressing gown. From her body language, this wasn't Chip's first approach.

"I see you've met our lothario," Wolfit commented as he joined Emily, wearing his full pirate's regalia.

"Bit of a philandering berk, that one," Emily muttered.

"Methinks Chip has concentrated so much of his efforts on what's below his shoulders that there wasn't anything left for what lay above."

Emily laughed. "Why Mr. Wolfit, are you calling Chip a meathead?"

Wolfit grinned through his dyed-blue beard. "I would never stoop to such an epithet."

"Emily, we're ready for you." Jerry, the 2nd AD waved her over to where a group of cast and crew stood around Werner.

"The hour approaches and we shall shoot the water scenes involving the escape of Bluebeard and Sarah." Werner looked right at Emily. "And Cindy," he added. "I want everyone to give me their utmost focus. If we are able to finish this sequence, then the three of you will be wrapped for today. Tomorrow, I will remain here to complete filming of the creature's attack on the ship."

"What are *we* doing tomorrow?" Cindy asked.

"First thing in the morning," Jerry said, "you three and much of the cast will be flying over to Little Cayman."

18

Boone waited beside the Jeep as the first of the chartered planes landed a half hour after sunrise. On Sundays, the first flight into Little wasn't until just after nine, so the production company had scheduled several flights back-and-forth with a rented Twin Otter, ferrying nineteen cast and crew at a time.

Giant sunglasses firmly in place, Emily came into view around the side of the little air terminal, rolling her small green suitcase. Her larger suitcase was being dragged along by Billy Faust, who walked beside her, a smaller bag over his shoulder. Em spotted Boone and quickened her pace.

"No, no! No autographs, please!" she said, raising a palm and averting her face.

"Fame's already gotten to you, huh?" Boone responded, taking her suitcase. He debated taking the other one from Billy, but the young actor was already angling toward the back of the Jeep.

"Mr. Fischer," Emily intoned in an over-the-top dowager's voice, "what is the meaning of the ratty T-shirt and shorts ensemble? I expect my driver to be well-dressed, with one of those silly little caps. Now, open the door for me, if you please."

"Yes, ma'am." Boone opened the back door for her, standing beside it like a limo driver.

"Thank you, my good man," Emily said, completely ignoring the offered door, going around Boone to hop into the front passenger seat.

Boone chuckled and took her suitcase around to the back, where Billy was waiting.

"Emily said she'd drop me off at my hotel. Hope that's okay."

"Sure," Boone said, putting the luggage in the rear compartment.

"Hey Cindy! Mister W!" The Jeep's top was down, and Emily stood in the seat, waving at an older gentleman and a strikingly beautiful brunette. "C'mon!" she shouted. "My chauffeur will take you to your digs! Sorry about how he's dressed. Hard to get good help, innit?"

The pair joined Billy in the back and Boone started the Jeep. "Where are they putting you up?" he asked.

"Don't talk to the passengers, driver!"

"Oh, we're still doing this, huh?"

"Very rude." Emily grinned, then leaned across and kissed Boone on the cheek. "Okay, *now* the chauffeur bit is over. Well, except for the actual chauffeuring. Our passengers are all at the Southern Cross, right next to us."

Boone drove onto Guy Banks Road and Emily gave a rap-id-fire version of the tour she'd given to Werner several days ago. As they passed the Little Cayman Museum, Boone interrupted her presentation.

"Hey! Remind me to tell you what I found on Owen Island."

"Boone, tell me what you found on Owen Island."

"Not now, later. Actually, Katja will want to hear this. I'm hoping I can catch her at Beach Nuts this evening."

"Ooh! Sangria Sunday!" She looked back at the trio. "You three are in for a treat!"

———◆·◆———

Fingers tapped a digital keyboard and a text exchange began.

"They're here."

"I know. I watched the plane leave Grand Cayman. Get to the airport in an hour. On the next flight over, there will be a locked road case labeled with your department. Everything you need will be inside."

"What about the next payment?"

"Inside the case. You remember what you have to do? Don't type it, just tell me yes or no."

"Yes."

"Good. Delete this thread."

The conversation ended and a finger swiped left, then tapped the trashcan icon.

———◆·◆———

"Billy and I are supposed to go over our scenes together this morning," Emily said, as she endured a vigorous tongue-bath from Brixton. "Werner wants us word perfect. And, honestly... I don't want him mad at me again."

"What's happened now?"

Emily recounted how she'd read the new sides and realized Werner was going to cut Cindy. "And when I pushed back on that, he was furious again. But then, the next time I saw him, everything's all hunky-dory!"

Boone nodded, remembering now what he had forgotten: Leonard had suggested something had gone wrong with the cancelled *Zombie Bigfoot* movie. *While Em is rehearsing, I'll Google around,* he thought. *See what I can find about that actress's nervous breakdown.* "Leonard said Werner could be difficult," he offered.

"Yeah, bit mood-swingy. Oh! Mr. Wolfit has been helping me navigate the filmmaking waters." Emily grabbed Brixton's clownfish squeak toy and hurled it down the beach. "And he and I have both made some suggestions that Werner liked, and they changed the script!"

"Hope they pay you extra for it."

"I don't think that's how it works, Boone."

"Hey, Emily!" A shirtless Billy Faust trotted over from the Southern Cross, bare feet kicking up sand. "You wanna run lines?"

"Sure! Let's do it in the hammocks."

Boone snickered at her word choice and Emily shot him a look.

"I meant run our lines in the hammocks, you randy prat."

Boone held up his hands in surrender, smiling. The first time he and Emily had made love, it had been an unmitigated disaster, courtesy of an overly optimistic fantasy about using the hammock in their tiny Saban cottage. Little Cayman's resorts had beachside hammocks aplenty, so the teasing was routine.

"Sounds good to me!" Billy followed Emily toward a pair of hammocks under a quartet of palm trees. Em looked up, no doubt checking the location of coconuts. One morning, she'd come out to discover one in a hammock, and it was easy to imagine an unsuspecting human experiencing death-by-coconut.

Brixton started to follow Emily, but Boone gave a whistle and called the dog into the condo. The pooch went straight to his water bowl, lapping messily, while Boone grabbed a Ting—a Jamaican grapefruit soda—and settled in front of the laptop. He Googled "zombie bigfoot" and glanced through the results. Apparently, it was a book that had been optioned for a movie, and there were several hits on sites that Boone considered to be gossipy tabloid trash. Ironically, he figured that was probably where he needed to look. One caught his eye, and he opened it.

Zombie Bigfoot in Big Trouble

Did director Heinz Werner drive his leading lady insane?

Production has been halted on the much-anticipated creature feature, Zombie Bigfoot. Shooting on location in Idaho, ZBF—as many expectant fans call it—was several weeks into its production schedule when filming was abruptly halted. Sources say that the lead actress, Michelle Reynolds, suffered a nervous breakdown on the set. There are conflicting versions of what brought the breakdown about. One cast member placed the blame squarely on director Heinz Werner, stating that his demanding directorial style bordered on abuse. However, several crew members stated that the only abuse they saw was substance abuse, on the part of Ms. Reynolds.

207

Boone skimmed through the rest of the article, which appeared to have been published right at the time of the production halt. He backed out of the web page and returned to the search results, entering "Michelle Reynolds" and "breakdown." That yielded several possibilities, and he tapped on the first one he saw.

Actress Michelle Reynolds Enters Rehab

The article began with a recap of the nervous breakdown and cancellation of production, but this one had an added rumor: Werner and Reynolds had been involved in a "showmance," with another source suggesting it had been going on before, and may have played a role in her being cast. Heinz Werner had flatly denied the suggestion. The story went on to say that one of the producers of *Zombie Bigfoot* had assisted Ms. Reynolds with admission into an upscale substance abuse treatment center in Malibu, California. There was a photo of Ms. Reynolds shielding her face in the passenger seat of a car. In the driver's seat, a man in a suit was yelling at the paparazzi taking the photo.

Boone popped back out and looked at the other search results. His heart sank as his eyes landed on:

Actress Michelle Reynolds, Dead at 35

◆ ◆ ◆

As Emily entered the condo, she found Boone at the computer. He swiveled around in the desk chair. "How'd it go?" he asked.

"Apparently I'm very good at memorizing. Good thing too! They're delegating the remainder of the Grand Cayman *Jolly*

Robert shoot to Dario, and Werner's just landed in Little. Everyone's heading to the *Puddingwife*! And you need to be starting up the *Lunasea*, Mr. Chase Boat Skipper." She grabbed her phone, which had been charging, and stuffed it in a pocket, then glanced over at the laptop. "Whatcha reading?"

"Oh..." Boone closed the laptop. "I'll tell you tonight. We better get a move on."

"Yes indeedy! You do *not* want to see Werner mad."

By mid-afternoon, the *Puddingwife* was to the west of Little Cayman, making her way north at a leisurely six knots. Emily was in her bikini for what she hoped would be the last time— on camera, at least. She had her leg up on a bench and a member of the makeup department was examining the "wound" on her calf and shin, from when her character was grazed by the imaginary Portuguese man o' war.

"Looks good to me. Don't get it wet."

"Water, water everywhere and not a drop on the makeup," Emily said with a grin. When the makeup lady just looked at her, Em added, "I won't get it wet."

Jerry, the 2nd AD, leaned down. "Sorry we sprung this on you. We all thought Werner would be shooting in Grand the whole day."

"No worries," Em said. "Is that a little weird, having someone else direct some of the movie?"

"It's unusual for Werner to do it. He's a bit of a perfectionist. But he's worked with Dario for years and trusts his eye. He's used him on a Second Team a few times. Plus, it's mostly fill shots and

B-roll of the attack. A lot of what happens during that sequence will be done in post by the computer graphics team, anyway."

"Ms. Durand," Werner interrupted, arriving on the tail end of a cigarette. When he looked around for somewhere to dispose of it, Jerry took it from him. "I apologize for the sudden decision to begin shooting here today, but I saw an opportunity to catch up after our production delays of last week. I hope you had a chance to study your opening scenes on the survey ship."

"I'm good. We're only doing two scenes, and I'm out cold for the first one, yeah? So, I'll run the lines for the second scene in my head while they're rescuing me."

Waiting nearby, Wolfit overheard this and chuckled, giving her a nod.

Werner cracked a smile. "A sensible use of your time," he said. "Let us make our way to the lifeboat."

The dinghy was currently sitting on the deck of the *Pudding-wife*, suspended from the crane at the stern. Cindy was waiting there, and gave Emily a little wave. In the "re-rewrite" that put her back in, her character had actually been the one to bring the boat over to Wolfit and Emily while invisible tentacles ripped the *Jolly Robert* and its passengers apart.

Jerry waved everyone together. "You three," he began, then gestured over to the animal wrangler, "and the monkey will board the boat, at which point the crane will lower you to the water. We have a small safety boat below, and they will follow you at a distance. You'll have a pilot aboard, and once you get into position, he'll transfer over to the safety boat."

"No need for that," Emily said. "I can skipper that dinghy easy peasy. Simple outboard, nothing fancy."

Jerry looked to Werner, who nodded. "Anything that saves time, I am in favor of."

"Okay," Jerry said. "The safety boat will still escort you out. Once in position, we'll begin shooting. The *Lunasea* will be doing most of the filming, although we'll have a drone overhead, capturing aerial footage."

"What if Ulysses jumps in the water?" Em asked.

"He won't be able to. He'll be tethered to Bluebeard's shoulder."

"Capital idea…" Wolfit muttered.

"There are a pair of oars in there," Werner pointed out. "At this point in the story, the dinghy's engine is out of fuel, and Bluebeard and Cindy have been rowing."

A sound guy leaned in. "We've rigged the boat with four small microphones. Try not to splash around too much."

"And you have the radio in place, yes?" Werner asked.

"Yeah." The sound engineer handed Werner a two-way radio. "We've put its mate out of sight in the bow of the boat."

Werner lifted the radio and thumbed the Push-to-Talk button. "Testing, testing, *eins, zwei, drei.*" From the boat on the deck, his words were mirrored from the unseen radio. "I will give you directions from this. If you have any questions about my direction, you may retrieve it and ask them."

"Right-o! Let's get this show on the road!" Em said. "Or 'ocean' or what-have-you."

◆ ◆ ◆

Twenty minutes later, Boone watched as Emily and her castmates were lowered into the water. Em took the tiller of the small boat and maneuvered her away from the *Puddingwife*. He watched as she crouched and retrieved a two-way radio and held it to her ear, shouted into it, then handed it off to Cindy, who tucked it back out of sight. Boone's own marine radio came to life.

"Lunasea, *you're up. The lifeboat is going to turn about and face the research ship. Please position yourself parallel to her. Your camera crew will tell you how close to get.*"

Boone acknowledged the order and maneuvered toward the dinghy. Emily looked up with a huge smile on her face and waved. After Boone returned the gesture, Em slowly swung her boat around one-hundred-eighty degrees and Boone mirrored the move, careful not to throw up much of a wake.

Amelia popped her head up from the flybridge ladder. "Marsha says you're almost a perfect distance. Come parallel to them, and about five feet closer."

"Got it." Boone nudged the throttle, then gave the wheel a slight turn, eyes on the dinghy.

Em throttled down as he came alongside, shouting across to him. "Don't swamp my boat, Boone!" Then she cocked her head, listening.

Boone could just hear a radio speaking aboard her boat, but couldn't make out any of the words. Emily said something to the others aboard and they laughed, and then Wolfit and Cindy retrieved the oars as Em looked up at Boone. She pointed two fingertips to her eyes, then tapped her chest; the dive signals for "Watch me." Then she raised the back of her hand to her forehead in an over-the-top rendition of a swooning damsel before carefully lowering herself to the bottom of the dinghy. The radio across the way said a few things, and Emily scooted herself closer to the bow before lying still.

A buzzing sound grew louder, and movement caught Boone's eye as a camera drone from the *Puddingwife* came to a hover over the dinghy. The *Lunasea*'s radio spoke.

"Hold position. We're rolling."

"Action," the radio squawked.

Emily found it funny that what she was doing was the *opposite* of action, but she kept her expression slack and eyes closed. The bright, tropical sun penetrated her eyelids with a pink-orange glow, and she sorely missed her sunglasses.

Wolfit and Cindy said their lines, and Ulysses chittered softly. Emily could do nothing but lie still and listen to the sounds around her: the white noise of the buzzing camera drone overhead, and to either side, the splash of the oars and the gentle lapping of the waves. These sounds all began to lull her to sleep. *No wonder. This past week's been a whirlwind.* Em didn't see any reason not to go with it—after all, she was supposed to be unconscious from the monster's venom. *Long as I don't snore.* She drifted off...

A pair of shrieks—one human, one simian—ripped her from sleep. A tiny part of her mind was aware of another sound ceasing: the drone's buzz. She opened her eyes and saw the quadrotor camera drone falling straight down, hurtling toward her face. Before she could move out of the way, Wolfit grabbed her shoulders and rolled her to the side as the drone smacked into the bottom of the boat, right where her head had been.

19

"Apparently, the battery wasn't charged," Emily said from the flybridge wheel of the *Lunasea* as it crossed the lagoon, headed for their dock. She wore her sunglasses and a spare Bubble Chasers Diving T-shirt over her bikini—hopefully she would be able to dress more modestly from now on.

"Something must be faulty in the charger or in the battery," Marsha, the best boy, mused. "The drone operator swears it had a full charge."

The sun was nearing the horizon and the day's shoot was done. Despite the malfunction of the drone, Werner was satisfied with the footage they had managed to get and had insisted that they continue with the schedule. The storyline advanced, as the dinghy was spotted by Ethan—the marine biologist aboard the *Puddingwife*—played by Billy Faust. The occupants were rescued and brought aboard the salvage/research ship, with Billy carrying Emily to the infirmary. One interior scene was shot, where "Sarah" is treated by "Ethan," who recognizes the type of sting and neutralizes the venom.

Boone had contacted the 2nd AD and pointed out that the channel was not something to be navigated in the dark, so this last scene was shot on the move as the flotilla of boats returned to the moorings near the entrance to the lagoon.

"Scene went well," Em said. "I managed to remember all of my lines, despite nearly being smacked in the gob by a drone."

"This your first scene with Billy?" Boone asked.

"It was. Now I get to slowly fall in love with him," Em teased.

"Good looking guy..." Boone offered.

"Yeah, well, I think he's got a thing for Cindy. Probably because he knows I'm already shackled to you."

"Thank goodness for shackles. I was afraid I'd lose you to a showmance." Boone turned to Marsha. "That's what they call it, right? Showmance?"

Marsha nodded, and Emily gave Boone a quizzical look. "Where on earth did you learn that terminology? Not something I'd expect to hear out of your mouth."

"I read it in an article this morning. Werner may have had a showmance with one of his actresses on a movie that never made it to the theaters."

"What?" Emily gasped.

"I'll tell you la—"

"If you say you'll 'tell me later' one more time, I'm going to track down a *real* Portuguese man o' war and shove it down your knickers."

"Okay, okay! But first, let's dock the *Lunasea* and get everyone ashore. I'm sure the M&Ms want to get everything stowed before sundown."

Emily wrinkled her brow above her sunglasses. "M&M's?"

Boone smiled. "Tell ya later."

———— ◆ ◆ ————

"What happened with the crane? I hear it lowered them into the water, safe and sound. That tells me you didn't do your job."

As the words appeared in the text thread, the recipient found an out-of-the-way place and responded: *"I was going to rig it tonight, but Werner changed his schedule and showed up early. The ship was already swarming with crew by the time I got aboard."*

"Yes, he caught me off guard too, leaving Grand when he did. Nice work on the drone."

"The operator almost spotted me swapping the battery out, but I finished just before she got back."

"You've seen the shoot schedule for tomorrow?"

"Yes. Just got it."

"Then you know what to do. Better get busy."

———— ◆ ◆ ————

"White or red?" the bartender asked.

"Gimme the lowdown on the fruit, Lilith," Em replied.

"Red has citrus and grapes, white has mango and pineapple."

"Sign me up for the white!"

It was Sangria Sunday at the Beach Nuts Bar, and the cast and crew had assembled there at Em's suggestion. A number of them were staying right at the Little Cayman Beach Resort, and the bar was centrally located for the rest, housed at the bordering resorts. Several groups of divers, as well as dive staff from Reef Divers, mingled with the visitors. Wolfit was holding court with several divemasters from the UK, telling tales of his time with the Royal Shakespeare Company.

Boone ordered an Ironshore Bock and took a stool next to Emily at one corner of the bar. He glanced around, hoping to spot Katja from the museum. No sign of "Iguana Girl," but there were certainly plenty of iguanas. In the landscaping nearby, a particularly robust-looking specimen was bobbing its head at a pair of smaller ones. *Katja would know who's saying what to whom,* Boone thought.

Emily sipped her sangria. "Oooh... tasty. Okay, spill it. Every bit. You found something on Owen Island, you read something about a Heinz Werner showmance, and you wouldn't tell me what you were looking at on the laptop." She turned in her stool. "Was it porn? It was porn, wasn't it?"

"I wish."

Emily snickered into her sangria. "You do? Boone, I never knew you were such a deviant."

Boone shook his head. When Emily was in a teasing mood, she could dance verbal circles around him. "No, I mean... porn would have been better than..." He sighed. "The article I was reading wasn't pleasant."

"Oh, sorry. What was it?"

Boone laid out what he had discovered about the aborted production of *Zombie Bigfoot*, and the breakdown, substance abuse, and eventual death of its lead actress, Michelle Reynolds.

"That's horrible. What did she die of?"

"Overdose. Possibly deliberate."

"Who found her?"

"A producer she was staying with."

"And the showmance with Werner... was it...?"

"Yeah. Same woman. But that was just a rumor. I couldn't find much about that, but a couple sites hinted at it."

"That's very sad," Emily said distantly.

"Sorry to bring it up, Em, but I felt you should know. There were some suggestions that Werner's treatment of her on set might have led to the nervous breakdown."

Em gave Boone a small smile. "Thanks for looking out for me. He can be a little brusque, and sometimes loses his temper like *that*." She snapped her fingers. "But I'm betting the tabloids blew things out of proportion, yeah?"

"Probably."

"I'm a big girl, Boone. I can handle a grumpy-pants German director." She pierced a piece of mango in the sangria with a toothpick and popped the orange morsel in her mouth. "Okay, that's two down. Now what's up with Owen Island?"

Boone spied a woman coming up the walk around the side of the restaurant building. "Let me include someone else when I tell you; otherwise I'll be telling it twice. Katja!" He waved to the newcomer.

Katja looked over, smiled, and started their way. She appeared to be coming straight from the field—her shorts and tank top were streaked with dirt, and several red scratches were visible along her forearms.

"Hello, Boone! Emily! Sorry about the mess. I had to pull an invasive green out of a thicket." Katja spoke with a touch of a German accent, though hers was quite a bit softer than Werner's Bohemian dialect. "Little bastard clawed me good." She showed off the scratches.

"Oh, that's nothing," Emily said. "Check this out." Em stuck out her leg and turned it, showing off her calf and shin.

"Good heavens!" Katja exclaimed. "What happened to you?"

Emily laughed and Boone gave her a playful shove. "Nothing happened to her. That's special effects makeup from the movie little Miss Meryl Streep here is shooting."

"I asked them if I could keep it on. Mess with the blokes at Reef Divers."

"I didn't know you were in the movie! Congratulations! Are you in it too, Boone?"

"I'm playing a supporting role. I'm ferrying some of the crew around while Emily hogs all the glory."

"Boone... enough stalling," Em prodded.

"Right. Katja, I'm glad you're here. Got something to ask you." Boone gestured to the taps. "Beer? Sangria?"

"I will take a Caybrew, thank you." She sat beside Emily while Boone ordered her beer and brought up the video he'd taken on Owen. He slid it over to where Em and Katja could both see it.

Katja's eyes went wide. "Burgess Meredith's sign! We've been looking for this! Where did you find it?"

"In the interior of Owen Island."

"What?" Katja frowned and pointed across the lagoon at the dark shape of the island, barely visible against the darkening sky. "Out there? That makes no sense. The house used to be on the north side of the island, near Ken Hall Road."

"Hang on," Boone said. "*Used* to be?"

"Yes. It was falling apart. A developer bought the property and there is a new house there. The sign with his signature was such a nice piece of Little Cayman history, we wanted it for the museum. Unfortunately, it went missing sometime between tearing down the old house and excavating for the new structure. But now, you've found it!"

"How long did Burgess Meredith live there?" Boone asked.

Katja took a sip of her Caybrew, thinking. "I remember he bought the house in 1967 and sold it sometime in the 90s. It was a place for him to escape to and unwind. Oh, interesting fact: after he bought it, he remodeled it, and they were digging a new well or cesspool. They dug in one spot, and the water was brackish. They dug in another spot... and found a skeleton!"

"Blimey!" Emily exclaimed. "Who'd it belong to?"

"If I remember correctly, the police thought it was the body of a youth who went missing shortly after World War II. We have newspaper clippings about it. But back to the sign—do you have it?"

"No, I figured I better leave it where it was until I talked to someone at the museum. The movie's going to be shooting a few scenes over there, if you want me to grab it."

"No, that's okay. I'll speak to the museum director first. She'll probably want to document it. We were hoping to have a small Burgess Meredith exhibit, but when that sign went missing, we stopped working on it."

"Did anything else go missing?" a voice asked.

Boone, Emily, and Katja looked up. At the corner of the bar beside Boone, the prop master was leaning forward with interest. Gone was yesterday's Batman T-shirt, replaced today with a blue shirt sporting a Superman logo.

"Sorry to eavesdrop, but I'm a huge fan of the original *Batman* series. Just curious if anything else went missing, other than the sign."

"Like what?" Katja asked.

"Well..." The man shifted on his stool. "There was a rumor a few props from the show went missing. It's not uncommon for actors to receive items their character used once a show comes to an end, so..."

"What, like Penguin stuff?" Emily asked. "Purple top hat, umbrella, that sorta thing?"

The prop master waved his hand dismissively. "It was only a rumor. Just curious if they found anything when they tore the house down. Memorabilia like that can bring in a fortune from collectors."

"Not to my knowledge," Katja said. "Mr. Meredith had not lived there in well over twenty years."

"Well, what about the sign? Is that for sale? I'm a bit of a collector myself."

"Oh, I don't think so. It is part of the history of the island."

The man nodded, picking up his soda and leaving the stool. "Cool. Thanks for the info." He raised his plastic cup to Emily. "Good work today. Nice dodge when that drone dropped."

"Oh, you saw that? Yeah, bit scary. But Daniel Wolfit saved the day!" Em turned on her stool and held her sangria aloft. "Wolfy!"

The old actor looked up from his rapt audience and smiled.

"Thanks for the save, Cap'n Bluebeard!"

Wolfit—his beard now more gray than blue—raised a pint in reply and inclined his head before returning to whatever theatrical yarn he was spinning.

"Emily!" Billy came toward the bar with Cindy beside him. Boone thought he saw him remove his arm from the brunette's waist just as they entered the pools of light around the open-air bar. "Great suggestion! This place is awesome! You know they have a hot tub right over there?"

"I'm well acquainted with it," Em replied. She wrinkled her nose. "What is that smell?"

"Oh, sorry," Billy said, holding up a vape pen. "It's probably this."

"Well, it's better than those European cigarettes Werner smokes," Emily said.

"Oh, hi Mr. Werner," Boone said nonchalantly, looking past her.

Emily froze, then turned and looked before promptly turning back and slugging Boone in the arm. "Wanker!"

Billy laughed. "Yeah, he's not here. He's back at his room, working on the next day's schedule with Jerry." He took another pull on the vape pen and Cindy giggled, waving at the air.

"What the sodding hell are you smoking?" Em asked.

Boone inhaled. "I'm getting a childhood sense memory of the Tennessee Valley Fair in Chilhowee Park, outside Knoxville." He sniffed the air. "Funnel cake?"

Billy touched his finger to his nose. "Bingo! I have all sorts of cool flavors."

"Ohmigod, you're smoking a dessert?" Em asked, disgusted and amused.

"Wait 'til I fire up some cotton candy."

"What are you drinking, Emily?"

"Sangria Sunday, Cindy-rella! Red or white, it's your night!"

Cindy laughed and dragged Billy to an open spot at the bar to order drinks.

Boone leaned over. "Ms. Durand… might I suggest a refill, followed by a stroll to the hammocks?"

"Why, Mr. Fischer!" Emily replied, poshing her accent up. "What a capital idea. So long as you deport yourself as a gentleman."

"No promises," Boone said, signaling Lilith for another round.

◆ ◆

Emily peered into the darkness near the shore. There was a little thatched roof that covered a pair of hammocks and she hoped they were free. Ropes hung down from the roof and allowed a person to grab hold and get a good swing going. Voices from the shadows revealed those two were taken.

"I'm telling you, it works better if the monkey bonds with Sarah."

"I suppose, but it changes a few things near the end."

The two writers from the meet-and-greet, Emily thought, recognizing the voices. As her eyes adjusted, she could see the two in the hammocks. The ponytailed writer had a leg over the side, a light blue Crocs sandal dangling from his foot. In the adjacent hammock, the younger writer had an impressive swing going. He reached up and grabbed the hanging rope, giving himself another pull.

"Evening, gents," Em said.

"Oh, hello Emily," the younger one said. "I was just saying how your suggestion about the monkey would work out well for the storyline."

"More rewrites," Ponytail groused. "This production is becoming more like *Jaws* every day."

"What, the shark movie?" Boone asked.

Ponytail craned his head around to see who had spoken.

"Oh, sorry," Em said. "This is Boone."

"Ah, yes, the other divemaster. Welcome aboard!" Ponytail said. "To answer your question, yes, I was referring to the movie that turned Steven Spielberg into a sensation overnight."

"How is this movie like that one?" Em asked. "Apart from both having a water monster, I mean."

"Well, like *Jaws*, we have a movie that started shooting without a finished script, and without our full cast. We're having to rewrite things nearly every day, and technical problems are plaguing us at every turn."

"The drone being the latest," the other said. "But there have been boat breakdowns, misdirected shipments, camera glitches, problems with our lead cast members. And I just heard one of the hard drives got wiped the other day. Fortunately, footage was already backed up in the Cloud."

"At least our monster is computer-generated," Ponytail said. "The mechanical sharks in *Jaws* kept breaking or sinking to the bottom. They collectively called them 'Bruce,' but some of the crew started using the name, 'The Great White Turd.' The shark was supposed to be waterproof, but it wasn't, and it broke down nearly every day. One time, Spielberg himself broke it, playing a prank on George Lucas when he visited the set."

"I heard about that!" the younger writer cried with a laugh. "Lucas stuck his head in the mouth as a joke, and Spielberg closed the jaws on him... and then it malfunctioned, and Lucas was stuck in there until they managed to pry it open."

"And the boat in *Jaws?* The one that sinks in the story? The stunt boat for it actually *did* sink!" Ponytail continued. "Lost some expensive camera equipment. The whole movie was supposed to be shot in sixty-five days, but ended up taking nearly two and a half times as long. And yet... it turned out to be the biggest box office success to date."

"How many days behind are we?" Emily asked.

"Surprisingly, only about a week," the young writer said, cutting loose with another rope-assisted swing. "Good thing for Werner, too. I think this is his last chance with the studio."

"Why's that?" Boone asked.

"Well, the last one was a box office flop. The one before did okay, but absolutely hemorrhaged money during shooting. And then there was that train wreck of a Bigfoot movie. Total dumpster fire."

"How are you liking shooting a movie in the Caribbean?" Boone asked.

"Well, it has its pluses and minuses," the younger writer said. "Certainly a nice place to be at the end of the workday. But there's a reason it's not often done."

"But there have been some big movies shot in the islands, yeah?" Emily asked.

"Oh, of course!" Ponytail said. "The James Bond movie *Thunderball* was filmed in the Bahamas. *Jaws 4* was shot there, as well."

"*Pirates of the Caribbean* was filmed all over the Caribbean," the other writer said.

"Well, that seems appropriate," Em remarked.

"I need to hit the restroom," Ponytail said, kicking the other leg over the side of the hammock and flailing like a manatee in a net. "Little help?"

Boone stepped in and assisted the man's escape. The other writer decided to grab another beer, and Boone and Em quickly claimed the vacated hammocks. They each hauled on the rope, pulling their hammocks all the way to opposite sides.

Boone counted down. "Three, two..."

"Stop!" Emily shouted. "Hammock time!"

They released as one, swinging down toward each other and colliding, laughing like schoolchildren. The swinging slowed and Boone reached across and took Emily's hand.

The lagoon protected the shore from heavier surf, but gentle waves lapped against the beach a half dozen yards away. The sky was brilliant with stars, and the Milky Way plainly visible, removed as they were from the lights of the bar area. The dark shape of Owen Island was dappled in the light of the moon.

They rocked in companionable silence for a while before an electronic chime interrupted the moment.

Emily sighed. "That'll be the call time for tomorrow. Probably the arse-crack of dawn." Her face glowed in the light of her phone, and she smiled. "Well, whaddaya know? They're shooting some underwater scenes with the treasure hunters and marine biologists"—she looked over at Boone—"*before* the part where I get rescued. I've got the morning off!"

"Great!"

"But you sure as hell don't," Emily snickered.

"Arse-crack of dawn?"

"Set the coffeemaker for stupid o'clock!" Emily replied.

20

"Okay, *Pudding*, we're passing the mooring ball for Joy's Joy," Boone said into the mic. "Amelia's pointing at it with a boat hook. Let me know when you've got eyes on."

"*We see it,* Lunasea."

"Good. That's yours. This site has the double eyebolts down below for your size vessel. We're going next door to Barracuda Bight while you get set up."

"*Roger.*"

Boone hung up the mic and turned to his skipper. "Are you going to remember how to be an actress, taking the morning off like this? You could've slept in."

Emily turned her face up to him, where Boone's reflection stared back at him from her sunglasses. "And leave you to wrap my boat around a safety diver? No, better to have me at the wheel. They gave me the morning off and this is how I want to spend it. And this way, Amelia can help out over on the *Pudding*; give the underwater camera crews information on the dive sites."

229

"Shouldn't you be running your lines?"

"I am." Emily pointed at a stapled stack of pages she had affixed to a spot beside the wheel. "Every so often, I look down and grab another bit to memorize."

Boone and Em were leading the *Puddingwife* to the north end to shoot a scene along the iconic Bloody Bay Wall. The Film Commission had agreed to a limited shoot with a range of restrictions, and Boone had suggested this particular site. Joy's Joy had the vertical drop-off the cinematographer wanted, and was also next to a gap between clusters of dive sites, so they'd be less likely to have any recreational divers straying into the shot. He'd also kept them away from some of the more popular sites like Lea Lea's Lookout, Marylin's Cut, or the East and West Great Wall, figuring he'd catch a lot of flak from the island's other dive ops if he plopped the film crew down on one of those.

After both ships had reached their respective moorings, Boone went below to speak to the M&Ms. The quadpod was still locked into place, but the four members of the chase boat camera crew—Marsha, Murray, Madge, and Mike—were currently occupied with an ROV camera on a tether. The group seemed tense.

"How's it going?" Boone ventured.

Marsha looked up. "We'll know in a minute. Had to reboot the little bastard. Baby Geek was working fine the last few days during the *Jolly Robert* shoots. Not sure what's up with it now."

Emily appeared at the top of the flybridge ladder and called down. "Hey, the script says there's a two-man submersible in this scene. Is that going to be real, or CGI?"

"There's a real sub over there, all right," Murray said. "Deacon got it on loan from a guy in Roatan, Honduras."

"Ace!" Em studied the *Puddingwife*. "Looks like they've got her on the crane." She winced. "Whoops."

"What? What kind of whoops?" Marsha asked.

"Well, it looks like one of the tethers broke loose, and one end of it hit the deck." She watched for a moment. "And now there's a lot of yelling going on. An-n-n-n-n-nd... Werner is throwing things."

"Glad we're over here," Murray muttered.

Boone climbed back up with Emily and went to the radio. "Uh, hey *Pudding*. Everything okay over there?"

"Uh... everything's under control. We had a slight malfunction, but uh... they're fixing it."

"Dammit to hell!" Marsha shouted from below.

Boone and Emily rushed to the aft side of the flybridge and looked over the rail.

"The reboot failed!" Marsha smacked the little ROV. "I'm getting nothing on the remote. Baby Geek is toast. We're going to need our computer tech to open him up."

"Werner's going to lose it," Mike said.

"Hold on a tick!" Emily shouted. She raced down the ladder.

"The UPC?" Boone guessed aloud.

"Yep! It's below!"

"What's a UPC?" Marsha asked.

"Underwater Personal Conveyor," Boone answered. "I know, terrible name. But it's high-tech, has a *very* high-res camera, and even though it was designed to be an underwater scooter, it can operate as an ROV. The guy who designed it was a genius. Also a criminal, but hey... that's how we ended up with it."

Emily came up from the Canaveral's bow cabin with a hard case and set it on the deck next to the camera crew. She popped the latches and opened the lid, revealing a foam-lined interior and a squat, black object. Its appearance brought to mind a manta ray with stubby wings, a number of controls and a screen deco-

231

rating its top. Emily lifted it out of the foam, unveiling a hand-held control panel in the bottom of the case. She set down the UPC and grabbed the controller.

"Looks flashy," Marsha said, "but tell me about the camera."

Em fired up the controller and a central screen lit up. She navigated to an "About" page and handed it over. "I'm a bit of a photog myself, but I only understand about half of this."

Marsha scanned through the stats. "This is... this is better than Baby Geek's camera."

"Oh, thank God," Madge gushed, as if she'd been holding her breath for the past five minutes.

Boone and Em spent some time answering questions about the device, and showed off several videos that were currently stored.

Finally, Marsha stood, wincing a bit at having been crouched for so long. "Okay, I need to talk to the cinematographer. Can one of you call over and get Alan Novak on the line? But don't tell them why."

"On it!" Emily scrambled up the ladder.

Boone looked across to the *Puddingwife*. "Looks like they've got the submersible reattached to the crane."

"We may survive today, after all," Marsha said, climbing the ladder to the flybridge.

<hr />

"A little to the left," Alan Novak said. "And back off ever so slightly... good! There!"

After learning of the failure of the studio's ROV and the proposed solution, the cinematographer had come aboard the *Lunasea* himself to oversee the undersea filming. When Emily had attempted to teach the M&Ms how to operate the UPC, Novak had quickly discerned that letting her operate it would be the safest—and quickest—option.

The shoot had gone well, with a two-diver film crew providing additional coverage. Billy Faust was aboard the submersible, along with an actress who played one of the treasure hunters who were also aboard the *Puddingwife*. A third occupant with a hand-held was stuffed into the cramped interior with them, filming their exchanges and ducking out of sight whenever the UPC or underwater camera crew shot any footage of the see-through cockpit.

Novak had a two-way radio and communicated with Werner and the other camera teams, although orders to the submersible had to be transmitted down its tether. If the underwater camera crew required instructions, these were relayed by the cameraman inside the sub, holding up a slate inside the cockpit. "We have some marvelous footage along the vertical wall," Novak said, "but I'd like them to go deeper so we lose more of the color. Let's take them to one hundred feet."

"*Roger that,*" a voice replied. "*Faust, we're taking the helm. Bringing you down to one hundred feet.*"

"The UPC's antenna only spools out to sixty," Em said.

"That's all right," Novak answered. "The divers will provide these final shots."

"They'll be close to deco, with the amount of time they've been down," Boone noted, referring to pushing the no decompression limits, or NDL. Decompression sickness could result if they didn't stage their ascent.

"They're professionals," Novak said. He raised the radio again. "Rotate the cockpit to face the wall. Have Wilson film the descent."

"Roger that." The channel remained open as the commands were given, but a garbled transmission was heard over the line.

"Uh… guys?" It was Billy Faust, a nervous quaver in his voice. *"We've got a leak in here. Make that two leaks."*

Jerry's voice shouted from somewhere in the background, *"Bring them up now!"*

———— ◆ ◆ ————

"Scheisse!" Heinz Werner shouted, red-faced. "Calamity stalks my every waking moment!" He tore a fresh cigarette from a pack, realized he already had a freshly lit one in his mouth, then crushed the unlit one to dust and tossed it on the deck. He turned to Dario, who had joined the shoot that morning. "I want someone fired. Find out who it should be, and do it!"

Dario nodded, keeping his cool. "I will look into it."

"Werner, we may have gotten sufficient footage before the leaks," Novak said. He had come aboard the *Puddingwife* as soon as the *Lunasea* could bring them alongside. "May I suggest that we skip ahead, and shoot some of the scenes with the mercenaries aboard the *Mako*? This will give maintenance time to examine the submersible, and I will have a chance to go over all of the footage."

Werner thought a moment. Novak was suggesting they shoot a scene intended for tomorrow; it was a point in the story when the mercenaries learn from an insider that the *Puddingwife* has discovered the treasure, and the mercs then go after the research ship to steal the loot. *"Ja, ja!* We skip ahead to shoot the *Mako*."

Dario grabbed the radio. "All right, everyone. Back to base."

In the early afternoon, Boone and Emily maneuvered the *Lunasea* between the shore and the Azimut 60, allowing the M&Ms a backdrop with nothing but ocean behind the mercenaries' boat. Most of the filming would occur aboard the *Mako*, but Marsha explained they needed some establishing shots, as well as a sequence where the yacht went from an idle to full speed as the bad guys raced away to intercept the *Puddingwife*. On board the *Lunasea*, a pair of safety divers were geared up, sitting on the aft ends of the dive benches. Amelia was back from her stint on the *Puddingwife*, and sat up top on the portside flybridge bench.

Boone glanced over at Emily: while one hand rested on the wheel, her other hovered near the throttle, like a gunslinger dangling fingers over the butt of a gun before a quick draw. "Managed to get the whole day off, didn't you?" Boone said. "That's not suspicious at all."

"Are you suggesting I sabotaged the sub to keep from acting this afternoon?" Em asked, dropping her hand to the throttle and nudging back the speed.

"How is Billy, by the way?"

"He texted me. He's fine. Said the leaks were small, but it's scary to see any kind of leak in a submarine, innit?"

"They figure out what happened?"

"I was there when they were examining it," Amelia said. "One of the seals was damaged in two places."

Boone frowned. "Are all movie shoots like this?"

"Well, you heard what that guy said about *Jaws*," Emily reminded him.

235

"Yeah, but... these things are happening every day. If I believed in that sorta thing, I'd almost think this movie was cursed."

Marsha poked her head up from the flybridge ladder. "Okay, they're good to go! Bring us in close to the *Mako*. Eight to ten yards."

"Right-o!" Em throttled up and swung the wheel to port, angling in toward the larger Azimut.

Marsha went back down the ladder, and Boone grabbed his binoculars from a cubby to look across at the *Mako*. A number of actors were standing in a circle on the aft deck of the yacht's flybridge, and two on-deck camera crews were off to the sides. A sound engineer had a boom mic on a long pole, his arms above his head, extending the microphone above the group. Werner stalked between the actors, holding his forefingers and thumbs up like goal posts as he framed the action about to occur. Even though the Azimut was a sizeable boat, the flybridge deck looked cramped with both cast and crew up there.

"What happens in this scene?" Boone asked Emily. He'd skimmed the script, but didn't remember many specifics.

"Well, you remember the *Puddingwife* has some researchers aboard, but that's mainly for show, 'cause she's really out there looking for a lost steamship full of gold, yeah?"

"Right," Boone said. "I remember that part. But what about this group of bad guys?"

"The mercenaries have a spy on board the *Puddingwife!*" Emily said, excited to tell the tale. "And they just heard that the treasure has been found, and so they're gonna go over there all piratey and take it!"

"So... the scene they're shooting is: 'They found the gold. Let's go steal it.'"

"Partly, yeah, but they also want to show just how bad the main mercenary is. One of his men questions his tactics, and the boss shoots him and dumps him overboard."

"And that's why we've got rescue divers aboard."

"Yep!"

Marsha popped back up, a two-way radio in hand. "Perfect spacing. Match pace with them. Speed..." She called over to confirm. "Four knots."

Emily throttled back even further. Boone could hear a flurry of commands, and the actors put on their mercenary gamefaces as the moment to shoot approached. An actor named Bernardo was playing the leader; a burly man sporting a goatee, hair buzzed close to his scalp. A crewwoman came up to the actor and brought a large semi-automatic pistol to him. Boone raised the binoculars and watched.

The woman removed the magazine and racked the slide three times, then angled the barrel up at the sun and peered inside the ejection port. Satisfied both barrel and chamber were empty, she thumbed one round out of the mag, looked at the back of it, pressed it back in, then returned the magazine to the pistol. She racked the slide, then pulled it back an inch to look into the ejection port again before finally returning the handgun to the actor.

"What on earth was that about?" Boone asked.

"Oh, that's Lucy, the armorer," Madge replied. "She's a specialist inside the props department, in charge of the firearms. We're going to have a gunshot, so she was making sure the barrel is clear and checking the blank round. This one's just a quarter load—they'll dub in a full gunshot later."

"Quarter load?" Boone asked.

"A quarter of the powder of a full blank cartridge," Madge explained.

"Is it dangerous?" Emily asked. "Shooting at someone with a blank?"

"Can be. The gases are still propelled outward with a lot of force, and could kill you if the barrel were pressed up against you. And occasionally, bits of wadding can be propelled into a target. One danger can be if an object is in the barrel at the time of firing: the propellant from the blank will blast the material out at great force, and that can be lethal. Just last year, there was a death on the set of a Western, although in that case it looks like some idiot introduced live ammunition to the set. Last I heard, they're still trying to figure out how it happened."

Emily visibly shivered. "Now you've got me nervous."

Madge waved a hand. "No need to be; Lucy's a pro. I've worked with her on three other movies. This will just be a single gunshot, and since the shot is happening at close range, the shooter won't actually point it right at the other actor. That's what alternate camera angles and edits are for."

Boone looked back across. Werner sat in a director's chair on the lower deck, the "set" above being much too cramped with actors, cameras, and the boom mic operator. The director leaned over in front of a monitor, lifting a cloth shroud over his head and the screen—no doubt to block out the glare of the tropical sun. He raised a hand to the side... then dropped it.

"Action!" Dario shouted from beside Werner.

Up top, the actors began their scene. They were speaking normally, so Boone couldn't hear them aboard the *Lunasea*. The dialogue escalated in volume, and tension appeared in the actors' bodies. The leader suddenly smiled and nodded, turning away from the man who'd been shouting at him. Boone had seen enough movies to know what would happen next.

The leader swung back around and raised his imposing-looking pistol, the barrel pointed just to the side of the man who had challenged him. A smile on his lips, the mercenary whispered a word... and pulled the trigger.

And then something clearly went wrong. The gun roared, bucking in the actor's hand. The *BANG* was extremely loud, even aboard the *Lunasea*, and the actors and crew were clearly caught off guard. The mercenary leader dropped the gun and grabbed hold of his ear, pushing a muffled scream through gritted teeth.

"Shit!" Marsha spat. "That was a full load. No one's wearing any ear protection—too many closeups!"

Emily pointed across. "Hey, there's that prop guy from last night at Beach Nuts."

The man who'd been wearing the Superman shirt the day before rushed up to the flybridge. Today's ensemble was a red shirt with a lightning-bolt Flash logo on the chest. The prop master picked up the gun and removed the magazine, staring into it. Dario dashed up to join the group. Another crewmember found the ejected round and brought it over to the armorer, who looked confused and shocked. The prop master pointed at her and said something in a tone of accusation.

The armorer held up the casing and shouted, "It's green!" loud enough to be heard over on the dive boat.

Werner remained below. Boone expected he'd be enraged, but oddly the director stared calmly over the stern, lighting up a cigarette. After a moment he shook his head. Werner appeared to be smiling, his mouth a thin line around the smoking cigarette. Boone had the impression of a tightly coiled spring. After a time, Dario came down and joined him, speaking rapidly.

Marsha came fully up the ladder to the flybridge, leaning on the port rail while she radioed across. "Talk to me. What's happening?"

"Adam is accusing Lucy of mixing up the rounds," The radio crackled back. *"But she says they're marked correctly and she test-fired one on shore. Wait one. They're trying to decide what to do."*

"You were saying something about curses?" Em murmured.

<hr />

Emily watched the activity over on the *Mako*, keeping a watchful eye on Werner. The director seemed strangely energized, snapping out commands. Dario listened attentively, relaying them via his own two-way. Activity increased on the Azimut's flybridge, and the actor who had played the victim of the leader's bullet-to-the-head shot came up to his original spot. Off to the side, another man wearing identical clothes was pulling a wig over his blond hair.

"Hey, check it out," Em said. "It's Chip, the karate Casanova stuntman."

Boone leaned on the rail and watched. "Guess they're gonna try to shoot something else..."

Marsha blew out a frustrated sigh and went to the aft railing. "Get set," she called down to the other three members of the M&Ms. "I think we're about to film the body falling in."

Across the way, Dario walked to the starboard side of the Azimut and waved at them, then adjusted his two-way and spoke. Marsha held the radio out so Boone and Emily could hear.

"Okay, listen up. First, while we set up the next shot, I need you to come alongside and pick up Lucy and Bernardo. Werner wants Lucy

off the ship—for now, it's best not to argue. And Bernardo may have burst his right eardrum. He can't hear out of that side. After you've got them, you'll return to your position and we'll shoot a scene."

"Have you lost the plot?" Em said. "You've got an actor who needs medical attention!"

"We're flying him to the hospital in Grand, and the next flight isn't for two hours. Besides, he insisted. So, we're going to shoot the victim being hit, and then the fall into the water. The safety divers will bring the stuntman aboard the Lunasea, *then you can all head into the lagoon. We'll have a car waiting for Bernardo at your condo complex. We'll continue shooting here."*

"What about the shot of the *Mako* zooming away?" Marsha asked. "You need us for that."

"We also need Bernardo for that. And we'd have to stow all of the gear out of sight, which would take a half hour at least. Werner wanted to do it, but I talked him out of it."

"Dario, you magnificent bastard. I owe you a drink for that," Marsha said, and ended the exchange. Taking in the look on Emily's face, she shrugged. "Welcome to show business." Starting down the ladder, she began barking orders. "Murray! We'll be tracking from their superstructure down to the waterline, so we need to elevate!"

Em took the wheel and slowly brought the *Lunasea* alongside the *Mako*. Boone and Amelia lowered fenders and tossed lines across at bow and stern, briefly securing the boats for the transfer. Bernardo, the goateed mercenary leader, was helped across by a well-muscled crewmember. The actor seemed unsteady, and held a wadded-up hand towel to his right ear. Em could see a bit of red on it as he came across. Lucy came over by herself, looking downtrodden.

The boats separated and the sequence began. First, the victim—the original actor—stood with his back to the starboard flybridge railing. Filmed from the front by a crew on the Azimut, and from behind by the M&Ms' rig, the man jerked and snapped his head to the side. They filmed this action of being shot over and over, with small variations, before a loud "Cut!" rang out.

Marsha was back on the flybridge ladder. "Okay, they got that one. They're going CGI for the blood. Emily, move us out about six more feet. Dario wants to get this stunt in one take, otherwise we'll be here all day, drying Chip off and cleaning up the wig."

Minutes later, the divers positioned themselves: one at the swim platform, the other sitting on the gunwale, ready for a back-roll entry. High on the Azimut flybridge, Chip took the same position as the actor he was stunt-doubling for, his back to the ocean. Cameras rolled and someone yelled "Bang!" in a loud voice. Chip jerked, went boneless, and pitched backward over the railing, hitting the ocean below with a loud smack of flesh on water.

Damn, Em thought. *The man might be a complete tosser, but he's good at his job!*

The divers went in, and moments later Chip ascended the stern ladder, bellowing a loud frat-boy shout, "Wooo!! Yeah, baby! That's how it's *done!*" He pulled the sodden wig off his blond hair and spiked it on the deck with a wet slap, like a soggy, deflated football.

Marsha rolled her eyes and triggered the two-way. "Did we get it?" The reply came in the affirmative and she turned to Emily. "Let's get the hell to shore."

21

"Tolstoy, what do you want for dinner?" Potluck called down the stairs.

"Cheeseburger and fries!"

Brooke sighed. "Could you maybe get something green, once in a while? Or sushi? I need my Omega-3s."

"What'd she say?" Potluck asked from above.

"Her Highness wants something green... or sushi. But I want a cheeseburger and fries."

"Hey, Brooke, I'll getcha a salad or something, and I promise we'll do sushi this week. And Tolstoy! Take the garbage to the curb tonight. You forgot last time."

"Go to hell!" he replied cheerfully. "Oh, wait! We are already there!"

Potluck came several steps down the stairs. "I swear, if you make that joke one more time, I will pound you flatter than hammered shit—don't think I won't."

"I love you too, *zaika*," Tolstoy replied. "Hurry back!"

Potluck shook her head and plodded back up the stairs.

Tolstoy settled in a chair and started playing some card game on his phone. Brooke adjusted the chain and lay down on the floor-mattress she'd been sitting on, arranging her shirt so it rode up her midriff a few inches.

"So... Tolstoy," Brooke began, allowing a little huskiness to kiss her vocal cords. "You and Potluck, are you... exclusive?"

"Exclusive?" Tolstoy asked, eyes locked to his game.

"I'm talking about *sex*," Brooke said, watching the word burst his bubble of card-playing concentration.

Tolstoy looked up at her and Brooke lifted a bare leg, pointing the toes and playfully sweeping them on the sheets atop her mattress. "Is Potluck the only one you have sex with? Or do you... sometimes...?" Her words trailed off and she let her eyes finish the sentence.

Tolstoy's own eyes gleamed with lust, but he suddenly smiled, shaking his head. "Ms. Bablin, you are trying to seduce me." He laughed. "Have you seen that American movie? Dustin Hoffman. Is very good." He shook his finger at Brooke. "No, no, no, little girl." He went back to his card game.

Brooke sighed. *It was worth a try.* "At least let me look at the latest gossip on the movie?"

"I am in middle of game of Durak."

"Please, Tolstoy? I'm going crazy in here."

"Okay, okay. One article only, you hear! Tell me web address."

Brooke directed him to TMZ's page and he handed her the phone. There probably wasn't anything new... but Tolstoy didn't know that. She typed in the search bar.

"What are you typing?"

"My name, silly. To find an article." She did so. But then, with the smartphone skill and speed of Generation Z, she opened a new window for Google, typed in a phrase, quickly scanned the result, then killed the window and returned to the article.

Tolstoy came around behind her and looked at the screen. "Is same photo as last time, yes?"

"Yeah," Brooke said, tinging her voice with sadness. "Nothing new." She sighed.

"Then I shall return to my game," Tolstoy said, plucking the phone from her fingers.

Well… now I know where I am, she thought.

Boone left Em at the wheel to navigate back to the lagoon and through the cut. They'd be at the dock in less than ten minutes. Below, the M&Ms were packing up camera gear, and Chip was regaling the safety divers with tales of his backward plunge— which, of course, they'd seen. Boone descended the ladder and stepped around the camera rig, making his way to Amelia, who was sitting beside a despondent-looking Lucy. He joined them on the dive bench and put a hand on the armorer's shoulder.

Lucy looked up at him. "I don't understand it. It was green. They were *all* green."

"I heard you shout that, back on the yacht. What does that mean, exactly?"

"The company we source our ammunition from marks the quarter loads with a green dot on the casing. Yellow for half loads, red for full loads. We didn't even *have* any yellows or reds on the ship! I loaded that pistol on the shore with greens and test fired it. Everything was fine. I topped the magazine off with a round from the same box!"

"Manufacturing error, maybe?" Boone suggested.

"It's not likely. They could have a lawsuit on their hands with a mistake like that. But what else could explain it?"

"The gunshot we heard..." Boone began, letting the sentence hang in the air.

"Oh, that was a full load, no doubt. And it doesn't help that it was a .44 Magnum round. The designers wanted Bernardo to have a big Desert Eagle for the intimidating appearance. Thank God they didn't go with the fifty-cal version." She shook her head. "I hope he's okay. We never fire full loads without earplugs." She wiped the corner of her eyes before saying again, "It was green."

Boone looked up and spotted Chip ascending the flybridge ladder, sparing a backward glance at Boone before vanishing up top. Emily was about to get a visitor. Boone returned his attention to Lucy. "Something screwy is going on with this movie, don't you think?"

Lucy nodded. "Things always go wrong on shoots, but... yeah. It feels like something's... odd."

Boone rose and went to Marsha. "Hey... you seem to get along with Dario, right?"

"Yeah, sure. We've worked together a bunch of times."

Boone nodded over toward the armorer. "Something was wrong with the ammo, and Lucy doesn't strike me as the kind of professional who would make that sort of mistake. Can you ask Dario to get ahold of that spent cartridge... and maybe one or two from the magazine?"

"I imagine Adam will want to examine them, in case we have to sue the ammo maker."

"Yeah, but... Em and I have a friend on the police force over in Grand. I bet we can get a professional examination from them... and it would be a neutral third party."

Marsha glanced sternward. "We're out of range for the two-way, but I can ask him on your boat's radio."

"Thanks." When she started for the ladder, he stopped her. "Wait. Better to stay below 'til we get through the cut. It can be rough."

———◆·◆———

"I can handle a little bumpy water!" Chip boasted.

"I'm sure you can," Emily said over the engine, as the *Lunasea* approached the gap in the surf. "But I'm telling you, you're going to want to hold on to something."

"You got that right." Chip leaned against the helm dashboard alongside the wheel and gave Emily a lazy leer. "I definitely wanna hold on to *something*. Know what I mean, baby?"

Em had spent the last few minutes listening to the young stuntman brag about his dead-body backward flop, even going so far as stripping off his shirt to show off the reddened skin from the impact. Then, Shirtless Chip had moved in close, claiming he didn't want to shout over the engine—he needed to save his voice, in case they asked him to replace Bernardo.

"Seriously, Chip. This is a rough passage."

"Good. I like it rough."

Okay, you tosser. I tried. Em reached the cut and floored it. Chip sat down hard, banging his tailbone on the flybridge deck with a surprised yelp. Emily spared a glance to make sure he grabbed hold of the bench beside him before locking her eyes back on the gap in the surf ahead. She'd actually timed things just right, and apart from a couple waves she had to crest, the transit was relatively smooth.

In the calm waters of the lagoon, Chip rose to his feet and jutted out his chin. "You did that on purpose."

"Well, yeah, 'course I did. I had to accelerate to make the first wave. I did warn you. Several times."

Boone appeared at the top of the ladder. "Nice one, Em! That was smooth sailing." He pulled himself up.

"You," Chip said. "You're supposed to show me your moves. While they're out there finishing the shoot, you 'n' me are going to spar." He pushed past Boone and descended to the main deck.

"Shite," Em muttered.

"What's wrong. Did he do something?"

"Just chattin' me up. Nothing I can't handle. But I may have bruised his tender ego, so watch yourself."

After Bernardo was driven away to the airstrip, Boone and Emily took Brixton for a walk along the beach. Returning to the communal area by the dock, Boone spotted Chip and his fellow stuntman, Ray, sitting in a pair of lounge chairs, a bucket of beers between them.

"There you are." Chip pressed one nostril closed and sniffed, then rose from the chair, polishing off the half a beer left in the bottle with three pulses of his Adam's apple. "I thought I told you we were going to spar when we got back."

Boone shrugged. "Had to walk the dog."

"Cute pooch," Ray said, and he seemed like he meant it. "What breed is he or she?"

"Brixton's a Belizean potlicker," Em replied. "Which is a fancy way of saying he's a mutt from Belize."

"I've got a Lab back home," Ray said. "She's a handful."

"Yeah, yeah, dogs are great," Chip said, tossing his empty in the bucket of beers with a clink. He rolled his neck and shook out his arms. "Okay, divemaster, show me some moves."

Boone glanced over at Emily and saw unease in her eyes. "Hey, Em, why don't you take Brix inside and give him his dinner."

"Aw, c'mon, you don't want to miss the show," Chip jeered.

"Let's go, Brixy." Emily led the pooch to their condo.

Boone kicked off his sandals and made his way toward an open patch of beach. He'd grown up with guys like Chip back in Tennessee, and had little doubt the "sparring" could get rough. And if Chip's boasts back at Rackam's about his martial arts rankings were truthful, he could prove a dangerous opponent. Removing Emily from the equation might deflate some of the alpha male display Chip was likely hoping for, and maybe he'd actually become interested in using some of Boone's techniques for the movie.

But just in case... Boone's bare feet reached the border between wet and dry sand. The unpredictable surface could make certain moves challenging, but he'd made a habit of training along the beach for years; the shifting sand required extra focus when it came to balance and weight distribution.

Chip stopped in the dry sand, his buddy beside him with a beer in hand. Boone stripped off his shirt and tossed it up the shore away from the surf.

"Damn, man..." Ray said. "Where'd you get that scar?"

Boone looked down, his fingertips tracing the line that ran diagonally along the ribs on his left side, the scar vividly standing out on his tanned skin.

"Machete."

Ray whistled, but Chip barked a short laugh. "Bullshit."

Boone shrugged again. "Believe what you want to believe." He started moving in a constantly shifting, triangular motion. "This is called the *ginga*. This is the standard footwork in capoeira, and many of your attacks and evasions will come out of this. The constant motion lets you rapidly change the center of balance, allowing for unpredictable moves. But I'm guessing this isn't of much interest, as far as movie-fighting."

"You got that right!" Chip crowed. "We're not shooting a music video."

"Yeah, you said that before," Boone remarked. He then launched himself into motion, whipping a butterfly kick through the air and continuing the motion into an *aú sem mão*, an impressive no-hands cartwheel that brought him to the side before finishing with a *macaco* back handspring, snapping another kick through the air as he retreated.

"Whoa!" Ray cried. "That is rad!"

"That's not *rad*, it's stupid," Chip scoffed. "You're not grounded at all. Looks more like a dance than fighting."

"Good eye," Boone replied, refusing to rise to the bait. "The slaves in Brazil incorporated dance into the moves to disguise the fighting techniques they were really practicing."

"Thanks for the history lesson, but you don't get to explain things to moviegoers. You have to *show* them."

Chip took a rooted, unmoving stance before exploding into motion. Pushing out gusts of breath with each move, he fired off a flurry of solid punches and kicks, even uttering a series of Bruce Lee-ish shrieks on one sequence. Boone recalled that Chip had mentioned tae kwon do, karate, and some other thing that started with a "K" that he'd never heard of. He looked like he knew his stuff, but when he attempted a spinning back-kick, the sand under his anchor foot slid and he stumbled back and fell.

Ray snickered, but Chip flipped himself from his back to his feet with an impressive handspring, called a "kip-up." He gave Ray a look, and the man stifled his mirth. Chip sniffed again, wiping his nose, then took off his sunglasses and held them out for Ray to take.

Boone now noticed Chip's pupils were very dilated, and he realized the stuntman may have preceded the beers with a little something up his nose. He decided to try flattery to cool the man down. "Great kip-up!" Boone said, smiling. "Flawless execution. That's almost a capoeira move, the *macaco mola*... springing monkey." Boone hurled himself back into the sand and sprang back up in an instant.

Chip watched the move. "Springing monkey, huh? Yeah, you've certainly got the look, Boone. What's that monkey with the super-long arms?" Chip waved his arms above his head and hooted.

"Gibbon," a voice answered. "But they're not monkeys. They're apes." Emily strode onto the beach. "Boone, I'm hungry. Let's get some dinner."

"Oh, no, no, no," Chip said. "Your boyfriend and I haven't sparred yet!"

"We can do this tomorrow morn—" Boone began, but cut himself off with a backwards cartwheel when Chip spun a kick at him, then launched himself into a sideways tumble when the stuntman kept coming. When Chip shot yet another kick at him, Boone suddenly halted his acrobatic retreats, stepping in to his attacker and sweeping Chip's supporting leg out from under him with a *banda de costas* before the stuntman's kick was even halfway to its target.

Chip went down hard. Laughing without mirth, he picked himself off the ground, brushing sand from his arms, nodding and smiling, eyes pointedly *not* looking in Boone's direction.

Classic sucker-punch fake-out, Boone thought. When the attack came, Boone simply shifted to the side and tumbled away from the three-punch combo. Frustrated, Chip came on. He switched up his techniques and when Boone came out of an evasive maneuver, Chip suddenly shifted his weight and executed a feint that Boone fell for, managing to land a punch with the other fist that Boone practically tumbled into. He sprawled out on the surf line.

Emily cried out. "Stop! That's enough!"

"Hey, Chip. Let's get back to the room," Ray urged.

"Aw, c'mon, it's just getting good!" Chip advanced on the prone Boone.

The lanky divemaster executed a fake-out of his own; Boone dug a size-thirteen foot into the sand before suddenly coming to life, whipping a *martelo de negativa* from the ground. The powerful ground-kick hurled a sizeable hunk of wet sand and salt water into Chip's face.

Chip staggered back. "Cheap shot," he gasped, grabbing Ray's beer from the man's hand and pouring some on his face and wiping at his eyes.

"This has gone far enough," Boone said, rising from the sand.

"What, afraid I'll drop you in front of your girlfriend?" Chip bounced on his toes, dancing around Boone's flank. "She's got a hot little body, doesn't she?" He spared a lecherous glance up at Emily. "Love those little pigtails she's got today—gives you something to hang onto, am I right?" Then he growled, soft enough that only Boone could hear: "Man… I would totally *wreck* that."

Emily could count the number of times on her fingers she'd seen Boone lose his temper. Chip looked at her and said something to Boone—she couldn't hear exactly what, but she guessed it was crude from the lewd look on Chip's face. As for the look on Boone's face... well, Em wasn't sure she'd ever seen it before. His eyes went dead, and his expression turned to stone.

Chip laughed, having finally gotten a rise out of his stoic opponent. He stepped in, shooting a trio of punches at Boone's face. Instead of evading or tumbling aside, Boone batted two away with simple blocks before weaving outside the third, catching Chip's punch in a painful wrist lock. Chip's face contorted in a grimace.

"We're done," Boone said. "Last chance." He released the lock with a shove and Chip sprawled back. Snarling, the stuntman came at him again.

"Ray!" Emily cried out. "Boone's not fucking around! Stop Chip!"

Unfortunately, Ray was too slow to act. As Chip attacked, Boone spun his body away from the stuntman's advance, but suddenly swung back toward him, slicing a kick through the air, a mere inch from Chip's face. As the man staggered back, Boone continued spinning, sending another kick, and a third, driving Chip back, each kick *almost* connecting. Emily didn't know the Brazilian Portuguese words for the capoeira moves, but she recognized this as a "compass half-moon kick," a move Boone had told her was very dangerous. Just when she thought a fourth half-moon was coming, Boone suddenly grounded himself and snapped a conventional-looking kick straight into Chip's abdomen. The man doubled over immediately, flopped to his knees, and retched into the sand.

Emily moved closer. "Boone...?"

Some of the tension seemed to leave Boone's body as he looked down at Chip. Ray stepped forward and Boone merely lifted his eyes, locking them onto the other stuntman.

"Hey, you and me got no beef," Ray said, raising his hands and moving forward slowly—like one might approach a snarling dog—even though Boone was dead still and making no aggressive moves. Ray knelt by Chip. "He can be an idiot. I'll take him back to the room."

Boone suddenly crouched, and Ray tensed as Boone placed his face level with him. "Whatever he's been snorting, flush it. This movie shoot's got enough crap going on as it is. If I see him coked up on the set, things will not end well. Hear me?"

"Loud and clear." Ray grabbed hold of Chip and hauled him away—still dry heaving—toward the street.

Emily reached out to Boone and he raised a hand, giving her a sad smile. "Gimme a sec." He snatched his shirt out of the sand and went over to Chip and Ray's bucket of beers. Grabbing one, he twisted it open, plinked the cap into the aluminum bucket, and drank a third of it before setting it back into the ice.

Em touched his lower back and gently rubbed the sand-covered skin. "Are you okay?"

"Yeah. Sorry about that. Kinda snapped."

"Most people would've snapped three or four times before you finally did. The man's an utter twat."

"I suppose. I don't like losing it like that."

Emily recalled Boone telling her of a time back on Bonaire when a drunk man with a knife had pushed his dear friend Martin to the ground outside of the old man's "snack," a type of simple eatery in the Dutch Caribbean islands. Martin had been a kind of father figure to Boone—his own father having left him and his mother when he was fairly young.

"You told me once… about that man who attacked Martin."

"Yeah. Lost it then, too. Fractured the guy's skull with a *meia-lua de compasso.*"

"Is that the same crazy kick that you did right at Chip's face?"

Boone nodded. "Same kick. But this time I wasn't trying to connect; I did those to get him off-balance. I guess I wasn't completely off the rails. I was planning on dropping him with that *pointeira* kick to the gut from the moment he came at me again. Wouldn't want to mess up an actor's pretty face."

"Or skull," Emily said, trying to lighten the mood. "Though a little 'dain bramage' might actually be an improvement for Chippy."

Boone huffed a little laugh.

There's my Boone, she thought with some relief. She grabbed the beer he'd started and took a healthy pull from it, then handed it to him. "Here. Quench that rage. Seriously, Boone, you were one scary-ass muthafucka."

"A what?" Boone gave her a crooked grin. "Who are you, and what have you done with Emily?"

"Just channeling a little Samuel L. Jackson. I'm not all-Britishy all the time, you know. Hey… um… what did Chip say, that…?"

"Nothing worth repeating." Boone drained the beer. "Let's go get dinner."

22

The sun rose to the left of Owen Island, splashing pinks and oranges across the sky. Boone stood at the gunwale alongside Emily, helping the last of the cast and crew across from the dock. They had a full boat, and would be shuttling a second load out to the *Puddingwife* once this group was delivered.

"All aboard who's coming aboard!" Em cried.

"I've got this," Boone said. "You're performing today. Better run your lines."

"Most of today is an underwater shoot," she replied. "So, mostly hand signals. And Amelia's skippering today, Boone. So don't hog the wheel."

"You're the wheel hog in this dive op."

"Guilty as charged. Oink, oink." Emily pushed her button nose up like a pig.

"Very attractive," Boone said with a smile.

"Oh, thank you, my good man," Daniel Wolfit said, as Boone helped the old actor come aboard from the dock.

"Mister W! Ready to do some acting?" Emily asked.

Wolfit launched into a brogue, graveling his voice and squinting an eye at her. "Bluebeard always be ready, young missy! Yaarrrr."

Billy Faust arrived, taking a last huff on a vape pen before taking Cindy's hand and passing her off to Boone. He followed, and Boone wrinkled his nose as he caught a whiff of what the young actor had been vaping.

"Whoa. What happened to the Funnel Cake?"

Billy laughed. "Hey, that's an afternoon dessert. It's breakfast time. I went with Maple Bacon."

"It's disgusting," Cindy said with a giggle, sounding more amused than repulsed.

"Back for you in a few!" Boone called to the M&Ms, who had arrived and were assembling their gear.

Minutes later, Amelia took the *Lunasea* through the cut and steered west, passing by the *Mako*, which was moored at Grundy's Gardens, close to the channel into the lagoon. Beyond lay the *Puddingwife*, which was being moored at the Black Hole dive site, south of the airstrip. They came alongside and Amelia snugged up against the stern platform. The crew had attached additional padding to that location, and they assisted in bringing the passengers across.

"See you around!" Emily said to Boone, as she took his hand and prepared to step over to the *Puddingwife*.

Boone maintained the grip for a moment before looking into her eyes. "Be careful today, okay?"

"I will," Em replied, giving his hand a little squeeze before stepping across. A young man with a radio snatched her up immediately, and Boone watched as she scurried toward a shaded area with makeup tables.

"Mr. Fischer!" The first assistant director, Dario, came to the stern and reached out a hand. "I've got something for you."

Boone held his hand out and Dario pressed a small, cold object into his palm. A blank cartridge.

"Marsha said you know someone with the police over on Grand Cayman?"

"Yeah," Boone said. "What about the one that was fired?"

"Props has all of them under lock and key. They want to do their own investigation. Probably sue the company."

"How'd you get this one?"

Dario looked over his shoulder, then back to Boone. "Something fishy is going on. So, I snagged one out of the box of spares Lucy had filled the magazine from before everything got locked up."

"Good thinking. Thanks. Hey, how's Bernardo?"

"An acoustic trauma, they called it. Not too serious, but the injury will affect his hearing and sense of balance. So, we'll need to reshoot, with one of the other mercenaries moving up to play his part."

"Not Chip...?"

"Chip? God, no. Besides, he's too valuable as a stuntman." Dario leaned in. "Running that blank by your police contact... please keep that under your hat. And you didn't get it from me."

Dario turned and was talking on his radio in moments, all business. Boone made sure it was just himself and Amelia left aboard, then they cast off, Amelia slowly motoring away from the *Puddingwife*. Boone climbed to the flybridge and sat on a bench, looking at the little brass object.

The cartridge looked like most handgun ammunition he'd seen, but instead of a bullet at the tip, there were six metal flaps bent toward the center, like the triangular petals on a budding flower. Boone guessed this was where the gasses that made the "boom" pushed through. On the base of the cartridge, a green dot had been added. Boone peered at it closely, looking for any scratches or signs that there might have been some red on there. He couldn't see anything amiss. He pulled out his phone and took some photos. When he was back at the dock and loading began for the second run, he would hop off and grab some Wi-Fi from the condo, sending the pics to AJ Bailey along with a message for Nora.

———— ◆ ◆ ◆ ————

"He really likes you," Silva said. Ulysses had jumped across from Wolfit during a rehearsal and perched on Emily's shoulder, playing with her braided pigtails. She'd suggested the hairstyle, since they were doing an underwater shoot after this short scene, and she wouldn't get it tangled in the mask strap. The monkey was fascinated with the braids, playfully tugging on the nearest one.

Werner watched Ulysses. "Very well. As discussed, if the monkey goes to you while cameras are rolling, play the scene accordingly."

"Will do!" Em said. "But before you yell 'action,' can we maybe change out his nappy?"

"Oh, thaaaat's what that is..." Billy said, wrinkling his nose.

"Sorry!" the wrangler said, taking Ulysses away to change the primate's diaper.

"Take five, then we will shoot this scene." Werner shook out a cigarette and started to leave.

"Mr. Werner, can I ask you something?" Em began, hesitant.

"Of course."

"Did you know an actress named Michelle Reynolds?"

Werner looked at her as he lit the cigarette. "I am assuming that you are very much aware that I knew her. Ask your real question."

Emily took a deep breath. "I just… well… I'm sorry, it's not appropriate. I shouldn't have brought it up."

"It is certainly an unpleasant topic of discussion," Werner said, looking more sad than angry. "And what happened to that poor woman was a tragedy." He blew out a cloud of smoke. "But if one of the questions skulking about in your head is 'Did I sleep with her?' the answer is no, a thousand times no!"

Emily nodded, waiting for more.

Werner sighed. "I knew she had a substance-abuse problem. This is something I struggled with myself at film university. It was affecting her work, so I met with her in her trailer on location in Idaho. I attempted an intervention. We were in there for hours. There were tears. In the end, she was better for several days, but then relapsed and production was called off."

"So… it was just a rumor. The affair."

"This rumor had good kindling. When I left her trailer late in the evening, a member of the cast saw me exit, and the whispers began." Werner gave a rueful laugh and shook his head. "Ironically, she was indeed having an affair during the shoot. With one of the producers, apparently. I never learned which one."

"And her death…" Emily let the half-finished statement hang in the air.

Werner smoked in silence before speaking abruptly. "This is not a subject I wish to discuss right before I am about to do my work. And you should be focusing on *your* work, Ms. Durand." He turned away and went around a corner of the ship's superstructure.

"You okay?" Billy asked, huffing on his vape pen.

Emily grimaced. "I *was*, but then you walked up with your stink flute. Blimey, it smells like… hickory-smoked farts."

Billy laughed. "Nope. Still bacon. But after the dive, I'll switch back to Funnel Cake if it'll make you happy."

"Happy, no… slightly less revolted, yes. Yeesh. Ulysses's diaper was better."

———◆•◆———

After the three-header scene with Billy and Wolfit was complete, Emily prepared for the underwater shoot. With Em's permission—and after a formal rental agreement and stipend was arranged—the camera department's drone operator had brought the UPC aboard, and would operate it from the *Puddingwife*. The scene would involve Ethan, the handsome marine biologist, taking Sarah on a dive to show her the wonders of the ocean while the treasure salvage part of the operation was prepared. Ironically, Em felt like she was the one showing him.

"You nervous?" she asked.

"Uh… a little, I guess. I finished my certification in New York right after I booked the gig. Did my open water dives in some rock quarry in Pennsylvania."

"So… you've never dived before? Apart from swimming pools and rock quarries?"

"I did a few dives in Grand Cayman, right after I came down."

"You know your signals?"

Billy gave her a smile and an enthusiastic thumbs-up.

"What is that?"

"Thumbs-up! I'm saying yes, I know my signals."

"Billy... a thumbs-up means ascend. You want the 'OK' signal."

"Oh. Jeez."

"You'll be fine. Stick close to me—we'll muddle through."

They suited up in their wetsuits. Emily had wanted to use her own gear—maybe one of her colorful dive skins—but the costume department had rightly pointed out that she'd just been rescued, wearing nothing more than a bikini. Realistically, she'd have to wear whatever the research ship had aboard, and most of Emily's personal gear trended toward eye-blinding lime greens and pinks. That being said, while Billy wore a full body, three-millimeter suit, they'd somehow managed to outfit Emily in a figure-hugging shorty wetsuit with a front zipper—something no self-respecting oceanography vessel would have on board. *Oh well... sex sells*, she thought, as she zipped it up as high as it would go.

The minutes ticked by, and Em watched an underwater film crew descend. The ship had gone to the north side and moored at Great Wall East, where they had gotten permission to shoot after Boone learned they wanted a shallow scene right on top of the drop-off. The top of Bloody Bay Wall at the Great Wall East and West dive sites was relatively shallow, and Emily knew the spot Boone had recommended: a patch of sand at about twenty feet in depth, just above a jaw-dropping vertical plunge. *Like looking over the edge of a skyscraper's roof,* Emily had thought the first time she'd seen the drop.

Across the way, the *Lunasea* kept station. Boone was below, talking with the camera crew. Two safety divers slipped into the water from the dive boat. Up top, Amelia caught Em's eye and they exchanged waves. A huffing sound over her shoulder drew her attention, and her nostrils were assaulted with fairground pastry.

"Really? Right before you stick a regulator in your mouth?"

"*Especially* right before I stick a regulator in my mouth." Billy took another pull on the vape pen. "It calms my nerves," he said through a cloud of exhaled vapor.

"At least you ditched the Rancid Pig's Snout flavor."

He laughed. "Yeah. I was going to switch it after the dive, but I think Cindy snuck over to my stuff and got rid of it. Funnel Cake was in the pen instead. She hated the Maple Bacon one."

"So... Cindy, huh?" Emily waggled her eyebrows.

"She's cool," Billy said, cagey.

"And drop-dead gorgeous."

"I suppose."

Pretending to cough, Emily barked out the word, "Show-mance!" then thumped her chest with a fist. "Sorry... little frog in my throat."

Grinning, Billy shook his head and went to grab the rest of his gear. Emily looked across at the *Lunasea*. One of the safety divers was returning and Boone was helping the man onto the swim platform. On the flybridge, Amelia was leaning on the aft railing, looking down with concern.

◆ ◆ ◆

"I'm okay, I think," the safety diver said, sitting on the swim platform of the *Lunasea*. "Just threw up in my regulator. Must've been something I ate."

Boone brought the man some water, which he drank carefully. "Do they have a backup?" Boone asked.

"Yeah, but by the time we got one... hell no. I'll go back down. If Werner has another delay, heads are going to roll. I'll be fine in a minute."

"You're green."

The man suddenly pivoted and vomited over the side. Boone turned and stepped around the M&Ms' camera quadpod, going below to the little storage cabin where he'd stowed his gear beside the marine head. Bringing it back, he set it by a bench at the stern and selected a tank. The man looked up at him, miserable.

"I've gotcha covered," Boone said. "Now tell me what to do."

◆ ◆ ◆

"You two ready?" Jerry, the 2nd AD, asked.

"Let's do this!" Billy said. He and Emily were sitting on a small, four-tank dive bench near the stern. Billy took a last pull on his vape pen and looked around for a place to put it.

Em plucked the evil contraption from his fingertips. "Here's a basic dive tip. Keep your gear bag under your bench."

"Oh… yeah. It's way back there…"

"And now you've got big flapping fins on, Fausty. No worries, I'll tuck it in my bag and mayyyyybe I'll give it back to you, if you promise to get some less-disgusting flavors." She leaned over and zipped it into a waterproof pouch at one end of her bag before shrugging into her BCD.

After Billy finished gearing up, two crewmembers helped them to the stern platform, and they stepped off with giant strides into the turquoise waters.

Emily was immediately aware of an underwater camera crew about ten feet down, capturing from below their plunge into the sea. Billy was to her side, and immediately began signaling her, as the script called for. He pointed with a flattened hand toward the coral below and flashed her a questioning "OK" sign. She replied back with an "OK" of her own, and followed the young actor down. Ahead of them, she could see the UPC drone, filming their descent from another angle.

Glancing off to the left through her mask, she spotted a safety diver keeping a respectful distance, but close enough to get to either actor in seconds with a fin-assisted sprint, if the need arose. Reaching Billy at the bottom, she leveled off near the vertical drop-off of Bloody Bay Wall. Billy sent some signals her way and she replied, pretending to be nervous. He took out a slate and wrote on it, then held it out for her—and for the camera she knew was behind her shoulder.

You'll be fine. Follow me.

She started to signal, but the other safety diver drifted just inside her field of vision on the sandy side of the drop… and his long limbs looked familiar. *Boone!*

A metallic *BONG BONG BONG* sounded in the water; the agreed-upon signal for "Cut!"

Shite. I must've reacted when I saw Boone. Knowing that shooting was halted, she turned to face him. Locking her eyes on his, she pointed at him, then gave an exaggerated shrug. *You! What are you doing here?*

Boone pointed toward the surface, then rubbed his stomach and waggled a hand like something was "so-so." He then tapped his chest and held his arms out, like he was saying "Ta-da!"

Emily took this sequence to mean that someone topside had gotten sick, and Boone had taken over. She flashed an "OK" just as another slate appeared near her mask. One of the underwater camera crew was alongside her, wearing a full-face mask. The *Puddingwife* had a transducer cable suspended over the side, allowing Werner to communicate with the camera crew when they were within range.

The underwater cameraman's slate read: *Werner says to stay focused!* And below that: *Ascend twenty feet, then descend to the same spot and do the scene again.* The crewmember showed it to Billy, then headed back to the rest of the underwater unit.

Emily held up an "OK" sign, first flashing it toward the UPC—where Werner was likely watching her from—then holding the signal back over her shoulder to the underwater camera unit. She ascended slowly, looking down at Billy. The actor was still in position, waving his palm at the bottom, making little whorls of sand float in the slight current. He glanced up at her and she jerked a thumbs-up.

He nodded, and held a thumbs-up back at her, then seemed to laugh into his regulator, swatting his head with his other hand and switching to an "OK" sign. He came up to join her—ascending a little too quickly for Emily's taste. She'd have to talk with him about that once the shoot was over. She looked over at his slate, which still had the lines he'd written on it. Em pulled her sleeve up over her hand and reached over, erasing the message so he'd have a blank slate for the next take. Billy watched, then said something garbled into his regulator that might have been: "Oh, yeah! Thank you!"

A single *BONG* rang out, the call for "Action."

Billy looked around. Emily flashed a thumbs-down at him. Behind his mask, she could see his eyebrows bunch up, but then he nodded and started down. In moments, they reached the same spot in the sand and repeated the scene. They got to the part where Emily acted nervous, and Billy wrote on the slate. He took a little longer with it, but eventually held it up.

Youl be fine follow me.

The handwriting was sloppier than before, and "you'll" was misspelled, but that wasn't what stood out. Underneath the words, Billy had drawn a smiley face.

Emily wrinkled her brow and tilted her head. She expected to hear the triple tank-bang calling for "cut," but it didn't happen. *They must've gotten Billy's slate in the first take,* she thought, *and they don't want to stop again.*

Billy turned and headed for the drop-off, kicking up a cloud of sand as he left the bottom. The slate dangled free, the actor not having returned it to the BCD pocket.

Something's wonky, Em thought. She started after him, as was called for in the shoot script. Without turning her head, she shifted her eyes to the side, spotting Boone. He was locked onto Billy, his posture alert. *Boone sees it, too.*

Emily reached the drop-off and angled down, only to discover Billy was not waiting at the top of the wall as planned, but was some twenty feet below her, upside down and kicking down along the vertical surface, arms out to his sides like an airplane. He somersaulted and inverted, looking back up along the wall. Seeing Emily, he waved, his eyes big behind his mask, a smile rimming the regulator's mouthpiece.

Oh, shite. Alarmed, Em broke character and raised a splayed hand horizontally level and vigorously rocked it back and forth, signaling *Something's wrong!* She found Boone above on her right, and the other safety diver above her on the left. Pointing down at Billy with her other hand, she inverted and dove down after him. Pinching her nose, she equalized quickly, trying to keep up with the rapid increase in pressure. Out of the corner of her eye, she spotted Boone already rocketing down.

Billy saw Boone coming at him and tensed. Turning, he kicked hard, angling down and away, bringing him close to the other safety diver. The man managed to cut him off, holding up his hands, signaling *Stop* and *Slow down/Calm down*. Billy plowed into him, and flailed at the man, knocking the safety diver's mask loose before kicking upward, ascending much too rapidly. The nitrogen in his blood—compressed from the greater pressure of deeper water—could expand and form bubbles, triggering decompression sickness.

Emily intercepted him, reaching out to grab his vest at the shoulder. She put her mask level with his and was about to signal him to calm down when he suddenly pushed at her, his hand connecting with her chin, rocking her head back and knocking her regulator free of her mouth. Em had lost her reg a number of times over the years and it was nothing to be concerned about just yet. She maintained her grip on his BCD, and tried to get through to the young actor, but his eyes were wild. He reached for her mask.

Boone arrived. Coming from over Billy's shoulders, he thrust his long arms down along the man's forearms, then pulled back as he dropped behind him, effectively pinning Billy's arms against his tank and arresting his ascent. The man struggled, losing his own regulator.

Quick as a flash, Emily plucked her yellow, spare regulator from her side and pressed it between the man's lips. *I'll need my own pretty soon,* she thought, releasing a gentle stream of bubbles from her mouth. *But first...* She put her eyes level with Billy's and reached out with a knuckle, giving his mask plate a gentle tap-tap-tap. He looked at her.

She backed off just slightly and signaled, slowly and deliberately, pointing at him, pointing at herself, then giving him a thumbs-up, followed by a flattened hand, gently moving up and down. *You. Me. Ascend. Slowly.*

Billy blinked, then nodded. The trio began to kick gently upward toward the sparkling glow of sunlight on the surface.

Emily felt rubber against her lips and opened them as she realized the other safety diver was pressing her lost regulator to her mouth. Holding onto the reg, she blew a blast to clear it, keeping her eyes locked on Billy's. Gone was the wildness of before, replaced by confusion or bewilderment.

Taking their time, the divers rose along the sheer wall, ascending toward shallower waters.

23

"**Y**ou're bleeding," Boone said, when Emily came to the surface. There was a trickle of blood on her upper lip.

"Am I? Thought I tasted something. He smacked me pretty hard when I lost the reg. I'll have supermodel lips in the morning."

"You have great lipssss…" Billy managed.

"Why thank you, Billy. Keep swimming, 'kay?"

Boone had fully inflated both of their BCDs, and now guided the actor toward the *Lunasea*. The other safety diver swam alongside, and Emily followed.

"What's the plan?" she asked Boone.

"I'm taking him straight to Salt Rock Dock. Amelia will radio for someone to pick us up. There's a flight across to Grand in about an hour. We'll pass the Little Cayman Clinic on the way to the airstrip, so maybe the nurse on duty can see him." Boone looked to the other diver. "Hey… it's Steve, right?"

"Yeah."

"Nice work, heading him off. You got down there fast."

271

"It's my job. Glad you two kept it together. What do you think? Nitrogen narcosis?"

"I doubt it," Boone said. "We weren't all that deep." Nitrogen narcosis, or "rapture of the deep," affected everyone differently, but usually, a diver had to be below one hundred feet for any extreme behavior, like hallucinations. And this had been a full-blown freak-out. "When he started descending down the wall," Boone continued, "you reached him at about seventy feet, give or take?"

"Sounds about right. I was too busy rescuing my mask to check."

"He was acting barmy in the sand, at just twenty feet," Emily noted.

"Hang onto his tank," Boone suggested to Steve. "Mark it and keep it separate. Maybe some kind of contaminant."

Boone reached the stern of the *Lunasea*. The safety diver who'd been sick was waiting on the swim platform, ready to assist. Everyone knew what had happened, of course; the entire incident had been captured on film.

Emily waited in the water while Boone and Steve got Billy up the stern ladder, and the other safety diver guided him to a bench to remove his gear.

"Emily," Boone said, helping Em over to a spot beside Billy, "stay with Billy. Keep him calm. I'm gonna radio the *Pudding*."

"Right-o," Em said.

Boone looked up to see Amelia at the aft rail of the flybridge. "Amelia, take us to Salt Rock Dock!"

"You got it!" she called back, disappearing from view.

"What happened?" Marsha asked, as Boone once more squeezed past their camera rig, heading for the flybridge ladder.

"Not sure. But we're taking him ashore." He went up the ladder and triggered the radio to the frequency they'd agreed upon, Channel 72. *"Lunasea to Pudding."*

"Pudding *here. Go ahead."*

"Billy Faust had some kind of episode. We're heading to Salt Rock Dock. It's only a mile from our current position. Contact the shore, and have someone send a car there, ASAP."

"Understood. Where are you taking him?"

"Clinic first, airstrip after, if needed. We'll fill you in once we're on the move."

With the *Lunasea*'s impressive speed, they'd be at the pier long before whoever they sent, but maybe they'd get lucky and be able to flag down someone. Folks on Little Cayman were a friendly bunch, and rides were freely offered.

Boone quickly stripped out of his wetsuit and pulled on his T-shirt and shorts. He felt for his phone and found it, along with an unfamiliar object. *Oh… right. The blank round Dario gave me.*

"Bugger me, my clothes are over on the *Pudding*," Em said, pulling off the shorty wetsuit. "And once again, I'm running around in nothing but a swimsuit."

"Well, we can't have that," Boone said, giving her his T-shirt, an XLT with an artist's rendering of the island of Saba on it, and the logo *I Climbed Mount Scenery.* "You steal this one all the time, anyway."

"I told you, I lost mine. Or Brixton ate it." She pulled it over her head and let it drop; on her diminutive body, the long shirt almost reached her knees.

In less than two minutes, the blocky chunk of concrete that served as Little Cayman's shipping port was in view, and the dive boat approached carefully. This wasn't a protected dock, like the ones in the lagoon. But the very calm seas that had tempted the production to begin shooting there early were still in play, and Amelia was able to drop off Billy, Emily, and Boone without too much difficulty. She then backed away from the concrete slab and headed back out to the *Puddingwife*.

"Werner's going to be pissed if I don't get back," Em said. "But I have to stay with Billy."

"Agreed," said Boone. The young actor had clung to her on the boat ride—if he went cuckoo bananas again, Emily's rapport with Billy would be more likely to calm him down.

As they walked from the concrete pier to the hot pavement of the offloading area, Boone spied a white pickup with lettering declaring "Department of Environment" along the truck bed's paneling. The truck was empty, but Boone could hear banging and clanging coming from one of the shipping containers that stood between the road and the dock, combined with a stream of curses in what sounded like German, capped by a triumphant cry.

"Ich habe dich, du kleiner Bastard!" echoed in the metal container.

"Katja?" Boone called out.

More muttering and banging, then Katja appeared, locks of her hair plastered against her sweat-soaked face, her tank top and shorts smudged from her battle inside the container. Triumphantly, she raised a small green iguana over her head.

"Boone! Emily! I got the little…" She trailed off. "What's wrong with him?" she asked, looking at Billy with concern.

"Not sure," Em said. "Can you take us to the clinic? And maybe to the airport?"

"Yes, of course! One moment." Katja carried the iguana toward the pickup. "I usually check the shipping containers when they come in for these invasive iguanas, but it occurred to me I hadn't looked in the two that have been sitting here awhile." She leaned into the truck bed and guided the little green reptile into a bag, which she then cinched closed. Satisfied, she went to the driver's side door. "Hop in!"

Although the pickup wasn't large, it was a four-door with a back cabin. Boone helped Emily and Billy into the back and joined Katja up front. Boone's phone rang just as Katja's tires crunched onto the hard-pack and headed east along the North Coast Road.

"Hello?"

"Boone, it's Dario. Leonard's on his way to get you."

"Actually, we just got a ride. Have him meet us at the clinic, okay? It's on Spot Bay Road, north of the airport. Right before the little police station."

"How is Billy doing?"

"One sec." Boone turned around. "Billy... talk to me. How are you feeling?"

Billy raised his head from Emily's shoulder, where he'd nuzzled in for a nap. "Hmm? Oh, hey Boone. Umm... I'm feeling... *really* good." He raised his glazed eyes toward the roof of the truck, as if he saw something there. "I think... I think I might be tripping."

"Yeah, I'd say that's a safe bet..." Boone said. He returned to the call. "Dario, he's all right, I think."

"What happened?" the 1st AD asked.

Boone was about to share his suspicions, but suddenly realized he didn't know much about Dario. He was a pretty good judge of character, and his interactions with the man had been positive, but still... he hesitated. Then he said: "Not sure. I'm just a shmuck who dives for a living, so I'm gonna get a professional to take a look."

"Okay," Dario said. "I'll redirect Leonard to the clinic. Talk soon."

Katja approached Spot Bay Road and slowed, turning right to head south toward the interior of the flat little island. "Hey, Boone... someone at Beach Nuts said you got into a fight."

Oh boy, here we go, Boone thought. But all he said was, "Really?"

Katja took her eyes off the road for a moment, giving him a knowing look. "Yes, really. And that you wiped the floor with him."

"He started it!" Emily protested from the back. "And yeah. Boone kicked his arse."

"Good," Katja said with a tight smile. "After you left on Sangria Sunday, he was hitting on me and every other woman at the bar. The man has a *Backpfeifengesicht.*"

"Yikes," Em said. "Is that contagious?"

Boone turned in his seat. "What on earth is... whatever you said?"

"*Backpfeifengesicht.* Face that needs a punch."

———— ◆ ◆ ————

The truck passed the small, gray building that housed the island's police station and turned into the next driveway, skirting the chain link fence to pull up next to the Little Cayman Clinic. Leonard was standing next to his rental car and waved at them as they came to a stop. Boone helped Emily with Billy. He seemed more alert, now... but a bit spacey.

"Thanks for the ride, Katja," Em said. "Now get back out there and keep making the world safe for iguanas!"

"Actually, I need to return to the museum. This was my lunch break."

And with that, Katja sped off to the south. Leonard went ahead of them to hold open the clinic door. "I spoke to the nurse. She's waiting for you."

After Emily recounted Billy's strange underwater behavior, the nurse—a Jamaican woman with a musical voice—took the actor's blood pressure and examined him closely. "Elevated blood pressure, pupils dilated... Mr. Faust, did you take anyt'ing today?"

Billy looked up from a close study of his palm. "Hmm?"

"I asked if you'd taken anyt'ing today?"

"I took a boat... to another boat. Oh! Wait, I know what you're asking. Uh..." He frowned, thinking. "A motion sickness pill?"

The nurse smiled and shook her head. "I'm not talking about somet'ing like that... did you take anyt'ing... *else?*"

Billy still seemed fuzzy, but he appeared to rouse at the implication. "What, like drugs? No, ma'am! I drink beer, but I haven't even done pot since high school."

The nurse glanced at a calendar on the wall and looked at her watch. Boone noted times written on every day of the month, and realized it was the current Cayman Airways schedule. "There's no lab here to test a blood sample, so I'd like to get you across to either the Brac or Grand Cayman."

"Boone said that might be needed," Leonard said. "We've already arranged two seats to Grand on the next flight."

"I'll go with him," Em offered.

"No. I'm going," Leonard insisted. "Werner was crystal clear; once Billy was taken care of, he wanted you two back."

"Well, whoever's going," the nurse said, "you'll want to get a move on. The plane for Grand will be coming over from the Brac right now."

Leonard helped Billy off the exam table and guided him toward the exit, Emily talking softly to him. Boone started to follow, but halted.

"You okay?" the nurse asked. "Don't tell me you took somet'ing, too."

"What? Oh, no… just wondered if you might have an envelope I could borrow."

The nurse seemed amused. "That's a new one. Usually, it's requests for free samples of painkillers or antibiotics." She went to a little office area, opened a drawer and slapped a stack of envelopes on the desk. "We used to send out bills, but everyt'ing's electronic nowadays. Help yourself."

"Thanks." Boone grabbed an envelope and pointed at a pen. "May I?"

"Nice manners! You may."

Boone smiled as he took the pen and wrote on the envelope. Then he reached into his pocket, took out the blank round, dropped it in the envelope, and sealed it.

Emily looked over at her seatmate. Billy Faust appeared more lucid now, but seemed somewhat anxious. Em decided to go the playful route to suss him out. "How are things in the brain of Billy?" she asked.

"Billy is not sure," he said. "Billy is seeing stuff he knows isn't there… but he's feeling pretty damn amazing." He managed to focus on her face. "What happened to your lip?"

"Oh, I probably bit it." Emily looked toward the clinic. *Where the hell is Boone—oh, there he is.*

Boone came out and jumped into the passenger seat beside Leonard, who put the rental car in gear and turned left onto Spot Bay Road.

"What were you up to, Boone?" Em asked. "Getting a free checkup?"

"Needed to grab something." He took out his phone and started texting.

"Who are you texting?"

"Nora. AJ Bailey gave me her number when I contacted her this morning. Gimme a sec. It's gonna be a long text and I suck at typing on tiny keyboards."

In minutes, they pulled up alongside the little air terminal and got out. An intern ran up to Leonard and handed him a small suitcase. "Thanks."

"Sure thing. Some extra clothes and toiletries, like you said."

"Here." Leonard handed the kid the car keys. "Take it back to Conch Club and leave the keys with the desk."

"Actually, hang on a tick!" Emily said, before the intern could hop in the car. "Werner wants us back out there, so can you take us up to the north side, once the plane's in the air?"

"Uh… sure."

"Thanks much," Em said, helping Leonard guide Billy toward the plane, but she paused as Boone stepped in front of Leonard.

"Got something for you," he said, handing him an envelope. "Well, not for *you*, exactly. But I need you to take this across."

"What is it?" Leonard looked at the writing on it. "Who's Constable Sommer?"

"She's with the Royal Cayman Islands Police Service. That's for her eyes only."

Leonard felt the bulge in the envelope and his eyes widened. "Is this…?"

"The constable's been told the envelope is sealed, so... keep it that way. She'll be waiting for you at the taxi stand; young, tall, blond hair. She'll take you to the hospital."

"Come on!" a Caymanian ground crewmember called out. "Time to go!"

———◆◆———

"What was in that envelope?" Emily asked. "And what was up with the novel-length text?"

"Dario gave me one of the blanks from the day they shot the scene that blew out Bernardo's hearing," Boone said, retrieving his phone from a pocket. "I got Nora's number from AJ this morning, and texted her some photos, but having a chance to give her the actual blank seemed like a good idea." They were standing on Salt Rock Dock waiting for Amelia to come back and pick them up. The intern had dropped them off before heading back to the south. "As for the text, here you go."

Emily took his phone and read it. "You want Nora to have that blank examined... and you want her there for the blood test." She looked up. "You don't trust Leonard?"

Boone took his phone back. "It just seems like too many things are going wrong. Something's... 'off,' and I can't get a handle on it. How about you? You're in the thick of things."

"Feels a bit dodgy, I admit." Emily shook her head. "But I dunno, Boone. After that writer told us about *Jaws*, I found a YouTube video about the making of the movie. It was a hot mess! Maybe this is just the way movies are."

"Maybe."

"I don't want to rock the boat for no reason," Em said. "This movie is important to so many people."

Boone nodded. "Okay, I hear ya. But if you need some boat-rocking, you just let me know." He pointed toward the northeast. "Speaking of rockin' boats, here comes Amelia in the *Lunasea*."

With Billy gone, there hadn't been much they could shoot. Nevertheless, Werner had been insistent on making use of the time he had and shot what he could with Emily, Cindy, and Wolfit, as well as some scenes with the treasure-hunting portion of the *Puddingwife* crew. Now, back at the dock, Boone and Emily bade the M&Ms good night and began removing gear from the *Lunasea*. Wolfit and Cindy lingered on the dive boat.

"Is he going to be okay?" Cindy asked for the twentieth time.

"Cindy-rella, he was doing great when we put him on the plane," Em reassured her. "Why don't you text him? I bet he'd love to hear from you."

"I did, but he doesn't answer."

"He's probably sleeping," Emily said. "It was an exhausting day for him, I bet." She grabbed her gear bag and stepped across to the dock with it, then set it down.

"You did yeoman's work today, young lady," Wolfit said. "Rescuing a co-star and performing flawlessly. And that monkey didn't bite me even once—I believe your presence has a mollifying effect."

"Aw, he's a lovable little imp. You probably just got off on the wrong foot." She picked up her gear bag. "I need to dunk everything in the rinse tank. Why don't you two come with us? We'll have a couple beers… grill some burgers. Maybe we'll hear from Billy, yeah?"

Cindy smiled. "That sounds wonderful."

"Whaddaya say, Wolfy? I bet we have a can of Guinness hiding in the crisper drawer of the fridge."

"Allow me to retreat to my room and purge this blue dye from my beard, and I shall return anon!"

Boone set his gear down beside the freshwater dunk tank halfway between the dock and their condo. "Cindy, wanna help walk a dog?"

"Sure!"

While Boone led Cindy into the condo to grab Brixton, Emily picked up Boone's mesh gear bag and pressed it down into the tank. She started to do the same with her own, but caught herself and checked the pocket on the end. She'd learned her lesson the time she'd forgotten she had tucked her phone in there; the poor thing had spent a couple days in a container of rice. Her fingers closed around a cylindrical object. Frowning, she removed it from the pocket. *Oh, right. Billy's vape pen.* She popped it in a pocket and dunked her gear, sloshing the bag around, her thoughts turning over in her mind. She took the bags out of the tank and brought them to their tiled porch area to sort through. Cindy came out from the sliding glass door and a lightbulb went off in Emily's head.

"Cindy, hold up a sec." She pulled the vape pen from her pocket. Cindy looked at it. "That's Billy's. God, I hate that thing."

"Did you by any chance switch out Billy's stinky bacon flavor and replace it with something else?"

"No. I have no idea how that nasty thing works."

Boone came out with an energetic Brixton, closing the sliding door behind him to seal in the precious air conditioning. He looked at Emily's expression. "What's up, Em?"

"Open up that text thread with Nora. I think I know what happened to Billy."

24

oone was awakened by Brixton's whine, accompanied by the
sound of his nails clicking against the sliding glass door. The
dog usually slept like a log, and he'd done his business outside
right after Wolfit and Cindy had returned home.

"Boone... walkies..." Em mumbled.

"All right, all right..." Boone swung his long legs down to the
cool, tile floor. He tapped the screen of his phone on the bed-
stand, and it lit up with the time: just past three in the morning.
Brixton never wanted to go out in the middle of the night. Boone
went to the door, slid it open... and froze. An orange glow flick-
ered out on the water. *Fire.* Voices were raised at some of the
nearby resorts. Brixton barked, roused by the unusual activity.

"Em! Get up!" He ducked back inside and pulled on his shorts,
yanking his phone from the charger and pocketing it.

"What is it?" Emily asked, rising from the sheets.

"There's a ship on fire, and based on where it is, I think it's the *Mako*! Throw something on and get to the dock. Bring your phone. Brix! Stay!"

Boone sprinted for the *Lunasea*, bare feet kicking up sand in the moonlight. In moments, he had the engine started and Emily came thumping up the dock, wearing one of her pullover hoodies.

"Take the wheel!" Boone called. "I'll cast off."

Boone left the lower set of controls as Em launched herself up the flybridge ladder. "You want to run the cut at night, I take it?" she asked as she neared the top.

"Probably. Start heading that way." Boone released the lines and stepped across, scrambling up the ladder to join Emily at the wheel. He took out his phone and called Deacon Brody, the man with the transportation department who had first shown him the various boats. It went to voice mail, so Boone hung up and tried again. This time, Deacon picked up.

"Boone! The Azimut is on fire!"

"I know, we're headed that way. Is there anyone aboard?"

"Yes! Me! And one other. We're doing our best to put it out, but... "

"We'll be there in five!"

"So... we're going through?" Emily asked.

"Yeah. You okay with that?"

Em chewed her lower lip a moment as they sped across the shallow lagoon toward the cut. "I've entered the cut after night dives, but I've never exited in pitch dark." She glanced back over her shoulder.

Boone knew what she was looking for: the range marker lights on shore, one set high, one low. If you were coming into the channel after dark, you waited until they stacked up and lined up your bow with the lights, then ran the channel, keeping between the red and green channel markers out in the water.

"The seas have been pretty chill. Let's do it." Emily looked at Boone. "Get the spotlight. I know we've got the channel markers, but better safe than sorry."

Boone opened a compartment and reached deep inside to snag the Goodsmann 4500 Lumens marine spotlight they'd picked up in Cozumel. He stepped up to the dash alongside the wheel and aimed the spotlight into the waters ahead of the bow. The powerful beam illuminated the surface to a respectable distance. "That gonna work for you?" Boone asked.

"Yeah, just keep the beam a bit further out. I don't want you shining that on our white foredeck during a wave bump and blinding me at a critical moment."

"Roger."

Emily maneuvered parallel to the channel until the shore lights were nearly lined up, then cut the wheel to port, lining up for the run, the red and green channel lights in sight ahead. The rule was "red, right, returning" and they were outbound, so the green marker was off her starboard bow, the red to port. In moments they reached the cut, and Boone swept the beam a little to either side so Emily could spot the shoals. She let out a long breath through pursed lips, then gunned it.

Moments later, Boone relaxed his tensed muscles. "We're through."

"Bit anticlimactic," Em said. "Not that I'm complaining, seeing as we're about to attend a boat roast."

The *Lunasea* now swung to starboard, aiming her bow at the flickering light of the fire. The *Mako* was moored at Grundy's Gardens, just to the west of the channel into the lagoon. The flames appeared to be coming from the stern, engulfing an area just forward of the swim platform. *Guess we won't be disembarking anyone from there.* Boone thought back to the quick tour he'd been given back on Grand. He was pretty sure the engine room was forward of where this fire was. A crewwoman was exhausting the last of a fire extinguisher on the blaze. Boone was glad to see she was wearing a life vest. Someone was in the wheelhouse—Boone assumed that was Deacon.

"Pull alongside," Boone said.

Em nudged the wheel to port as she idled closer. "What are you going to do?"

"Not sure yet. But I want to get over there." Boone scrambled down the ladder and grabbed a small extinguisher they kept forward. "Ahoy! I'm coming aboard," he called across.

"Okay..." the crewwoman said, backing away from the flames.

The Azimut's gunwale was higher than the Delta Canaveral's, so Boone stepped up onto the side of the *Lunasea*'s bow, where he'd get a little extra height. Stretching out a long arm, he grabbed hold of the *Mako*'s railing and put a foot on the gunwale, muscles cording as he pulled himself across, precariously hanging onto the fire extinguisher in his other hand. The crewwoman quickly took it from him, and he joined her on the deck. Deacon poked his head outside.

"Thank God you're here. Danielle and I were in the VIP stateroom when the smoke alarm went off. We were, uh... well, not important. Dani, take over the radio. Keep sending out a mayday on 16."

"Where exactly is the fire?" Boone asked, pulling the pin from the fire extinguisher.

"In the crew berth," Deacon said. "It's a small compartment with two twin beds. No idea what could start a fire in there."

"Where's the entrance to the berth?"

"Right in the back, off the swim platform."

Boone stepped along the aft seating area, but couldn't make it past the flames to reach the platform. He tried to knock it back with a few blasts of the extinguisher, but even if he managed to get around to the crew berth, he doubted he'd have enough retardant to put it completely out. He sniffed the air. *Gasoline? Or "petrol," as Em would say. Arson?* He turned back. "Deacon, where are the fuel tanks?"

"Too close for comfort. Either side of the engines, just forward of that crew berth."

Boone thought for a moment, looking toward shore. He could just make out the dark shape of the Hungry Iguana restaurant and the cottages of Paradise Villas. Just beyond lay the airport, as well as the solitary fire engine for the island. *This just might work.* He handed the extinguisher to Deacon. "Here. Try to keep it from spreading any further forward. It's probably burning below deck, but maybe we can slow it for just a few minutes."

"What's the plan?"

"First, I need to get her off the mooring. We can't have her sink onto the reef; this is some of the most valuable diving real estate right below us. Besides... I think we might be able to save this beauty."

"Beach it?"

"Sort of. Little Cayman isn't exactly known for its beaches, but I've got an idea." He rushed into the wheelhouse, where Danielle was beside the radio. "Can you drive this boat?"

"Yeah. Deacon let me pilot it several times."

"Good. Start her up. We need to come forward to the mooring ball so I can unhook us. Keep it just above idle for that. I'll direct you."

Boone dashed forward to the bow, snagging a boat hook on the way. Emily—*God bless her*—could see what he was doing and shined the marine spotlight across at the mooring ball. Boone looked back toward the windscreen and directed Danielle toward the ball, holding up his hands for her to stop as they coasted up to the mooring. Boone stepped to the bow and quickly unhooked their line, then dashed back to the wheelhouse.

"I got the police on the radio!" Danielle cried.

"Great! Go to the starboard side. I want you and Deacon to transfer over to the *Lunasea*."

"What are you—?"

"I'm sorry, there's no time to explain!" As Danielle ran out, Boone grabbed his phone and speed-dialed Emily, putting it on speaker. Fortunately, the Azimut 60 had a handy-dandy phone-holder right by the wheel. On the northside reef sites, cell service could be spotty, but this close to the lagoon resorts, phones worked just fine. "Em! You there?"

"Yeah, Boone!"

"Come closer again and pick up D&D."

"D and…?"

"Deacon and Danielle."

"Oh… okay. What's the plan?"

Boone started to reply but the radio crackled to life.

"Attention Azimut yacht, this is the Royal Cayman Islands Police Service on Little Cayman. Please respond."

Boone grabbed the mic. "Macy, is that you? It's Boone Fischer." There were only two police constables on LC, one male and one female, and Boone knew them both.

"Boone, what's happening? Where is the person I was speaking too?"

"She's transferring over to our dive boat. Listen, Constable, this needs to happen fast. Emily? Can you hear all this?"

"Yes!" the phone barked.

"Go ahead, Boone," Macy said over the radio.

"First, get the fire department at the airport to drive their truck down to the Hungry Iguana. Have them take it around the side and get it as close to the water as they can. And leave the headlights on! Actually... if someone can get over to Paradise Villas and the Iguana and turn on as many lights as you can, that'd be a big help."

"I'm by the airstrip now," Macy said. *"The fire department crew is already alerted. I'll handle the lights."*

"Boone, what are you going to do?" Em asked.

"I'm at the wheel of the *Mako*, an Azimut 60. Fire in the crew berth behind the engine room. We don't want it sinking on the reef and ruining a big patch. And we don't want to risk running the channel and wrecking it there, blocking Little's primary way in and out of the lagoon. I'm going to beach this sucker on the far-left side of the lagoon, where the shoals are right up against the shore. It's shallow there, and I should be able to get it in close enough that we can put the fire out."

"That'll probably rip up the hull," Em said.

"Better than the alternative."

"Deacon and Danielle are aboard," Emily reported. "What do you want me to do?"

"Follow behind me, just in case this idea turns out to be incredibly stupid."

Boone brought the engines to life and throttled up, swinging the wheel to starboard and pointing the bow toward shore. He scanned the controls and found multiple options for lights. Flipping several switches, he found one that cast a bright light on the waters ahead.

"Constable, you still there?"

"Yes, but I'll need to leave the radio to go get those shore lights on. Just spoke with the fire truck. It's on its way. I'm pulling into Paradise Villas right now."

"Okay. Seeya on the shore, Macy! Emily, I'm going to do this from the flybridge so I can better see where to thread the needle." He grabbed the phone and headed back to the flybridge steps, which were uncomfortably close to the flames. Dashing up, he raised the phone. "Wish I had your skippering skills, Em."

"Hey, I may take the piss out of you about your boating abilities, but you're plenty good, Boone. I'm better, of course."

"I know," Boone said, taking the wheel and slipping the phone into another convenient phone holder. "Any advice?"

"Yeah. Don't floor it. No need for that. And when you get to the shoals and find your spot, gun it when you feel the bow rise. There's not much wave activity, thank goodness—but what little there is, make it work for you."

"Okay," Boone said, taking slow, easy breaths. He sensed movement on his portside and glanced left. The *Lunasea* was rapidly overtaking him, heading in toward the shore. "Em, what are you doing? I thought I said to follow me."

"You did. And I tossed your suggestion for a better idea. Your plan's not half bad, but if you go too far left, you may make a dog's dinner of it and end up on the jagged ironshore. I'm going to station myself just to the west of where I think you should go, and have Deacon illuminate the best spot to attempt the crossing, 'kay?"

"Yeah. Better plan." On shore, a pair of headlights appeared to the left of the Hungry Iguana as the fire engine arrived. To the right, lights began popping on, and Boone could see guests emerging from the cottages. The restaurant itself lit up, and Boone could make out wisps of white in the waters near the shore.

"Okay, Boone," Emily's voice said. "Throttle back and line your-self up with the Iguana while Deacon and I find the sweet spot."

Boone watched as Emily slowed to a stop near the shoals and Deacon shined the marine spotlight along the expanse ahead of the *Lunasea*'s bow. Looking back over his shoulder, the orange glow below the aft edge of the flybridge reminded him that they didn't have all day. Boone returned his eyes to the *Lunasea*. Dea-con's beam of light suddenly halted, then switched back and forth between two spots before finally settling on a single location.

"Boone! There!" Em cried. "Take 'er in at about six knots! Don't forget to goose it when the bow pitches up right before the spot of light."

Boone pushed the throttle forward, watching the glowing knot meter until it hovered at about six, then locked his eyes on the water ahead. As Emily had pointed out, there was very little wave action, but he could feel a gentle rise and fall and quickly attuned his mind to it. On the shore, he could see figures lining the little beach, many with raised smart phones as they filmed the spectacle. The headlights of the fire engine grew brighter.

"Almost..." Emily's voice coaxed.

Boone placed his hand on the throttle.

"Now!"

Boone was already shoving the throttle forward as Emily's voice rang out. The boat bolted forward and Boone braced himself, wincing at the shriek that rose from below as the keel of the fiberglass hull scraped across razor sharp limestone. As discon-certing as that sound was, Boone knew the plan had worked. The bow of the yacht reached the shallows and nuzzled into a mixed bottom of sand and limestone rubble. The *Mako* came to a halt and tipped over slightly on its port side. Boone watched two Cay-manian firemen charge into the waist-high water near the stern.

Emily's elated cries rang out, both from the phone and from out at sea, her doubled soprano voice making a triumphant chord. "You did it! Woooooo! Now get your arse off that thing!"

Boone grabbed the phone and pocketed it, then vaulted the dashboard and slid down the sloping windscreen to the bow. In two strides, he reached the rail, clambering over and carefully lowering himself into the shallows, where the water came up to above his knees. The temptation to do a flashy, action-star jump had been there, but the last thing he wanted to do was spoil the whole adventure by spraining his ankle in the chunks of old coral that littered the bottom.

"Way to go, Boone!" Murray, of the M&Ms camera crew called out. Several of them were staying in the villas, and he now saw a camera pointed at him and the boat.

"Did you get it?" Boone asked with a laugh, as he made his way to shore.

"All of it! On my low-light. Been filming since we heard there was a fire out there. Don't know how much we can use, but it'll make for exciting viewing for the blooper reel!"

Emily's muffled voice spoke from his pocket and Boone retrieved his phone. "Yes?"

"I said, see if the Iguana will open early and whip up some breakfast."

Heinz Werner staggered out of the shadows, a bathrobe clinched at his waist. He stared at the wrecked yacht in disbelief. "*Gott im Himmel,*" he gasped.

Boone jerked a thumb back over his shoulder. "You're gonna need another boat."

A pair of eyes watched from amongst the gathered onlookers. Walking away from the group, a cell phone was extracted and a text composed. *"It's done."*

"Anyone hurt?"

"No."

"Good. Did it sink?"

"No. Those local divemasters managed to beach it and the fire is out. But the boat's a wreck."

The text field lay fallow for a long while. Then, finally: *"Good enough. For now."*

25

The combination of Billy's absence and the fire aboard the *Mako* brought production to a halt. While the production team hunkered down with the creatives to come up with a strategy, Boone, Emily, and Cindy went to the airport to greet the morning flight from Grand. They'd heard Billy was returning, and Boone and Em found they weren't the only ones waiting for the plane.

"Macy!" Boone said, as he got out of the Jeep. "Thanks for saving my bacon."

"You were fortunate I was already close by," the constable said. "That was a nice bit of piloting."

"I just had my hands on the wheel and throttle." Boone jerked his thumb at Emily. "Em was calling the shots."

"You make a good team," Macy said with a grin.

"Only when he listens to me," Emily replied.

The Cayman Airways turboprop appeared in the western sky and descended onto the airstrip, the deep thrum of the propellers changing in pitch as it taxied over to the little terminal. In moments, Billy exited the plane, but instead of Leonard, someone else accompanied him. He appeared to be a Caymanian, his skin on the lighter side of brown. Wearing a light gray suit, he was slender, with salt-and-pepper hair. Behind his glasses, eyes shone with keen intelligence, scanning the faces of everyone around.

Macy stepped forward to greet him. "Detective Whittaker, welcome to Little Cayman."

"Thank you, Constable. Where is your partner?"

"Over on the Brac, sir. Taking care of his mother after a surgery."

Cindy rushed forward, nearly bowling Billy over with a hug. The young actor looked over her shoulder at Boone and Emily. "Listen, uh… thanks for saving me down there."

"Do you remember what happened?" Em asked.

Billy looked sheepish. "Uh, no… but Leonard managed to get some footage from the underwater crew, so… I got to watch myself being a complete jackass."

"Where is Leonard?" Boone asked.

"He stayed on Grand. He was booked on this flight, but after what happened to the *Mako*, he's trying to track down a replacement."

"On that subject," Whittaker said, "Constable, what is your opinion of the cause of the blaze?"

"Arson is strongly suspected, sir. The chief of the fire department is fairly certain. I'm no expert, but it certainly looked like someone doused something in the crew berth with some kind of accelerant. Maybe the twin beds that were in there."

Whittaker shifted his eyes from Macy to Boone and Emily. "You are the friends of AJ Bailey, yes? The ones who have been in contact with Constable Sommer?"

"Yes, sir," Em said. "Emily Durand and Boone Fischer."

"Pleased to make your acquaintance. I am Detective Roy Whittaker, of the Royal Cayman Islands Police Service. I have been tasked with investigating a number of incidents that have occurred on Little Cayman over the past few days, and I will be the acting scene of crime officer for the duration. Normally, we have another detective who is our primary SOCO, but she is handling a case in West Bay at the moment." Whittaker spoke with a very slight Caymanian accent, but his words had a crisp precision to them.

The detective took out a folded piece of paper and opened it. "I have here a series of texts from you, Ms. Durand. To Constable Sommer. Do you have the item in question?"

"Yes sir, Detective sir."

The detective smiled, appearing amused. "No need to be so formal, Ms. Durand."

Emily enjoyed the irony of Whittaker informing her so formally that she didn't need to be formal. "Right-o, then." She took out a Ziploc bag with the vape pen in it. "Here you go, Roy."

Whittaker raised an eyebrow at the use of his given name, but reached out and took the bag.

"I tucked it in that Ziploc after I had my eureka moment. I've touched it, of course… but no one else, apart from me and Billy."

"Excellent." Whittaker looked around the area at the other passengers and airport staff. "Constable, let's go to the station before we say anything further."

Minutes later, they arrived at the little police station situated north of the airstrip. Macy led them into a small conference room, and the five of them sat around a table. Whittaker set the bag with the vape pen in front of him. Opening his valise, he retrieved a soft black case about the size of a toiletries bag, unzipped the sides, laid it out flat and extracted several items.

Then, after slipping on a pair of disposable gloves, he removed the vape pen and set it on a pad. As he opened a smaller, zippered bag, he spoke.

"Mr. Faust's blood test came back positive for lysergic acid diethylamide—or LSD—and in sufficient quantities to explain the hallucinations and unusual behavior during the dive. He has sworn that he is not a user of hard drugs, and I believe him. Ms. Durand..."

"Emily." Em smiled sweetly at the detective. "Informal, yeah?"

The detective smiled as well, but kept his eyes on his work. "Emily... your contention is that someone 'dosed' Mr. Faust by contaminating his electronic cigarette with a psychotropic drug."

"Yeah. Billy was vaping this awful Smoked Buttocks flavor..."

"Bacon," Billy mumbled.

"And then, all of a sudden, it was this other smell. Still disgusting, but not as bad. I think someone dosed his other flavor, then swapped out the Bacon Barf with the wacky juice."

Whittaker had opened the vape pen and dipped a cotton swab into the reservoir before transferring the tip into a clear vial. "This is a simple Erlich reagent test, which can detect psychoactive compounds in seconds." He swirled the swab around and the liquid turned purple.

"Congratulations, Emily. Your hypothesis appears to be correct." Whittaker reached into his little black bag and removed a Ziploc of his own. "And then, there is this." He set it down. It was the blank round Boone had sent over in the envelope.

"One of the crew grabbed that for me," Boone said, "but it's not a round that was in the gun."

"No, I understand. Nevertheless, it has been tampered with." He removed the round from the bag and held it up so that Boone and Emily could see the underside of the casing. "We contacted the company and confirmed that a green dot indicates a 'quarter load,' or one quarter the powder of a full load. Yellow for half, red for full."

"I see red," Boone said. "But it was green when I sent it over."

"We dabbed the green with paint thinner. The red dot had been painted over with green. Likely from a paint pen, given the precision of the green dot."

"And the *Mako*..." Boone said. "Looks like arson? Plus, that same boat had fuel lines cut, back in Grand. And there have been other suspicious occurrences as well."

"Yes. Constable Sommer mentioned you hypothesized about a number of them at Rackam's."

"And don't forget the drone that divebombed my face," Emily added. "And the submersible that sprung a leak. And the ROV whose circuits were fried."

"I was not even aware of those incidents," Whittaker said.

Emily swallowed. "Whaddaya think, Roy?"

The detective leaned back in his chair. "All the circumstantial evidence points to the same thing: your movie has a saboteur."

———◆◆◆———

While Detective Whittaker was setting up a series of interviews with cast and crew, Emily had gotten a call that she and Billy would be needed for an afternoon shoot. Apparently, the production crew had figured out something they could film: one of the last scenes in the movie, when the survivors of the *Puddingwife* manage to wash ashore on a deserted island. The location to be used: Owen Island.

Ahead of the *Lunasea*, Boone watched eight kayaks nose into the sandy shore; Emily, Billy, Cindy, and Wolfit had gone over in the kayaks to stay dry, along with one member each of the hair and makeup departments, and Alan Novak, the cinematographer. Wolfit had taken some coaxing and coaching from Emily, but the old actor had acquitted himself quite well in the kayak. Bringing up the rear, Heinz Werner and Dario entered the shallows in a two-seater.

"I'm surprised Whittaker didn't shut down the shoot for the day," Boone remarked to Jerry, as he ferried additional cast and crew as close to the island as he could get them.

"He tried," the 2nd AD replied. "But Mr. Scott, the producer who lives in Grand, pulled some strings."

Boone frowned. "Isn't he the one who owns the Azimut? Does he know it might have been arson?"

"Yeah, but I think that just pissed him off. He's as determined as Werner to get this shoot done."

Boone cut the engines as he reached the shallows near the little island. "Okay, this is as close as I can get without churning up the bottom. From here, we'll wade ashore. This is one of the few spots I'm allowed to drop an anchor, so we'll leave the *Lunasea* here. Amelia, you want to keep an eye on things?"

"Sure thing."

The M&Ms and an additional camera unit gathered up their gear. Boone hopped into the shallows and helped each person down. "Keep an eye where you're stepping and shuffle your feet a little. We get little yellow stingrays and an occasional southern stingray in here."

The prop master stepped down, carrying a case. He was sporting another comic book T-shirt and Boone did a doubletake. A red shirt with gold eagle wings with a stacked pair of Ws. "Wonder Woman?" he asked.

"Like William Marston, the creator of the comic, I too am a feminist," the man said matter-of-factly. "Plus... a classic is a classic."

"Can't argue with that," Boone said, reaching for the next crew member.

"Thank you, Boone," Marsha said, as he lifted her down.

"No problem. Give me something to carry, and I can save somebody a trip."

"Great! Grab that box there."

In minutes, the movie crew was on their way toward the beach. Boone followed behind the animal wrangler, Ulysses perched atop Silva's shoulder. The monkey looked back at Boone and lifted his brows several times. Boone imitated the gesture and Ulysses chittered at him.

Silva looked at Ulysses, then back at Boone. "He's greeting you."

"Well, I don't speak monkey, but let him know I'm pleased to make his acquaintance. I hear he's a big fan of Emily's, which is a gold star in my book."

◆ ◆ ◆

Emily watched as Heinz Werner stood on the beach, lifting his face to the sun. He beamed, gazing around the little island. *He looks ten years younger*, Em thought.

"Ah... this takes me back," Werner said as Dario dragged the kayak up onto the beach. "When I filmed *Wrath of Dreams* in Venezuela, we spent three days shooting from canoes. Sometimes, I feel we have lost track of the down-and-dirty art of filmmaking." He looked out at the approaching crew members shuffling through the shallows and shouted, "This will need to be a deserted beach, so please exit the water on either side of this expanse of sand!" He turned to Dario and indicated their own footprints. "We will rake this smooth, *ja?*"

Dario nodded, unclipping his two-way and making his way back to Emily, Wolfit, Billy, and Cindy. "We've got about three hours of usable light. Everyone have the new pages?"

"Yeah," Em said, "but it was hard to bone up on my lines while paddling."

Dario smiled, nodding. "Why don't the four of you find a patch of shade and look over the sides while we get set up."

"Shade sounds delightful," Wolfit said, eyeing a copse of palm trees.

"I bet you're glad to be rid of the blue dye, aren't you, Wolfy?" Emily said as the group made their way to the dappled shadows beneath the palm fronds.

"Yes, thank goodness. I have blue stains on the collars of half of my shirts, as it is. And not having to wear twenty pounds of pirate garb is a godsend." Once aboard the *Puddingwife*, the script called for "Bluebeard" to drop his piratical persona.

The group was about to sit in the sand when a shout brought them up short. A member of the costume department had arrived ashore and spotted them. "*Don't...* sit on the ground in your costumes," she yelled. "We'll bring you chairs!"

Emily and the other actors stood beneath the palms and looked over the scene together. It looked fairly simple: the group washes up on the shore after the mutated man o' war rips the *Puddingwife* apart.

"Uh..." Cindy began, "why was the costume lady concerned about us sitting in the costumes, if we're about to wash up on the beach?"

"Fair point," Em said. "Do you want to make the argument to her?"

Cindy shook her head. "No, I'll just wait for the chairs."

"Oh, excellent!" Wolfit stabbed a finger at the script in his hand. "Here's a rewrite I wholeheartedly endorse."

Em looked where he was indicating. In this new version, Emily woke up to find Ulysses staring down in her face. "Oh, yes... Ulysses revives *me* now. But before, it was you, yeah?"

"Yes... and I was fully expecting that little monster to peel my eyelids off while I pretended to slumber." Wolfit abruptly tensed. "Speak of the devil. Literally."

Ulysses came scampering through the sand and launched himself onto Emily's shorts, scrambling up her tank top to her shoulder. "Why, hello, Ulysses!" She offered a fingertip and the capuchin engulfed it with his ten tiny fingers.

"Sorry about that!" Silva said. "The clasp on the leash is rusting and sticks open sometimes."

"Salty, humid air will do it," Em said. "I've got a couple carabiners on my dive gear that are like that."

The handler retrieved Ulysses and reattached the leash to his tiny collar. Like Daniel Wolfit, the monkey had lost his booze-cruise paraphernalia—the tiny pirate hat and bandolier of drink umbrellas—and now only wore his diaper, in addition to the collar that would be removed when the cameras rolled.

Boone came into the shade, helping the costumer carry several collapsible canvas chairs. As he set some up, the prop master approached the group, carrying several personal props their characters would have close at hand when they washed up. After he handed them over, he caught Boone's eye. "This is the island where you found that Burgess Meredith sign, right?"

"Yes."

"Whereabouts is it?"

Boone stepped away from the palms and looked toward the interior before pointing. "It's way back there, in that thicker foliage. Unless the museum sent someone to fetch it."

The prop master nodded and headed back to the beach, where the crew was setting up.

"Anybody need anything?" Boone asked the actors.

"Yes, intern," Emily said, affecting an imperious tone. "Go back to the mainland and fetch me some sparkling water... and a bowl of M&M's. But just the green ones."

Boone smiled, popping open a chair. "That joke doesn't work when we're calling the camera crew by that name."

"Don't speak to the talent!" Emily spat, then burst into giggles.

"Oh, boy," Billy said. "This is going to be an interesting shoot."

In half an hour, the "set" was nearly ready and the four actors rehearsed their scene off to the side, in an effort to keep the footprints in the sand to a minimum. Once the crew finished the setup, the actors went to the water's edge and lay down on their marks; little Xs in the sand that had been made with a long pole. Strewn about were pieces of flotsam, washed ashore from the sunken *Puddingwife*. Emily lay on her back, her face turned to one side. Right before the call for 'action,' one crewman used a push broom on a pole to sweep away footprints, while a second crewman stood in the shallows and doused each of them with buckets of seawater. Werner had placed his director's chair in the shallows just beyond the surf line, its folding wooden frame sunk into the sand in several inches of water.

A familiar series of phrases rang out from various members of the crew, and Werner cried: "Action!"

Silva released Ulysses and the monkey dashed over to Emily and sat on her chest. During rehearsal, the wrangler had placed a treat under her cheek that lay against the sand, and the monkey had learned to get at it by pulling on her face. Ulysses reached out, then suddenly froze and looked off toward the interior of the island. With a shriek, the capuchin jumped off Emily and bolted into the brush.

"Cut, *Gottverdammt*, cut!"

Silva sprinted into the interior, clicking a little clicker that usually meant a treat was forthcoming.

"Hold, please," Dario said. "Everyone stay where you are."

Emily looked up at the vibrant blue sky, listening to the distant shouts, simian shrieks, and rustling of foliage. Minutes later, Em was aware of a rush of movement as Ulysses dashed back to the set and leaped onto Emily's stomach. The capuchin only weighed a few pounds but she "oofed" as the unexpected weight landed on her. She raised her head to look at him and the monkey chittered happily, offering her something cream-colored and fuzzy.

"Oh, thank you, Ulysses. What a... baffling little gift."

"What is it?" Jerry asked.

"A glove. A furry, white glove."

"Throw it out of frame, Ms. Durand!" Werner called out. "The monkey is in place, so let us see if we can shoot this scene!"

Em frisbeed the glove off to the side and the crew sprang into action, attempting to shoot the scene before Ulysses decided on another treasure hunt.

"And... action!"

———————◆•◆———————

Boone watched the glove plop into the sand. Curious, he took a few steps toward it, but the prop master got there first, snatching the object off the beach. The man examined it closely, then stuffed it into a fanny pack belted under his bulging mid-section, glancing furtively around. The man in the Wonder Woman T-shirt saw Boone observing him and gave the divemaster a friendly smile before heading over to the snack table off to one side.

Odd. Boone resolved to ask the man for a look at the object, but his attention was drawn to the action on set, as Emily rose from the sand and began to revive her marooned shipmates. She spoke her lines in a far less "blue-collar" British tone than she normally used, and Boone suddenly realized she sounded a lot like AJ Bailey. Boone lost himself for a time, watching the woman he loved perform in front of the cameras. What might this mean for her, if the movie took off? *If she has to move to Hollywood, guess I could work for a company running dives on Catalina Island.*

The scene was reset and shot again. When that second take ended, Dario took Werner aside and showed him something on his phone. Whatever it was sent Werner into a rage, and he stomped into the tropical scrub of the interior, obscenities ringing amongst the palm trees. Boone sidled over to the 1st AD and Emily joined him.

"Umm... may I ask...?" Emily ventured.

Dario sighed. "Technically, we weren't supposed to do this shoot today," he said, holding up his phone. "I got this email while we were coming over, but I deliberately held off opening it until we'd finished. Unfortunately, I've gotten a follow-up, and I can't put it off any longer."

"What is it?" Boone asked.

"In light of the fire on the *Mako* and several other 'incidents of concern,' the Cayman Islands Film Commission wants to send someone out to go over our safety protocols, and the Department of Environment wants to examine the area where the *Mako* was burning." He looked at Boone. "And the spot where you... um... 'docked' the boat."

"That's on me," Boone said.

"So, what does this mean for the movie?" Em asked.

"Until they are satisfied, the Film Commission is calling for a temporary halt to production."

26

"Hello, I am calling for specials. Yes! It is me! Yes, I miss you, too! But maybe I come for Happy Hour today, yes? What you have?"

Brooke watched Tolstoy as he listened intently to the specials, either shaking his head with disinterest, or practically salivating, depending on what he heard.

"What about the scallops, you have those, *da*? I mean... yes?" He listened. "Okay, I will maybe come later!" He hung up. "They sound very busy!"

"You can go *now*, if you want," Brooke said, jangling the cuff on her wrist. "Not like I'm going anywhere."

"What, you don't enjoy my company?"

"You're more fun than the other one," Brooke said dryly.

"This is true! But I will remain until Potluck returns with groceries. If still Happy Hour, I will go in search of scallops and rum. Maybe I bring you back a dog bag."

"Doggy bag?"

Tolstoy frowned. "No, I think it is dog bag. American idioms. So strange."

"Hey, Tolstoy..." Brooke said, shifting a bare leg across the mattress. She didn't want to be overtly seductive; that tactic had already been tried without success. Criminal and occasional drunkard he might be, but Tolstoy was devoted to his partner. Nevertheless, he was a heterosexual male, so a little display might short out a few neurons. She winced, and rolled her shoulders, arching her back. "Can I see what they're saying about me? Please?"

Tolstoy's eyes slid to her legs, but popped right back to her face. "You celebrities. So vain. Here you are, a captive, and you want to know if you are... what is word... trending?"

"Hashtag Guilty-as-charged. Hashtag Bored." When Tolstoy's face went into full-confusion mode, Brooke quickly followed up with: "Sorry. Stupid social media lingo. I'm just bored and I want to know if anyone's missing me." She managed to summon a sheen of tears—she might star in a lot of schlock, but she was damn good. "I need to know... if anyone cares."

Tolstoy sighed. "H'okay, what site?"

"TMZ will be fine."

Tolstoy brought up the website and handed her the phone.

"Thank you. And, hey... I'm sorry I've been so mean about the cigarettes. You can smoke one, if you want."

"*Spasibo!* I was dying for one!" He extracted the box of Black Russians and searched for his lighter.

Brooke looked down at the smartphone. Over the past few days, she'd established a pattern of asking to borrow it to Google herself once or twice a day. She had familiarized herself with the phone, and now she put her plan into motion. Brooke quickly typed her name into the TMZ search bar and tapped on the most recent story, then immediately closed the browser and tapped on the phone icon. Hitting "Recent," she selected the number he'd just called, the restaurant and bar he frequented. Brooke immediately pressed the volume button, dropping the sound down low so the rings would not be audible to Tolstoy. *They're not picking up,* Brooke thought, holding the phone close so she could just barely hear the repeated rings.

"Ahhhhh… I needed this," Tolstoy said, as he fired up one of his eccentric cigarettes.

Brooke fought the urge to cough, waiting until she heard the soft sound of a voice on the phone. With the volume down, and holding the phone like she was reading an article, she couldn't hear the exact words, but could tell it was a voice mail. *They must be busy. It will have to do.* As the outgoing message ended, she coughed to cover the beep, waving a hand in the air.

"Forgiveness," Tolstoy said, moving even further away from her with his cigarette.

Perfect, Brooke thought. She looked at the phone, speaking clearly. "No news stories at all about how you followed Brooke Bablin home from Rackam's, kidnapped her, and stuck her in a basement. So, I guess you got away with it."

Tolstoy cocked his head, smirking slightly. "What you mean?"

"The only stories on TMZ are about how Brooke Bablin must have quit and no one knows where I went. And nothing at all about some Russian guy smoking black-and-gold cigarettes sneaking into my villa and chloroforming me. So, like I said. I guess you got away with it. And here I am… what's that joke you're always making? Oh, yeah… so here I am, 'in hell,' wondering when you'll let me go."

Brooke heard an engine outside. Potluck was back. Heart pounding, she tapped the Hang Up icon and reopened the browser window to the TMZ article. She glanced down at it, actually taking it in. Another picture of the girl who'd replaced her took up a good bit of digital real estate. *She's beautiful,* Brooke thought, an irrational stab of jealousy poking her in the back of her brain.

———————◆◆◆———————

"Honey, I'm home!" Potluck called as she opened the door and clomped down the stairs, a quartet of grocery bags split between her hands. "I finally found some decent cheese on this island..." She halted at the bottom. "You're smoking."

"*Da.* She say I could."

Potluck narrowed her eyes, then dropped the bags and crossed the room in two strides, snatching the phone from Brooke's hands. Tolstoy might be a whiz with hacking and lockpicking, but he could be a bit of a child at times. Potluck had seen the comely actress try to manipulate her man on several occasions, so she immediately checked the text and call logs. There was nothing out of the ordinary; texts to and from their employer and calls to that blasted bar.

"Is okay," Tolstoy said. "I let her read gossip about herself, is all."

"Uh-huh," Potluck said dubiously, reopening the web page Brooke had been on. Eyes widening, she stared at the image in the article. It was the divemaster who had replaced Brooke, and this photo showed more of her face than the last one Potluck had seen. "You have got to be kidding me."

"What?" Tolstoy asked.

"This little hottie that took her place..." Potluck said, staring at the photo. "I remember her now."

Tolstoy came over and looked at the photo. "She look familiar to me too..."

"I shot at this blond bitch on that mega-yacht off the coast of Cozumel. She dived into a laundry chute."

"Cozumel!" Tolstoy shouted. "She was at Coconuts! The bar with the book of breasts! She was telling me about flashing her..." He cleared his throat. "I remember her too, is all."

Potluck thought back to that botched mission. One team member dead, and the majority of the payoff up in smoke. She wasn't about to screw this one up.

"I am thinking of going to Rackam's."

"Think again." She tapped the phone's screen. "If we recognized her... she might recognize us!"

"But she's not even in Grand Cayman," Brooke said. "That article is from today. It says they're shooting over on Little Cayman right now."

"Scallops!" Tolstoy shouted as he mounted the steps. "I not be gone long, I promise!"

"Oh, no you don't," Potluck said, well-muscled arms folded across her chest. "You promised this young lady we'd do sushi tonight and that's what we're gonna do."

———◆·◆———

Boone and Emily treated Detective Whittaker to a meal at the Hungry Iguana before bringing him back to their condominium. With most of the island's hotel rooms being taken up by cast and crew, as well as a few dive groups, Detective Roy Whittaker had reluctantly accepted Boone and Emily's offer to stay with them.

"AJ lets us stay at her place all the time," Emily insisted. "Only fair for you to stay with us, you being a mate of hers. We've got a guest room; couple movie blokes stayed there a few days ago, before we were suddenly whisked away to Grand. I can change out the sheets for you, or we've got a foldout right there in the sofa."

"The foldout will fine. Thank you. It is appreciated," Whittaker said. "My lower back was not looking forward to a cot at the police station."

"I'll get some sheets and a nice gushy pillow." Emily went into the bedroom to fetch them.

"Can I offer you a drink?" Boone asked.

"Water would be most welcome."

Boone grabbed a bottle of water from the fridge. Plastic was a monumental problem for the world's oceans, so he hated to buy bottled water. Grand and the Brac had desalination plants and most resorts on Little had reverse osmosis desalination systems, but Boone and Emily's condo used rainwater cisterns for their water. He'd never gotten sick from drinking it, but he didn't risk it with guests.

"Anything come out of the interviews?" Boone asked, handing the bottle to Whittaker.

"I was only able to complete a portion of them, with the Owen Island shoot taking many of the crew away. Nothing conclusive. A number of the crew suspect something nefarious is occurring, but no clear motives have emerged thus far. I did have a fascinating conversation with the writers." He took a sip of the water, shaking his head with a smile. "A giant, mutated Portuguese man o' war?"

"Yeah, a bit out there," Boone said with a chuckle.

Emily returned with a stack of sheets and a pillow. "Let's get you set up, yeah?"

"I'll walk Brix," Boone said, grabbing the dog's lightweight harness and leash from a hook. The slightest of jingles issued from the items, triggering Brixton to rocket from his doggy bed in the corner, his nails clicking as he reached Boone by the door and paused to stretch. Boone slipped the harness onto the pooch and the two of them stepped out into the humid air, the gentle lap of the waves competing with night insects. Boone took Brix along the shoreline to the east, where the sand quickly gave way to low scrub and dense foliage. The dog did the deed, and Boone turned around and headed back the other way, walking across the beachfronts of the Southern Cross Club and the Conch Club.

At the midpoint of the two properties, Boone noticed an area in the sand that looked like something had been dragged between the beach and the surf. The Milky Way was splashed across the sky above; between the moon and the starlight, there was sufficient illumination for Boone to spot the disturbance in the sand at a distance. It was reminiscent of the tracks a sea turtle made when going ashore to lay her eggs, and this very stretch of beach was known to have a few nests each year. *But egg laying doesn't happen until May and June,* Boone thought. *Months away.* As he got closer, he felt silly; the human footprints within the scrape were now apparent. But instead of barefoot prints, these had a tread of some kind. A kayaker, maybe. But at night?

Boone paused, staring out into the dark waters of the lagoon. It was still early enough that the resorts had their lights on, but ironically, that made it difficult to see anything beyond a hundred yards out, spoiling one's night vision. Boone could only just make out the dark shape of Owen Island, and the shoal line beyond occasionally caught a glimmer of moonlight. He closed his eyes and listened, and might have heard the gentle splash of a paddle, but with the constant lapping of the surf at his feet, he couldn't be sure.

Brixton's patience was exhausted, and the energetic pup pulled on the leash.

"Okay, okay. Let's go back."

———◆◆◆———

Boone woke from a fitful sleep. Normally, he was dead to the world once his head hit the pillow, but something was gnawing at his mind. He rose from the bed, pausing to snatch his phone from the nightstand and a pair of shorts from a nearby chair where he'd flung them. He pulled them on, quietly opened the bedroom door, then crept across the tiled floor toward the sliding door to the patio, doing his best not to wake the detective. Unfortunately, the heavy glass door was not a stealthy model.

"Can't sleep?" Whittaker said, sitting up in the foldout bed.

"Yeah. Brain won't stop chattering at me," Boone replied. "Figured I'd get some air. Sorry if I woke you."

"You didn't. I've never been adept at sleeping in strange rooms when my head is full of questions. I'll join you."

The two men stepped out into the night. All the resort lights were off at this hour, and the stars seemed even brighter than before.

"It is beautiful over here," Whittaker said, a note of reverence in his voice. "So peaceful. None of the bustle of George Town. I hope this island remains undeveloped."

"You 'n' me both. It's why Em and I chose it. We seem to be drawn to the sleepy corners of the world." Boone snorted a laugh. "Not feeling too 'sleepy' tonight, though, that's for sure."

"Anything in particular that is bothering you?"

Boone started toward the dock. "Actually... yeah. Join me up on the flybridge for a sec?"

Whittaker followed Boone to the dock, boarding the *Lunasea* and climbing the ladder. Boone opened a compartment and took out the small birding binoculars he'd had since his time in Bonaire.

"You won't see much with those," Whittaker observed. "Not enough light."

"Actually... light is what I'm looking for." Boone aimed the lenses toward Owen Island, just over a thousand feet from the dock. With all the lights on shore now doused for the night, he had a much easier time making out the little islet. *There.* He lowered the binoculars, squinting. "Don't even need these, actually." He pointed toward the island. "Look a little left of center."

"I don't... wait. I see something. A torch?"

"Flashlight, yeah. That'd be my guess," Boone said. Emily often said 'torch' instead of flashlight, and this being a British Overseas Territory, Boone figured Whittaker meant the same. He raised the binos once more. "Back in the interior. Which is where I thought I might see something."

"Is this what was keeping you up?"

"Probably," Boone said, dropping the binoculars for another naked-eye look before refocusing them on the patch of beach on the nearest side of Owen Island. "Sometimes my hunches aren't fully formed, y'know? I just see something 'off' and it gnaws at me. Earlier, when I was walking Brix, I thought maybe someone had taken a kayak out into the lagoon. And I might be wrong, but..." He smiled. "But I'm not. There's a two-person kayak in the trees a little ways off the beach. I can just make it out."

"Who on earth would be out there in the middle of the night?"

"I've got a guess about that too," Boone said, dragging his phone from his pocket and bringing up a search engine. He'd waited to do this, not wanting to spoil his night vision until he'd spotted the boat. He typed in a phrase and ran an image search. "Bingo."

"What on earth are you two doing out here?" Emily's voice rose from the dock. Barefoot and sporting another stolen T-shirt, she looked up at them, the moonlight reflecting in her eyes. "It's two in the bloody morning!"

Boone leaned on the rail and looked down at her. "Hey Em… how do you feel about a little late-night kayaking?"

27

Under the moon and stars, the trio paddled silently through the shallows, speaking in low voices.

"Okay Bobo Boone, spill it. Why are we in kayaks instead of beds?"

Boone quickly recounted the tracks on the beach, and what he and Whittaker had spotted from the flybridge. "Remember what the monkey brought to you after running off into the interior?"

"Yeah. Some kind of fuzzy glove."

"Well... after you tossed it aside, I went to pick it up, but the guy in charge of props grabbed it before I could get to it. And I saw something in his eyes when he got a good look at it. Remember when we were talking to Katja at Sangria Sunday, about the Burgess Meredith sign?"

"Yeah? Oh! The prop master was there, asking questions about... well... props. Missing props. From the original *Batman* show."

"Batman?" Whittaker asked.

"The American TV show in the late 60s," Boone explained.

Whittaker chuckled. "We have television here too, you know. But what does that have to do with anything?"

"The actor Burgess Meredith lived on Little Cayman for a while. And he played a villain called The Penguin."

"Yes, I remember," Whittaker said. "He wore a purple top hat and carried an umbrella."

"And he wore a tuxedo," Boone added. "With gloves. White, furry gloves."

"I don't remember that," Whittaker said. "The gloves, I mean."

"I didn't either," Boone said. "But television wasn't Hi-Def back then. That's what I was looking at on my phone. I found a detailed photo, and you can clearly see white fur on the backs of the gloves."

"Yeah!" Em said loudly, then quickly lowered her voice. "The fur was on the back! And wait… at the bar, didn't he ask if anything other than the sign had been found?"

"He did. Right before he asked if he could buy the sign."

"And when we were sitting in the shade on Owen Island, working on our lines before the shoot… he asked you where the sign was."

"Yep. And that's where that flashlight glow was coming from."

"So… what? He's looking for the other glove?" Em asked.

"I'm not certain that is a crime, in and of itself," Whittaker said.

"Well… Owen Island is private property," Boone pointed out. "And anything Burgess Meredith-related could be considered a historical artifact."

"Then I suggest we stop speaking," Whittaker said in a low tone as they approached the beach. "We have a potential trespassing treasure hunter to catch."

As quietly as they could, the three slid their kayaks onto the beach. All carried flashlights, but kept them extinguished as they crept toward the sparse tree line. Boone paused beside the two-person kayak that was pulled up beside a large native agave plant. He reached down and took the double-bladed paddle, gesturing for the others to come close. "Only one paddle. So, he's probably alone." He pointed at their own kayaks. "Actually... grab all the paddles. Let's tuck them out of the way somewhere, in case he gets past us."

They gathered the paddles and pushed them into a thick clump of sea grapes before moving into the interior. In moments, the sound of digging could be heard, and a single, dim light shone from a clump of foliage—likely a flashlight, propped against something to provide light for the digger's work.

"What if he's armed?" Emily whispered.

"I doubt he will be," Boone said.

"Although, from the sound of it, he does have a shovel," Whittaker cautioned. Like most RCIPS officers, he did not regularly carry a service weapon.

Abruptly, the digging noises ceased. Boone crouched, signaling the others to hold up while he listened. Muttering... a grunt of effort... and a cry of triumph.

Whittaker rose and moved toward the sounds, beckoning the others to join him. Once they were within ten feet of the man, he triggered his flashlight; Boone and Emily did likewise. Boone was carrying his SEAC R30 dive light, whose beam was particularly bright on its highest setting.

Like a raccoon caught rooting in the trash, the prop master's pasty face whipped around, his eyes blinded by the trio of lights. Gone was the red Wonder Woman shirt; the Batman T-shirt was back in the rotation—perhaps chosen for its stealthier black color.

"I am Detective Roy Whittaker of the Royal Cayman Islands Police Service. You are trespassing on private property."

"We've got permission," the man said. "I'm with the film crew. Adam Dozier. Property master for the production."

"Yes, I recognize the name. You were on my list for questioning, but I understand you decided to join the shoot on this island yesterday afternoon."

"Just doing my job."

"And this?" Boone asked, directing his light to a shallow crater in the sand. "Is this part of the job description for a prop master, digging stuff up in the middle of the night?"

"What's in the bag, Batman?" Emily asked. "You find the other glove?"

Dozier looked confused. "I know that voice. You guys aren't cops."

"I assure you, Mr. Dozier, I am very much a member of the police force," Whittaker stated. "Mr. Fischer and Ms. Durand are merely assisting me." The detective's beam dipped, spotlighting a heavy-duty, waterproof duffel bag in the man's hand. The bulky zipper was open, and it appeared to contain items wrapped in plastic. "Set the bag down and have a seat where you are, please."

Dozier did as he was told and Emily stepped forward to reach into the bag. The first thing she brought out was the other furry glove. She gently laid it aside and pulled out a long object, wrapped in clear plastic. Holding it up, she played her flashlight beam along it. "An umbrella!" She shined the light down into the bag. "And a purple top hat! And quite a few other things. This looks like a full set of Penguin costume pieces and props."

"I was going to bring them to the museum," Dozier said.

"Sure you were," Boone said, looking around the area. "Where is the glove from yesterday?"

"Back in my room."

"Good to know." He looked down at the shallow crater in the sand. "Why was the glove not wrapped up like the rest?"

324

"I wondered that myself," Dozier said, obviously trying to sound helpful. "The other glove was in a Ziploc that had been torn open, and it was only partially covered by sand. Maybe someone came back and added it to where they'd buried the bag."

Boone shifted the light to the side where a shovel lay, tossed down alongside a wooden post. Beside that, a prybar. And beside that...

"Look, all I did was dig up some stuff on a deserted island that I have permission to be on. I haven't committed any crime."

"How about destruction of property?" Boone held up the No Trespassing sign with Burgess Meredith carved in cursive. "You pried this off the post it was attached to. Probably to make it easier to get it out of the country."

"No! To make it easier to take it back in the kayak," Dozier insisted. "To give to the museum," he added belatedly.

"I suggest we continue this conversation back on Little Cayman," Whittaker said, stepping over to Boone and retrieving the shovel. "I'll take this. Leave the post. Everything else goes in the duffel bag."

"You can put it in the two-man kayak," Dozier offered. "That's why I chose it, in case I needed to bring things back."

"Excellent suggestion. And Ms. Durand will pilot that kayak. Mr. Fischer and I will escort you back."

"Fine by me," Dozier said.

He doesn't think anything about this is "fine," Boone mused, reading the man's vibe.

After loading up, the four kayaks paddled back toward the dock, Emily leading the way, Whittaker and Boone flanking Dozier.

"So... where are we going?"

"Just somewhere quiet where you can answer a few questions," Whittaker replied.

"I've got an early call tomorrow," Dozier protested.

"Do you? I heard the production was on hold. But not to worry, this shouldn't take long."

For a few minutes, the night was silent, save for the dipping of paddles in the water. Boone could feel the prop master's rising nervousness across the few feet of distance.

"Look, I told you," he blurted, "I was going to donate all of this to the museum."

"Then why didn't you do this in the daytime?" Whittaker asked. "Perhaps ask the museum to help?"

"We were too busy today, and I'm a night owl. Look, I'm a collector, but I'm not a thief!"

"How about a saboteur?" Boone asked.

"What? What are you talking about?"

Boone could see Whittaker abruptly look across Dozier's kayak at the divemaster, but he said nothing.

"That blank round that damaged Bernardo's hearing: you had access to the ammunition, didn't you?"

"Lucy was in charge of that!" It was a simple fact that Dozier could have stated in a calm and reasonable tone, but he shouted it instead.

"Yes, she was, wasn't she?" Boone said. "But she works under you, correct?"

Dozier shifted in his kayak seat. In the darkness, Boone thought the prop master dipped a hand into a pocket. Alert, Boone hefted his paddle in case he had a weapon. Instead, the man let his hand drop to the water, then returned it to his own paddle. The moon was nearly gone, but the starlight was still bright enough that Boone could just make out the bottom. Like much of the lagoon, it was extremely shallow here. He allowed himself to fall behind.

Whittaker began asking Dozier some questions as Boone back-paddled, coming to a stop where he thought the prop master had dipped his hand. There was a dark object there, to the left of his kayak. Eyes locked on the spot, he retrieved his dive light, dipping it under the surface and flipping it to its lower setting. The dark object was revealed to be a queen conch, pulling in its eyes at the sudden intrusion of light. *Damn.* He shined the light to either side, and there it was! A small smartphone lay in the sand. Memorizing the spot, Boone doused the light and set it by his feet. Eyes still locked on the spot, he crossed his right arm over with the paddle, pressing it into the sand on the left side, setting it as an anchor to keep from overturning. He snaked his left arm out, the kayak tilting on its side. Emily often teased him about his lanky frame and impressive wingspan, but it came in handy now, as he tweezered the phone between two fingertips and brought it aboard, sliding it into a pocket. The whole procedure had taken mere seconds.

With long strokes, Boone quickly ate up the distance and came up behind the other two kayaks, his night vision slowly returning. Dozier glanced over his shoulder at him.

"There was a big stingray back there!" Boone said. "Haven't seen one that size in the lagoon before."

Dozier looked back toward shore as Emily's kayak reached the beach.

◆ ◆ ◆

While Whittaker contacted Constable Macy to swing by and transport him and Dozier to the Little Cayman Police Station, Boone dashed into the condo, Emily right on his heels.

"Whoa, that was a *rush*!" Emily gushed. "I feel like Nancy Drew! And you can be one of the Hardy Boys, if you want to."

"Rice!"

"What?"

Ignoring Brixton dancing at his feet, Boone grabbed a kitchen towel and dried off the exterior of the phone.

"What's that?"

"A cheap-looking smartphone. I bet it's a burner. The prop guy dropped it in the lagoon when I mentioned 'sabotage,' and I managed to grab it. It was down there less than twenty seconds, so maybe... *damn*. Dead."

Emily was already taking down an airtight container of rice and another empty container. Working together, they entombed the phone in rice and sealed it.

"You think this guy is behind the sabotage?" Em asked.

"I wouldn't bet against it, and I don't think he's alone," Boone said, tapping the container. "And if we can get this working again..."

"Actually, even if it isn't working..." Emily trailed off, thinking. "Hey, does Whittaker know you have this?"

"Not yet."

"And did Prop Guy see you find it?"

"No."

"Ace! Mwah-wah-wah!" Emily chortled in an over-the-top rendition of the Penguin's laugh. She grabbed the container. "C'mon, let's get to the police station! This little treasure will make him talk."

Five minutes later they strolled into the police station. The front desk was vacant, but the door to the conference room where they had met earlier was open. Emily could see Adam Dozier on the far side of the table, Macy and Whittaker across from him.

Emily snuck up to the door and rapped on the frame as she peeked in. "Knock knock!" Dozier jumped, nearly spilling the Coke can he was just taking a sip from. "How's it going, Roy?"

Roy Whittaker gave her a bemused smile. "I was just asking Mr. Dozier if he would consent to my searching his room, but he seems oddly reticent."

"Huh. That's curious," Em said, stroking her chin theatrically, "seeing as he's just a hardworking professional in the film business who sometimes digs for treasure... which he promptly hands over to local museums out of the goodness of his heart."

"Look, I haven't done anything wrong. And you can't go poking around my stuff without a warrant. I know my rights!"

"You are not in the United States, Mr. Dozier," Whittaker explained. "Since you were on private property in the middle of the night, and damaged a piece of Little Cayman history, I have sufficient probable cause that a crime was committed. That being said, it is always preferable to obtain either permission... or a warrant."

"Then I guess you're going to need a warrant," Dozier said.

Whittaker leaned back, glancing at Constable Macy. "What do you think, Constable? Recreational drugs?"

"Perhaps," she said.

"What are you talking about?"

"I'm trying to determine why you wouldn't allow a simple search of your room."

"I don't do drugs."

"Not even LSD?" Boone asked.

Dozier blanched, rapidly blinking his eyes. He quickly recovered, but Emily was sure everyone had seen the reaction. She decided the time was right.

"Hey, you three hungry? I brought brownies! Me mum's old recipe. The secret is a pinch of cayenne!" Em set down the container and opened it. "Oh, silly me! This isn't brownies. This is some rice with a mobile in it." She fished the phone out and waggled it in her fingers.

Dozier went white as a sheet. His brain knew he had to simply deny everything, but his body clearly had its own agenda.

"That's not mine."

"You sure?" Boone asked. "I plucked it out of the water right after you dropped it."

"I don't feel so good..."

"Hey, you know what's good for nausea? White rice. I suppose we could cook up some of this for you."

"The phone must be dead, or you wouldn't have it in rice," Dozier managed, sweating profusely.

"It wasn't in the water long enough. We were able to fire it up just fine," Emily lied. "The rice is just to make sure it stays functioning. Before we powered it down and riced the sucker, we found some very interesting texts." Emily was completely free-styling at this point. She took a chance, and went with the most recent sabotage. "A delightful little chat about a fire..."

Dozier's eyes wobbled, looking into the middle distance, appearing to think about what he'd last texted.

"And another amusing conversation about the battery on a drone..."

"Bullshit! I deleted that one—" Dozier practically choked off the last of his outburst. If his skin had been pallid before, he now paled into the realm of Frosty the Snowman. He swallowed. "Lawyer," he croaked.

28

While Macy and Whittaker waited at the station for a search warrant to be issued, Boone and Emily managed to catch a few hours of sleep. With no shoot that day and no dives, they planned to sleep in, but Boone's phone rang at a few minutes after seven. Looking at the screen, he saw the call was from a Cayman Islands number, but he didn't recognize it.

Blinking away sleep, Boone grabbed the phone and put the call on speaker. Emily scooted over onto his side of the bed to listen in.

"Hello?"

"This is Detective Whittaker."

"Hey, it's Boone and Em. You're on speaker."

"Sorry if I woke you. I have the search warrant and I would welcome additional eyes. Constable Macy's partner is still on Cayman Brac, so she needs to remain with Mr. Dozier at the police station."

"He didn't strike me as much of a flight risk."

"Perhaps not, but it is proper procedure. Mr. Dozier is renting a room in what used to be a hotel, but now offers long-term rentals, often for divemasters and resort staff. He had access to some of the same housing the cast and crew had, yet he chose to stay there."

"Far from the prying eyes of his fellow crewmembers at the resorts," Emily noted.

"My thoughts exactly."

"We'll see you in ten," Boone said.

Twelve minutes later, they parked the Jeep in front of a row of three one-story buildings; a duplex on the right, and two four-room buildings to the left. Neat little cottages with simple porches in front, the units were tucked away on a dirt road behind the liquor and grocery stores, tropical trees encroaching in spots and providing a great deal of shade.

Whittaker was standing beside one of the island's two police vehicles, sipping from a travel mug. "Thank you for coming." He set his mug inside the patrol car and offered a plastic bag full of disposable gloves. "If you'd be so kind?"

"Putting on rubber gloves to find a fuzzy glove," Emily remarked, pulling one on with a snap.

Boone grabbed a pair. "I'm hoping we find more than that."

Whittaker reached into the passenger side and retrieved the little black case he'd had when they'd first met in the police station. "This way." The detective approached the far-left unit and produced a key, opening the door into the little apartment. The room was stuffy, since most air conditioners in rentals had an automatic shutoff to prevent tourists from leaving them on all day. The shades were drawn; Whittaker opened them and flipped on the light before turning and taking in the room.

"Look, Boone," Emily said, "he tosses clothes on the floor just like you."

Boone smiled. He didn't floor-ditch clothing often, but when Emily caught him, she was on him in an instant. His eyes scanned the room, taking in a suitcase lying open atop a black trunk.

Emily crouched, looking under the bed. "Not much to see, apart from the discarded shirts and undies."

Whittaker set his case down and approached a closet, looking within. "There's a chance he stored things in another location. But I'm hopeful that—"

"May I move this suitcase?" Boone interrupted.

Whittaker looked back. "Set it on the bed. I should go through the contents myself."

"Actually, I'm more interested in this trunk below it. It looks a lot like the ones the camera crew stores their gear in. Has a strip of tape that says 'Props Department' on it."

"Oh, yeah, that's a road case," Em said. "There are tons of those around."

Boone tried the clasps. "Locked." He looked at the black box, its edges banded in silvery metal. "Can we break it?"

"One moment," Whittaker said, exiting the room. He returned with a sturdy-looking slotted screwdriver. "Constable Macy is to be commended for having a toolbox in the trunk." He jammed the tip under the clasp and wrenched it, breaking the simple lock plate with ease.

Inside were a variety of small props and tools, paints, adhesives, rolls of tape. Whittaker examined various items, returning each to its precise placement.

Emily stepped back, looking at the trunk. "My Nancy Drew senses are tingling. The inside and outside don't match. There's more space under the bottom you're looking at."

Boone nodded. "She's right. May I?" He reached inside and gripped two of the ridges in the compartment, lifting it straight up. The interior came out, revealing a false bottom several inches deep.

Inside was a treasure trove of items: A red box of full-load blank rounds and a green paint pen. Wire cutters, bolt cutters, a hacksaw, small bottles of sulfuric acid, and two squeeze bottles of lighter fluid. A number of USB flash drives in a small container, and another container with a variety of fuses. Rechargeable lithium batteries of various sizes. A small, unlabeled bottle with an eyedropper top. A familiar-looking smartphone, still in its packaging—no doubt, a disposable burner.

And tucked in the corner, a furry white glove.

"Houston, we have a scumbag," Boone muttered. He reached in and picked up the little bottle with the eyedropper. "Detective, do you have that magic stuff in your bag? The test you used on Billy Faust's vape pen?"

Whittaker set his case on the bed and unzipped it, retrieving the reagent test kit. "I'll do this at the sink," he said, taking the bottle from Boone and exiting into the bathroom.

"Bet I know what's on these." Em tapped the container with the USB flash drives. "The computer glitch on the ROV... and one of the writers said a hard drive had been wiped. These probably have all sorts of nasty malware on them."

"The lighter fluid bottles are full," Boone noted. "The *Puddingwife* might've been next on the arson menu."

Whittaker reentered the room. "Purple. Positive for psychoactive compounds."

"So... what's next?"

"In light of these discoveries, I will officially arrest Mr. Dozier, and transport him across to Grand Cayman on the next flight."

"What if he has an accomplice?" Emily asked. "You can turn up the heat on him with all of this."

"Mr. Dozier has requested a lawyer, and further questioning should be done in the presence of counsel. In addition, I'll need official statements from the two of you."

"Well... we do have the day off," Boone suggested.

"RCIPS will cover the cost of the flights, if you'd care to accompany me."

Boone smirked and pointed at the road case. "You just want someone to carry that for you, while you handle the prisoner."

Whittaker returned the smile. "And the Burgess Meredith memorabilia. And the rice container with the phone. And my carry-on."

"I've got a lot of experience being a pack animal for this one here," Boone said, aiming a thumb at Emily. "Fine by me. Amelia can look after our dog while we're gone."

"Always happy to pop over to Grand," Em said. "See what AJ's up to."

Suddenly, multiple chimes sounded as a text message arrived on all three of their phones. Emily got to hers first. "Well, that's a coinkydink. It's AJ. 'Call me ASAP.'"

Whittaker looked at his phone. "We're all on the thread. Go ahead and call her."

Emily dialed and tapped the speakerphone icon. "Whassup?" she asked when AJ picked up.

"Hey, I just got a weird call from Maeve at Rackam's," AJ said. "Is Roy still over there on Little?"

"Yeah, we're playing detective with him right now! We may have solved The Curse of the Movie Shoot!"

Whittaker cleared his throat. "Best not to go into details about an ongoing investigation. AJ, this is Roy... what is the nature of this unusual call?"

"Well, apparently someone called and left a message during happy hour. Maeve didn't catch it until she showed up to receive a liquor shipment this morning. It might have been a prank call, but..."

"But what?" Boone asked.

"She says it was a woman's voice, talking about how Brooke Bablin had been kidnapped."

It was a scramble, and Constable Macy had to request a ten-minute hold on the take-off, but Boone, Emily, and Whittaker managed to make the 8:50 a.m. flight, Dozier in tow. The prop master sat sullenly beside the detective in a rear window seat, his hands cuffed in front of him. Thirty-five minutes later, the plane landed at Owen Roberts International and they were greeted in front of the entrance to arrivals by Constable Tibbetts, Nora's partner. To avoid parading a handcuffed man through the main terminal, airport security escorted them to a staff parking lot off to the side, where Constable Nora Sommers waited in a second patrol car alongside the one Tibbetts had arrived in. Together, they drove to the Central Police Station on Elgin Avenue in downtown George Town.

Boone and Emily began to follow Whittaker and Tibbetts, who had Dozier between them, but the detective turned back. "I will need your statements later, but I'd like you to accompany Constable Sommer. I've asked her to look into this voice message the bartender called AJ about."

Nora opened the rear door of the patrol car she'd driven. "I requested you. You both had some insight when last we spoke, and I believe Boone has a rapport with the bartender."

"Maeve? I only just met her."

Nora simply shrugged and gestured to the car. "Please."

◆ ◆ ◆

Rackam's didn't open for lunch for another hour, but Maeve was waiting for them at the outdoor bar, busily scrubbing glassware as they came around the corner.

"Oh, good, you're here! I'm sorry I missed the call when it came in during Happy Hour, but we were so slammed with a cruise ship group, it went to voice mail. I called AJ as soon as I listened to it this morning; figured she'd know how to get in touch with you, Constable... since you were in here with her the other day."

"What time did the call come in?" Nora asked.

"Close to six o'clock in the evening. Look, it may just be a prank call. It's really weird, how things are phrased." She swung the hinged bar gate up. "Come on back and have a listen."

They gathered around the cordless phone base, where a red "1" glowed.

"One moment. I will record this," Nora said, taking out her phone and opening a simple voice memo app. "Ready."

Maeve pressed the button, and the machine announced in a robotic voice: *"Wednesday, six-oh-three p.m."* The message began with a woman coughing. Then:

"No news stories at all about how you followed Brooke Bablin home from Rackam's, kidnapped her, and stuck her in a basement. So, I guess you got away with it."

There was a muffled sound, like someone else nearby was speaking, then the female voice continued:

"The only stories on TMZ are about how Brooke Bablin must have quit and no one knows where I went. And nothing at all about some

Russian guy smoking black-and-gold cigarettes sneaking into my villa and chloroforming me. So, like I said. I guess you got away with it. And here I am... what's that joke you're always making? Oh, yeah... so here I am, 'in hell,' wondering when you'll let me go."

There was a pause, and then the call ended.

"She mentions being held in a basement," Nora said. "There are no basements in Grand Cayman. I learned this on a recent case. The water table is just below the ground."

"Maybe she's in a room that *looks* like a basement." Boone said. "Besides, that's not a prank call."

"How do you know?" Maeve asked.

"Like you said, the wording is strange. Too many odd specifics, and no prank caller would phrase things like that. She begins the call talking about Brooke Bablin in the third-person, and then switches to 'me' and 'I.' She's in the room with her kidnapper and doesn't want him to know she's on an active call, so she's talking about what he did as if it's something she hoped would be in the news."

"Betcha she's looking at a smartphone, pretending to read an article," Emily said, her own phone out as she tapped away. She looked up. "I've had some experience misdirecting kidnappers."

Nora raised an eyebrow, but didn't ask for Emily to elaborate.

Em looked back at her phone. "Play the message again? Just the first part?" When Maeve did, hitting pause in the middle, Emily held up her phone and tapped the screen. She had pulled up a clip from one of Brooke Bablin's movies and let it play for a few seconds.

"That is her voice," Nora said. She gestured at the cordless handset. "Does your phone store the numbers of the incoming calls?"

"Yes." Maeve picked it up and scrolled back through them. "Here it is. 6:03 p.m. It's a local number." She held it up for Nora, who recorded it in a small notebook.

"Can you play the rest of the message for me?" Boone requested, stealing a cocktail napkin and a pen. As the remainder of the message played, he scribbled notes. The call ended. "Black-and-gold cigarettes," he said softly. "A Russian guy."

"Holy shite snacks…" Emily breathed. "Is it possible?"

Nora frowned. "Whatever you two are talking about, I would like to know."

"Let me be sure, first." Boone looked over at the seating area beside the bar, where he'd seen the loud-talking foreigner sitting with the well-dressed man when they were last here. "Maeve, do you have security cameras set up?"

"Yes, we do."

Boone felt his heart rate ramp up. "Please tell me you have footage of last Friday."

"Probably. Everything's on the Cloud, and I think they're stored for at least thirty days. Follow me to the office."

In moments, they were gathered around a computer monitor as Maeve scrolled through thumbnails of videos, sorted by date and camera location. They found the previous Friday and Boone pointed at a particular frame.

"This one, please. We want to look at this table here." He pointed at a spot on the image. "The sun was about to set when I got there, so let's start a little before, at six."

Maeve adjusted the time to six, but the table had two unfamiliar occupants.

"Can we nudge it forward?" Boone asked.

Maeve advanced the video a few minutes at a time, the image changing slightly: The diners looking at the check, a busboy cleaning the table, and after the next click on the time line, the table was occupied. A black-haired man in a dress shirt had his back to the camera, but the man in a ballcap and tropical floral-print shirt was plainly visible, gesturing grandly. He had a cigarette, but it seemed to be of the standard white variety.

"That's him," Boone said.

"Who's him?" Nora asked.

"Oh, that's Lev," Maeve said. "He's a real character!"

"You told me he was a regular," Boone recalled. "Is he Russian?"

"I suppose he could be."

"And does he ever smoke unusual cigarettes?"

Maeve thought a moment. "You know… I think he did." She paled. "Black and gold. Like that message said."

"It's him, innit?" Emily gasped.

"*Him* who?" Nora asked, clearly losing patience.

"He went by Tolstoy," Boone said. "We don't know his real name."

Emily jumped in. "He was one of a group of mercenaries that tried to kidnap a bunch of billionaires on a mega-yacht between here and Cozumel. Three of 'em got away."

"Oh… yes… I remember hearing about this."

"It was right after that we met AJ Bailey," Boone added. "At Rackam's, actually." He thought back to that day. There had been remnants of those odd cigarettes in an ashtray at the bar, he was sure of it. "It's possible the surviving mercenaries hid out on Grand. They were on a long-haul tender from the yacht, last we saw them. This would've been the nearest land."

"You mean… Lev…?" Maeve seemed bewildered. "But he's such a fun guy. He calls in all the time, asking for the daily specials."

"Does he, now?" Emily said. "How about yesterday?"

"Yes... he asked if we had scallops. He called right as that big cruise ship group arrived."

Em grabbed a cordless near the computer. "Is this phone on the same line as the one we were looking at?" When Maeve nodded, Emily tapped backward in time through the calls. "Here's the 6:03 p.m. call... and before that..." She tapped the back button once. "Boom. Same number. 5:59 p.m. Brooke must've redialed after his call."

Boone thought for a moment, remembering. "Maeve... last time I spoke to you, your waitress Lily said that 'Lev' had asked for Brooke's autograph, and she seemed annoyed at him."

"Ohmigod, yes... that's right."

"Can you pull up footage from that day? Lily said it was a Tuesday. It would be the same week as this footage. Sunset again."

"I remember the table she was sitting at. It'll be this camera, here." Maeve clicked on the Tuesday video for that view. The camera was westward-facing, so she advanced the time until the sun neared the horizon. "She really does look a lot like you, Emily," Maeve remarked, as they watched Brooke Bablin enjoying a tropical drink and a salad.

In minutes, 'Lev' appeared, wearing a Hawaiian shirt of a different color from the other footage. Smiling broadly, he spoke with the actress for a time, appearing to be an excited fan. Then he came over to her and raised his camera for a selfie. Things happened quickly. He bumped the table and looked apologetic, bending down to retrieve something and return it to her table, the flat object appearing to be a card wallet.

Nora grunted. "This man is very skilled. Play it again."

"There... he bumps the table with his thigh, but flicks his finger against the card holder," Boone observed. "That's what sent it off the table."

"Yes, and he appears to linger with the wallet beneath the table," Nora added. "Longer than necessary. He may have had some form of magnetic skimmer."

"Maybe her room card?" Emily suggested. "That message said something about him chloroforming Brooke in her villa."

"Do you think this man was working with the one Whittaker just arrested?" Nora asked.

Boone thought for a moment. "Not directly. I think we're missing a pretty big piece of the puzzle. Maeve, can you go back to the other video?"

As the bartender brought it up, Nora leaned in. "Ah yes, I meant to ask who the other man at the table was." The video filled the screen, the timestamp still at the point where they'd left off.

"His back is to the camera," Maeve said.

"I remember him bringing the check and some cash to the bar," Boone replied. "Nudge it forward until they get up from the table."

Maeve did so, and the handsome man approached the bar, setting down the bill. The camera had a good view of his face and Maeve paused it. "Not a regular. Sorry, I don't recognize him."

"I do," Em said. "That's Maxwell Beck. One of the producers."

29

"One of the producers?" Nora said. "An investor in the film?"

"Well, let's see..." Emily said, pulling up one of the many emails she'd gotten from the production staff. "Says he's the field producer, which is pretty hands-on, I think. More about supervising and coordinating than investing."

"So... he'd know what's being shot when," Boone mused. "Might even be the one *deciding* what's shot when?"

"Maybe," Emily said. "Although it seemed like Werner was calling the shots, most of the time."

"Maxwell Beck..." Boone said softly. "Distinctive name. Familiar." He borrowed a pen from the office desk and added the name to his napkin of notes.

"I need to call all of this in." Nora took out her phone. "Needless to say, these videos are now evidence." She stepped outside.

"I need to open up the bar," Maeve said, rising from the computer. "Oh dear, I hope they find her!"

Boone and Emily followed the bartender out, Emily immediately slipping on her sunglasses as they returned to the outdoor seating area. The glorious Caribbean Sea sparkled under the late-morning sun.

Nora was just finishing up her call, and she gestured brusquely at them. "Come. Detective Whittaker wants us back at the station immediately."

Emily and Boone followed Nora into Detective Whittaker's office. He gestured for the constable to close the door.

Em looked at a familiar airtight container on the detective's desk. It was open. "The rice... did it work?"

Whittaker smiled. "It did. I was able to power up the mobile. It appears that Mr. Dozier had been systematically deleting texts and records of calls, but there are two texts that appear to have come in at the time he was digging on Owen Island."

"What do they say?" Nora asked.

"One word only. 'Report.' The texts arrived an hour apart."

"Was it from the number Brooke called from?" Boone asked "The one that may belong to 'Lev,' or whatever his real name is?"

"No. The numbers are different... however..." He referred to a printout beside him. "The numbers *are* related. The one you provided me, and the number that texted this mobile, and also, the number for the mobile itself... all are prepaid phones that were purchased on the same day. Six in total, from a store in George Town. I haven't yet had time to check, but I imagine the packaged one we found in the road case is one of the six."

"So... have you called it?"

"Absolutely not. We don't want to alert any co-conspirators."

At that precise moment, the phone vibrated on the desk, causing Whittaker to jump. "Another text. 'Report.'"

"Well, that's a sticky wicket," Em said. "Although... not really. You could text back: 'Sorry. Phone fell in toilet last night. Can't talk now.'"

Whittaker looked at the others dubiously. When Nora shrugged, the detective typed the suggested message. After a moment, the phone dinged again. "They say 'What about the spare?'"

"Just shut him down," Em advised, reaching out for the phone. Whittaker handed it over. She spoke as she typed, "This phone fine now. GG."

"GG?" Whittaker asked.

"Gotta go," Em explained. "It implies you won't respond to any immediate follow-up."

"This generation," Whittaker muttered, looking at the rest of his notes. "I listened to the voice mail from Ms. Bablin... if it is indeed her. The mention of a 'basement' is unusual."

"Yeah, Nora here said that wasn't a thing in Grand Cayman," Emily said.

"Yes, that is what I thought, as well," Whittaker said, "but I decided to call a realtor my wife knows. She said a very small number of new dwellings are built with basements, although they are really more of a recessed ground floor. Apparently, many new buyers who are used to basements find them desirable. She said most of the ones she knows about are in South Sound. So that gives us somewhere to start."

"*Dritt!*" Nora barked a Norwegian curse. "We should have checked the restaurant security cameras situated on the street. To see if 'Lev' got into a car. Then we could look for it in South Sound."

"Good idea. We will do that," Whittaker said. "And what about the man he was with?" He checked his notes. "Maxwell Beck? He is a producer on *Man O' War*. Why would he be involved in sabotaging his own movie?" The detective rotated to the side and brought up a window on his laptop. "I have been looking at the Internet Movie Database. He has many producer credits."

Emily watched as Boone moved around the desk, staring at the screen, eyes wide.

"Boone? What is it?"

<hr>

Boone leaned in close, then realized he was crowding the detective at his own desk. "Sorry. May I?"

"Be my guest." Whittaker slid the laptop closer to the divemaster.

Boone scrutinized the headshot on the site. The producer's picture was a younger-looking man than the one on the security tape, but just as the name "Maxwell Beck" had struck him as familiar, this photo also looked like something he'd come across. "Wait a minute..." He started scrolling through the man's credits. "I don't know if they have movies that weren't released, but... ah, here we go, looks like they do." He opened the page for the movie that had caught his eye.

Whittaker rolled his desk chair closer. "*Zombie Bigfoot*? I've never heard of that."

"No reason you would've," Boone said. "It was cancelled. But here's a connection for you, detective." He tapped the director slot. "Heinz Werner." He scrolled up to the cast photos. "And here is Michelle Reynolds, the actress who reportedly had a break-down during filming."

"Wait a minute," Em said, coming around the desk. "Remember you told me there were rumors of a showmance between Reynolds and Werner? I asked him about it. He swore they never slept together, but someone told him she was intimate with one of the film's producers."

"This is starting to make sense." Boone was already bringing up another window on the laptop. "And I know where I saw Beck's name before." He found the tabloid article about Michelle Reynolds entering rehab in Malibu, California. "Okay, so his name isn't in this one... it just says one of the producers for *Zombie Bigfoot* assisted with admitting her to the addiction treatment center. But look at this photo." He centered the article on a photo of Reynolds in a car, with a man in a suit shouting at the paparazzi. "That's Beck driving the car. And the place where I saw his actual name would be..." He typed and clicked and brought up the actress's death notice. "This article."

Nora had joined them, and the four scanned through the story.

Boone found the phrase he was looking for. "Ms. Reynolds was discovered by her partner... Maxwell Beck."

"Ohmigod..." Emily reached up and wiped away a tear that had snuck up on her.

"This is why he's doing it," Boone said. "He blames Werner for her death."

Maxwell Beck tapped a manicured fingernail against the prepaid phone, thinking. The unexpected communications blackout with

Adam Dozier had been concerning, but there wasn't any immediate need for the man's services. And in all honesty, Dozier struck Beck as *exactly* the sort of man who would drop his phone in a toilet.

And in any event, things were going well—better than expected. Obviously, he'd hoped the one-two punch of taking out the leading man and leading lady would have been sufficient. But after Cliff Van Dorn's unfortunate "mugging," and Brooke Bablin "quitting," the production had lucked out recasting so quickly. Billy Faust was a star-in-the-making, and that little divemaster, Emily Durand... who would have thought Werner could get so lucky? *But now, his luck has run out.*

The Cayman Islands Film Commission and the Department of Environment *both* jumping in to halt production in the wake of the arson on the *Mako*... that had been a gift he hadn't anticipated. *That pretentious Kraut must be losing his mind,* Beck thought. *Maybe he'll just have an aneurism and get it over with.* But no, that would be too easy. What Beck wanted for the man was career death.

Heinz Werner had burned a few bridges of his own over the last few years, and the eccentric director had called in a lot of favors to get this shot at redemption. A series of box office flops and cost overruns, coupled with the man's caustic personality, had left Werner on shaky ground. If *Man O' War* hit it big at the box office, the director might stand a chance of regaining his former heights. *But not if I have anything to say about it.*

"Max? Maxwell!"

Beck looked up from the burner phone that lay beside his laptop, returning his gaze to the face that stared out at him from the screen. "I'm sorry, Mrs. Barclay. You were saying?"

"I was saying a great many things, Max. You asked for this meeting. The least you can do is give me your undivided attention."

"I apologize, Mrs. Barclay. With everything that's gone wrong in the last week, I haven't been getting a lot of sleep."

"You're not the only one losing sleep. This production is turning out to be an unmitigated disaster. Now... tell me truthfully... is this going to be *Zombie Bigfoot* all over again?"

Beck sighed, putting on a show of great contemplation and soul-searching. He knew the scuttlebutt inside the inner circle of producers and studio execs. If this production imploded, it would take Werner with it. *And then no one will touch him with a ten-foot pole. And he will know how Michelle felt.*

Maxwell Beck had only been a lowly assistant producer when he had fallen in love with the mercurial actress on the set of *Zombie Bigfoot*. And from the wings, he had watched her world fall apart, her big chance at stardom crumbling around her. Sure, she indulged in recreational substances from time to time, but who didn't? No, the deterioration he'd seen in her all started after she'd met with Werner in her trailer one evening. What exactly occurred in there, Beck couldn't be sure, but Michelle had sworn that nothing inappropriate had happened, saying only that the director had chewed her out about her profession-alism. And within a week, she had suffered a breakdown and the movie was called off.

After that, no one wanted to hire her, and while Beck had risen up the show business ladder, Michelle had spiraled down into a deep depression. By then, they were living together off-and-on, although Beck kept the relationship quiet, and they each had their own places. He'd done everything he could for Michelle, from paying for a rehab program, to lining up auditions. Beck had even set up an audition for a movie for her, and she'd actually been hired to play a medium-sized part; unfortunately, the director had bowed out and been replaced by Heinz Werner, who had insisted on recasting the role. Michelle sank into a suicidal depression. That had been the last straw.

Beck had been attached to that movie, and with some creative accounting, he'd managed to inflate the costs, embezzling some of the overages. Even though that film had done moderately well at the box office, it had barely broken even. He was even more successful financially hamstringing Werner's next film; that one was a complete and utter flop. Beck had been surprised when the studio brought Werner in to direct *Man O' War*. Apparently, Jeffrey Scott, the local Cayman Islands producer, liked Werner's work and had pulled some strings for him.

Wonder how Jeff feels about his choice now? Beck thought with a smile. The beautiful Azimut yacht Dozier had torched belonged to the man.

"Max! I need an answer. Do we pull the plug, or no?"

Beck shook his head, playing the tortured soul. "I can't do this to Heinz. It would destroy him."

"You don't work for Heinz, you work for *me*! And I want an honest assessment."

Beck nodded. "Very well. Morale is crumbling. And looking at the numbers... the schedule... I just don't see how this has a happy ending."

Barclay sat back in her chair, deep in thought. "Damn," she finally muttered. She sat forward. "I will call the producing staff together immediately. Be back on the conference in one hour." Her window went black.

Beck closed his eyes and let out a long, slow breath. After a moment, he picked up the phone and sent a message to the other number he had stored. *"How is your guest?"* There was a short pause, then:

"She is fine. How much longer?"

Beck thought for a moment. It might take a short period of back-and-forth skirmishing, but he'd be surprised if *Man O' War* survived the weekend. Once the movie was well and truly dead and the cast and crew dispersed, Brooke would be driven to a remote part of Grand Cayman... and released. No need to harm the actress any further. He typed: *"I believe your guest's stay will end early next week."*

"Good. And the rest of the payment then."

"Of course. We will speak later."

Beck deleted the exchange, then rose from the desk in his hotel room and put on a lightweight sport coat, slipping the phone into an inner pocket. His regular phone chimed with a notification from the production crew. Taking it from his pants pocket, he opened the message. Apparently, Werner had flown back to Grand from Little Cayman and was downstairs in the hotel bar, day-drinking. Beck smiled and headed for the elevator. *Cracking already, and he hasn't even heard the worst of it. Couldn't hurt to give him a little nudge. This time...* Werner was finished.

30

"So, what's the plan?" Emily asked, as they exited the police station. Constable Jacob Tibbetts, Nora's partner, had joined the other four.

Whittaker walked briskly to his car. "We must act quickly, before Mr. Beck discovers his lackey has been arrested. Constable Sommer, you will return to Rackam's and see if you can match up a car with this 'Lev' person. Constable Tibbetts will accompany me to confront Beck. We suspect he is in the defunct hotel the production is using for housing and offices."

"Can we come, too?" Em asked. "I've met Beck... might get him talking, yeah?"

"Perhaps," Whittaker said. "You wouldn't be out of place."

"Then I will take Boone," Nora said matter-of-factly. "Since you are taking my partner. Plus... he has nice eyes." When Boone raised his eyebrows, Nora blew out an exasperated breath. "Don't flatter yourself. I meant you are good at spotting things. Looking at security footage, you will be useful."

"Yeah, go make yourself useful, Boone," Emily chided.

Whittaker opened his car door. "Very well. Keep me apprised. We will follow you out."

The two patrol cars turned north on Elgin and made their way to West Bay Road. Rackam's was only a half mile from the station, and Nora and Boone turned left through a gate into a small parking area, while Whittaker continued north. The hotel was two and a half miles further along, but thanks to George Town weekday traffic, the trip took several minutes.

"If Mr. Beck is responsible for all of this sabotage," Whittaker asked, "what exactly does he have to gain?"

"Revenge, plain and simple," Emily said from the back seat. "We talked to a pair of writers on Little Cayman, and one of them said Heinz Werner's last few projects didn't go so well; this movie might be his last chance."

Turning off onto Piper Way, the detective brought the patrol car to a halt in a parking spot out of view of the entrance to the hotel. Emily followed the policemen into the lobby, where they gathered off to one side.

"The movie crew is using the business center and the conference and banquet halls for their offices," Emily offered. "He may be in one of those."

"Constable," Whittaker began, "go to the front desk and ask which room belongs to Maxwell Beck. Make it clear this is a discreet inquiry. And see if you can acquire a keycard."

"Yessir."

Tibbetts crossed the lobby, while Whittaker scanned the people coming and going. He did a doubletake. "That is a monkey."

Paulo Silva had just left an elevator and was heading for a side exit that led to a restaurant and bar.

"That's Ulysses," Emily said. "He's in the movie."

The monkey either heard or spotted her and shrieked, yanking forcefully on Silva's ear, practically steering the man to face Em.

"Emily! You flew over, too?"

"Yeah, well... the shoot was put on hold, so..." She held out a hand and the capuchin grabbed her finger. The handler let the creature scamper onto Emily's shoulder. "Hi, cutie! Wait, who else came over?"

"I came to Grand because Ulysses ate something he shouldn't have, and Little Cayman doesn't have a vet. He's fine, now. But when I got on the plane, Werner was on board. And Dario came rushing up at the last second and joined us. I got the impression it was all a little unplanned. They're in the bar right now. I was going to join them, see what's up."

Just then Constable Tibbetts returned and took Whittaker aside. While the detective was in plain clothes, Tibbetts was in full uniform. Silva leaned over to Emily and took back Ulysses. "Is... is everything all right?" he asked, indicating the constable.

"Oh, yeah, no worries," Em said. "Hey, head on over to the bar, maybe we'll join you."

"Okay, sure." As he exited the lobby, Whittaker finished his exchange with Tibbetts.

"We have a room number, but the constable and I will examine the offices first. Wait in the bar with your monkey friend while we search. If we spot Beck, I will text you."

"Right-o!"

Emily went out the door Silva had exited through and headed along a short outdoor walkway to a free-standing bar, surrounded by small tables with umbrellas. Inside, the walls of the little bar were painted sky blue and yellow, while the bar itself was decorated in a mosaic of brightly colored chunks of tile. Werner sat on a barstool, his demeanor a stark contrast to the cheery interior. He slumped, his arms crossed in front of him, a thousand-yard stare directed into the golden liquid in the glass that sat before him.

A shrill squeak sounded from Emily's left, followed by shushing sounds. She turned to find the animal wrangler sitting at a table, Ulysses perched atop it, playing with a paper drink umbrella. A number of closed umbrellas were lying around the table, with some opened ones stuck into grapes. Emily remembered the script talking about the bartending monkey putting umbrellas into drinks on the rum cruise, and she smiled. *Someone's still rehearsing his part.*

Dario sat across from man and monkey. After glancing over his shoulder at Werner, he beckoned brusquely for Emily to join them and leaned forward as she sat.

"Heinz is not in a good place at the moment," he said softly, "so I'm giving him a wide berth while he sorts through some things." Then he seemed to truly take in the fact that she was sitting there. "Wait... why are you in Grand Cayman? You're supposed to be in Little."

"Well, I figured with the production on hold..."

"No, you can't just... you should have asked permission from one of the ADs!" Exasperation slid into resignation. "Oh well, it doesn't matter. The Film Commission said the hold will be for at least forty-eight hours. And one of the producers is about to have a talk with Heinz. They may be about to pull the plug."

"Oh, no! But... we've shot so much! Even with all the, uh... all the *stuff*... happening."

Dario looked at her quizzically, then sighed. "This movie's been cursed from the beginning."

"Wait." Emily lowered her voice even further. "*Which* producer is coming to talk with Werner?"

"Maxwell Beck."

—◆—◆—

"Try another one," Nora said, her voice tinged with frustration.

Maeve sighed. "Pick a day."

Boone crossed his arms, thinking. They'd watched footage from three days when 'Lev'—the man Boone knew as Tolstoy—had come to the bar to drink and smoke. Each time, he had arrived and departed on foot. He didn't ever get out of a cab, but if the man had driven, he'd parked his car somewhere out of view of the street-facing camera.

"This one." Nora pointed at a video and Maeve pressed play. Boone looked at it, but his mind was elsewhere. There was something he'd missed. *Something incredibly obvious,* his subconscious taunted.

"Boone? Boone!"

Boone blinked. "Hmm?"

"I've been talking to you," Nora said, sounding annoyed but looking amused. "Nothing in this video. Should we try another?"

"Sure. Wait... no..." He reached into his pocket and pulled out a wadded napkin full of his scribbles, spreading it out and looking at it. "I'm such an idiot," he breathed.

"What?"

"Play the... uh... play the..." He couldn't get the words out, instead reaching across and picking up the cordless phone. "This."

"The voice mail?" Maeve asked.

Nora was already bringing up her phone, triggering the voice memo she'd recorded of the message. They listened to the whole thing, but it was the last part Boone was waiting for:

And here I am... what's that joke you're always making? Oh, yeah... so here I am, 'in hell,' wondering when you'll let me go."

"Hell," Boone said. "She's in Hell."

"The tourist trap in West Bay?" Nora asked.

In the middle of the peninsular outcrop on the northwest side of Grand Cayman, a desolate patch of jagged black limestone had clawed its way up from the depths, the sight so bleak and inhospitable that at some point a person may have said, "This must be what hell looks like." And then a second person probably said, "Ha, that's a good one! Let's make money off it." Now, signs proclaimed "Welcome to Hell." There was a Hell Road, and a Hell gift shop, and even a Hell post office—complete with "postcards from hell" and official postmarks from "Hell, Grand Cayman."

"Nora, can you get that realtor's number from Whittaker? If there's a property in Hell with some kind of pseudo-basement—"

"Yes, yes!" Nora was a step ahead, already dialing the detective. She waited a moment, then spoke. "Detective, it's Nora. I need the number for that realtor friend of Rosie's." She listened a moment, then answered the question she'd been asked, with: "We think the kidnappers are in Hell."

———◆•◆———

Emily finished typing a text just as Maxwell Beck strolled into the bar. His eyes locked onto Werner and a smile tugged at the corner of his mouth. It wasn't a pleasant smile. Glancing to the side, he spotted Dario, Emily, and Silva and came over to their table.

"I didn't expect to see you here, Emily."

Emily had to fight her instinct to say something that implied she was on to him; instead she smiled and infused her voice with enthusiasm and naivete. "Hi, Mr. Beck! Yeah, I heard the shoot was on hold, so I'm just back here for the day. But I'm working on my lines, I promise!"

"Good, good." He glanced over at Werner, then leaned in toward Dario and lowered his voice. "How is he?"

"Right now? He's doing as well as can be expected. But I guess it kind of depends on what you have to tell him."

Beck nodded, considering. That unnerving smile flirted with his face for a moment, but he straightened and said, "Well, the news is mixed, as you might expect. I'll be diplomatic about it."

He made his way to the side of the bar, several stools away from Werner, and ordered something. After a moment, the bartender brought the drink, a sparkling liquid in a flute.

Are you bleeding kidding me? Champagne? Emily ground her teeth.

Beck took the glass and sat at a stool beside Werner. He spoke in low tones. Emily couldn't hear what was being said, but Werner's posture became rigid, and the rising anger was palpable across the room. Emily glanced down at her phone. When she had learned Beck was on the way, she'd texted Whittaker. No reply just yet.

"Those bastards!" Werner abruptly shouted. "They wouldn't dare!"

Beck shrugged and said something else in low tones.

Heinz Werner went ballistic. He rose from his seat and hurled his half-finished whiskey, the glass shattering against a sky-blue wall in a shower of liquor, ice, and jagged shards. Ulysses shrieked, leaping onto Em's head, and from there to a ceiling fan above. Thankfully, the fan wasn't on at the moment.

Spittle flew from Werner's mouth as he shouted, "I will *not* have another movie cancelled on me by a bunch of *verdammte* bean counters in suits!" He stormed out of the bar.

After the outburst, Dario shot up from his seat and dashed after the director. Silva stood on a chair, trying to reach Ulysses, but the capuchin stubbornly retreated to the fan blade furthest from his reach.

"I... I'm going to see if the front desk can get a ladder," he said to Emily. "Will you keep an eye on him? He may come to you when he calms down." Silva dashed off.

"Sure, no worries," Emily said distantly, watching Beck as the producer methodically polished off his champagne, setting it down on the bar with a satisfied sigh.

"Sorry about that," Beck said to the shocked bartender, a young Caymanian girl. "Here, this should cover the drinks and the broken glass." He pulled several bills from a money clip and set them beside his empty champagne flute. Then he turned from the bar, looking up at the monkey with a bemused smirk.

"What did you say to him?" Emily asked.

"I'm sorry, but I was relating an internal communication between the producers. Not something I can share with talent." He straightened his jacket and started to go.

Em's phone dinged and she flicked her eyes to the screen. *On the way.* She rose. "Wait! Mr. Beck?"

He paused, hand on the handle of the glass door. "Yes?"

"Can I... can I talk to you?" She slipped a lock of blond hair over an ear and batted her eyelashes. Immediately, she felt icky.

Beck released the door handle and gave her a lingering glance before replying, "Usually, when a beautiful young actress in a bar asks me if we can talk, she's hoping I can 'help' her with her career. If this is one of those conversations, I'm sorry, I'm far too busy."

"No, no, it's not that at all..."

"Then what is it?" he asked, an amused smile on his face. The hand returned to the door handle.

Got to keep him here for just a few more minutes. "It's about... Michelle Reynolds."

His cocky expression darkened, and the smile vanished. Silently, he came to the table and sat beside Emily, locking his eyes on hers. "You have my attention."

31

Nora's phone rang in her hand. Boone had been watching her stare at it with tense impatience, ever since she'd made her information request to the realtor, a woman named Patricia McField.

"It's her," she told Boone, answering the call on speakerphone. "Constable Sommer."

"Hello Constable, this is Patricia. I didn't expect to find anything with a basement-type room in the Hell area, but guess what? There is a new construction, replacing a structure that had been damaged in a fire. It went up for long-term rentals last November, and the description boasts of a 'ground-floor basement with laundry.' It was rented last month."

"Who rented it?"

"I'm sorry, our database doesn't have personal information like that, only prior sales, dates of purchase, square footage, number of bathrooms... that sort of thing."

"Do you have an address?"

"Yes. 21 Miss Daisy Lane. It's a dead-end street off Hell Road. The house is the last on the left, just before Bodden's Heavy Equipment Services."

"Thank you, Mrs. McField. This is very helpful." Nora hung up and nodded to Maeve. "Thank you again for the use of your cameras. Boone, let's go."

"Shouldn't we call for backup? Let Whittaker know?"

"We will, once we're on the road." Nora was already exiting the office and entering the bar area.

A light tropical shower had started, the pungent zing of ozone in the air. Boone and Nora sprinted around the side of the bar area and got into the patrol car. Nora grabbed the radio. "I will direct the Firearms Response Unit to join us at the scene. Please text Detective Whittaker with the details."

While Nora spoke to the dispatcher, Boone began composing a text to both Whittaker and Emily, with a short synopsis of what they'd learned and where they were headed.

❖ ◆ ◆

Maxwell Beck continued to stare at Emily. "If you have something to say, say it."

"Well... I heard a rumor—*oh*!" Em jumped as Ulysses dropped down onto her head from the fan, then hopped to the table. Snagging one of his umbrellaed grapes, he pulled the toothpick loose and discarded the decoration, snacking on the little fruit. "Sorry! He scared me!"

"You heard a rumor..." Beck prompted, looking impatient.

"I'm sorry... this is hard!" Emily decided to take what she'd learned over the past week and dial up the acting. In seconds, she felt tears trickle down her cheeks. *Well, how do you like that? Wolfit would be proud!* She tried to speak, crying throughout. "Michelle... what happened to her... it's just so sad!" Then she burst into tears. Every extra second she could milk out of this would give Whittaker time to reach the bar.

Rather than evoking sympathy, the display seemed to anger Beck. "Stop crying!" He grabbed her wrist in a tight grip, grinding the bones together. "Why did you mention Michelle Reynolds to me?" he hissed.

With her Krav Maga training, Em could very easily have turned the tables on him, but she didn't want to tip her hand. Instead, she squealed, "Ow! You're hurting me!"

"I'll let go, if you tell m—aaaahhh!"

Beck and Emily both looked down at the pink umbrella sticking up from the back of Beck's hand, blood starting to pool around the toothpick. Ulysses shrieked at the producer and grabbed for another. Beck let go of Emily, stumbling back from the table and upending his chair. Wincing, he pulled the umbrella from his hand and tossed it on the table. Warily eyeing the monkey, he spoke to Emily. "You haven't answered my question."

As the sentence left his mouth, Detective Whittaker entered through the glass door, Constable Tibbetts on his heels. "Maxwell Beck?" Whittaker asked.

"Yes? Who are you?"

"I am Detective Roy Whittaker of the Royal Cayman Islands Police Service. I'd like to..." He frowned. "What happened to your hand?"

Beck was already sliding back into a calm and cool demeanor. "It's nothing. Just monkey business." He nodded toward Ulysses. "I'm afraid he's not as well trained as we would have liked." He took several steps toward the bar. "Can I trouble you for a stack of cocktail napkins?" he asked the bartender, who quickly handed him a wad.

Emily noticed Tibbetts had countered Beck's move, positioning himself closer to the staff door at the back. Whittaker glanced at Emily, a look of concern coming over his face. "Are you all right?"

Oh, bollocks, I'm probably red-faced, sniffly, and teary. She waved a hand. "I'm fine!" She dabbed at her eyes with a T-shirt sleeve. "Just practicing my acting."

Beck gave her a wary look as he held the napkins to the back of his hand. "What can I do for you, detective? Is this regarding the fire on the yacht? Extremely unfortunate, that. Have they determined the cause?"

"Actually, I have a number of topics to discuss with you, Mr. Beck. I wonder if you'd be willing to accompany me to my office?"

"No, I'm sorry, that would be impossible. The producers are meeting by videoconference within the hour. In fact, I should go and prepare. I need to tally up the latest costs for the week." He started to go.

Whittaker stepped into his path. "I really must insist on a few minutes of your time."

Beck stepped back. "Do you realize one of our producers is very good friends with members of your government? What would they think of this harassment?"

"Harassment, Mr. Beck? I haven't even asked a question yet. Or made an accusation."

Just then, both Whittaker's and Emily's phones chimed simultaneously. The detective's attention stayed locked on Beck, but Em took hers out and checked it.

"Mr. Beck, please have a seat," Whittaker said, politely but firmly.

366

"I'm sorry, but as I said, I have a meeting."

"Roy!" Emily cried. "Boone says they think they found Brooke!"

Whittaker looked over. "Where?"

Before Emily could answer, Beck tried to push past Whittaker. The detective had clearly had enough of Beck's song-and-dance, and took hold of the producer. "Constable! Arrest this man for assaulting a police officer."

◆ ◆ ◆

"Looks quiet," Nora observed. They had arrived at the dead-end lane and parked just up the street from the house the realtor had found. A light drizzle fell on the windshield.

"No car that I can see," Boone observed. "That could be good. Maybe the kidnapper is out getting supplies."

"Or it may mean we have the wrong location."

"Look at the stairs leading up to the front door," Boone said. "And the cinderblock layer below it, all the way around."

"A pseudo-basement. No windows in the cinderblock on the front or the near side."

"Maybe there's a window or an access around back."

"Let's go see," Nora said, exiting the car.

"Wait! We should wait for the… whatever you called it."

"The FRU. Firearms Response Unit," Nora said. "They were at an incident in Bodden Town. It will take them forty-five minutes to get here, even if traffic cooperates. I'm not waiting." She strode into the brush that neighbored the plot.

"Do you at least have a gun?"

"No." She tapped a baton at her side. "I have this."

"That's reassuring," Boone said, following. AJ Bailey hadn't told him all that much about Nora, but he recalled one conversation where their friend had suggested the young Norwegian had a reckless streak, and had hoped that joining the police force might temper her tendency to charge headlong at a problem. *Not yet, apparently,* Boone thought.

They reached a point where they could make out the rear of the house, a scraggly backyard fighting a losing battle against the encroaching tropical foliage. The light rain continued, cooling the tropical air.

"There is a back door to the main house, but I see no basement entrance," Nora said. "So that leaves the north side we haven't checked."

Boone's phone suddenly chimed, and Nora's head whipped around, a strand of blond hair coming loose from beneath her constable's cap. "Sorry!" Boone hissed. He silenced his phone, but glanced at the message. "Whittaker says he'll be on the road shortly. They arrested Beck."

"Good."

"So, maybe we should wait for… an-n-n-n-d you're already crossing the yard." Boone hustled to catch up. If there was some sort of window or door on the far side, great. If not, he'd insist they hunker down and wait for the cavalry.

"So… you're going to let me go?"

"That's the plan, Princess," Potluck said, chowing down on the jerk pork she'd picked up from Undra's Takeout nearby. "In fact, that's why Tolstoy's hitting the bar for a little celebration. Our big payday is coming!"

"Did someone pay the ransom?"

Potluck laughed. "I guess you could say that. Sure you don't want any of this? It's delicious."

Brooke had a plate of the jerk pork on her mattress but hadn't touched it. "I don't do pork. Smells good, though."

"Aw, shoot, I woulda gotten you the chicken if I'd've known." Potluck's phone chimed with a notification that one of the Wi-Fi cameras had picked up motion. *Probably another iguana,* she thought, but opened up the app just the same.

The video started up with a live feed and there was nothing unusual in view. There was a delay on the activation, so if a single critter had run across the yard, the camera might not have caught it. She paused for another mouthful of jerk pork, then backed up the video to the activation point as she chewed.

"Uff da," Potluck muttered, setting the pork aside. A tall, lanky man in shorts and a T-shirt was sneaking across the yard, south to north. "Looks like we have company." Potluck rose and headed up the steps to the main floor, removing the Beretta M9 from her waistband and racking the slide to chamber a round.

After borrowing a bandage from the bar's first aid kit and applying it to the producer's umbrella wound, the group took Maxwell Beck into the lobby. Whittaker had intended to take the man straight to the patrol car, but the movie production's own security staff had appeared, summoned to assist the animal wrangler in his efforts to "wrangle" Ulysses. As it turned out, that assistance wasn't needed, as Emily appeared in the lobby with Ulysses clinging to her neck. While Silva retrieved the monkey, the security men set the ladder aside and turned their attention to the sight of one of their producers being frog-marched toward the main exit.

"Security!" Beck cried. "Stop these men!"

Constable Tibbetts's uniform gave the two security men pause, but nevertheless they moved to intercept. Whittaker eyed their bulging arms. Both men clearly knew their way around a gym, and would probably prevail in a physical conflict. The detective sighed, retrieving his badge. This would take precious seconds.

"What seems to be the problem, Mr. Beck?" the larger of the two asked.

"These men are kidnapping me!"

"These men are Caymanian police officers," Whittaker interrupted, holding up his badge. "And we are arresting this man."

"What'd he do?" the slightly smaller of the two inquired.

"Assaulted a police officer," Tibbetts said.

"Bullshit! I tried to go out the door to a meeting and brushed against one of them. The cameras in the bar will confirm it. You have no probable cause to arrest me."

Whittaker smiled. "Do I not?" He looked at the security men. "You are tasked with protecting the security for everyone involved with this production, is that correct?"

The larger man puffed out his chest and nodded.

"So, if an individual were responsible for numerous acts of sabotage, that would certainly be someone you would want to protect the movie from, yes?"

"What are you blathering about?" Beck asked, but his complexion had visibly paled.

Emily grinned as Whittaker took out the burner phone. She hadn't known he'd brought it with him from the police station. *Smart cookie, this one.*

"This mobile was taken from a man who has likely committed numerous acts of sabotage over the past two weeks. He is currently in custody. He deleted most correspondence but there are a few remaining texts from the same number in the message log."

Beck started to struggle, but Tibbetts held him firmly.

Whittaker navigated to the number and held up the phone, tapping the call button so that all could see. No phone rang.

"See? They're crazy!"

"Shhh..." Emily said, cocking her head, listening. Playfully stalking forward, she put her ear to Beck's suit coat. "Now, I'm just a simple divemaster and amateur thespian, but... I think I hear a mobile on vibrate." She looked at Whittaker. "May I investigate?"

Whittaker's professional veneer slipped and a grin escaped. "You may."

Emily reached into Beck's inside jacket pocket and took out a burner phone identical to the one that Whittaker held. "Blimey, what have we here?" She answered the call in a high-pitched voice. "Hellooooo, who is it?"

"Justice," Whittaker said into the phone.

"He'll have to call you back," Em said, hanging up. "I think you're allowed a phone call, right Roy?"

Whittaker laughed and hung up, repocketing Dozier's phone and taking the one from Emily. He held it in front of Beck's face. "Probable cause."

32

"It is locked," Nora said.

Boone had turned the corner to the north side of the house to discover the constable staring at a pair of slanted basement storm doors. In keeping with the odd construction, the doors were somewhat raised from the ground, with a single concrete step in front of them. Wrapped around the handles of the two doors was a loop of chain, secured by a sturdy-looking padlock.

"You would think it'd be locked on the inside," Boone mused, wiping some rain from his eyes.

"Unless you have someone on the inside that you don't want getting outside," Nora said. "I have tools in the patrol car. Wait here." She went around the front of the house, the most direct route back to the street.

Guess we're not doing the sneaking thing anymore, Boone thought, although he figured the absence of a vehicle made it possible that they had the place to themselves. No sooner had he thought that than the universe proved him wrong.

"Can I help you?" a woman's voice came from behind him.

Boone turned to find a powerfully built woman coming around the corner from the back. He immediately recognized her as one of the mercenaries that had been with Tolstoy. She'd been the only female member of the team, code name "Potluck." Boone noticed she wasn't facing him square-on, and had one hand behind her right hip. He smiled, putting on his best "Aw, shucks" face. "Oh, hello! Sorry, I heard this place was for rent and I was just checking it out."

"Afraid you're out of luck…" She abruptly went silent, eyes widening. "You!"

Boone saw her body tense, and as she started to bring her arm around, he lashed out with a kick to the woman's midsection. He connected, but it was like hitting a boxer's heavy bag; the blow barely staggered her, and left him off balance. Grimacing, the mercenary replied with a kick of her own, smashing her booted heel into his ribs just as Boone was beginning an evasive capoeira move. Caught mid-tumble, Boone went sprawling into the wet sand and scrub. Wincing, he tried to regain his feet, only to find a handgun pointed at his face.

"Oh my garsh, I know you." Potluck said, an Upper Midwest accent on full display. She shook her head in amused disbelief. "You're the boyfriend. You and that little cutie patootie were on the mega-yacht my team infiltrated… and she's the one that took over the movie part from…" Potluck frowned. "What the hell are you doing here?"

Boone caught movement out of the corner of his eye; through the light rain, he could see Nora was at the nearest corner at the front of the house. He made a concerted effort to not look that way.

"You better start talking, Beanpole, or I'm gonna start with the kneecaps."

"Okay, okay!" Boone said. He held up his hands and got to his knees, slightly to Potluck's left. *Got to get her to turn a little more...*

"Did I say you could move?" Potluck shouted.

"Easy! I'm not armed. I was told to come here!"

"By who?"

"Maxwell Beck."

"Bullshit."

"I can prove it! Here." Keeping one hand held high, he carefully brought the phone out of his pocket. "I'll unlock the phone... open the message... and hand it to you. Okay?"

"Not okay. Unlock the phone and put it on the ground. Then lie on your face, hands behind your head."

Boone unlocked the phone, opened his most recent text from Whittaker, then laid the phone on the ground, subtly turning as he did so and placing it even further to Potluck's left. She pivoted, reaching out with her left hand, the pistol still pointed at Boone. *Now or never, Nora*, he thought.

In two strides of her long legs, Nora came around the corner of the house, her collapsible baton extended, the steel tip whistling through the air as she brought it down in an arc, smashing it into Potluck's right wrist. The crunch and Potluck's cry of pain made it clear bones had been broken. The pistol landed with a clatter and Boone reached for it, but Nora was already kicking it clear of Potluck. The move brought her closer to the mercenary, who whipped her left fist around and rocked Nora's head to the side, sending her constable's cap flying and blood spraying from a split lip.

Boone was concerned the blow would drop the young constable, but instead she growled with feral rage and whipped the baton in a backhand motion, catching the merc across the temple. Potluck staggered but grabbed Nora's baton-wielding arm, bending it back.

Still on the ground, Boone executed a capoeira kick that was designed to come from a partially prone position, snapping a *martelo de negativa* into the side of Potluck's knee joint. Something gave under the force of the powerful kick, and Potluck howled, involuntarily releasing her grip on the young woman.

That was all Nora needed. A precisely aimed thrust took Potluck in the throat and she doubled over, gagging. Boone sprung to his feet and drove her face down into the dirt, holding her there while Nora cuffed the mercenary in record time. Divemaster and constable both collapsed on the wet ground beside the prisoner, gasping for breath.

"Thank you," Boone managed.

"You as well," Nora replied, panting. "You must... teach me... that kick."

"You seemed to do just fine without it."

Nora held a fingertip to her bloody lip, looking at it for a moment before launching herself into action. "There is a toolbox around the corner. Get it while I deal with her gun."

Boone grabbed the tools and came back around to the storm doors. Nora had Potluck's weapon and removed the magazine before ejecting the round that had been in the chamber. "Beretta M9. We find these on the island from time to time. It's hard to get a gun on Grand Cayman, but not impossible." She tucked it into her waistband.

Boone opened the toolbox, looking at his options. "You know, rather than break in here, we could just go inside the house at this point."

Nora elbowed him aside and took out a prybar. "I prefer the direct route."

"That lock looks pretty solid."

"Yes, it does," Nora said, jamming the prybar under an edge of the plate that held one of the handles. A few seconds of wrenching and she popped the handle free of the door, the padlocked chain still attached.

"Okay, that works too," Boone said, opening the doors and revealing a short flight of concrete stairs descending to a tile floor. Fluorescent lights illuminated the room with a pale glow.

"Hello?" a voice echoed from below. "I'm in here! Help me!"

Ignoring Nora's shout to wait, Boone rushed down the stairs.

———————◆ ◆ ◆———————

"Take the highway," Whittaker ordered.

Constable Tibbetts laughed as he left West Bay Road, turning right onto Lawrence Boulevard. "Are you telling a Tibbetts to use Esterly Tibbetts? I've lived here all my life, Detective."

They hit the roundabout and got onto the Esterly Tibbetts Highway, heading north.

"How far are we from Hell?" Emily asked from the back seat, then snorted. "Hard to ask that with a straight face."

"Should be there in ten minutes," Tibbetts said.

Whittaker's phone rang and he glanced at it before answering. "Constable Sommer, we are on the highway. ETA is..." Whittaker stopped talking and listened as they approached the next roundabout. He lowered the phone for a moment. "Constable Tibbetts, take us back to West Bay Road!"

Tibbetts had just passed the turn, but the nature of roundabouts allowed him to simply circle around, exiting off the highway onto Gecko Link on the second pass.

377

Whittaker returned to the call. "Well done, Nora! Secure the scene. Rasha is already en route. I'll have Dispatch send an ambulance." He hung up and grabbed the radio on the dash. "Southbound, Constable," he directed, before summoning an ambulance to go to Nora's location.

"What's happening?" Emily asked. "Who's hurt?"

"Constable Sommer and Mr. Fischer have rescued Brooke Bablin and apprehended one of the kidnappers. The ambulance is for her."

"Wait... 'her'? The kidnapper wasn't Lev? Or 'Tolstoy' or what-have-you?"

"Apparently, there were two. A woman was guarding the house, but a second kidnapper—the Russian you and Boone identified— was not there. According to Ms. Bablin, he left for his favorite bar shortly before Nora and Boone rescued her."

"So, where are we going?" Tibbetts asked, as he headed south along West Bay Road.

Emily answered before the detective could: "Rackam's!"

———— ◆ ◆ ◆ ————

Brooke Bablin stood in the mid-afternoon sun, stretching her limbs and taking the humid air into her lungs with deep breaths. The tropical shower had passed, remnants of the light rain sparkling on the leaves fringing the yard. Brooke burst into a flurry of jumping jacks, laughing. "I can't tell you how good it feels to move around again!"

"Did they mistreat you?" Nora asked.

"You mean, apart from snatching me up and chaining me to a metal pipe for a week and a half?" She looked over at Potluck, who now sat slumped against the front corner of the house. "Actually, they fed me well. Let me use a little half-bath to shower and do my business. The other one let me borrow his smartphone every once in a while, to surf the web. He usually kept an eye on me for that."

"Except that one time," Boone said with a grin. "That was a pretty slick move, calling Rackam's right after he did."

"I was afraid the bar would think it was a prank call."

"They almost did. No one had any idea you'd been kidnapped. The media all thought you'd just up and quit."

"I know. I've been reading those articles. And they went right out and replaced me with a pretty face with no acting experience!"

"Uh... yeah... I heard that." Boone eyed Nora, who was looking at him with a wry smile. Further awkwardness was interrupted by new arrivals. "Oh, look, the cavalry's here."

Coming up the lane were an RCIPS patrol SUV and an ambulance. A plainclothes female detective stepped out of the SUV and Nora waved her over.

"Who's that?" Boone asked.

"That is Rasha, the island's main SOCO... scene of crime officer. She will take command here. We will hand over the prisoner to one of the arriving officers, to accompany her in the ambulance to the hospital."

"What about me?" Brooke Bablin asked.

Nora jerked a thumb toward the road. "First, we'll take you in for a medical evaluation. We'll also need a statement from you, but I imagine you'd like to do that somewhere away from this place."

Brooke let out a whoosh of breath. "You got that right. Please, let's get out of Hell."

Arriving at Rackam's, Emily and Whittaker left Tibbetts in the patrol car, covering the gated northern exit; Whittaker didn't want the man's constable uniform to spook their quarry, and most regular bar patrons tended to come and go by the southern entrance, just to the left of the Outpost Rum Bar, a small specialty tasting room.

Whittaker and Emily walked around the south side of the bright yellow restaurant, and as the Caribbean Sea came into view, their ears were greeted with the sound of loud, exuberant laughter, and a thickly-accented voice bellowing a punchline, "So the duck says... got any duck food?"

More laughter, mostly from the joke-teller, but a smattering of others laughed politely. Emily and Whittaker reached the patio area and looked at the U-shaped bar. Maeve wasn't there at the moment; a different bartender was tending to the patrons. The laughter was coming from a man in a garish, tropical shirt, smoking a distinctive black-and-gold cigarette.

"That's him," Em said, just as Tolstoy blew out a cloud of cigarette smoke and queued up another joke.

"Here is another! An Englishman, a Frenchman, and a Russian are in museum, looking at painting of Adam and Eve in the Garden of Eden. The Englishman says, 'Look how calm and dignified they look. They must be British.'"

Emily moved over to a table and picked up a menu, looking at Tolstoy over the top. Whittaker joined her as the joke continued.

"The Frenchman says, 'Nonsense! They are naked and unashamed, and so beautiful. Clearly, they are French.'"

Emily examined the man's garish shirt—at the waistline, under the printed palm trees and sea turtles, she could make out a slight bulge.

Tolstoy tapped his cigarette on the ashtray, grinning expectantly. "So, the Russian looks at Adam and Eve picture and says, 'No shelter, no clothes, only apple to eat, and they are being told this is paradise. These poor souls are Russian!'" With that, he burst into gales of laughter.

The bartender chuckled politely. "Good one, Lev." He pointed at Tolstoy's empty drink. "Can I get you another?"

"Is not yet Happy Hour, no?"

"No, not until five."

"In his waistband... I think he has a gun," Emily observed quietly.

"Yes," Whittaker concurred. "And I do not. The Firearms Response Unit is en route to Hell... and in any event, I would prefer not to involve them in a popular establishment."

"And Tolstoy might just up and leave before they got here, anyway," Emily said. "I'm gonna sit down on his right. Have a little chat. Once he's focused on me..."

"I'll come behind him and take his gun. I understand the plan, but what if he recognizes you?"

"I'm counting on it. And I don't think he'll pull his gun if he doesn't have to, yeah? He's got to know he'll be finished in Grand Cayman if he does that."

"I will text Constable Tibbetts to come to the south entrance and wait just around the corner."

While the detective moved behind a potted palm, Emily approached and leaned against the bar a few seats to the right of Lev, aka Tolstoy. She nodded at the bartender. "Caybrew, please."

Maeve arrived and let herself into the U-shaped bar, her face going pale as she spotted Lev. Emily managed to catch her eye and raise a finger to her lips, smiling broadly. "Hi, Maeve! Good to see you!"

Tolstoy heard the name and looked up from his drink menu. "Maeve! My favorite bartender! Which drink you think I should get?"

"Lev! Good to see you!" Maeve said, a little too chipper, a forced smile plastered on her face. "How about the rum runner? On me."

"You are like angel of booze!" He tapped his cigarette into an ashtray.

"Cool-looking cigarette," Emily said, easing onto the stool beside the man.

"Yes, I know! It is a Black Russian. I love them and..." he trailed off. "You. I know you." His festive attitude began to drain from him, replaced with confusion. "You are dive girl who is in movie. You were in Cozumel..."

"Hey, I'm not looking for trouble," Emily said. "Just a drink. Y'know, I remember you from Coconuts." Em turned sideways to face him, giving him a flirty look. Coconuts was a popular waterfront bar in Cozumel, known for having several albums containing photos of a risqué nature. Emily wasn't actually in them, but she had led Tolstoy to believe she was. "Did you ever find me in the special photo albums?"

"No," Tolstoy said, a glimmer of amusement in his eyes. "You trick me to open book with rubber snake."

Emily giggled. She'd actually forgotten that. "Sorry, couldn't resist."

"Later, on yacht... your boyfriend broke my nose," Tolstoy said, remembering.

"And you guys were gonna kill us, so I think we're even. Chill out. Max Beck's got me doing stuff for him, too. How do you think I got the job on the movie? In fact, that's how I knew where to find you."

"*Shto?* Who is this Beck?"

"Good answer," Em said with a smile, and sipped her beer. She lowered her voice and leaned in, whispering near Tolstoy's ear. "Beck is the good-looking guy paying you to babysit a certain actress. And thanks to you, I'm starring in a movie. And getting paid to sabotage a few things on the set."

"I read about these troubles on the T, M, and Z," Tolstoy said.

"I'm here to tell you, whatever he's paying you... he should be paying you a *lot* more. Beck is *loaded.*"

"Go on."

"I'm thinking... between what you know... and what I know... we could blackmail the bloke. If we both put the screws to him at the same time..."

"Put screws?"

"Turn up the heat. Put pressure on 'im. Once he shuts down this movie and starts to relax, we threaten to talk to the media, yeah? Unless he pays us some more."

Emily could see dollar signs in Tolstoy's eyes. She could also see Whittaker slipping from behind the palm tree and closing in.

"How much more?"

"A million, easy."

"Really?"

"This guy's so rich, it won't even make a dent. So, what do you say?" Emily held out her right hand, offering to shake. Tolstoy's left was holding the cigarette, and after a moment, he turned a little more toward Emily, accepting her handshake.

Whittaker struck. In an instant, he flipped up Tolstoy's shirt and plucked the handgun from his waistband. As he did this, Emily called up her Krav Maga training, turning the handshake into a wristlock, sliding off her barstool as she inverted Tolstoy's arm and locked the elbow. The man cried out in pain as Constable Tibbetts turned the corner, handcuffs at the ready.

Whittaker unloaded the gun and pocketed it. "Lev... Tolstoy... whatever your real name is. You are under arrest."

Tolstoy glared at Emily, then burst into laughter as he was led away. "You are very good actress, *krasotka*," he called over his shoulder.

33

THREE DAYS LATER.

Boone swung gently in one of the hammocks beside the shore at the Little Cayman Beach Resort. Brix was lying in the shade of the thatched roof over their heads, panting happily. "Are you disappointed?" Boone asked.

"Well… sure," Emily admitted, rocking in the hammock beside him. "But also relieved, honestly. Is there a word for that? Relievappointed? Disappieved? But a contract's a contract, and after what Brooke went through… I was happy to step aside."

Upon the arrest of Beck, Dozier, and the two kidnappers, things had moved quickly. The preponderance of evidence was sufficient that a pretty clear picture had emerged: Maxwell Beck had indeed done everything in his power to sabotage Heinz Werner's movie. What's more, he had been embezzling from the studio on three other movies, and a team of accountants had tracked down much of the ill-gotten funds. The amount was substantial.

385

The spectacular sequence of events would make for a marvelous story of its own, and one of the producers was already sketching out a four-part series on "the making of" *Man O' War.* Of course, to really make that work, the movie would need to be completed. And apparently, it would be... but not with Emily Durand in the starring role.

"Are you two going to hog the hammocks the whole time?" AJ Bailey asked, coming down from the Beach Nuts bar area, a bottle of Savanna Cider in hand. Nora Sommer followed close behind with a bottle of her own. Boone had suggested the two come over from Grand for the day, to catch up on everything that had happened, as well as giving Emily some company.

Em extracted herself from one hammock and joined Boone on his. "Budge up, Bobo." The two turned sideways, arranging themselves side by side, bare feet in the sand, using the hammock like a bench swing.

AJ and Nora took the other hammock and mirrored the two divemasters. "Good cider," AJ remarked, peering at the bottle's label. "From South Africa."

"Sorry they didn't have any Strongbow," Boone said.

"It's good to branch out and try new things," AJ replied.

"I quite agree," said Emily. "Case in point, before we flew back over..." She lazily stretched out a bare leg, elevating and pivoting it to show off her ankle.

"You actually did it!" AJ said.

On Emily's ankle was a small, reddish tattoo of a mermaid, the fishy tail wrapping around toward her heel.

Boone nudged her. "Fess up, Em."

"Okay, okay. It's just a henna tattoo. Probably last a couple of weeks. I completely chickened out."

"I told her I didn't see it that way," Boone said. "Em's such a free-wheeling free spirit, I figure this way she can change it up on a whim."

"I tried to convince Boone to get one, but he wouldn't. Stick-in-the-mud wanker."

AJ laughed. "So, Emily... you had a taste of celebrity. How was your time in the spotlight?"

"Fleeting!" Em said with a grin.

"You don't seem too broken up about it," AJ observed.

Emily shrugged. "I have a damn good life. And I don't want to do anything to cock it up."

"Like dashing off to Hollywood and becoming a movie star." AJ said. "Yes, that would be terrible."

"Well... it might be! Terrible, I mean. I dunno... this whole experience... it just fell into my lap. And now it's just fallen out. Werner was always going on about fate; maybe this was all supposed to happen."

"What exactly happened, then?" AJ asked. "They'd already shot quite a lot with you, hadn't they?"

"Yeah, but Brooke Bablin didn't quit, did she? So, once the police had taken her statement, she marched right over to the production offices and got on a conference call with her agent and representatives for the studio. Being the only real star in the production, she had a pretty ironclad contract. And the payout penalty for a potential cancellation of the movie was *hefty*, I heard."

"Where did you hear that?" Boone asked.

"Daniel Wolfit has been keeping me apprised of all manner of occurrences behind the veritable curtain," Emily said, dropping into the posh accent that the old Shakespearian actor had helped her with.

"Didn't you also have a contract?" Nora asked.

"Well, yeah. I still get paid."

"So, are they going to reshoot everything?" AJ asked.

"Well, no... Alan Novak—he's the director of photography or cinematographer or what have you—he's working with the editors to determine how much of the footage they can use. Basically, anything without *this* ugly mug." Em jerked a thumb toward her face.

"Oh, yes. You are objectively hideous," Nora deadpanned. This caught everyone off guard and they erupted into laughter, Emily most of all.

"I know, right?" Em twisted her face into a grimace before continuing. "But turns out, I'll probably be in the movie after all! Well, sort of. Werner has insisted my spontaneous dive over the side to rescue Wolfit has to stay in."

"How's that going to work?" AJ asked.

"Well, it's mostly my body you see, just some of my face in profile. Apparently, they're gonna CGI it a bit; throw a little Brooke on my face. They wanted to use some of my underwater footage, too... but I braided my hair into pigtails and Brooke said she wouldn't be caught dead in those. Plus, that was the LSD dive, and Billy went off his trolley pretty early in the shoot, so I think they'll start from scratch. But at least you can take your mates to see the movie and shout 'I know that arse!' when I dive in."

AJ laughed. "So, this movie is actually going to get made?"

"Funny thing, it turns out all the media buzz on crazy kidnappings and sabotage and revenge... it's turned this production into a potential blockbuster! And the studios will be reclaiming quite a bit of money that Beck was siphoning off, and that's cool for two reasons. One, they're gonna pop a lot of it right back into *Man O' War*. And two, it means that Werner's last two projects for them did much better than first thought!"

"I have not seen any moviemaking going on in Grand Cayman in the last few days," Nora said.

"Oh, yeah, the production is on hiatus," Em clarified. "They're going through the footage, they have to unwrite some of the rewrites, replace the *Mako*, recast a few parts. The producers and the studio are basically giving them two weeks to 'reboot' the shoot."

"And you won't be involved?" AJ asked.

"Actually..." Em paused for a sip of Caybrew. "Boone and Amelia are gonna run the *Lunasea* as a chase boat again... and I will be hired for Second Team."

"Second Team?"

Emily readjusted herself in the hammock, crossing her legs in the netting. "There's a lot of time spent setting up camera angles and lighting, yeah? So, the Second Team is a group of actors they hire to stand in for the main cast members. Usually, they look a lot like them, and they need to be the same height."

Boone laughed. "Which is sorta why you got hired in the first place."

Emily affected a look of mock indignation. "I'd like to think it had more to do with my sparkling personality and innate talent. Well, that... and my smoldering sexual chemistry with Billy Faust."

"Aw shucks! You never got to shoot the big seduction scene, did you?" Boone teased.

Em gave him a mischievous smile. "Not with Billy. But the Second Team sometimes gets to do the scenes for the camera crew, so... who knows? Hey, maybe the stand-in will be even hotter than Billy!"

"So, you'll get to do a little more acting after all," AJ said.

"Yeah! But I get to hold a script, so no more memorizing lines! And I'll be able to hang out with the good friends I made. And my mate, Ulysses! Although Paulo is concerned that monkey is too bonded to me, so I'll have to make myself scarce when they shoot."

Boone took a sip of beer and looked out across the sparkling waters of the lagoon to Owen Island. "One thing I don't get… what was a bunch of Burgess Meredith Penguin props doing out there?" He gestured with his beer.

"Ah, that I can help with," Nora said. "Although the theft of the sign and the burial of the items predates this movie and was unconnected, Whittaker asked your Constable Macy to look into it. Several locals were involved in the demolition of the old house and she questioned them, showing them pictures of the sign and the Penguin props. They all recognized the sign, and remembered it being there until the demolition was nearly complete; but then, one morning when they began work, they noticed it was gone."

"Was it only locals working on the teardown?" Boone asked.

Nora smiled. "Good question. No. There was also a man from the States. From California. He had arrived on the island a month or two before and offered to help, claiming he was a carpenter looking for work. The locals remembered he knew quite a lot about Burgess Meredith but not much about carpentry. And they remembered something else about him, too. Do you remember the bag the items were stored in?"

"Yeah," Boone said, thinking back. "It was a heavy-duty, waterproof duffel bag. Almost like a drybag, but large."

"Exactly. None of the locals remembered seeing the props. But two of them *did* remember seeing that bag. In the rental truck of the so-called 'carpenter.'"

"Maybe the guy was a collector," Boone mused. "But why stash things over there?"

"It's out of the way," Nora said. "No one around to see him burying it. And, as it happens, somewhat convenient to where he was staying."

"Which was?" Emily asked.

"Your condominium complex," Nora said with a smile. "One of the other workers remembered he was staying there. We haven't identified the man, but Whittaker assumes he was a collector much like Dozier, who suspected that props from the show were kept in Meredith's cottage. He probably intended to return for them, but for whatever reason, he never made it back to the island."

"What's going to happen to the props?" AJ asked.

"They are still material evidence in the trial of Mr. Dozier, but at some point, they will be returned here and given to the Little Cayman Museum."

"Yeah, Katja said they're planning on creating an exhibit for them," Boone said with a smile. "Better than winding up in Dozier's basement."

Emily snorted a laugh. "And you just *know* he would've played dress-up with them."

"Or sold them to other collectors," Nora suggested. "Our inquiries have revealed an interesting connection between Beck and Dozier. Apparently, Dozier absconded with several high-value props from a movie that Beck was a producer on. We suspect he had some leverage over Dozier, and his inclusion in this sabotage scheme was carrot-and-stick, paying him well, but keeping the threat of turning him in in his back pocket."

"If the movie's not starting up for a couple weeks, what are you two going to do between now and then?" AJ asked.

"Well, we run a dive op," Boone said. "Figure we'll do some diving."

"We already have a charter for tomorrow morning," Em said with a sideways glance at Boone. "Should be interesting."

The following morning, the *Lunasea* prepared to put to sea for a two-tank excursion to the north side. AJ and Nora decided to come along, and AJ was huddled with Amelia Ebanks, discussing their favorite dive sites on their respective islands. Emily flipped her green sunglasses up on her head as she held up the clipboard and called roll for their chartered divers.

"All righty! It's a small group but I like to do things by the book, so when I say your name... please reply with your favorite color."

"That's a new one," Boone, leaning against the flybridge ladder, said with a laugh.

Emily cleared her throat theatrically, and called the roll in what she hoped was a fair approximation to the accent Wolfit had been helping her to attain. "William Faust."

"Here. Oh, I mean... blue."

"Cynthia Trudeau."

Cindy giggled and responded, "Also blue."

"See, I knew you two had a little Kismet thing going. That being said, Billy... if I see that vape pen, I'm gonna send it on an anatomical journey which you will not enjoy." Em grabbed the next name off the list. "Sir Daniel Wolfit."

Wolfit laughed and waved a hand. "Purple. But I'm not a 'Sir.'"

"Well, not yet anyway. Wait'll the Queen gets a load of Bluebeard. And finally... Heinz Werner. Favorite color?"

"Gray," the director said, a smile on his lips.

"Called it!" Emily flipped the clipboard and pointed at where she'd written "Grey," in the preferred British spelling, with the letter "e." Em set the clipboard down. "But I do hope you favor a lighter shade of it, now; after all, things turned out pretty well for you, yeah?"

"They did indeed. And I understand I have the two of you to thank, in no small part."

"Well, maybe a teensy bit," Em said.

"There is still so much to do, but I needed a break. I want to thank you sincerely for making time for us."

"Got nothing but time," Emily replied. "Oh, I meant that in a good way! I'm glad things worked out the way they did."

"And I am glad we will all be seeing you again shortly," Werner said with genuine warmth.

"Is the movie on schedule to start back up?" Boone asked.

"Yes, I believe so. Everything seems to be on track. Much of the footage will be usable and most of the cast is still available. Bernardo is returning; his hearing is on the mend. Even Brooke Bablin has decided to stay in Grand Cayman until we start back up, and I must say, her overall demeanor has improved."

"Ohmigod, I just got it!" Emily cried. "Brooke Bablin. A babbling brook."

"Even I got this pun, and English is not my first language," Nora teased.

"It was something we all laughed about at the very first meet-and-greet," Wolfit said with a grin. "She swore it was a coincidence."

"So, where are you taking us?" Werner asked, looking out across the lagoon.

393

"Bloody Bay Wall, of course!" Emily said. "Can't come to this little corner of the world and not experience it. Let's cast off, Boone!"

Minutes later, they passed through the cut, and Werner joined Boone, Emily, and Amelia on the flybridge. To starboard, the Azimut was plainly visible along the shore at the edge of the lagoon. Several men were working on the hull, applying patches.

"They're going to refloat it and carefully bring it out through the channel," Boone explained. "A salvage ship will secure it in a cradle and deliver it to Grand for proper repairs."

"Good to hear," Werner replied.

As they neared the western tip of Little Cayman, Boone asked, "Hey, did they find a replacement for the *Mako* for the shoot?"

"Yes, the agreement came through just last night," Werner said. "Another Azimut 60."

"Over on Grand Cayman?" Emily asked.

"No, they're bringing it down from Providenciales."

"Turks and Caicos..." Boone mused. "Always wanted to go there."

Keep reading for The Afterword, but first:

If you enjoyed this book, please take a moment to visit Amazon and provide a short review; every reader's voice is extremely important for the life of a book or series.

Boone and Emily will return in another installment of

The Deep Series!

If you'd like advance notice of their next adventures, head on over to

WWW.DEEPNOVELS.COM
or
WWW.NICKSULLIVAN.NET

where you can sign up for my mailing list. If you're like me, you hate spam, so rest assured I'll email rarely.

And check out other authors who set their tales on the water, near the water, or under the tropical sun at

WWW.TROPICALAUTHORS.COM

Looking for a little more Boonemily? Watch them team up with characters from Wayne Stinnett, John H. Cunningham, and Nick Harvey! Check out *Graceless*, the first Tropical Authors Novella, a collaborative work from four of your favorites!

Curious about *Zombie Bigfoot?* As you can probably guess, it is not in the same vein as *The Deep Series,* but you'll find much of my humorous touch and action-packed scenes in this wild romp of a creature feature. Available on Amazon.

Want a little more Boone, Em, AJ, and Nora? Nicholas Harvey and I have you covered. Check out our Tropical Christmas Novella, *Angels of the Deep.*

Finally, if you're looking for more with AJ, Nora, and Detective Whittaker, go check out Nicholas Harvey's A J Bailey Adventure Series.

AFTERWORD

They say, "Write what you know," and while I know a fair amount about diving, marine life, and numerous Caribbean islands, it occurred to me that I ought to draw from something else that has been a large part of my life. Many of my readers may know this—but I suspect just as many might not: I have been a professional actor for the past three decades. I've appeared in numerous television shows and films, performed in a few Broadway shows, and have been an audiobook narrator since the days of cassette tapes, having voiced over five hundred titles. I had always been an avid reader, and had some interest in writing for television and film, but it was my audiobook narration—and the exposure to so many genres and writing styles—that led me to try my hand at writing my own novels.

I had a screenplay kicking around that I'd never done anything with, but I thought the story was a hoot, and decided to novelize it. The name? *Zombie Bigfoot*. And yes, it's as ridiculous as it sounds, an action-adventure horror comedy creature feature. It did fairly well, and I was about a third of the way into the sequel when a completely different inspiration struck. I had another idea in my head, based on a screenplay that I had not yet written. Many years ago, I'd read an article about an advanced narco sub that had been found in the jungle, and I wondered what would happen if one of those was taken over by terrorists. *Deep Shadow* was born. Setting it on the unique island of Bonaire was a no-brainer for me: it was the first time I'd dived fully certified (I had dived before that, but that's another story) and Bonaire's proximity to Venezuela made it a perfect choice. Fun fact: it was the backstage crew guys at a Broadway show who talked me into getting certified, and led to that Bonaire trip.

Which brings me back to "write what you know." I've been involved with many film and television productions, and it occurred to me it would be fun to drop Boone and Emily into the world of moviemaking. Numerous films have been shot in the Caribbean, including several in Grand Cayman. Of course, I'd need a fictional maritime movie to shoot. As luck would have it, *Man O' War* was another screenplay idea in my back pocket— one that had been fleshed out over beers with horror writer Chris Sorensen. And this led me to reflect on what I'd heard about the making of *Jaws*, and what a train wreck the production had been. Although… it worked out very well, didn't it? *Jaws* was the highest-grossing movie to date, until *Star Wars*.

As I like to do in my Afterwords, here I will say a little about what is based on fact, and what I've fudged in the name of fiction. Let's start with the fudging. As you may have guessed, I had to greatly oversimplify the filmmaking process in order to move the narrative along. Replacements of major characters are rare, but they do happen. In *Aliens*, Sigourney Weaver's co-star, the Colonial Marine "Hicks," had to be replaced after they'd already begun shooting. A more widely known replacement occurred in Stanley Kubrick's *Full Metal Jacket*. R. Lee Ermey had been an actual Marine Corps staff sergeant and was brought on as a consultant—he ended up replacing an actor, taking over the role of Gunnery Sergeant Hartman, and delivering a performance that is easily the highlight of the film, in my humble opinion. And in *Back to the Future*, the lead role of Marty McFly was originally played by Eric Stoltz, and they shot for over five weeks before recasting with Michael J. Fox. There are numerous group scenes in the movie where original footage was used—where Stoltz wasn't in frame—and new reaction shots with Fox were spliced in. There are also plenty of examples of a non-actor being cast as a major part in a movie. But a non-actor coming in as a last-minute replacement? None that I know of, so Emily broke new ground!

Location scouts: production would've been finished with their scouting by this point, but for obvious reasons I needed Leonard Berezinski to discover Emily.

Inter-island Cayman Airways flights: If you read my foreword in *Deep Devil*, you'll know I am not addressing Covid-19 and its effects on travel and tourism (because don't we have enough of that in our lives?) but alas, Covid was affecting tourism in the Cayman Islands at the time I was writing this book, and my flight arrivals/departure times were based on a schedule that will likely be different once the Cayman Islands open back up to more visitors. Taking a boat across to Grand from Little: this is done very rarely. But where's the fun in that? And hey, Boone and Em have a former drug runner's dive boat, so I gave myself some leeway.

Basements in Grand Cayman: I put Brooke in a basement... then learned there were no basements on GC... then found some listings for a couple places with these "pseudo-basements." Anyway, that initial blunder actually gave me a way for our heroes to narrow down their search.

The Cut—or the channel—into South Hole Sound. While the transit in and out of the lagoon can be hair-raising, it's something the dive ops do multiple times a day. It's not a passage a novice should attempt, but I nudged its difficulty up a notch for the sake of drama.

And the Royal Cayman Islands Police Service would not likely allow two civilians to participate so heavily in their investigation (and arrests), but hey... if your heroes aren't police or military, you have to bend the rules for the sake of a good mystery-thriller.

How about something that combines fact *and* fiction? Burgess Meredith did indeed have a house on Little Cayman: a skeleton was discovered when they were digging a cesspit, there is a dive site called Penguin's Leap situated out from the house's original location, and there certainly was a No Trespassing sign with his carved signature that went missing when the old house was torn down. Or at least, no one on LC I've talked to knows what happened to it, including the Little Cayman Museum. But I made up everything about a set of props being stashed in the old house and stolen by a collector. Well, not everything. I found an expired auction lot for Meredith's purple top hat and gloves—and yes, the gloves had fur on them! That was news to me.

Things based on fact: The full-load blank round. I was in a stage show where the property guy put full loads into a character's Colt .45 Peacemaker (it was supposed to be filled with quarter loads) and an actor lost most of the hearing in one ear. In that same production, I fired a pistol nightly, a hefty cap-and-ball Navy Colt. Fortunately for me, my blanks were just the caps, and my barrels were plugged. And... life imitates art. I'd written the full-load blank round scene back in August of 2021, and on October 15, I turned my completed first draft over to my beta readers. On October 22, a terrible accident happened involving a handgun on the set of the movie *Rust*, where a cinematographer was killed as she and the director were framing a point-of-view shot of the gun being pointed toward the camera, that pistol being a .45 revolver in the hands of actor Alec Baldwin. Since the events of my book take place in January of 2022, I felt my armorer would have to mention it, so I had to go back in and add a sentence or two.

As I write this afterword, the incident is still being investigated, but it's looking like live rounds made their way onto set. This was actually something I had considered in *Deep Focus*, but an unexpected, lethal shooting is horrific, and you may have noticed this book was lighter in tone than my previous ones, with no one meeting their demise, apart from some dastardly lionfish. I decided my own experience with a non-lethal mishap would be better for the book, as a death at that point in the story would have brought the production (and the plot) to a crashing halt.

Daniel Wolfit: this character is based in part on an erudite Shakespearean actor I once worked with, as well as the character of "Sir" in *The Dresser*—and *that* fictional character, played by Albert Finney, was based on actor-manager Sir Donald Wolfit... see what I did there? I also had Sir Ian McKellen in mind. I've met him twice—for a miniscule micro-second each time—but a friend who'd worked with him said he was the kindest, gentlest soul and very helpful, so I figured Emily could use a moviemaking mentor.

Emily's audition: I put it inside Boone and Em's home because I was channeling a memorable theater experience from my younger years. I was up for Clifford Odets's play *Golden Boy*, auditioning for the great Joanne Woodward in her living room in a swanky NYC apartment on the Upper East Side. I remember hearing what sounded like a soda can being opened behind me while I was acting my little heart out, and only later did my friend who was with me tell me, "Dude... Paul Newman was standing behind you in the doorway to the kitchen, drinking a beer and watching the audition." Full disclosure: I didn't get the part.

The *Jolly Robert*: Down in Barbados, when I was a teen, I took a cruise on a popular excursion boat, the *Jolly Roger*, a red-sailed party barge made to look like a pirate ship. Yes, it had a plank to walk, lots of rum punch, and a pirate (no monkey, thankfully). I figured a drunken booze-cruise full of college partiers would be an ideal target for a maritime monster.

The idea of a treasure hunting salvage ship having marine biologists on board: This plot point in *Man O' War* is based on the salvage of the SS *Central America*. My undergrad zoology teacher was on board to do surveys of marine life on the wreck... but the nine tons of gold in the hold of that side-wheel steamer (and its 1988 gold-price value of $126 million) was clearly the focus of the expedition.

And finally, Iguana Girl: Yep! She's real! When I was in Little Cayman for a dive trip back in 2017, we had a German bartender at Beach Nuts who knew everything there was to know about the local Sister Islands rock iguanas, and gave a very detailed presentation one night on the struggle to control the invasive greens. When I began this book, I reached out to the Little Cayman Museum, and an employee responded to my email. She was very helpful, and knew a surprising amount of detailed information on the iguanas. I noticed her name's spelling was German and asked if she used to bartend at Beach Nuts. The world is a funny place. It was the same person. She now works at the LC Museum and continues her quest to save the local iguanas, working with the Department of Environment. Two weeks after I handed my first draft over to my betas, she was awarded Conservationist of the

Year in the National Trust's Governor's Conservation Awards. A bit of Little Cayman trivia: there are quite a few iguana burrows behind the museum itself!

Hammocks on Little Cayman: did I mention them a bunch just to bring up Boone and Emily's disastrous hammock sex again? No! Well, maybe a little. But there are hammocks everywhere on LC. Every resort I saw had a bunch. In fact, my trip to Little Cayman in 2017 is probably the reason that the hammock bit ended up in the finale of *Deep Shadow* in 2018. Wait... not for *that* reason! Get your mind out of the gutter.

A huge thank you to Nicholas Harvey (or as I call him, "Brit Nick") for sharing his knowledge about Grand Cayman, and for the use of his characters. AJ Bailey, Nora Sommer, Detective Whittaker, and constables Tibbetts and Macy are all his creations. You may remember Emily meeting AJ at the end of *Devil*, and I couldn't very well have "Boonemily" in the Cayman Islands and not have them buddy up with Harvey's crew. If you enjoy my books, go check out Brit Nick's AJ Bailey Adventure Series! It'll give you something to read while I take forever to write my next.

And, as I finish up this afterword, Brit Nick and I are putting the finishing touches on a co-op Christmas novella! By the time you read this, it will already have been out for several weeks! So if you'd like a little more Boonemily and AJ, go out and grab *Angels of the Deep*! And yes, the audiobook is narrated by yours truly.

You may have noticed that this book took *less* than a year to write, unlike prior titles. In addition, *Focus* is longer than any of my previous books, by a substantial margin. I am trying to increase my writing output; for this book, at least, it worked. And, actually, I was writing more than this book this summer. I teamed up with three other Tropical Authors—Wayne Stinnett, John H. Cunningham, and Nicholas Harvey—to create a story that wove together our characters and locations. It takes place before this book, with Boone and Emily still in Cozumel. Grab your copy of *Graceless*! And if you'd like the audiobook—narrated by yours truly—you can pick up the audiobook.

Speaking of Tropical Authors, I want to thank everyone in that community. If you're interested in beach reads set by the sea, under the water, on a boat, or along the coast, then head over to TropicalAuthors.com and find some new storytellers. We've got about thirty-six or so last I looked, with mysteries, thrillers, action-adventure, romance, and more on offer. Tragically, we lost one of our founding members this year: Dawn Lee McKenna was one of the original ten we started with, and she will be sorely missed; not just by her loyal readers, but also by all the authors in the TA group. She was always available to everyone with sage advice or a witty remark.

A big thank you to Tanja Laaser of Little Cayman Museum for all her assistance in getting "the little things" right on Little. Thanks also to Cameron Akins of Caradonna Dive Adventures for putting me in touch with some of her contacts in Little and on the Brac. And a huge thank you to Tim W. Jackson for his detailed information about operating boats in LC. Tim is not only a scuba instructor and dive captain for Little Cayman Divers... he's also a novelist! Check out his novel *Blacktip Island*!

Thank you to all of my beta readers: Chris Sorensen, John Brady, Kevin Carolan, Mark Aldrich, Stuart Marland, Alan and Joan Zale, Mike Ramsey, Dana Vihlen, Patrick Newman, Drew Mutch, Jason Hebert, Glenn Hibbert, Deg Priest, Alan Fader, David Margolis, Bob Hickerson, and Malcolm Sullivan. Many of you have extraordinary backgrounds in diving, boating, and writing and you all kept me on my accuracy-toes and made some wonderful suggestions.

A big thank you to Shayne Rutherford of Wicked Good Book Covers for helping this picky ol' author with the cover design he was looking for! Once again, I've got a cover that makes me giddy! And additional thanks to John Brady for a brilliant mockup to send us down the right path toward the design.

Thanks to Marsha Zinberg of The Write Touch for her top-notch editing, keeping me on my toes with my grammar, punctuation, and plotting! And to Colleen Sheehan of Ampersand Book Interiors for her beautiful formatting, and Gretchen Tannert Douglas and Forest Olivier for their hyper-accurate proofreading skills.

Thank you to Paul Berezinski, dive instructor at BonScuba, who helped get my paperbacks into bookstores on the spectacular island of Bonaire. My thanks to Karl Cleveland for his work on my DeepNovels.com website, and thank you to everyone at Aurora Publicity, who are taking some of the marketing load off my shoulders so I can spend more time spinning words into stories.

And finally, as always, thank you to my readers (and my listeners, you audiobook fans). I know where "Boonemily" will be next—and having read this book, I suspect you may have a pretty good idea, too. Until then, stay safe, stay sanitary, stay sane... and keep seeking the sun.

ABOUT THE AUTHOR

Born in East Tennessee, Nick Sullivan has spent most of his adult life as an actor in New York City working in television, film, theater, and audiobooks. After narrating hundreds of titles over the last couple of decades, he decided to write his own. Nick is an avid scuba diver, and his travels to numerous islands throughout the Caribbean have inspired this series.

For a completely different kind of book, you can find Nick Sullivan's first novel at:

WWW.ZOMBIEBIGFOOT.COM

9 780997 813272